LONG HIDDEN

SPECULATIVE FICTION FROM THE MARGINS OF HISTORY

EDITED BY ROSE FOX
AND DANIEL JOSÉ OLDER

Crossed
Genres
Publications

Framingham, MA

LONG HIDDEN: Speculative Fiction from the Margins of History

Print ISBN-13: 978-0991392100 / Print ISBN-10: 0991392108
Ebook ISBN-13: 978-0991392117 / Ebook ISBN-10: 0991392116

FIRST EDITION: May 2014

Edited by Rose Fox and Daniel José Older

Cover design by Kay T. Holt
Interior layout by Bart R. Leib

Cover art copyright © 2013-2014 by Julie Dillon
http://juliedillonart.com

Interior art copyright © 2013-2014 by:

Esme Baran (http://fungiidraws.tumblr.com)	Pgs 268, 304
GMB Chomichuk (http://comicalchemy.blogspot.com)	Pgs 1, 106, 160, 342
Janet Chui (http://www.janetchui.net)	Pg 8, 174
Jennifer Cruté (http://jennifercrute.com)	Pg 222
Sasha Gallagher (http://chienoir.deviantart.com)	Pg 150
Kasey Gifford (http://killskerry.deviantart.com)	Pg 276
Daria Khvostova (http://hotrodsfromheck.tumblr.com)	Pgs 32, 80, 90
Nilah Magruder (http://nilahmagruder.com)	Pgs 122, 244
Alice Meichi Li (http://alicemeichi.com)	Pg 18, 50
Eric Orchard (http://ericorchard.blogspot.com)	Pgs 40, 134, 188, 290, 320
Aaron Paquette (http://www.aaronpaquette.net)	Pg 208
Kaysha Siemens (http://www.kayshasiemens.com)	Pgs 62, 198, 258

The editors would like to thank Sara Schwartzkopf; Dmitri Zagidulin; and v. Kosho George Finch, Koyasan Shingon Buddhism, for their thoughtful conation and insight.

TABLE OF CONTENTS

Introduction

INTRODUCTION

Before *Long Hidden* was a book, it was a conversation. Really, it was many conversations, over the course of many different lives; these fed into one conversation in particular, a back-and-forth on Twitter in December 2012 about representations of African diasporic voices in historical speculative fiction, and the ways that history "written by the victors" demonizes and erases already marginalized stories. That discussion became an idea that became the book you're about to read.

(We are especially grateful to Cassandra Taylor for starting and spearheading that conversation, the entirety of which you can read here: http://dft.ba/-LH-spark)

We grew up reading stories about people who weren't much like us. Speculative fiction promised to take us to places where anything was possible, but the spaceship captains and valiant questers were always white, always straight, always cisgender, and almost always men. We tried to force ourselves into those boxes, but we never fit. When we looked for faces and thoughts like our own, we found orcs and deviants and villains. And we began to wonder why some people's stories were told over and over, while ours were almost never even alluded to.

Our discomfort and confusion turned into anger and frustration. We were tired of being pushed to the margins. We were furious at the complicity of publishers who whitewashed covers, and booksellers who shunted any book by a Black author to the "African-American Literature" shelves in the back of the store. Our hearts ached for all the writers who had been actively discouraged from writing characters that didn't fit the norm, even as readers like us clamored for those stories.

Slowly we gathered a few rare gems by authors who really seemed to know us and understand what we needed. We reveled in works by Octavia E. Butler, Diane Duane, Gael Baudino, Tobias S. Buckell, Nalo Hopkinson, Ellen Kushner, Samuel R. Delany, Caitlín R. Kiernan, Lawrence Schimel, and N.K. Jemisin, and anthologies like Sheree Renée Thomas's *Dark Matter* and M. Christian's *Eros ex Machina*. These authors and editors—and the publishers, booksellers, and librarians who took chances on them—showed us that splendid, exciting, rich speculative fiction could be written about people of color, queer people, trans* people, and others too often neglected and ignored.

But too many other supposedly diverse stories had generic faux-multicultural casts where everyone sounded the same. Our lives and personalities and voices were shaped by our cultures, our ancestry, and the history of people like us. We wanted more speculative works that reflected those truths. Only an anthology, a book that encompassed many voices, could speak to both the vastness and the underlying unity of our need for fiction that reflects all people and makes room for everyone to be a hero.

The journey from conversation to idea to book took a year, and a lot of hard work; and since we're stuck in a capitalist world, it also took a lot of money. Once we all agreed we were in, we set up a Kickstarter to fundraise.

Crossed Genres said it would cost $12,000 to purchase and publish 100,000 words of fiction. We added stretch goals to make it longer, get illustrations, and cover the book in gorgeous wrap-around art by Julie Dillon. We had a month to raise the money. In three days, we'd cleared the initial $12,000. Support came in from all over the world. It came in tiny donations and huge ones. Tweets and blog posts were posted and reposted, and by the end of the month we'd blown straight through almost all our stretch goals and raised a stunning $31,597 from 1,181 different funders. So this book is the result of many collaborations, many contributions, many conversations, many voices.

We're not celebrities (though a few genuinely famous people were kind enough to boost the signal). We don't have enormous followings. But the idea rang true. People wanted to read *Long Hidden* as much as we did, and they eagerly joined us in making it happen.

Once we'd met our funding goals, we set out spreading the word about *Long Hidden* as far and wide as we could. We extended our call for submissions internationally and posted it in places that don't normally get solicited for speculative fiction anthologies. We reached out to writers who have never felt at home in a genre that often demonizes or erases them. And all those years of reading misrepresentations turned into an extensive set of guidelines: we demanded that our writers treat their characters and settings with respect, take care with depictions of sex and violence, and explicitly address difficult and complex topics.

Accordingly, we were then swamped with awesomeness: brilliant, unpredictable, courageous, elegant, hilarious, and heartbreaking awesomeness. Over 250 authors submitted stories, writing from their hearts, their experiences, and their family histories. We were humbled that so many people trusted us to read their deeply personal and often emotionally wrenching stories. From this amazing mountain, we drew 27 stories that spoke to the true heart of what *Long Hidden* is: a book of counter-narratives. It is an act of literary resistance. In whispers, shouts, and moans, these stories combine into a collective outcry that is both joyous and mournful, a forgotten praise-song that puts flesh on the bones of our hidden dreams.

As first-time anthology editors, we learned a tremendous amount about crafting a book like this. From our authors' meticulously researched work, we learned astonishing things about the lives of marginalized people around the world and throughout history. And from the outpouring of support from writers and readers, we learned that the longing to see ourselves and our history in fiction is bigger than any one book could encompass.

Many conversations became an idea that became a book, and we hope the book will spawn many conversations that will become many ideas, many stories, many dreams. If one of those dreams is yours, write your *Long Hidden* story. Send it to an editor, a friend, the future. Post it online, paint it on a wall, or whisper it into a loved one's ear. We are done being silent. We will revel in our messy, outrageous, complicated truths.

Thank you so much for joining us on this marvelous journey.

Rose Fox and Daniel José Older
New York City, 2014

Art by GMB Chomichuk

OGRES OF EAST AFRICA
SOFIA SAMATAR

1907
Kenya

Catalogued by Alibhai M. Moosajee of Mombasa
February 1907

1. Apul Apul

A male ogre of the Great Lakes region. A melancholy character, he eats crickets to sweeten his voice. His house burned down with all of his children inside. His enemy is the Hare.

[My informant, a woman of the highlands who calls herself only "Mary," adds that Apul Apul can be heard on windy nights, crying for his lost progeny. She claims that he has been sighted far from his native country, even on the coast, and that an Arab trader once shot and wounded him from the battlements of Fort Jesus. It happened in a famine year, the "Year of Fever." A great deal of research would be required in order to match this year, when, according to Mary, the cattle perished in droves, to one of the Years of Our Lord by which my employer reckons the passage of time; I append this note, therefore, in fine print, and in the margins.

"Always read the fine print, Alibhai!" my employer reminds me, when I draw up his contracts. He is unable to read it himself; his eyes are not good. "The African sun has spoilt them, Alibhai!"

Apul Apul, Mary says, bears a festering sore where the bullet pierced him. He is allergic to lead.]

2. Ba'ati

A grave-dweller from the environs of the ancient capital of Kush. The ba'ati possesses a skeletal figure and a morbid sense of humor. Its great pleasure is to impersonate human beings: if your dearest friend wears a cloak and claims to suffer from a cold, he may be a ba'ati in disguise.

[Mary arrives every day precisely at the second hour after dawn. I am curious about this reserved and encyclopedic woman. It amuses me to write these reflections concerning her in the margins of the catalogue I am composing for my employer. He will think this writing fly-tracks, or smudges from my dirty hands (he persists in his opinion that I am always dirty). As I write I see Mary before me as she presents herself each morning, in her calico dress, seated on an overturned crate.

I believe she is not very old, though she must be several years older than

1

I (but I am very young – "Too young to walk like an old man, Alibhai! Show some spirit! Ha!"). As she talks, she works at a bit of scarlet thread, plaiting something, perhaps a necklace. The tips of her fingers seem permanently stained with color.

"Where did you learn so much about ogres, Mary?"

"Anyone may learn. You need only listen."

"What is your full name?"

She stops plaiting and looks up. Her eyes drop their veil of calm and flash at me – in annoyance, in warning? "I told you," she says. "Mary. Only Mary."]

3. Dhegdheer

A female ogre of Somaliland. Her name means "Long Ear." She is described as a large, heavy woman, a very fast runner. One of her ears is said to be much longer than the other, in fact so long that it trails upon the ground. With this ear, she can hear her enemies approaching from a great distance. She lives in a ruined hovel with her daughter. The daughter is beautiful and would like to be married. Eventually, she will murder Dhegdheer by filling her ear with boiling water.

[My employer is so pleased with the information we have received from Mary that he has decided to camp here for another week. "Milk her, Alibhai!" he says, leering. "Eh? Squeeze her! Get as much out of her as you can. Ha! Ha!" My employer always shouts, as the report of his gun has made him rather deaf. In the evenings, he invites me into his tent, where, closed in by walls, a roof, and a floor of Willesden canvas, I am afforded a brief respite from the mosquitoes.

A lamp hangs from the central pole, and beneath it my employer sits with his legs stretched out and his red hands crossed on his stomach. "Very good, Alibhai!" he says. "Excellent!" Having shot every type of animal in the Protectorate, he is now determined to try his hand at ogre. I will be required to record his kills, as I keep track of all his accounts. It would be "damn fine," he opines, to acquire the ear of Dhegdheer.

Mary tells me that one day Dhegdheer's daughter, wracked with remorse, will walk into the sea and give herself up to the sharks.]

4. Iimũ

Iimũ transports his victims across a vast body of water in a ferry-boat. His country, which lies on the other side, is inaccessible to all creatures save ogres and weaverbirds. If you are trapped there, your only recourse is to beg the weaverbirds for sticks. You will need seven sticks in order to get away. The first two sticks will allow you to turn yourself into a stone, thereby escaping notice. The remaining five sticks enable the following transformations: thorns, a pit, darkness, sand, a river.

["Stand up straight, Alibhai! Look lively, man!"

My employer is of the opinion that I do not show a young man's proper spirit. This, he tells me, is a racial defect, and therefore not my fault, but I may improve myself by following his example. My employer thrusts out his chest. "Look, Alibhai!" He says that if I walk about stooped over like a dotard, people will get the impression that I am shiftless and craven, and this will quite naturally make them want to kick me. He himself has kicked me on occasion.

It is true that my back is often stiff, and I find it difficult to extend my limbs to their full length. Perhaps, as my employer suspects, I am growing old before my time.

These nights of full moon are so bright, I can see my shadow on the grass. It writhes like a snake when I make an effort to straighten my back.]

5. Katandabaliko

While most ogres are large, Katandabaliko is small, the size of a child. He arrives with a sound of galloping just as the food is ready. "There is sunshine for you!" he cries. This causes everyone to faint, and Katandabaliko devours the food at his leisure. Katandabaliko cannot himself be cooked: cut up and boiled, he knits himself back together and bounces out of the pot. Those who attempt to cook and eat him may eat their own wives by mistake. When not tormenting human beings, he prefers to dwell among cliffs.

[I myself prefer to dwell in Mombasa, at the back of my uncle's shop, Moosajee and Co. I cannot pretend to enjoy nights spent in the open, under what my employer calls the splendor of the African sky. Mosquitoes whine, and something, probably a dangerous animal, rustles in the grass. The Somali cook and headman sit up late, exchanging stories, while the Kavirondo porters sleep in a corral constructed of baggage. I am uncomfortable, but at least I am not lonely. My employer is pleased to think that I suffer terribly from loneliness. "It's no picnic for you, eh, Alibhai?" He thinks me too prejudiced to tolerate the society of the porters, and too frightened to go near the Somalis, who, to his mind, being devout Sunnis, must be plotting the removal of my Shi'a head.

In fact, we all pray together. We are tired and far from home. We are here for money, and when we talk, we talk about money. We can discuss calculations for hours: what we expect to buy, where we expect to invest. Our languages are different but all of us count in Swahili.]

6. Kibugi

A male ogre who haunts the foothills of Mount Kenya. He carries machetes, knives, hoes, and other objects made of metal. If you can manage to make a cut in his little finger, all the people he has devoured will come streaming out.

[Mary has had, I suspect, a mission education. This would explain the name and the calico dress. Such an education is nothing to be ashamed of — why, then, did she stand up in such a rage when I inquired about it? Mary's rage is cold; she kept her voice low. "I have told you not to ask me these types of questions! I have only come to tell you about ogres! Give me the money!" She held out her hand, and I doled out her daily fee in rupees, although she had not stayed for the agreed amount of time.

She seized the money and secreted it in her dress. Her contempt burned me; my hands trembled as I wrote her fee in my record book. "No questions!" she repeated, seething with anger. "If I went to a mission school, I'd burn it down! I have always been a free woman!"

I was silent, although I might have reminded her that we are both my employer's servants: like me, she has come here for money. I watched her stride off down the path to the village. At a certain distance, she began to waver gently in the sun.

My face still burns from the sting of her regard.

Before she left, I felt compelled to inform her that, although my father was born at Karachi, I was born at Mombasa. I, too, am an African.

Mary's mouth twisted. "So is Kibugi," she said.]

7. Kiptebanguryon

A fearsome yet curiously domestic ogre of the Rift Valley. He collects human skulls, which he once used to decorate his spacious dwelling. He made the skulls so clean, it is said, and arranged them so prettily, that from a distance his house resembled a palace of salt. His human wife bore him two sons: one which looked human like its mother, and one, called Kiptegen, which resembled its father. When the wife was rescued by her human kin, her human-looking child was also saved, but Kiptegen was burnt alive.

[I am pleased to say that Mary returned this morning, perfectly calm and apparently resolved to forget our quarrel.

She tells me that Kiptegen's brother will never be able to forget the screams of his sibling perishing in the flames. The mother, too, is scarred by the loss. She had to be held back, or she would have dashed into the fire to rescue her ogre-child. This information does not seem appropriate for my employer's catalogue; still, I find myself adding it in the margins. There is a strange pleasure in this writing and not-writing, these letters that hang between revelation and oblivion.

If my employer discovered these notes, he would call them impudence, cunning, a trick.

What would I say in my defense? "Sir, I was unable to tell you. Sir, I was unable to speak of the weeping mother of Kiptegen." He would laugh: he believes that all words are found in his language.

I ask myself if there are words contained in Mary's margins: stories of ogres she cannot tell to me.

Kiptebanguryon, she says, is homeless now. A modern creature, he roams the Protectorate clinging to the undersides of trains.]

8. Kisirimu

Kisirimu dwells on the shores of Lake Albert. Bathed, dressed in barkcloth, carrying his bow and arrows, he glitters like a bridegroom. His purpose is to trick gullible young women. He will be betrayed by song. He will die in a pit, pierced by spears.

[In the evenings, under the light of the lamp, I read the day's inventory from my record book, informing my employer of precisely what has been spent and eaten. As a representative of Moosajee and Co., Superior Traders, Stevedores and Dubashes, I am responsible for ensuring that nothing has been stolen. My employer stretches, closes his eyes, and smiles as I inform him of the amount of sugar, coffee and tea in his possession. Tinned bacon, tinned milk, oat porridge, salt, ghee. The dates, he reminds me, are strictly for the Somalis, who grow sullen in the absence of this treat.

My employer is full of opinions. The Somalis, he tells me, are an excitable nation. "Don't offend them, Alibhai! Ha, ha!" The Kavirondo, by contrast, are merry and tractable, excellent for manual work. My own people are cowardly, but clever at figures.

There is nothing, he tells me, more odious than a German. However, their women are seductive, and they make the world's most beautiful music. My employer sings me a German song. He sounds like a buffalo in distress. Afterward, he makes me read to him from the Bible.

He believes I will find this painful: "Heresy, Alibhai! Ha, ha! You'll have to scrub your mouth out, eh? Extra ablutions?"

Fortunately, God does not share his prejudices.

I read: *There were giants in the earth in those days.*

I read: *For only Og king of Bashan remained of the remnant of giants; behold, his bedstead was a bedstead of iron.*]

9. Konyek

Konyek is a hunter. His bulging eyes can perceive movement far across the plains. Human beings are his prey. He runs with great loping strides, kills, sleeps underneath the boughs of a leafy tree. His favorite question is: "Mother, whose footprints are these?"

[Mary tells me that Konyek passed through her village in the Year of Amber. The whirlwind of his running loosened the roofs. A wise woman had predicted his arrival, and the young men, including Mary's brother, had set up a net between trees to catch him. But Konyek only laughed and tore down the net and disappeared with a sound of thunder. He is now, Mary believes, in the region of Eldoret. She tells me that her brother and the other young men who devised the trap have not been seen since the disappearance of Konyek.

Mary's gaze is peculiar. It draws me in. I find it strange that, just a few days ago, I described her as a cold person. When she tells me of her brother she winds her scarlet thread so tightly about her finger I am afraid she will cut it off.]

10. Mbiti

Mbiti hides in the berry bushes. When you reach in, she says: "Oh, don't pluck my eye out!" She asks you: "Shall I eat you, or shall I make you my child?" You agree to become Mbiti's child. She pricks you with a needle. She is betrayed by the cowrie shell at the end of her tail.

["My brother," Mary says.
She describes the forest. She says we will go there to hunt ogres. Her face is filled with a subdued yet urgent glow. I find myself leaning closer to her. The sounds of the others, their voices, the smack of an axe into wood, recede until they are thin as the buzzing of flies. The world is composed of Mary and myself and the sky about Mary and the trees about Mary. She asks me if I understand what she is saying. She tells me about her brother in the forest. I realize that the glow she exudes comes not from some supernatural power, but from fear.
She speaks to me carefully, as if to a child.
She gives me a bundle of scarlet threads.
She says: "When the child goes into the forest, it wears a red necklace. And when the ogre sees the necklace, it spares the child." She says: "I think you and my brother are exactly the same age."
My voice is reduced to a whisper. "What of Mbiti?"
Mary gives me a deep glance, fiercely bright.
She says: "Mbiti is lucky. She has not been caught. Until she is caught, she will be one of the guardians of the forest. Mbiti is always an ogre and always the sister of ogres."]

11. Ntemelua
Ntemelua, a newborn baby, already has teeth. He sings: "Draw near, little pot, draw near, little spoon!" He replaces the meat in the pot with balls of dried dung. Filthy and clever, he crawls into a cow's anus to hide in its stomach. Ntemelua is weak and he lives by fear, which is a supernatural power. He rides a hyena. His back will never be quite straight, but this signifies little to him, for he can still stretch his limbs with pleasure. The only way to escape him is to abandon his country.

[Tomorrow we depart.
I am to give the red necklaces only to those I trust. "You know them," Mary explained, "as I know you."
"Do you know me?" I asked, moved and surprised.
She smiled. "It is easy to know someone in a week. You need only listen."
Two paths lie before me now. One leads to the forest; the other leads home.
How easily I might return to Mombasa! I could steal some food and rupees and begin walking. I have a letter of contract affirming that I am employed and not a vagrant. How simple to claim that my employer has dispatched me back to the coast to order supplies, or to Abyssinia to purchase donkeys! But these scarlet threads burn in my pocket. I want to draw nearer to the source of their heat. I want to meet the ogres.
"You were right," Mary told me before she left. "I did go to a mission

school. And I didn't burn it down." She smiled, a smile of mingled defiance and shame. One of her eyes shone brighter than the other, kindled by a tear. I wanted to cast myself at her feet and beg her forgiveness. Yes, to beg her forgiveness for having pried into her past, for having stirred up the memory of her humiliation.

Instead I said clumsily: "Even Ntemelua spent some time in a cow's anus."

Mary laughed. "Thank you, brother," she said.

She walked away down the path, sedate and upright, and I do not know if I will ever see her again. I imagine meeting a young man in the forest, a man with a necklace of scarlet thread who stands with Mary's light bearing and regards me with Mary's direct and trenchant glance. I look forward to this meeting as if to the sight of a long-lost friend. I imagine clasping the hand of this young man, who is like Mary and like myself. Beneath our joined hands, my employer lies slain. The ogres tear open the tins and enjoy a prodigious feast among the darkling trees.]

12. Rakakabe
Rakakabe, how beautiful he is, Rakakabe! A Malagasy demon, he has been sighted as far north as Kismaayo. He skims the waves, he eats mosquitoes, his face gleams, his hair gleams. His favorite question is: "Are you sleeping?"

Rakakabe of the gleaming tail! No, we are wide awake.

[This morning we depart on our expedition. My employer sings – "Green grow the rushes, o!" – but we, his servants, are even more cheerful. We are prepared to meet the ogres.

We catch one another's eyes and smile. All of us sport necklaces of red thread: signs that we belong to the party of the ogres, that we are prepared to hide and fight and die with those who live in the forest, those who are dirty and crooked and resolute. "Tell my brother his house is waiting for him," Mary whispered to me at the end – such an honor, to be the one to deliver her message! While she continues walking, meeting others, passing into other hands the blood-red necklaces by which the ogres are known.

There will be no end to this catalogue. The ogres are everywhere. Number thirteen: Alibhai M. Moosajee of Mombasa.

The porters lift their loads with unaccustomed verve. They set off, singing. "See, Alibhai!" my employer exclaims in delight. "They're made for it! Natural workers!"

"O, yes sir! Indeed, sir!"

The sky is tranquil, the dust saturated with light. Everything conspires to make me glad.

Soon, I believe, I shall enter into the mansion of the ogres, and stretch my limbs on the doorstep of Rakakabe.]

Art by Janet Chui

THE OUD
THORAIYA DYER

1633
The Shouf, Ottoman Empire

My dead husband's demons are seeking to sink into my daughter's bones.

Inside our stone hut, Ghalya is yet to wake. Outside it, the pine forest also. Sunrise catches dewdrops hanging from dark needles. Gazelles slip through shadows and wildcats settle silently in tree forks to sleep.

But pebbles roll where there are no feet, human or animal, to disturb them. Cracked shapes shift, breaking free of their concealment against scale-patterned bark.

The morning steals the feeling from my fingers as I pluck the strings of my oud with a risha of smooth bone. The music of grief emerges, keeping the demons at bay. Legend says that the ribcage-like shape of the instrument was inspired by the bleached, hanging bones of a grandson of Adam. The dead boy's father constructed the wooden skeleton of the oud in imitation of the terrible source of his mourning.

I have not worn mourning colours, for the Christian villagers must not know that my husband has died. They would send another family to take my place in this part of the wood. That family would collect the unopened cones of the wild pines, extracting the nuts when the dried cones open, cutting the dead wood to keep the forest healthy. It is food, it is income, it is safety for a larger family than mine – now just Ghalya and me – but they do not know of the dozen others I must feed and keep hidden.

They do not know that the secret cave where a Druze leader died is now a refuge for his defeated son.

At last, the demons lie still. Rays of light touch the tree bark and it is only bark, again. I hold the instrument in the moment of quiet before the birds swoop in, to quarrel and to sing, now that the sense of unease that warns them of demons is lifted from their thin, feathery skins.

I can keep no tame fowl in the forest. The goats, in contrast, never shrink from looking a demon in the eye. I pack the oud away in its leather case and sling it across my shoulder as I move to unlatch the gate of the goat pen. As time goes by, as my grief fades, the song becomes less powerful. Sometime soon, maybe even now, it will not last a full day.

The oud must be within arm's reach when that time comes.

Inside the hut, bags of straining yoghurt make the same milky *drip, drip, drip* as the limestone daggers of the cave. It makes me shiver in foreboding but I cannot falter. I pack my hand cart with flat loaves of bread, pastries stuffed with goat meat and pine nuts, soft cheeses, cucumbers, sesame seeds, and olive oil.

When the Janissaries raid the village, they take great casks of wine. Those elite infantrymen serve the Ottoman Sultan, Murad IV. I do not take wine with me, to the place where I am going.

"Time to wake, little squirrel," I whisper into the soap-soft scent of my sleeping child. Ghalya frowns and tries to turn her back, but I shake her shoulder until she's awake enough to ride on my back without falling, her five-year-old fingers knotted around my neck.

We set off with the goats trailing after us. If any early risers from the village of Bkassin see us, they will think we go to the base of the terrible north-facing cliff to fill waterskins from the mineral waters. Or to let the goats find what nourishment they can from the mosses growing in the southern end of the valley. It is perpetually in the shadow of the mountain, pounded by waterfalls in spring when the snow melts.

When we reach it, I pay no attention to the goats as they scatter. They know how to find their way home. A thin spray of water from the stream, which winds its way through the village of Jezzine and then falls off the edge into emptiness, seeds my shawl fringe with diamonds and rouses Ghalya.

"Are we there?" she murmurs. "I don't like the men. They smell bad. I don't like the dark."

I wish I could leave her at the base of the falls. I wish I could trust in the song. If the demons come when I am not with her, they will sap the strength of her muscles, as they did with Hisham, so that he could not rise from his bed.

They will take her mind, as they took Hisham's, so that he could not recognise anyone. He screamed Satanic songs until his eyes bulged and his lips turned blue.

Ghalya is heavy. Healthy. Strong. But her legs aren't long enough to cross the broken gaps in the mountain path. I hitch her up higher; I must carry her, despite the ache in my back and the burning in my thighs. The cart I hide in its usual place behind the bushes.

"Not yet, little squirrel. Hold on tight. Don't let go until I say."

Only I can see the firebirds, with their great hooked beaks and flames for feathers. Each one is ten times the height of a man. The pair are petrified, part of the cliff face, one on either side of the waterfall. They are the guardians of Jezzine. Mother warned me they could be woken by my sorrow.

The song I am giving to you, she said sharply. *You must never sing it near the firebirds. It is for holding back the stone demons. The bone demons. Not for holding back the Ottomans. Not for setting the firebirds against the Sultan. You understand?*

What did I care about Ottomans? I had cradled the oud as if it was Hisham's sweating brow, and cried and cried under the critical, dry eyes of my mother. Her face was framed by the fall of the black veil from the inscribed silver tower of her tantoura and her robes were belted with silver, too. She had risen far in the ranks of the Knowledgeable since I had disobeyed her and fled the foothills to marry a Maronite Christian.

If this can keep the demons away, I sobbed, *why didn't you bring it while Hisham was alive?*

He was not my blood. She shrugged. *He was not mine to save. In a dream, I saw my hands putting the instrument into your hands. Your father taught you how to play. You haven't forgotten. All you need is the right risha with which to pluck the strings.*

You didn't have a dream! Admit it. You wanted him to die because he was not a Druze. You sent the demons!

Silence! Her voice was an avalanche. *Your false baptism was blasphemy enough without such accusations. And do not let me hear this word, Druze, pass your lips again. We are the Muwahhidun. Ad-Darazi was a heretic. Do not call us after him. He interpreted the Koran poorly. We do not need the sword to spread the faith.*

No, I whispered. *Only to cut off your hands and feet when they do not obey you.*

You cut yourself off, Zahara. From me and from God. For now, your grief will keep Ghalya safe, but when you finally forget your husband – and you will forget him, forget his smile, forget the sound of his voice, forget the shape of his face – then you must come home to us, to forge a new sorrow with which to fight.

I do not wish to forge any new sorrows. I have had enough of them. Instead, I will borrow the sorrow of others. I am not as ignorant as Mother thinks. It is not because I care, as Fakr-ad-Din does, about my country becoming united – Sunni Muslim, Christian, and Druze – that I feed the fugitives in the cave. Nor do I feed them in order to defy the Ottoman Sultan, nor the Pasha from Damascus who rules with the Sultan's authority.

No. I feed them because Fakr-ad-Din's son has been recently killed. His grief is raw. His grief is new.

Hisham's demons are old. They were his mother's. I don't know how long they have been in his family and I don't know any way in which they can be destroyed. All I know for sure is that my song of grief has lasted almost three years and is beginning to fade. Might the song of a prince, even a prince defeated and in hiding, not last for thirty years, or more?

God loves Fakr-ad-Din, I think, *or he could not have been the prince. He could not have conquered from Palmyra to the sea, built mighty castles, or beaten the armies of Damascus.*

"It is the woman," calls a low voice from the mouth of the grotto.

"Weapons away," another voice murmurs. "It is only the woman. Come. We will go down to the valley and unload the cart."

I hesitate at the cave mouth. Inside, it is cold. Wet. Dark. A screen for the bloody shadow-puppet show of my unexorcised memories. Hisham died in a cave like this one. The Jesuits chained him to the wall. In the Cave of the Mad, they said, the healing powers of the saint would save him.

The saint did not save him.

"The beautiful Zahara," says the man who can only be Prince Fakr-ad-Din. Each time I have come before, it has been full dark, and the prince has been engaged in secret meetings, but his supporters do not dare visit in day-

11

light.

He takes my hand, kisses it. Christian women permit such things. My mother would have clawed out his eyes.

The prince has a woman's height. He has a curling white moustache and a waist-length beard that obscures the thread-of-gold embroidery decorating his silks. He carries a lantern in his left hand. A scimitar hangs at his waist. "It is a gift of heaven to meet you at last," he says. "My nephew told me the story of how he shot one of your goats. Instead of bringing the Janissaries, you vowed to keep us from starving, and here you are, true to your vow. Is your husband in good health?"

God loves Fakr-ad-Din.

"My husband is blessed with excellent health," I say by rote.

See me, God. I give bread and cheese to the one that you love. Will you give me some crumb in return? Or has my baptism truly cleaved me from you? Can you truly be turned aside by water?

"And your children?"

"My daughter is also blessed, your Highness. Is your royal family well?"

There it is. The mouth slackened by distress. The tic in one eye. The breath in his lungs that is suddenly not enough. Finally, he wets his lips and speaks.

"My... my nephew is well. Nephew!"

The middle-aged cavalryman who killed my goat comes out of a side-passage. He carries a Turkish bow and a musket. It has been three months since I first saw him and though he still wears the same brown tunic, baggy black trousers, and knee-high boots as he did on that morning, his neat black beard is no longer neat.

He quirks an eyebrow that is sliced in half by an old scimitar scar.

"Yes, Uncle?"

"You did not tell me that the talented Zahara is also a musician. You did not tell me she carries an oud."

"Do you think music is prudent in this place, Uncle?"

"She will play for me in the inner chamber. My soul is weary."

"As you wish, Uncle."

If Fakr-ad-Din fears his father's demons, it does not show. He leads me deeper and deeper into the cave. My foot slips on uneven ground and the jostling wakes Ghalya fully. Though soldiers cannot, in general, be trusted, I have no fear that these will harm her. They depend on me.

"I don't like the dark," she says in a frightened voice by my ear.

"Hush, little squirrel," I say, struggling wearily to find my balance. "I will play some soothing music, soon."

"But Aunty Rafqa says—"

When we reach the inner chamber, I let Ghalya slip down to the carpet. She stretches, but stays hiding behind me, peeping around me as I unsling the oud case and sit with my legs crossed beneath my many-layered skirts. White beards frighten her.

"What would you hear, your highness?" I ask.

"You hold your head tilted back," Fakr-ad-Din observes lightly. "You wore a tantoura when you learned to play."

"Conversion is permitted, O Prince of the Druze."

"This Prince of the Druze only wonders if the talented Zahara knows any verses of the Koran."

"Yes. Of course."

I begin to play, with the risha I made from my husband's breastbone, and to sing, with a voice that the Sunnis would say is heretical. To them, the voice of a woman is the voice of temptation. And not just to them; Hisham's sister Rafqa is Christian, but she never passes up a chance to declare to me that my singing is a sin and a scandal.

The Muwahhidun, on the other hand, do not care, so long as the songs are not sung to outsiders.

Until al-Hakim returns, I think, *the curtain is drawn, the door closed, the ink has dried up in the inkwell, and the pen is broken.*

At first, I think the howling is the howling of my husband as the demons torture him in the Cave of the Mad. Then I realise it is Ghalya.

"No!" she scolds, little fists on my back. "Aunty Rafqa says God wishes women to be silent. You must not sing God's songs, Mama!"

"Ghalya," I hiss. "You are angering the prince! Be quiet or I shall slap you, hard!"

But the prince is smiling.

"Never mind," he says. "Hush, child. Hush, Zahara. It was wrong of me to ask. You are a Christian woman now. I only thought to distract myself from dark thoughts with prayers from my childhood. They make me feel a boy again, playing warlord in my father's jeweled costumes."

I understand with a thrill that this is the key to my new song. The black, unshelled kernel of his grief. If he will only show it to me, I can weave it into my protective music. Then all I will have to do is steal one of his son's bones for my new risha, and Ghalya will be safe.

No pine nut was ever shelled without first hitting it with a rock.

"Did your son dress in your robes, as a boy?" I ask with false hesitancy, my heart galloping.

"Yes, he did," Fakr-ad-Din says hoarsely.

"In your castle by the sea?"

"No. In the Palace of the Moon. He laughed, even when he grew tangled in them and fell. He cut his lip. Kept laughing, even as he bled."

"Is that where you buried him?" I prompt softly, dangerously.

But Fakr-ad-Din's gaze is vacant. He travels along the river of his grief. I must put my waterwheel into that flow. I must harness the power of it.

The Prince's nephew returns and the moment is lost. He guides me out of the Prince's inner sanctum and pays me for the food in gold coins I can never use, never show to anyone. I carry them back down the cliff face with my dangle-legged daughter, my oud, and my frustration. I am so close.

Next time. Next time, he will tell me.

When I get back to the stone hut in the pine forest, half my goats have been trussed and slaughtered. My jars of flour and oil have been loaded onto donkeys for transport to the town.

Bristling with edged weapons and hostility, the Janissaries are waiting.

***

The pasha's narrow face is impatient.

He taps his palm with a riding crop. The end of his jewelled turban tucks under his grey-bearded chin. The beard boasts to all who see him that though he leads the uniformed Janissaries, he is not of them.

He is a pasha of Damascus, a Muslim and a free man, not a Christian conscript sworn to celibacy, trained for war, and severely disciplined since childhood to owe his loyalty to the Sultan alone.

"I told you, I haven't seen anyone," I say again, my throat shrivelled with thirst. Forced to kneel before the pasha with a yatagan sword resting lightly on the nape of my neck, I glance at the huddle of villagers behind the pasha's retinue, Ghalya among them, restrained tightly by her terrified Aunty Rafqa and Uncle Estefan.

"Where is your husband?" the pasha demands. "Consorting with the rebels, no doubt."

"He is a woodcutter, my lord! He is cutting wood in the forest!"

"We will see. Take the instrument from her."

The sword at my back slides beneath the knot of the sling. If they take the oud, it will mean my daughter's death. My fingers fly over my shoulder to the knot, to seize the sling, and are sliced through for their troubles.

My blood is everywhere. Men are shouting. I am frantic.

"No, my lord! Please, my lord!"

Somebody kicks me between the shoulder blades. Somebody else drags me away from the green where the Pasha holds court. I smell incense and fowl droppings. My right hand, before my eyes, is a fountain of red. The fingers do not function.

They have taken my oud. I will never play again.

Stones are cold against my back. Rafqa and Estefan have propped me against the side of the little church. Bkassin's church was paid for by the coins dribbling back to the village from all the sons taken to be Janissaries.

Sons like Rafqa and Estefan's son. His name was Yusuf. Now it is Mehmed, but I still recognise him. I remember how Rafqa cut her hair when he was taken, as though he had died. Now, his face swims in front of mine.

Young. Handsome. A bare, cleft chin.

"Wind it tighter to stop the blood," he tells Rafqa. "I will beg my lord for the use of his Jewish physician."

I realise Rafqa is ruining her best striped sash by binding my bleeding hand with it. Estefan looms behind her, muffling Ghalya's face against his paunch.

"Kill her," I gasp to my dead husband's brother. "Kill her, or find a way to bring my oud back to me."

"You should not have been carrying it, Zahara," Estefan answers, stricken. "You gave up women's witchcraft when you married Hisham. Music is for men only."

14

"My son risks his life for you," Rafqa says, crushing my hand between both of hers. "He betrays a lingering affection for his former family simply by speaking to his own mother, and now—"

I watch her mouth moving but the sounds lose their meaning. In the white clouds overhead, I see the shapes of snow-covered pine trees, and Hisham standing beneath them, swinging Ghalya into the sky. I see him drinking from the mineral spring.

Then the spring dries up. Hisham digs a well behind the stone hut. Down in the dark, that is where the demons find him. They slip from the stone into his bones. They make him scream and writhe.

The Jesuits hear him in passing. They hold long conversations, not with me, but with one another and with the God they say has led them through the valley. I don't hear their God speak, but the brothers say that Hisham must go with them to the monastery.

I trail after them with Ghalya like a milk goat with a kid at foot, ignored by them, until they are forced to bar me from the Cave. My woman's blood will pollute it, they say.

"Run away, Ghalya," I try to say. "Run away. Don't go to the cave. Don't go to the cave, Hisham. You'll die there. You'll die in chains."

Whiteness is everywhere. The clouds have come down. They are all around.

"Which cave is she talking about?" Rafqa says sharply.

"My God," Estefan says. "She is speaking of the grotto. The grotto of Fakr-ad-Din's father. She knows where he is. The pasha spoke true. Hisham is a traitor."

"We must tell the pasha, right away. With this information, we can protect our son. We can protect the village."

And then I do not hear or see anything at all.

***

When I wake, frogs are crooning to a crescent moon.

The bed by the open window is a heap of layered blankets on a swept clay floor. My right hand is a heavy lump of bandage and clotted blood. I can't feel anything inside. There is no sign of Ghalya, but then, she would not be allowed to sleep with me. I am a bad influence. Rafqa will be her mother, from now on.

For as long as she has left to live.

Crawling to the storage shelves behind the closed door, I take Rafqa's funeral garb from its wrappings and put it on. My husband is dead. I have never worn mourning colours for him, but the night is black, and the robes are black, and I must reach the grotto to warn Fakr-ad-Din of what I have accidentally done.

Is that why? Mother's voice demands in my imagination. *Is it to warn him, or to find out, at last, where he has hidden the bones of his son? Is it to warn him, or to beg him to bring his soldiers down into the valley and murder the pasha, murder all his Janissaries, including your own nephew, so that you can have your oud returned to you and save Ghalya from the stone demons?*

I climb out of the window. Take the forgotten road out of Bkassin, far enough that the pasha's guards will not see me, before circling around, heading for the southern end of the valley where the mighty cliff waits.

It takes hours to cross the valley floor. There are no wolves in the pine forest. They will not come where there are demons.

I see no demons.

"Where are you?" I wonder aloud; I wonder if I am still delirious. Or walking in a dream, for I do not grow thirsty, or tired.

I find the base of the waterfall by its spray on my face, and climb the perilous path between the sleeping firebirds. The path is treacherous enough by day. It is foolhardy to attempt it by moonlight. Yet I make no missteps in Rafqa's curled, black satin slippers, and when I find the grotto I call Fakr-ad-Din's name into its empty depths.

For, of course, it is empty. There were no scouts to give warning of my approach. No lanterns live in the dripping dark.

I stand there, a pillar of futility and pain, wondering if I should simply throw myself off the edge. It is a long way down. There is no chance I would survive.

***

When I arrive back at the village, it is emptied of the pasha and his soldiers.

I realise that the shapes of men I avoided on my way to the valley were the bodies of villagers who had defied the pasha, tied to upright halberds before being stoned to death.

Placing one foot after another, one ruined slipper after another, between the uneven stones of Bkassin's main street, I collapse by the building that houses the village spring, drinking spilled water from broken buckets out of a dust-flecked pool while reflected sunlight spears my gritty eyes. The village water is tasteless. Not like the mineral water that rushes from the mountain.

After a short rest, I stagger back to Rafqa's house.

"I curse the day that Hisham ever laid eyes on you," she cries. "I curse the day your house was joined to mine."

Ignoring her, I seek another source of crying, one that comes from a room that once belonged to Rafqa's son. His toy wooden animals still sit on the window sill. Ghalya lies limply in a bundle of furs. Her face is flushed and her eyes are staring.

I see the stone demons move inside her. I see them eating her from within. Estefan moves back from her. His eyes are wild.

"We should not have done it," he says. "We should not have helped the pasha. Now the girl has no father to guide her. No wonder she has gone mad."

I feel my knees touch the floor beside the bed. I gather Ghalya into my arms.

Let them leave her body, I beg wordlessly. *Let them leave her body and enter into mine.*

But they do not leave her body. Three days later, she is dead.

***

Standing before the stone firebirds, I take the oud out of its sling.

Every movement that I make is slow and deliberate. I have only half a thumb and my two smallest fingers remaining on my right hand.

It was months before my wounds healed and I was able to steal the oud back from the wedding celebrant who had taken it. After that, it was only a matter of desecrating Ghalya's grave. The stone cover, placed there to prevent her demons from infecting anyone else, was no barrier to the demons, though it was to me. I used a woodcutter's axe in my left hand — the hand furthest from God, the hand closest to the Devil — to break through the stone, and then through the ribcage of the perfect daughter I had borne.

With her breastbone for my risha, I knew the song of my grief would be powerful enough to move mountains.

I look up at the firebirds. When they awaken, fire will cover everything that falls into their line of vision. The pine forest will burn. Gazelles and wild-cats will flee for their lives. Villagers, too.

My mother told me the music was not for setting the firebirds against the Ottomans, but that was before they murdered my child. Her granddaughter. She cannot stop me.

She will not stop me.

"Awake, spirits of the mountain," I sing. "Children of the sun. Fakr-ad-Din is taken to Constantinople. There is work to be done."

The great birds shiver. They ripple. They begin to glow.

In the always-shade of the cliff face, the firebirds open their eyes.

Art by Alice Meichi Li

FREE JIM'S MINE
TANANARIVE DUE

May, 1838
Dahlonega, Georgia

"He out yet?" Lottie's husband, William, breathed behind her, invisible in the dark.

Lottie's heart sped, a thumping beneath her breastbone that stirred the child in her belly.

"Don't know," Lottie said. "Hush."

She stared from her hiding place behind the arrowwood shrubs, heavy belly low to the soil. They had slipped past the soldiers at Fort Dahlonega, and now they were twenty yards west of the mine's gate, which stood open wide as miners escaped the cavern's mouth for the night. Shadowy figures ambled toward them, unaware.

Would she know her Uncle Jim in the dark? Lottie had not seen her father's brother in five years. Until then, he'd come to see mama two or three times a year after Lottie's father died. But now he was a freeman – the only free Negro she knew. Free Jim, everyone called him.

Mama said God shined light into his massa's heart one day and he wrote up Uncle Jim's freedom papers after church. But most said Uncle Jim bought a mojo and poured a powder with calamus, bergamot, and High John the Conqueror root in his massa's morning tea.

As tiny feet kicked at her, Lottie vowed she would name William's baby Freedom. If only she could find Uncle Jim and survive the night, they could all change their names.

A few white miners remained huddled at the gate while she waited and hoped to see Uncle Jim's beard or his shock of white-splashed hair. One by one, the miners untied their horses. About a dozen colored men emerged last, but they did not have horses. Instead, they shuffled down the road as fast as they seemed able, lanterns swinging. Uncle Jim, born a slave, had slaves working for him? *What makes you think he'll help you?* The forlorn call of a bullfrog hidden somewhere nearby reminded Lottie of swinging from a rope on a rotting oak branch, slowly to and fro.

They would not make it without Uncle Jim. Would not make it to the state line, or to the farmhouse in North Carolina where the Quakers would come fetch them. The last few days' horrid rain had stopped at last, but they would be cold tonight. Lottie couldn't remember when her clothes last had been dry.

"Go to 'em, William," Lottie said to William. "Say you lookin' for a few days' wages. Say you wanna talk to Free Jim." Panic made her voice sound

19

twelve instead of seventeen.

"They'll know that's gum," William said.

Without the wagon, they had been forced to go to Uncle Jim in Dahlonega, where William had been reared. Cherokees weren't welcome since the Army started marching families off. William said he'd rather die running with her than let the white man choose his home.

"Whatever you gonna say, hurry and say it, Waya," she told him.

William's mother had given him a Cherokee name, Waya, though he used William outside of his boyhood home to set white men at ease. William pressed his palm to the side of her belly, head bowed. Then he stood and crept past the brush and up the road toward Lot 998 – Free Jim Boisclair's mine.

The chatter at the mine entrance went quiet when William walked up. Lottie tried to hear, lying so still that she didn't brush away the insects that tickled her ankles and calves. But she couldn't hear a word over the bullfrog's warble, vexing her like a haint.

A sign, it was. A bad sign.

Then she heard the low, snapping bark that followed her into her dreams. Dogs were on their trail again! "Damn, damn, damn," she whispered to the dark.

Next, the men came. On the road, two white riders trotted north, their *clop-clopping* steady and loud. If not for the brush, she would be in plain view. The angry barking drew closer, crisper. And William was surer with his knife!

Lottie's frightened heartbeat shook the earth.

They would be found! Her eyesight dimmed. She would beg mercy from the slave-catchers. She was carrying a child, plain as day. One of them might have brains enough to realize that cow-hiding her might kill the child – and then what would they tell Marse Campbell about his lost property? She would never see William again; he would be sent away with his people. But he would not be alone. She'd wanted freedom, but at least she and her baby would live.

The plan was hard, but anything was better than dogs.

The riders stopped in the road, barely six strides from where she hid.

Two shadows walked from the mine's gate to meet the men, one carrying a lamp. Lottie saw the paunch of a man's middle beneath a brightly-colored vest, pocket watch swinging. She had seen that pocket watch before. Please, Jesus, was he the one?

"Evenin'." Uncle Jim's voice! His pocket watch winked in the lamplight.

"Evenin'." The lead rider spoke in a manner reserved for other white men.

"Need you at the ice house. Injun'll stand watch here."

The riders circled Uncle Jim and William on their horses. Uncertain, it seemed.

"All right, then," the lead rider said after a long while. He made a kissing sound for his horse, and the second man followed him up the road. Lottie had never seen white men do what a nigger told them. Uncle Jim had a mojo for sure! *Had* to.

Uncle Jim thrust the lamp into the brush, his wide nose nearly pressed to hers. "You're damn fools. 'Specially *you*, Lottie."

Uncle Jim's first words to her in five years.

Five years ago, he'd told Mama he would keep his promise to his dead brother. He'd gone to the back door of Marse's house and tried to talk to him, even offered him a bank note, but Marse Campbell had turned him away. Lottie and mama both had cried themselves hoarse. Lottie had not, could not, forget Uncle Jim's last words to her.

Don't you fret, Lottie. I'll come back for you.

***

Uncle Jim cursed a fury as he led her and William around a bluff on the brick-lined path to a wooden door. A preacher should know better than to blaspheme, and wasn't he a preacher? Wasn't he the one who'd taught her to read Scripture? Wasn't he the one who had left her in Augusta when he'd promised to buy her freedom?

Once the door was closed behind him, they walked a narrow corridor on a wood plank floor until Uncle Jim stopped at a door made half of glass. JAMES BOISCLAIR, the glass read in script so fancy she could barely make out the lettering.

Inside, he lit lamps and brought daylight to the small room. The desk buried in papers, bookshelves stuffed with books. Lottie hadn't realized she was shivering until Uncle Jim laid a warm blanket across her shoulders, and her trembling stopped.

"Look at you," Uncle Jim said. He'd fussed away his anger; now he only sounded sad. "You thought you'd get to the state line?"

"Got this far," Lottie said.

Uncle Jim's eyes lashed fire at William. "What are you going to do for her and a baby? *You*? She has kin in Augusta."

"Ain't his fault," Lottie said. "I wanted to come. Had to. I couldn't wait no more."

Marse Campbell had refused to let her take William as her husband. When her belly showed, he told her he would drown her half-breed baby if she gave him trouble. Drown her baby! William had been telling her she should run all along. He knew the roads and the woods. The first day she'd seen William, he'd sat perched in his driver's berth with the promise of faraway places.

"I saw a runaway notice in town!" Uncle Jim said, fingers twisting his beard. "Someone will piece it together. Those men you saw were not stupid men."

"We saw those crackers do what you told 'em," Lottie said. "Jumped right quick."

"Those," Uncle Jim said, "are white men who would turn in a stray Cherokee and his nigger runaway for a whole lot less than Campbell's reward. For shillings!"

Outside, the rain started its cruel pounding

21

Uncle Jim went silent when William took a step to him. She hoped Uncle Jim would not lay hands on him. Her husband would show his knife.

"Jim Boisclair's a big man," William said. "The mercantile. Eating house. Ice house. And this gold mine. Jim Boisclair's got his name, Lottie. No time to fool with you. My uncle was a big man too – had a dozen slaves. Now where is he?"

"I know you," Uncle Jim said. "Injun Willie the driver. You've hauled for me. My men were wondering why you're not on your way to Ross's Landing with the rest. Or Tennessee. Where you gonna' hide in Dahlonega?"

"It's *talon-e-ga*, not Dahlonega," William said. "You steal the word and destroy it."

"I ain't stole a damn thing," Uncle Jim said.

"Stealing from our grandfathers' mountain is nothing? Stealing land is nothing?"

Their words sounded like blows. It was all going terribly wrong.

"William, please," Lottie said.

"You're big enough to move the mountain," William said. "To take the gold. We ask a small thing from a big man."

When William glanced her way, Lottie begged him with her eyes: *Stop vexing him.*

"We jus' need a roof for the night," Lottie said. "We move on at daylight. William had a wagon, but we had to leave it cuz of the paddyrollers and all the soldiers on the road. We'll walk if we gotta, but if'n a body could ride us up closer to North Carolina..."

"Then why don't I snap my fingers and make pigs fly?" Uncle Jim said. "Didn't you hear me? I can't be seen with–"

"We could sleep in the mine."

Lottie wondered who'd said it, but it was her own tiny voice. From Uncle Jim's face, she might have said they should light themselves afire.

Uncle Jim shook his head. "It ain't fit, Lottie."

"Fit?" Lottie said. "What I care 'bout that? You think I'd rather be drug through the woods by dogs? Me an' my baby?" When she said *baby*, Uncle Jim cast his eyes to the floor.

William brushed his fingertip across the colorful book spines on Uncle Jim's shelf. "You afraid we're gonna steal your gold, big man?"

"Git away from there and mind your business," Uncle Jim said.

William reached up to a higher shelf, which was empty except for a small sack of burlap bound with twine. William took the sack and weighed it in his hand.

"*Don't touch that,*" Uncle Jim said. He tripped over his rug rushing to William, knocking books to the floor as he snatched the sack away. He hid it beneath his shirt, his whole body shaking. "That's not for anyone but me to touch!"

Lottie had never laid eyes on a bag of luck before, but she was sure William had found Uncle Jim's. He kept his mojo in plain sight. He might have feathers or bones in the sack, or powders, or strands of his old massa's hair. She knew people who'd bartered food or shoes to heal maladies and turn a beau's head their way, or to wish ill luck on their masters, but she had never imagined such a mighty mojo. With so much power, could the creature who'd sold it to Uncle Jim be called human?

"What that cost you, Uncle Jim?" Lottie whispered.

Uncle Jim looked at her with tears, bottom lip quavering. "I can't help you, Lottie," he said. "It's not I don't want to, girl – I *can't*. Every time I do... when I try... it goes wrong. You hear me? *I'm* free. Just me. I can't share it with nobody else – even you. Especially you, girl. Don't you see?"

"You turnin' us away?" Lottie said. "To the dogs and patrollers?"

"Might be better," Uncle Jim said. "You hear? Might be better'n staying with me."

Lottie had seen survivors of dogs with rent limbs, missing eyes, and ruined faces. She didn't want to believe dogs could be better than anything, even death, but the mine's stink seeped beneath the closed door: sour water full of rot.

"Told you he wouldn't help us," William said. He'd been wiping his hands on the seat of his pants since Uncle Jim took the bag of luck, as if his palms were sticky from its touch.

Lottie raised herself to her feet so fast that she felt dizzied.

"We gotta leave this place," Lottie said.

Uncle Jim's heartbroken eyes said *Yes, thank the Lord you understand, child.* But his lips twitched, as if against his will, and his mouth said, "Into the cold night? The rain? How can I?"

That was how the plan was settled.

Before the first miners arrived at dawn, Uncle Jim would hire a wagon master he knew, an Irishman named Willoughby who had no fondness for slavery or the Cherokee relocation. Willoughby would drive them to the train – "I'll be up the whole night to devise the papers and think of a pretense!" – and try to ride with them as far as Charlotte. Uncle Jim would pay Willoughby handsomely for his silence and peril, greater than the advertised reward.

But arrangements would take until morning. A long night lay ahead.

"Tonight," Uncle Jim said, "you must sleep in the mine."

***

Under the ground, Lottie met the purest lack of light she had ever known. Every step, it seemed, was blacker than the last.

Lottie steadied herself against the pocked wall, which felt as damp and slimy as a water snake. William stayed close to her, offering his hand, but instinct made her hold his arm instead. William wiped his unclean palms still, as if they itched from the bag of luck.

Uncle Jim's lamp was a poor defense. A flickering, sickly light.

"With the storms, the whole mine was flooded," Uncle Jim said. "Where we're going, water's still as high as your ankles. Higher, in some places. Lottie, mind where you walk. Don't get that dress wet."

Lottie's dress had been wet for two days. She would have laughed if she hadn't been so desperate to run back up the narrow steps as quickly as she could. She almost stepped on the dead, bloated rat at her feet, halfway under the water, a flash of light fur against the void.

"At least the flood killed the rats," Uncle Jim said. "But they're raising quite a stink."

"Water is good," William said. "It fools the dogs' noses."

Nothing was good about this water. No rainwater or creek bed carried the stench of the water in the mine. Lottie thought she might bathe for days and never be clean of it. She hoped the smell couldn't reach William's baby inside her, but it seemed all too certain her unborn could smell it too.

"Well..." Uncle Jim said. "You needn't worry about dogs down here." He huffed a breath when he said *dogs*.

"What, then?" Lottie said.

Uncle Jim looked back at her, his face and eyes invisible.

"Breaking your necks," he said. "Blowing yourselves to bits. Touch *nothing*, hear?"

The narrow cavern opened to release them to a wider space where a mining car smaller than a wagon sat on the tracks, empty and still. If only the Underground Railroad were truly underground, she thought. If only they could ride to freedom unseen by any human eyes.

"Where's the gold at?" Lottie said. The walls did not look golden.

"Deep in the rocks. T'ain't plain to the eye."

Black water pooled just beyond the mining car, shimmering tar in the light. Dripping echoed around them endlessly. Again, Lottie fought the urge to run.

"We ain't gonna drown down here, is we?" Lottie said.

"Not so long as you do as you're told and don't wander," Uncle Jim said. "Come on."

As he led them past the mining car, water seeped into her worn shoes, cold enough to tingle her toes. Water dripped just beyond her nose, and Lottie looked up: sharp rock formations like swords above them stood poised to fall and slice them in two. The next water droplet caught her eye, and she panicked as the cold stung and blinded her. With a gasp, she wiped her eyes clear. Her lungs locked tight until she could see Uncle Jim's lamp again.

William pointed to a narrow enclave, a shelter to their right. "Here?"

"No," Uncle Jim said. "Not far enough in. That's where the men crouch during the blasts. We'll find you another like it."

The corridor forked, and Lottie tried to map their location the way she did in the woods, but by the next fork she was confused. No landmarks guided her here.

The sloshing grew deafening as the floodwater rose to their shins. Lottie gathered her dress at her waist to try to avoid soaking it in stink. Mama had warned her not to stay wet, that she could get sick and die. But even though both she and Mama knew death might await her, Mama had said *Yes, let William take you and that baby away. There ain't nothing for you here. Go see Jim at his gold mine. At least it's a chance.*

But the longer Lottie walked, the less it seemed like any kind of chance. Death above or death below, it didn't matter – dying was dying. And Lottie felt death down here.

William gave a start, staring into the water near his feet. "Y'all see that?"

"What?" Lottie said.

William probed the water with his foot. "I saw... something."

"Quit your daydreaming," Uncle Jim said, but he sounded frightened. He still had the bag of luck snugly beneath his shirt. Holding it tight.

The water was higher now, at her knees. The damp fabric she carried was a heavy load. Her shins hurt from walking downhill, and the baby's bulk nearly toppled her with each step.

"What that bag do, Uncle Jim?" Lottie said. She raised her voice to be heard over their steady wading. "How you get it? Can I get one too?"

Uncle Jim faced her. The lamplight aged his face, made his eyes appear to burrow into his skin. His transformation startled her. "Stop that talk."

"You say when you try to help, it always go wrong," Lottie said. "How it go wrong?"

"You got to sell your heart for freedom, Lottie," Uncle Jim said. "Just like me."

"We're not like you," William said.

"Sure you are, red man. I've been watching them round up your people. Soldiers come knocking at the door, don't give nobody time to gather clothes. Everything you had is gone. They take the children in one wagon, the parents in the other, just to make sure nobody runs. You think they dreamed that up special for you? The ones who run – well, they don't listen to their hearts, do they? Their hearts are cold as ice."

Lottie blinked away tears. She tried not to think of Mama getting lashed because Marse Campbell would never believe she didn't know where her daughter had run to. Tried not to think about how Mama would never see her first grandchild. And that was just the best of what might come. Lottie's shaking started again, her knees knocking like clapping hands. In a few steep footsteps, the water reached above her thighs; dark slime in her most unwanted places.

"How it gonna go wrong for us, Uncle Jim?" Lottie said.

When Uncle Jim was silent for a time, she gave up on having an answer. And when he spoke, she wished he hadn't.

"It always goes wrong, girl," Uncle Jim said. "Don't get it in your heads you'll both make it up to North Carolina – and then what? Philadelphia? You're fools if you think this ends well. You never should've come. Think of the last words you want to say to each other, and be sure to say 'em quick. You won't both survive the night."

***

They had to stoop to enter the boxy blast enclave.

In the far back corner, the water didn't creep as high. A narrow, uneven ledge was raised enough for them to sit out of the stinking muck. Lottie hoped the water would drop by morning. Uncle Jim had said it might – if the rain let up. She couldn't tell if it was raining outside, but it was surely raining *inside*.

The only sounds were the chorus of dripping water and Uncle Jim's sing-song prayer as he walked back up to the world above.

"...Lord, take pity on your poor servants on this long night..." she heard his voice echo through the passageway. The words collided and faded, but she could make them out well enough to feel the prayer move her spirit. "Do not punish this poor shepherd, Lord, for we all have suffered enough.... Do not punish the innocent, Lord, for all they desire is the freedom to serve you better..."

Every few words, his voice hitched in a sob. He was the very sound of despair.

Then it was a faraway whisper.

Then he was no voice at all.

All around her, the dark.

Uncle Jim had given them two lamps, but the two hundred miles since Augusta had taught them to save kerosene for dire necessity. They had checked their matchsticks before blowing out the lamps, and while Lottie's had gotten wet in her pouch somehow, William had kept his dry. Lottie had fewer possessions now than ever. Before this night, she had never wanted for moonlight or air to breathe.

But Lottie was glad for the dark, since she didn't want William to see her tears. He was helpless to soothe her, so why should they punish each other? She huddled against the best man she knew, hearing Uncle Jim's prayer in her mind, rubbing her belly.

Uncle Jim had said that in the morning he would give them a treasure chest in the Irishman's wagon: dry clothes, a packed traveling bag, food, boxes of matches, a new compass. And money – how much she could only guess, if Uncle Jim's hired man didn't steal it first.

Neither of them had a timepiece, but she thought it had to be ten o'clock. At least.

In seven hours, Uncle Jim would come back for them. Seven hours. Seven years, it might as well be. But he would come. He *would* come, this time.

Seven hours, Lord. Let them last seven hours.

Don't let her mother's lashes be for nothing. Don't let William's grandmother's cries in her sickbed when the soldiers came be for nothing. Let it all matter for something.

Unless he means to drown you both here. For your own good.

And didn't he? Hadn't she heard his soul's guilt in his weepy prayer?

Lottie couldn't swallow away her sob, and William slid his palm against her hot cheek, all tenderness. Did he know it too? Did he know Uncle Jim had sent them into the mine to die?

Loud splashing flew toward them. Gone as soon as they heard it.

They sat closer, their bodies hard as stone. The splashing had come from directly outside the mouth of their enclave. Had Uncle Jim come back so soon? No more than half an hour could have passed.

"Uncle?" she whispered.

William covered her mouth with the palm. His heartbeat pulsed through his skin.

The next splash sounded like two limbs colliding. Then an undulating motion, one spot to the next. And sudden, impossible silence. They could be back out in the forest, jumping at bears and bobcats.

"That ain't a man," William said. "Didn't I say I saw somethin'? He saw it too."

"What it look like?" Lottie said. "A snake?"

"Too big for a snake," William said. "Too wide. Can't say what it looked like, but it wasn't no fish or snake. It looked 'bout as long as me."

"It's a man, then," Lottie said. "Somebody chasin' us."

"No," William said. "Not a man."

William calmly struck a match and lit his lamp. In the brightness, colored circles danced across Lottie's eyes.

Her vision snapped to focus when she heard the splash again. The creature was beyond the poor reach of their lamp, but she could hear its size – the front end slapping the water first, then the back. Like William said, as long as a man. But maybe wider. Beyond reason, she expected a bloodhound to come flying from the water, teeth gnashing.

William sucked in a long breath.

"You see it?" Lottie said.

William shook his head, waving his lamp slowly back and forth across the water.

Lottie's heart tried to pound free of her. "Maybe it's a gator!"

"No," William breathed. He stayed patient with his lamp's spotlight, which showed only brown flecks floating in the murk.

"What, then?" Lottie said.

"As a boy," he said quietly, "I heard stories about Walasi. A giant frog. My mother told me, her mother told her, her mother's mother, through time. To the beginning."

Ain't no damned frog that big, Lottie's mind tried to tell her, but she remembered the bullfrog's call she'd heard outside. An omen after all.

William pointed left. "Look there," he said, calm beyond reason.

Ripples fluttered in the lamplight. Then a frothy splashing showered them. Lottie screamed, but did not close her eyes. She wanted to see the thing. A silhouette sharpened in the water, like giant fingers stretching, or a black claw. Her hands flew to cover her eyes, but she forced her fingers open to peek through.

The creature churned the water, tossing its massive body. A shiny, bulging black eye as large as her open palm broke the water's plane, nestled by brown-green skin.

The creature flipped, its eye gone. Was this its belly? Pale beneath the water, smooth as glass. Too big to be anything she could name. The mine's thin air seared her lungs.

"Did you see it?" William's grin made him look fevered. His eyes seemed as wild and wide as the water creature's. "The frog?"

It can't be, she tried to say, arguing with her eyes. But her mouth would not move.

Lottie was whimpering, a childish sound she hadn't made since the day

Marse Campbell turned Uncle Jim away. She sat as far back as she could from the water, her arms locked around her knees. Her bones trembled as she rocked.

William whipped off his tattered shirt. His readied knife gleamed.

"Leave it be!" she said.

"Any child knows about Walasi, but no one has seen him. And now... here he is!" William's excitement unsettled Lottie. "Walasi tries to kill everyone in the village. But a warrior slays him."

Lottie felt a fear deeper than the mine's darkness. Maybe Uncle Jim's mojo had confused his mind. Had that come of touching it?

"Waya..." She called him by his mother's name, hoping he would hear her.

William clasped her upper arm and squeezed. His face wore an eerie grin. "When the warrior kills Walasi, it turns to little frogs. Harmless. They scatter. The village is saved."

"All your people is gone far away," Lottie said. "You ain't got no village. Ain't nothin' you can do!"

"What else should I do, dear Lottie?" he said. "Should I run and hide like a boy?

He laid his head across her belly, and she breathed him up and down. Lottie tried to summon words to bring sense to him, but she had no strength to speak.

Then he slipped from her, holding tight to his knife. He dove into the black water.

Lottie screamed. "*Waya!*"

Endless silence, except for the dripping water.

Every evil Lottie could dream felt certain: The creature was pulling strips of her husband's flesh with its teeth, far worse than any dog. And it would come to take her next. It would tear the baby from her and scatter its limbs. Uncle Jim had bargained his freedom with a curse. He had sacrificed them.

The world spun, the mine's darkness fighting to take her thoughts too. She felt dizzy enough to faint, but she could not. Could *not*. Lottie kept her mind awake by counting off in her head as she waited for William to pop up from the water. *Eleven... twelve... thirteen... fourteen...*

William could hold his breath a long time. He swam like a fish in the pond near the road where he drove past Marse Campbell's farm once a month. Showing off for her.

Thirty-five... thirty-six.... thirty-seven... thirty-eight...

Lottie stood as close to the water's lapping edge as she dared, using William's lamp to try to see. She tried calling both of his names. After a time, fingers shaking, she lit the second lamp too. His absence only grew brighter. The water lay still and silent.

Ninety-one... ninety-two... ninety-three...

"No..." Lottie whispered. "No..."

At five hundred, she stopped counting.

She felt too breathless to sob. Even tears shunned her misery.

How could she have let William go? Why hadn't she let him drag her down with him? How dare he go to freedom without her!

Time passed uncounted. Lottie only realized she had slept when the water woke her with a start.

Just beyond her haven, something was moving – a steady gliding from one side to the next, back and forth. But even bleary-eyed, confused, and sick with sorrow, Lottie knew the sound was not from William. No man could glide so quickly or make such a sound.

Her lanterns made no impression on the water's void, showing her nothing.

"*Git on away from me!*" she shrieked at the dark, as if monsters heeded commands.

The water's splashing told her that the creature still lurked. Watching her? Preparing to make her and her baby its next meal?

"You give me my husband back!"

She tried to shout again, but her throat's tatters produced only a whisper, more frightened than angry.

How had she forgotten her knife? She prized the ivory-handled pen knife William had given her as a wedding gift, of sorts, when they decided they would run. Their time in the woods had dulled the blade from too much hacking and cutting, but she still had it. The knife was all that remained of William now.

Lottie grasped her knife and held it out like a sword toward the churning water. Like her, the blade was weak and small, but she wielded it as if they both had greater power.

"You hear me?" she said, and this time her voice was stronger too.

The thing in the water did hear. It swam closer to her, splashing water over the ledge in its huge wake. Lottie had not believed she could feel greater terror, but the advancing creature awakened such a childlike fear in her that she wanted to cover her eyes.

But she did not. Arm outstretched with her knife, she watched. And waited.

The bulbous eye appeared again before the water swallowed the sight of it, much closer than it had been before. Gone before she could lunge at it. Then came a wet slapping on the stone as the creature hoisted itself nearer to her with shiny green-brown skin. It was not a claw, nor a human hand, but a large and sinister blending of the two that fanned across the ledge as if to reach for her.

Lottie had no time to scream. She stabbed at the closest – digit? – and hacked at it, feeling euphoria when a piece of the creature fell separate from the rest. The creature howled, muffled under the water, and the limb retreated to escape her, snatched away. Lottie kicked the cursed tendril away from her, back into the black pool.

Her laughter was not true laughter – just a desperate, gasping cackle – but the sound of it filled the cave. Then Lottie collapsed into sobs that joined the chorus of falling water droplets from above.

Drip-drip. Drip-drip.

A plan came to Lottie. With a plan, she stole shallow breaths. Her sobbing eased.

She would stay away from the water.

Drip-drip.

She would teach their child his father's Cherokee name. *Drip-drip.*

She would teach their child that Waya's family had lived in peace along the Etowah River before soldiers took them away. *Drip-drip.*

She would feed their child the corn and hickory nuts Waya loved so much, alongside mama's corn cakes. *Drip-drip.*

Minutes passed, then hours, while Lottie made her plans for freedom that she would win at such an unfathomable cost.

"Lottie? You still here?"

When a voice came, Lottie shrieked. Hope swelled in her. But, no.

Not William. Not Waya.

Had she slept again? Her body was stiff against the stone.

Hours must have passed. Lamplight swayed in the passageway. The water had receded to a thin sheet. She smelled pipe tobacco. Her uncle's shadow floated on the wall.

"We got to hurry, girl."

Uncle Jim did not ask about William. He was not surprised her husband was gone.

"Waya," she whispered to the ravaged cave.

"Come on, Lottie – my man's outside waiting."

As Free Jim reached for her, his two gold rings flared like droplets from the sun.

His pinky finger, a bloodied crust, was freshly sliced away.

Art by Daria Khvostova

FFYDD (FAITH)

J. LYNN

1919
Swansea, Wales

Always more work than hands willing to turn to it, even in your own bloody kitchen. "Is that the last of the milk, then?"

Chorus of complaint and sighs from my husband's sisters. Lily and Iris and Violet have been looking after the home front, they're not used to being ordered about like relief-workers, not to scrub and fetch and stretch a ration *proper*. Not that it's not all the same war we've been fighting against. But.

I'd thought it would be less blood and worry, to be home again.

We fall silent as my husband edges into the room. Still a wisp, for all they've fed him since he's been home.

Still not even a shadow of him to reflect in the spoons.

Trevor smiles, hesitant as always. Still the same crooked eyeteeth. Still his. Unshaven. Iris shattered all the mirrors in a fit of rage, or pique, I never entirely know with Iris. Though no mirror ever helped his hair *before*, it's always been a hayrick. He looks like a naughty schoolboy.

He's barely met my eyes since I've been home, my husband. As hard to bear as how he's been lying beside me like a stone these last few nights. I'd been holding so fast to the memory of his eyes, the colour of that single word for what other languages slice up into *blue* and *grey* and *green*. But how can you divide the slate, the sky, the sea.

He'll never see those eyes looking back from a glass again. And there's not a word at all for what he is.

He's changed, they'd written. (Not *come home*, no, they credit me that much, but... but could I stop myself thinking about what they wouldn't say right out, till I had to tell myself I'd do no one much good working myself into a state. Better to think of it as seeing he's fit to join me at the relief efforts. Even if the leaving felt like an admission of unseriousness of purpose, just because I'd a husband to go home *to*.) And it's true. Not the sort of change one might have expected when a man's been in gaol over his conscience, neither. *That* one could understand – sudden starts at nothing, weeping when he'd think no one could hear? Seen my share of *that* this past while.

But Trevor, Trevor's is none of that.

How of a sudden he's the one offering to butcher the hen who'd stopped laying – how he'd come back in with blood round his mouth. He'd not denied it. Couldn't, *wouldn't*, not if it's simple truth. Just asks us to come clear in our own consciences, whether he's still the boy they loved, the man they knew.

That there itself should tell us that.

Trevor's looking round in that terribly polite way of a bloke who's only dared come in with us cooking because he's that desperate to see if the kettle's on. When he clears his throat Iris slams the cheese-grater down in the bowl hard enough I worry for her knuckles. "Put it on your own bloody self, why don't you? Ned manages."

Ned doesn't manage and we all know it, we know that Violet will be acting as her brother's lost arm for the rest of her days and the worst is she'd rather that than admit there's barely a lad left to marry proper and live her own life instead. Iris *has* cut her fingers on the grater. Trevor is watching his sister's hand as she sucks at her knuckle, teeth dimpling his lower lip till the blood beads. And, ah, the *hunger* in his eyes, until Iris finally says, abrupt and sharp, "Go see to the chickens then."

Trevor pushes out the back door into the courtyard without another word. I'm sure Iris doesn't mean to be hateful, well, I'm almost sure Iris doesn't mean to be hateful. I feel it low in my own stomach, our desperate fear of this uncharted future. Lily and Violet can see to the rest of our tea, or to Iris, whichever they please; I dust the flour from my hands and step out the back door after him.

It's a bright day, as it goes. Not raining yet at any rate. Trevor's sat on the step cuddling one of the hens in his lap. The cockerel's watching him from the wash-line, clearly not on with the notion that this sudden threat to the back-garden flock has hold of one of its wives or daughters, however gentle the embrace. I wave a hand for the bird to get off the washing and it flaps down to peck at the bricks as if we're the ones here on its sufferance. "I've not seen Iris *this* cross," I say.

"She's missing William." Trevor looks up, then ducks his head back down as if he'd not meant to meet my eyes for even that instant.

"Suppose I can understand that." I pause, steel my nerves with as deep a breath as I can draw through the knot of my chest. "I'd have minded it, if I'd lost you."

I can see it on his face, that thought he's not so certain I haven't. I smooth my skirts and tuck myself down onto the step beside him, just enough room not to crowd though he still shifts away. The chicken in his arms gives a small chortle of uncertainty and he pats her soothingly. "Reckon we're luckier than some," Trevor says.

Which I suppose is true, he could have been Daisy's husband, to make it all the way through the war and then die of the 'flu. Nor the health of his body ruined, quite. It's a scandal how those who refused to fight have been treated, the misery, the few who'd not come home, though of his own troubles Trevor's said as little as the men back from the trenches with no words to explain to those who'd not seen.

And of the other, only, *Someone took offence.*

Lily's husband comes out of the toilet at the bottom of the garden, nodding at the door with a wry grin beneath his bristling moustache; "I'd not go in there for a bit, aye?"

Dear Herbert. At least he's not mentioned the chicken. Yet. Instead he pauses in the act of pulling open the back door to squint at his wife's young brother with a keen eye for a sorry state: "Trying to grow out your whiskers?" Trevor reaches up to brush his dusting of stubble, and Herbert laughs, not unkindly. "Never mind, lad, you'll get the knack of it someday. Lil? What's on for tea, then, love–"

Trevor's not smiling back when I look to him from the closing door. "Ah, 'nghariad, he didn't mean anything by it, you know Herbert." He's shaking his head, small, but enough to make me shiver from it. "Hm? What is it, what's the matter?"

Trevor looks at the cockerel. Meets *its* eyes, square on. It tilts its head at him, jerky, puzzling – takes a step towards Trevor, another, until he can reach out a finger to chuck it under the beak. "I did this to the prison barber," Trevor says, so low I want to ask him to repeat it. "The mirrors, he was frightened of me, and I *looked* at him, and..." A bone-deep shudder. "I could have told him to slit his own throat and he'd have done it. I could smell the blood inside his skin..."

This man who'd paid near two years of his life to witness with his body that to raise a hand against another is never the way – "What did you do?"

He looks up, picture of misery. Scratch of nails on the bricks as the cockerel takes wing. "Asked him for a short back and sides."

The smile startles out of me like the flapping cockerel. "Not enough ruddy brilliantine in the world to make *that* look right with you."

He sets the hen down onto her feet on the cobbles, leaving her to make her unsteady affronted way back towards the coop. "Wouldn't know, would I."

Can't but put my arm round his shoulders, can I, my husband, my Trevor. "Come back in?"

Lily is the only person in the kitchen now, mopping at a spill of jam on the table with a furious glower on her face. "Why do we marry them, I ask you? – Not you, bach," she adds when she sees I've her brother with me, small fond smile for the ridiculousness of our lives. (Hard sometimes not to be envious of Lily, thirty soon and married to a house-holder. Do we claw at each other because we've not got all that we wanted? Or do we retreat into our separate troubles?) "Trevor, I was talking with Helen and we're thinking that even if Meeting can't spare the money to send the both of you back over to the Continent, I'm certain they'll at least be able to help you sort out what you mean to do for work and all?"

Been weighing on her mind something terrible, what her brothers are to do with themselves now. Though Ned's his soldier's pension, small token for it all but more than anyone would grudge for my husband. Trevor half-turns from where he's gone to wash barnyard-smelling hands under the tap. From his face he's picturing what even Friends will be able to do to find positions for anyone from this notorious family of conchies and suffragists. "Not the civil-service I don't think," Trevor says. The irony, that *he'd* have the vote now if he'd not chosen to go to prison. "Go back to helping Aled-mawr maybe?" (And how long will it be that we're still calling his uncle that, when will we forget the *why* of it now Aled-bach rests in Flanders?) "Or Da."

"You're wasted as a builder *or* a baker and you know it," I say.

Lily's pinched look speaks to how she's more than ready to see any of the men in her life find bloody *something* already. Thread of normality to pluck at, as if one small worry can displace all the greater. I take Trevor's hand and tug him towards the stairs. I can hear the denial of tears in Iris's voice in the front room, where Violet must be giving her as much of a talking-to as I imagine Violet capable of. But upstairs all is still, just quiet breathing from the room where Trevor's aunt's been looking after Lily's girls and poor Daisy's little Rhys. As well to have got them all down at once, Nora's still not been up to much after the 'flu. We creep past that door, and then the bedroom that Iris still shares with Violet, and Ned's ajar and a shambles, to our own scant refuge from care.

Suppose we can get on with setting up house on our own now the war is behind us. Suppose we all can, except Iris. Funny how that's not even occurred to me till just now, where she'd go. We're all still travelling on the rails the past laid down when the train's lost its bloody wheels. I'll be organising another march for the vote next.

We've still not got electric in the bedrooms. I strike a match for the lamp and set it back beside the basin, doesn't altogether chase aside the grey dim of a day that's never going to go fair but enough for this. The dressing-table arches into an accusing void where a mirror ought to be. I've been fixing my hair in the largest shard Iris missed, sliver now of myself standing alone at the edge of the bed beside my husband.

His shaving-soap's not been touched since he's been home, or nearly – he'd have *tried*, surely, but I can guess how that had gone, without having the sight of his face in a glass. Trevor's brows crease into a dark question when I reach to pick it up. "No, Helen, why...?"

"Herbert *is* right, you know, you're a bit of a sight. I *think* I can help you get tidied up?"

The frown is deepening into a proper scowl. "Hardly an invalid."

"We have to do *something* with you, can't go about looking as if – as if you're about to run off to the hills to paint yourself *blue*."

That's got me a smile, at least. Both of us that proud streak all the way back to when it was the Romans we were wanting out of our country. When I come back in from fetching hot water from the bath Trevor's sat himself in the chair at the dressing-table, gazing absently at the blank-faced oval of the missing mirror as he twirls in his fingers the white feather of cowardice that chit had handed him, when the shame ought to have been hers. "Suppose I ought to get on with learning, yeah. Blind men can do it, after all."

I'm not going to tell him what I'd seen a blinded man do, in one swift moment when his nurse had set down the razor. I dampen the brush and draw it in sturdy swirls across the face of the cake of soap. How many times I'd watched my new husband do this in those few blissful months before the review-board and the letters from the ambulance-corps and the decision we'd made that even this service was still complicity in the act of war. Better to go to prison, than make it one bit easier for someone else to kill in our names.

(He'd come to see me in my sentence over the demonstration and when we were only stepping out, but I'd not been let to visit him. Barely given leave to write, he was. Should have been there to meet him – should have been there with our baby in my arms. Should, should, should. First casualty of war.)

Trevor closes his eyes as I touch the lathered brush to his face, as if he can't bear to look at me. (No, he's just imagining how to guide his own hand without a glass.) "Smells nicer than the barber's soap," he says.

"Keep yourself still, do you want to lose an ear?"

I have a go at pulling the safety-razor in a slow stroke down his cheek. At least he's young enough never to have even tried to fuss with a cut-throat for himself, father a sensible enough man to have started his sons straight on the newest miracle of modern invention. Trevor reaches up to join his fingers to mine on the handle, easing the angle. "More like..."

And then it's just the soft rasp of the blade against whiskers, his patient submission to a necessity he'd never have asked of me. Not a drop of blood spilt, when I've finished. I'm proud of that, I believe.

We'll sort what's to be done for his hair when it comes to it.

Trevor's still not looking at me even as he wipes his chin with the flannel. "Can imagine Ned's first go at shaving," he says.

It had involved muttered words that I'm ashamed to admit I knew and Violet on her knees in the bath quietly sweeping up bits of the one mirror in the house that Iris wouldn't get to break. (We try not to think badly of Ned, that if he'd felt led to run out and bloody *enlist* it was his to say. But I know we've all thought it. As well we're not Ireland, I can only think what he'd be off about.) "Ned's still Ned," I say. "More's the pity."

"Least he can walk down the shops and go to a barber. Be happy to see *him*, call him a hero and all." And at last he lifts those great slate-coloured eyes to mine, moody as a storm coming in over the water. "You deserve better than this, Helen, you should leave me."

I've seen this look before, in Rouen and Cologne and the streets of my own city. Glaring limbless men feeling themselves useless, dangerous, un-manned. Women who only stared at nothing our innocent eyes could see. The children who'd given up hope of love or bread. "Stood up in front of Meeting and *promised*, we did. Not forgotten that?" I can't but *tch* at him, the look dawning in those glorious eyes. "I love you, Trevor, always have, since you brought me the sandwiches. Though why you brought me a pot of tea when I was chained to a *bloody* railing–"

He's laughing in a way could have been sobs, only the flash of those dear crooked eyeteeth as his mouth turns up with every breath tells me which. "Ought to have known you'd be that stubborn."

His lips taste of soap when I lean forward, soap and old iron and the promises we'd made to one another in that naive conviction that the world couldn't really be so mad as all that. Bother being proper anyway, his cool hands warming against my skin as we sort our way out of suddenly too many clothes (could have been my Nain's old corsets, catch *me* outside of a shirt-waist ever again) until at last at last we lie tangled in touch, the old bedstead singing our joy to the rest of the house and half the bloody street for all that we're minding it. Thinking only, *this. I want this. I want* you.

And, in the sudden breathless quiet after, somewhere from down below a voice sounds like Iris shouting that we can bloody well shut it. Trevor rumbles a chuckle and buries his face in my neck. Barest hint of teeth brushing my skin, before he sighs, and tucks his head against me, with a murmur: "*Wi wedi golli di.*" *I have missed you.*

O, Lord, I have my husband back, and he is himself. Whatever else he may also be, he is himself, and we shall relearn what that means, to us both, together.

S. LYNN – FFYDD (FAITH)

Art by Eric Orchard

ACROSS THE SEAM
SUNNY MORAINE

1897
Lattimer, Pennsylvania

So I might forget time, forget the world
My native land
My beloved land
I might find again, as in a blessed dream
      – Petro Trokhanovskii
      trans. from the Russian by Elaine Rusinko

It was not a battle because they were not aggressive, nor were
they on the defensive because they had no weapons of any kind and
were simply shot down like so many worthless objects; each of the
licensed life takers trying to outdo the others in the butchery.
      – Inscription on monument erected at Lattimer, 1972

    In his dreams, Baba Yaga sets fire to the seam and dances with him as it burns.

    This is the last thing she does, after the rest of the show she puts on for him – a show, she has always given him to understand, that she does not organize for his entertainment but hers. That first night, cold and alone and curled against a stoop with black dust choking his nostrils and coating his throat, without even yet the hard bed at the boarding house to make sleep a less terrible thing, she had come to him in her chicken-legged dacha, waving her spoon and laughing as if he was the funniest thing she had ever seen.

    Well, look at this. All curled up like a cat – except no cat would ever put up with such cold. You're a long way from home, little dochka.

    I'm not your daughter, he would have said, but one didn't argue with Baba Yaga, not even in dreams, unless one wanted to find oneself up to the neck in a soup pot. Instead he kept silent, then, and looked at the knobby chicken knees of her house and not at her crouching on her porch like a hunched black bird, pointing at him with her spoon.

    The streets of the coal camp are muddy now and they were muddy then, only then the mud was half ice and somehow sucked and pulled even worse than when it was merely waterlogged. Men lost shoes. But the house of Baba Yaga seemed entirely unconcerned as it stood there.

    But of course, it was a dream.

    Don't you turn your gaze away from me, dochka. Don't sulk. I came a

41

long way for you, and bad manners make a good supper. Look up at me, curtsy, and pay me a proper thank-you when you meet my eyes.

It was as if the spoon had become a sword and pierced him through. She knew. Her eyes were like brittle knives when she laughed at him again. Every part of her was sharp. Every part of her might carve, slice, alter.

So now he looks forward to his dreams.

***

Every day is much the same.

Out of bed before the sun; cold coffee and bread so dry it crumbles in his mouth. The boarding house smells like unwashed socks and stale drink, but he no longer notices it. He has been in the camp two weeks but his overalls are already worn as if he's had them for years and his boots badly need resoling. He covers his head with the hard shell of his helmet. He rubs the chin stubble that he's come to hate, but as yet he doesn't have enough company scrip to afford a good straight razor.

He is sixteen years old.

Iwan. Sometimes he's sure the shafts are whispering his name under the growls and coarse laughter of the other men. It began his first time down and he hasn't talked to anyone about it since then. Many days, he's sure that he's insane. When he sees the chicken-legged dacha in the center of the street. When the shafts speak to him. When he looks at the dresses of the boarding house's proprietress, her neatly coifed hair under her scarf, her hands — somehow both rough and delicate — and feels a yearning that has nothing to do with wanting her the way a man should want a woman.

He knows that he's broken.

Iwan, Baba Yaga murmurs to him as he staggers home under the weight of the coal dust and the low ceiling of the shaft, his back bent for so many hours that it is as though he carries the weight of the entire mountain on his shoulders. *My little Iwanka. They don't know who you really are. Let us discuss what might happen if they find out.*

***

The low mountains of western Pennsylvania are greening now, coming out of a winter so brown and barren and long that he had wondered if it might end at all. A few times there had been snow — which at least was familiar — but there was much more ice than snow, cold rain that leached into the bones and settled there, and everywhere dead vegetation like the earth herself was dying. At first, looking at the mine, seeing the dark scar of it and the black hell inside, he had wondered if its poison was seeping outward and infecting everything.

What have I come to, he had wondered then. *God.*

He no longer believes that God cares about him.

So now green life is creeping back into the mountains, but in his dreams, perhaps to torture him, Baba Yaga sits him behind her on her spoon and they

42

fly across the ocean and back to the rolling green mountains, dear and distant – and his heart aches as if it wants to burst from his chest and bury itself in the soil of his birth.

You have to remember, Baba Yaga says, no mocking laughter in her voice now, *where you came from. Such things can sustain you when nothing else does.*

He shakes his head, in his dream, in his sleep, on his flat boarding house pillow, his thin blanket gathered around his shoulders. *I have nothing now. Not even this. Why are you showing this to me?*

Baba Yaga does a little jig, more to prove a point than out of any personal glee. She lowers her spoon and scoops up the earth, pours it into his outstretched hands. It is nothing like the coal. *Iwanka, you are soft and deep like this here. And you can be hard like the mountain into which you dig. You must be both in order to survive.*

***

On the worst nights he dreams of the ship pulling into the harbor, the great statue lifting her torch over everything, the cold look in her eyes. Everyone else leaned over the deck and chattered, excited, and he thought of little birds flitting through his dense forests. She was welcoming to them, or they thought she was. But he looked up at her and he saw no welcome at all, and began to wonder if he had made a mistake.

The same coldness in the man with his many papers spread out in front of him.

Name? Place of origin? Are you literate? Where are you going? Is anyone meeting you there? He had stumbled through it in broken English, the little he had managed to scrape together in the passage. Iwan Charansky. Austria-Hungary. No. Lattimer.

No.

I am alone.

It was like confession. He hung his head and felt his cheeks burn.

***

The warmth of the stove in the early mornings. The lowing of the cattle, the soft jangle of their bells as he takes them to the fields. The sun rising over the mountains. Fresh paskha and pirohi with cheese. His father fixing prosfora and seed inside his pouch as he goes to plow the field, without which a good harvest will not be assured. Candlelit gilt and wood in the church, the knowing eyes of the saints in the ikonostas. Trying on his mother's best dress alone in the house, the terror of being caught. A scatter of grain in the sunlight like little beads of gold. Ice silvering the trees.

Screams. Fire – fire to consume a family that to others were always strangers, fire to consume the worrysome and the unwanted. Fire to consume the world.

Baba Yaga hands him this fire, like a fist, like a little burning heart in his

43

cupped palms, and he understands that he has carried it with him from the green hills and across the ocean, and it is part of him now.

The seam, dochka. Give it to the seam.

This place is almost ready to burn.

***

Nights in the boarding house are becoming more interesting. Louder, more people, squeezing together in Big Mary's kitchen, listening to her talk. Sometimes he stands in the doorway and listens too. What's done to them. What might be done. Big Mary is offering fragments of another world, holes through which to glimpse it, like gold nestled in the coal. Something he has never imagined, let alone seen. Big Mary offers exhortations to the promise of America, to the rights of men, and the men nod and bang their mugs on the table and cry agreement. Some. Others sit silently, their arms folded, and he can tell that they have yet to be convinced. But they're listening.

Behind him, he can feel Baba Yaga folding the spindles of her fingers and grinning. She whispers, *This is also my dochka. She knows me, even if she doesn't call me by name. Look at her: wouldn't she make a tasty stew? But her spirit is too big for my pot, and I have other uses for her. She is also carrying the fire. My fire.*

You should watch her. You are sisters, you and she. Even if she can never know.

More and more, Baba Yaga is coming to him in his waking hours.

This should perhaps frighten him more than it does.

***

Every night, now, the seam burns. The whole mountain runs with flame like a river. He watches it, and it seems to him that there are figures in the flames, bright and beautiful. They are not in pain. They are dancing, and they are holding out arms of cinder and glowing coal and beckoning to him to dance with them.

His mother is there. His father. Their faces are alight with pride as they behold their only son. Only now they see him for what he truly is, and there is no blame and no shame and not a hint of rejection. They love him as he is. *Iwanka,* his mother sings, her fingers like sparks as she whirls through the dying trees. *I have a lovely little dress for you, and look, I made for you this scarf. Look how bright it is.*

If anyone touches you after this, to harm you, they will burn, and not with us.

He wakes up with tears scalding his cheeks. They smoke and steam.

***

Goddamn hunkies.

When at last he has enough scrip saved to buy a razor, the man in the

44

company store overcharges him. He expects it, would have even borne it as yet another in a long line of harsh treatments, except that the amount the man is demanding is more than he has. He's been borrowing a razor from one of the other men in the boarding house, but it's too blunt and it hurts him, and the shave it gives is nowhere clean enough. It's a small thing, and he doesn't even know why it should be so important to him, except that he does.

Baba Yaga is teaching him to face hard truths. He's not the quickest of learners when it comes to things like that but he does learn.

Goddamn hunkies, the man growls when Iwan tries, stuttering through the words, to explain, to try to convince the man to take what he has as sufficient for the blade. *You come here, think you don't have to speak the language, think you're special. Owed special treatment. You won't get it from me, you little rat. Give me the price of it or get the hell out of the store.*

But it *is* special treatment. It always has been. *Hunky. Polack. Little rat.* For a long time now he's been used to it, but Big Mary is suggesting that he shouldn't be, that he's more than just some hunky rat crawling on his belly through the shafts. And there's Baba Yaga, folding all the hunky rats into her arms, her hands black with the coal, giving them firesides and warm porridge with milk, chalky with powdered bones.

There is something else that his saved scrip will buy. He stares at it for some long minutes the next time he goes to the company store to buy what little food he can. He stares at it for as long as he can, for as long as he thinks is safe, before he's noticed. A pair of lady's gloves, white and soft, very plain and, he knows, not fine. It seems strange to find them in a store that only stocks the necessities of the working people of Lattimer, but there they are, and to his weary eyes they seem to shine as if they were made of ivory. They are free of coal dust, pure, like the polished bones of someone long-dead. Of the stuff that Baba Yaga grinds for her porridge.

Strange things are beautiful to him now.

He wants to buy them. He wants them more than the razor. He imagines sliding his hands into them, the hair on his knuckles and the callouses on his palms and the black dust packed under his fingernails hidden by that elegant white. They would make his fingers look slender, he knows. Delicate. Before he turns away he reaches out and runs a fingertip along their backs.

Hey, hunky. He pulls his hand back as if he's been burned; his face *is* burning, his neck and ears, and he's praying that the big man behind the counter won't see. *Buy something or get out. You here to browse like a fucking woman?*

Take me home, he whispers to Baba Yaga as he slinks out of the place, feeling her heat and her glee at his side. In the shadows of the town he could swear he sees a *dacha* shuffling, out of the way like any other house but for its legs. *Take me back and bury me in the ground with the ashes of my family.*

No, dochka, she laughs. *Better for you, given that you're mine. The things you want will be yours. They will have to be.*

***

45

She tells him stories about ordeals, in the shafts, in the lukewarm water he uses for his quick baths, in the doorway of the boarding house kitchen. She tells him stories of walking on hot coals to prove one's innocence, of burning women as witches and trusting to God to care for their souls if they proved free of the influence of the devil. *They were all my daughters, Iwanka. They danced with me in the moonlight and the fire, as you do.*

I'm not a witch, he insists. But he lifts his blackened hands and, as if they are someone else's, his own fingers trace ancient symbols across his arms, his face. He smears coal over his lips, turning them dark and full. Baba Yaga nods in approval.

Not a witch, no, maybe. But were they *witches? I tell you truly, dochka, there have always been those of us who simply didn't fit, and those ones tend to be of a kind. And you are my sweet little daughter, and you will never be one of them. The others.*

Why would you want to be?

She places his burning hands against the seam and Lattimer fails its test in an orgy of flame.

***

It comes in the fall, with the rain and the cold wind. The trees are aflame, red and gold, and as the strike is called, as the marches begin, he marches with them but his gaze is locked on those burning branches, each one like the embodiment of God sent to give him a message. Big Mary cries out to them, her arms lifted, praising them as if they are her children and newly learned to stand on their own. There is word that the company will shortly send in the strike-breakers, but there is fearlessness on the sharp wind, at least for the moment, and they tell each other to be strong. Even him, no longer just a hunky rat but, for a short and precious time, a brother among brothers.

He accepts this with certain reservations. Baba Yaga leads the march in her chicken-legged dacha, standing on the porch and waving her spoon like a general.

What would his mother think of this? His father? If their spirits could travel from dust to dust, emerge from the mountain and see him now? Would they be proud? Would any of this surprise them? Their lost son, marching with the lost and demanding to be found again?

Still more lost than any of them, though they can't see it now?

Does he still care?

***

Yet the actual moment, when it comes, isn't in the rain or the cold wind but on a warm, sunny day in early September that still contains hints of dying summer, the last of the green before the fire begins to turn it to gray ash. It's a big march – nearly three hundred of them, or so the rumor goes – and there is such a sense of quiet strength among them all that even Baba Yaga ceases her cackling, though he senses that this is not out of any particular respect so much as it is that she is waiting. That the world around them is holding its breath.

That the ground is heating under their feet.

There are fires far below, Baba Yaga whispered once, *that have burned for hundreds of years. Longer. There is a single great fire beneath it all that has been burning since the birth of the world.*

When the sheriff issues the call to disperse, Iwan barely hears it. It's a voice far removed, present but ultimately not very important, and at any rate no one is dispersing. From somewhere far away there's a scuffle, the sound of feet scrabbling and the grunt of bodies hitting bodies, but this, too, seems unimportant. Everyone around him is standing, standing like stones.

Then. "Give two or three shots!"

Now a murmur. Now people turning to each other, alarmed, the quiet strength drifting away like ash. And as the shots ring out, he looks to Baba Yaga and sees her grin eating up her face. *Grandmother Chaos,* he thinks. *Grandmother Fire.* And the people scatter into madness.

It's the spark. He can feel it. It warms him as he runs with the crowd down the muddy streets, as more shots and screams ring out, pain and anger, the sound of fighting. He looks behind and sees fallen bodies, clothes streaked with blood; he turns away again and keeps running.

He has always been running, since he was set into motion. Now it ends.

It comes to him that Baba Yaga has left the porch of her dacha and is on his back, riding him, beating him with her spoon like a horse. He goes where she points him, breaking away from the fleeing crowd, and isn't surprised to find himself standing in front of the shop. Baba Yaga leaps up on his shoulders and shatters the glass of the front window with her spoon.

The razor. The gloves. In a few seconds he has them, though now his arms are bleeding from stray shards. It feels like fair trade. If trade was even necessary; perhaps these things are his, his from the very birth of the world, like magical things waiting for him in a dragon's cave.

And to the dragon's cave she is now driving him.

He runs past the fleeing bodies in the streets, running against the flow. No one notices him or the things in his hands. Once he thinks he hears the cry of Big Mary rising over the shots and screams, and when he turns at the bottom of a little hill he sees her standing there above him, her arms raised and tears streaming down her face. She's muddy, dirty, but somehow she is shining in the sun like a piece of cut anthracite. Their gazes meet and he knows that she sees him, and that she sees him for what he is. Their fundamental kinship.

In this moment he has her blessing.

Give it to the seam.

He turns and runs again, and the shaft opens up like a mouth and swallows him.

***

It is so very much like a story. Baba Yaga has drawn him into it, him and his true self that waits for him in the shadows. She has spun it around herself like a cloak, from coal seams and fairy gold. This is his journey, from the green hills and forested mountains of his homeland to the coal and the black and the fire, and for once he feels that it is exactly as it should be.

And here in the glittering dark anything might be possible.

The line between truth and story is so thin, Baba Yaga whispers. *Here, thinner still. You are a child of the story, dochka, half in and half out of the world. No one will tell your tale, but I will keep you safe and tell it to myself within the walls of my house; I will feed it to my oven and bake it in my black bread.*

Now give the fire to the seam and dance with me in the ashes.

Iwan, Iwanka, Janus-faced and true to herself at last, presses her hands against the coal and finds a hard stone that holds a spark within its cold heart. She lifts the razor and strikes, and gives what lies inside to the seam that has run through her life and her world. She turns them both to ash and dust.

***

Wagons carry the dead into the lands beyond like fallen heroes. There are cries for vengeance. There are ordeals that are failed and others that are passed, there is condemnation and a trial, and in the end there is memory of a kind, though no one tells the story of Iwan-who-was-not-Iwan and who was no fool, and how he vanished into the dark after death came to Lattimer.

But there is fire. There is fire that burns forever in that dark, and in the flames Iwanka dances with Baba Yaga and eats her black bread and her porridge of powdered bone and sweet milk. She dances in the arms of her parents and the other dead, and she dances all the way back to the mountains, to the green and the trees, to the older fires and the memory that sits in the stones like glowing coals. She is with the scattered ones, even the ones who have been forgotten, and the great secret that Baba Yaga sings to those who can hear is that even they have a way of living forever, until, like wheat, they emerge from rich earth, green and new and reaching their arms toward a clear sky.

Art by Alice Meichi Li

NUMBERS
RION AMILCAR SCOTT

1919
Maryland

1.

Out in the middle of the Cross River there is an island. It appears during storms or when the river's flooding or sometimes even on clear summer days. And sometimes it rises out the water and floats in the air. The ground turns to diamond and you can hear the women playing with the sparkling rocks. The skittery clatter of diamond on diamond and the high laughter of the women – I call them women, but they are not women. So many names for them: Kazzies. Shuantices. Water-Women. The Woes. I like that last name myself. The poet Roland Hudson came up with that one in the throes of madness. Dedicated his final volume, *The Firewater of Love,* to

> *Gertrude, Water-Woman, my Woe who caused all the woe... even though, my dear, you are not real, I cannot accept that and will never stop believing in your existence and beautiful rise from the river into my arms.*

Drowned himself in the Cross River swimming after Gertrude and there's something beautiful in that. Dredge the depths of the Cross River and how many bones of the heartsick will you find along the riverbed? So many poisoned by illusion. Don't tell me there's no island and no women rising naked from the depths, shifting forms to tantalize and then to crush. I've seen their island and I've seen them and gangsters love too; gangsters are allowed love, aren't we? Sometimes there's a fog and I know the island's coming and I snap out of sleep all slicked with sweat and filled with the urge to swim out there to catch a water-woman and bring her back to my bed. If you pour sugar on their tails they can't shift shapes on you and they have to show their true selves and obey you completely. If I had to do it all over again I'd dust her in a whole 5-pound bag and spend eternity licking the crystals from her nipples. And Amber, a man lost in delirium. Poor, poor Amber.

2.

Last year, 1918, ended bad for me and for Amber, and to think, it began

51

with so much promise. My mother got me a job driving Amber around town in February and by summer I expected to be collecting numbers slips for him, and then Amber Hawkins fell in love with Joyce Little and became something like a lovesick pit bull puppy. Joyce's brother Josephus got the money-making position I had my eye on and I was stuck being yelled at from the backseat as I swerved about the road. Amber was a killer, as was everybody I worked with. I tried to forget that, but sometimes it made me nervous, especially when I drove.

I figured Joyce would turn Amber into something akin to a decent human being once they were married. Most married people I knew became boring soon as they put on the ring; they lost some of their humor and spontaneity, but I had to admit they grew a little more humanity.

September 15, 1918: that was supposed to be the day. He booked the Civic Center for the wedding – displacing a couple that had reserved the place months before, but it was Amber Hawkins, nothing anyone could do. He ordered up nearly a hundred pastries. So many tulips arrived on the eve of the wedding that I joked a hillside in Holland suffered a sudden baldness. Hundreds of people swarmed the Civic Center that Sunday. Everything was to begin at noon. Those of us who worked for Mr. Washington, and even people who worked for Mr. Johnson and Mr. Jackson, put aside our differences to show up for Amber. Joyce's family sat in the front. Mostly, I remember her cute little sister and the short socks resting against her tan skin. Her tall skinny father sat stoically holding the little girl's hand. Joyce's jellyrolled mother wiped at her wet eyes every few minutes.

And then nothing.

No word from Joyce up on through the wedding day. Amber made us get all dolled up and festive-like for his big humiliation.

Josephus was the best man. He stood near the altar wearing a twisted guilty smile as he swayed back and forth fingering a big, ugly purple flower pinned to his lapel. He was an arrogant fucking shitstain, but I hated seeing him squirm.

At about five in the evening it was clear all was lost, Amber's father ambled to the front where Amber and Joyce should have been standing. His movements were sheepish and slow. For the first time, the ruthless killer looked as frail and as wispy as the old man he was. There were rumors that his lifestyle – the women and the whores he kept around town – had left him so syphilitic that his once sharp mind had rotted and his body was beginning to twist and fail too. I didn't believe or engage in the talk. He'd been nothing but good to me.

Thank you for coming, people of Cross River, Elder Mr. Hawkins said to the wedding crowd. You have been more than generous to my family and all connected with us. I'm sorry, but there will be no celebration today. Again, I thank you for spending your time with us. We all slowly dispersed that night and the next day Amber was back to work, mumbling the day's numbers from the backseat. Never mentioned Joyce or showed any signs of sorrow or pain. I knew the sadness was there though. Had to be.

Amber waited a month. He waited three. Then he had Joyce's whole family killed.

A single bullet to each of their foreheads and their bodies dumped in the Cross River. It was deep in December, near Christmas, and thin white sheets of ice skimmed along the river's face.

Three days after their disappearance, the family came bubbling to the surface, just as Amber wanted. The cold-hearted bastard didn't spare even the 10-year-old girl. Amber's own best man paid the ultimate price for his sister's desertion.

With Josephus dead, I expected a promotion, but he gave that to Doc Travis Griffin's son. I let it pass without complaint; at least Amber hadn't tasked me with taking the lives of four innocent people. Frank and Tommy did the hit, I heard, and when I saw them I watched their muddy boots and thanked the Lord I didn't have to walk in them. But who am I kidding, though? I stood amongst the killers and the dirt was all over me just as it was all over them. I would have done the job with sadness and emptiness; with revulsion and cold rage toward Amber, but still I'd have done it.

Loretta and I used to stand at the river's edge sometimes and watch the sky reflecting on the water. Did it through all types of weather, but a pleasant March day was definitely a reason to be out. Felt I was safe from the river when I was with her, like it wouldn't dare open up and devour me whole.

What if you die, she asked on this day when Amber had missed another payment to Mr. Washington, putting all of us who worked for him in danger. What if they kill me?

I didn't look up from the river. Amber's falling apart, I said.

And he should fall apart, she replied. Baby, this is not your problem. He made this happen. Brought it all down on himself. So you gotta fall on his sword? My cousin, he in St. Louis, we could go up there. I could work for him and you could find a job—

Shining white people's shoes again? The type of job I got is the only way a negro can live decently. At least negroes who came up poor like us anyway.

On her face I could see the passing hellfire that she – an angry God – was condemning me to for all my mistakes. I suppose I have to take some credit or some blame, as it were, for how things happened. I've been known to blame Loretta for eventually leaving me, or Miss Susan – it was her *Little Book of Love Numbers* that got all those thoughts cranking through our heads. I've blamed Mr. Washington for his harshness and even the whole society of water-women and their wicked nature. But really, if I had left the whole business behind like Loretta wanted, how could things have been any worse? Truth was, I couldn't leave Amber, the one who was destined to sit on the throne if only he could do something as simple as overcome heartbreak. His face sweating constantly now. His limbs shaking. This damn compassion. This damn empathy.

A March breeze passed over Loretta and me. It was filled with heat and something that made me feel like a lover, like I could take Loretta into the water and after we finished she'd trust my word forever. Loretta kicked at the river with her bare feet.

Still cold, she said.

St. Louis, huh? I said, pitching a rock into the water. Can't put your feet into the Cross River in St. Louis.

You worry about the silliest things, she replied.

Girl, you know Elder Mr. Hawkins called me a poet when me and Amber met with him. He say that 'cause I like to daydream. I never rubbed two words together and made them rhyme, but he right, you know. I wonder how he know I'm a poet at making love, though?

We talking about our future and you want to make jokes? Even if Amber get himself together and you do move up in the organization, you want to end up a dirty old mobster like Elder Mr. Hawkins?

I knew Loretta was right — at least somewhat right; Amber did bring this problem on himself — but I could never give Loretta her due.

I took a deep breath while Loretta lectured me; the sound of my own breathing helped to cancel out her voice. The day was one of the spring's best, but I didn't expect the air to be so floral and I mentioned it to Loretta. Then I said what had been on my mind in the last several months:

I ain't never been nothing and nobody ever expected anything from me at all. Not you. Not even my mother. You all think I'm not that smart and that's OK. I'm the underdog. I stick with Amber I could be up there in the organization in the number two spot like Elder Mr. Hawkins. Shit, I could be the next Mr. Washington if Amber don't make it. Don't doubt me. You could be the Washington Family First Lady. How about that, Loretta?

If that's what matters to you then—

In my memories, Loretta turns to white dust mid-sentence and blows away, leaving behind the sweet scent of flowers in bloom. My mind is so damaged I can't tell memories from hallucinations; daydreams from nightmares.

3.

Mr. Washington was so furious over the Little family killing that he carved up our territory and threatened to give over our remaining operations to Philemon if we couldn't pay a $5,000 fine and restitution to the Littles.

Elder Mr. Hawkins delivered the news coldly and sternly in January — the very top of 1919 — at the funeral for Frank and Tommy, Amber's best shooters.

Who the fuck am I supposed to pay restitution to? Amber asked. The Little family is dead! And Mr. Washington didn't have to kill Frank and Tommy—

I canceled Frank and Tommy, Elder Mr. Hawkins said. I laid their bodies out by the river myself. They were stupid enough to follow your order to cancel Joyce's peoples, they had to — trust me, Amber, it was best for you that they go.

On top of the fines, Mr. Washington stripped us of half our territory and reassigned much of Amber's personnel. And still we were responsible for kicking the same amount to Mr. Washington every week.

The debt became a millstone dragging Amber's operations to the bottom of the Cross River. It's as if Mr. Washington didn't want to see us live. Like the folks high up could no longer abide by Amber's success after the death of the Little family. I wondered why Mr. Washington didn't just put a bullet in him. Would have been more merciful than this slow usurious homicide.

Amber sent a fleet of prostitutes into the juke joints and commissioned truck hijackings, but it was never enough. Never did he look less like the heir to the throne. When all seemed lost, Carmen shot into our lives, a little brown-skinned bolt from a cannon. Woke us up when we didn't even know we were sleeping. I was never clear on where he found her. It seemed as if she had always been there on his arm.

Carmen was a pretty number. From a certain angle her head appeared perfectly round. Her hair — shiny, black and smooth — stopped where her head met her long neck. Carmen stayed draped in a green dress. Said it was the color of spring. And the spring of Carmen indeed felt like a rebirth.

It was an April afternoon and Carmen's green dress had been on my mind for several hours. Three sets of ledger books sat before me — Amber asked me to make the numbers work, but there was no making sense of these numbers so I daydreamed and when I got tired of that I leafed through *Miss Susan's Little Book of Love Numbers*. When I got to the chapter titled, "Can A Woman Make a Man Lose His Mind?" I was damn sure for a few minutes that Loretta and Joyce were water-women. They made you fall so deep you never wanted to ever gasp for air again and then they disappeared, leaving you disoriented with your mind buzzing with madness until the end of your days and that's if you're lucky. Everyone else they lure to the Cross River and persuade to bury themselves beneath the waves. Loretta and Joyce hid their gills well. I thought of the creased skin beneath Loretta's breasts. Where was Carmen hiding her gills? They could shift shapes, you know. Maybe Carmen was Joyce returned. No. Amber walked into the office holding tight to Carmen's hand and her sweet smell deranged every thought I had of the water-women until the images slid from my brain into my throat and tasted like the smoothest ice cream.

You got time to be reading that witchcraft? he asked. Amber moved as if he had no control over his body and fell into the chair across from me, breathing heavy and sighing before speaking again. What my numbers looking like?

I couldn't immediately answer him. I noticed Carmen's slant smile. Amber too had grinned when he walked through the door, but talk of business had twisted his lips into a grimace.

I'm not sure how we're gonna make Mr. Washington's payments again this month, I said.

It was a fair enough guess. With the reduced territory there were fewer businesses to intimidate, fewer lottery customers, and Amber had fewer people working for him bringing in any revenue.

Carmen rested her soft hands on the back of Amber's neck.

You need to get yourself a woman, Amber said.

I'm sorry I can't get these numbers to make sense, I replied. I'll keep try—

I'm talking about what's really important in this life and you stuck on business. I don't remember you being this stiff. Didn't my father call you a poet or something?

Amber was telling me about Loretta, Carmen said. You been out with anyone since then? Amber's a good guy, he asked about my friends for you. I got a whole army of nice girls. You don't like one, the next one will be better. They all could use a guy like you.

See, what I'm talking about, Amber said. This is a firecracker of a woman. What you think of my woman?

I looked up at the sweep of her hair resting on her cheeks. The black, breathing lines beneath her eyes.

She hides her gills well, I said.

Amber and Carmen laughed. I'm glad they took it in the spirit of a joke. Sometimes it was hard to tell what was going to make Amber lose it.

You know there's no such thing as water-women, right? Carmen asked with her slant-smile lingering and hanging over me. I didn't reply.

Loretta wasn't no water-woman, Amber said. She just ain't like your ass no more. Same thing with Joyce. We got to live with that. It takes a special woman to be with guys in this life. Loretta and Joyce wasn't special enough, but my baby Carmen — he grasped her by the waist and pulled her tight — my baby Carmen ain't going nowhere.

Mean-fucking-while, I said. Philemon is the toast of the family.

Outrageous! Amber slapped the desk. What would happen if I walked right up to him and shot him in his face right in front of Mr. Washington?

You know something, Carmen said, looking up to the ceiling, her voice all distant and spinning with childlike innocence. There hasn't been a good firebombing since your dad ran the streets, has there?

In a different world, Carmen could have run this organization, I'm sure. I feared her and I wanted to devour her.

To us this was nothing serious; just a prank like streaming lines of toilet paper through his trees. We didn't mean for it to happen, but Philemon's house burned. Perhaps I daydreamed too intensely about Carmen's green and put too much gasoline into the Molotov Cocktails. No one was hurt, but Amber yelled at the old-faced teenagers we hired to do the job: What was in that shit, sunfire?

He never gave them the second $10 he promised and still they kept their mouths shut and everyone assumed the Johnson Family did it as retaliation for Philemon moving into their Northside strongholds.

Mr. Washington took Philemon's advice and ordered all guns turned on the Johnson Family in a sort of unbalanced warfare. When they largely retreated, most of our crew leaders were left with bigger territories, except for us. Somehow our territory shrank and we found ourselves scrounging for every dollar we came across.

Amber shrugged it all off. I still have this vision of him with his feet up on a table in the office, staring at the air above the ledger as if the numbers were twirling before him, nodding, grimace-smiling, saying, Carmen got this all figured out. Every damn piece to the puzzle. Every piece.

4.

Shortly after I began working for Amber, before he became translucent to me – the way Josephus appears in my dreams – my mother sent me to see Miss Susan. She had seen Miss Susan before she married my father (and probably before she started seeing Elder Mr. Hawkins) and said everyone should see her when they think they're in deep with a lover. I hadn't even been paid yet and was still living off shoe-shining so my mother gave me money for that old witch. Miss Susan told me to go into the Wildlands and bring her three roots. My mother said, That witch crazy if she think I'm sending my only boy into that old spooknigger forest. She went down to the market and bought three roots and ground them into the dirt so they looked fresh.

Ms. Susan stared at me. She fingered my naps. Squeezed my face and then she turned my roots in her hand. I had heard rumors that she made you drop your pants and she stared right into the eye of your penis. I silently prayed she let me keep my pants on and thankfully, she did, but, God, the power of this woman! She looked nothing like the grinning old crone they had pictured on her books. Miss Susan looked young and serious. Smooth-skinned. I would have done anything she asked just because of the forceful-ness of her voice. So, I said, is Loretta the one? She looked up from my roots with her glowing gold eyes and said, You're in danger.

You know who I work for, I said. You not telling me nothing I don't know.

That's not why you're in danger. It's your heart. If you know what's good for you, you're gonna stay the hell away from the river.

I left with a bunch of her books and walked straight to the river to sit and read. And that's when I heard them calling me. A wispy sound rustled in my ears and I felt drunk, pleasant drunk without the anger or the bitter taste on my tongue or the physical burn of liquor corroding my insides as it passed through.

The world looked wavy, but I saw it – that diamond island rising from the Cross River like a ghost ship out the fog.

And those water-women dove from land and swam to me. They rose out the water, brown and nude, their skin shining with the life-giving water of the river.

Numbers-boy, the water-woman in the front said. Hey, Numbers-boy. You got a number for me?

All those women turned into one. She reached for me and caressed my face. You're beautiful, she said. Anyone ever tell you you're beautiful?

She grabbed my hand and placed it on her naked hip.

Don't be afraid, she said. When I looked into her eyes, we lived a whole life, from awkward first steps together to deep deep commitment. I could never look at another.

Loretta, a voice called from the island.

Your name is Loretta? I asked. Like my Loretta?

No, she said. I'm better than your Loretta.

Without another word, she turned and dived back into the river. Perhaps she didn't have all of me. Some of me was back with my Loretta because I realized this was a trap. This was exactly how Miss Susan described water-woman seduction in her books. So many lovers, like the poet Roland Hudson, dived to their ends after these deadly tricksters. I took a step toward the water. Then I stopped. Self-preservation kicked in and I remembered they weren't even women or human, but evil-intentioned beings with secret gills tucked away somewhere.

The island descended from mid-air into a thick fog, sinking slowly into the black water. And even though it nearly caused my death, the feeling I had there by the Cross River was the greatest feeling any man could ever experience. I cried hot tears that night waiting for the water-woman's return.

I knew nothing in life would ever feel like staring into her brown eyes, touching the warmth of the flesh at her hip. Nothing. I would chase women, try to experience bliss in all things, but no experience I ever had could fill my soul this way. But if I ever returned to the river and that island decided to rise up, I knew I would die.

Not a bad way to go, huh? Drowning in a water-woman's light.

5.

Carmen disappeared, not by train, but by wind. To hear Amber tell it, they had spent the afternoon downtown on the way to purchase a ring when she walked out ahead of him. She smiled, not the slant-smile, but a broad true one and then she stretched out her arms like a bird preparing for flight. Oh, Amber were her last words before the soft brown of her flesh turned into a fragrant white powder. When the breeze came, scattering pieces of Carmen throughout the town, Amber grabbed clumps of her powder and tried to put her together, but the grains of Carmen slipped between his fingers, leaving traces of her in the creases of his hands, embedded between the threads of his clothes and curled always in the coils of his hair.

It's like my dream, I said the night of her disappearance. Water-women. A plague of them.

I need to smoke, he said, walking to the door. Come and get me in ten minutes so we can finish the ledger. Business first, right. I'll be OK by then.

It only took two minutes to figure out that he was going out into the pitch of the night to find Carmen by the river. He had left the car, so I figured he was walking briskly south toward the bridge. Their voices would soon be screaming through his head, crowding his lonely thoughts.

Turns out there couldn't have been a worse time for Carmen to blow in the wind. I took two steps into the street and felt a hand grab my arm: it was Fathead Leroy, a guy who took numbers for Amber over on the Southside.

Man, he said. I got rolled for my numbers slips. I don't know that shit by heart like Amber.

Who got you? Somebody with the Jacksons?

Naw, look, you know Todd who work for Elder Mr. Hawkins? Him and a guy I never seen before. A white guy. I think he from Port Yooga. They looking for you and they looking for Amber. Told me to tell you not to burn nothing you can't pay for. Cracker punched me and threw my betting slips into the river. I don't got the standing to do nothing against someone as high up as Todd. You and Amber gotta get this right for us out on the streets.

I looked over Leroy's shoulder. It started to play as a setup. Not too far in the distance I saw Todd with a big white man who stomped toward us like a gorilla. How could I leave the office without my piece? Loveblind Amber probably hadn't spent two thoughts on packing. I dipped my head and turned from Leroy before breaking into a jog. Perhaps they ran behind me, but I wasn't willing to spare a glance. The shadows of the Wildlands called. When I entered them, the dark grew heavy and I swore as I dashed through the stream that pieces of the dark flaked off and covered me. I came out into a clearing and could see the gleam of the moon casting down on me. This was a circuitous route to get to the Hail Mary Bridge, but it would keep me alive long enough to find Amber. I imagined him standing above the waters, waiting for Carmen to beckon him beneath the choppy surface.

The closer I got to the river, the louder the buzzing vibrating in my head. I felt as if something kept lifting me into the air with every step. It was a beautiful tone shooting from the depths. My skin grew warm, suddenly flush with blood. Part of my mind called me to turn around to save myself. Who would I be if I bowed to the gods of self-preservation when Amber was in danger? But Amber could already be a bloated corpse, the beasts of the river tearing at his dead limbs. What a liar I am. This death march felt good, that was the truth. That's why I plowed deeper into the forest. It felt just like floating on my back beneath the sun in an ocean that rocked with a loping rhythm. All that remained was for me to dip my head under.

While I indulged this daydream as one of the last I'd ever have, I came out of a long blink and before me stood Amber with his ankles steeped in the river.

That's when the whispers began. Images of Loretta. My Loretta. Then the water-woman Loretta.

I wanted to call out to Amber, but what if I missed my Loretta speaking to me?

A burst. A loud popping, like fireworks. I looked to the cloudy black of the sky, now hiding the stars and obscuring the moon. Another pop, or rather this time it was a bang, closer to me now. I wasn't shot, but for a second I thought I was as the rhythm of the bang vibrated first at my feet and then in my chest.

Amber didn't move. Didn't react at all as if he hadn't heard the sound. He just stared down at the river, trying to see the whole world in the water.

Another shot burst toward us, this time from a different angle and there was Todd on a hill looking down upon us.

Amber, I called. Amber! Run! Save yourself!

The whispering in my head grew louder. I saw the white man approach, an albino gorilla burning with murderous intent. There was nowhere we could run; Todd and the White Gorilla were tactical geniuses, cutting off our paths of flight.

I wondered if Mr. Washington would give us a twin homegoing full of lavish food and celebration.

My skin warmed and I figured since my death was upon me, I'd shut off my mind and give in to the creeping pleasures of the world around me.

Just as I decided my time lay at an end, the water parted and up in the sky rose that diamond island, the land of the water-women. Scores of them — brown and nude and river-slicked — floated down to us. Two of them caressed Amber. I locked eyes with a woe and she whispered my name. Tall and skinny with a sharp, gaunt face. She bounce-walked and after a few steps her movements nearly resembled floating. The woe put her arm around me, softly touching my chest. With my eyes, I searched her naked body for gills, but soon I gave in and began softly kissing her neck and kneading her soft wet flesh, growing more aggressive with the increasing intensity of her breaths and her moans. Together they sounded like a new language.

There was that pop again. Another pop, itself a language I no longer cared to understand. I placed my tongue gently into my water-woman's mouth. We were melting into one being. Pop. She shuddered and I felt a hot wetness at the side of my lover's body. I gasped. My heart felt as if it had shifted and now beat in the center of my body, somewhere near the back. My water-woman went limp in my arms, her head flopping to the side, her skin turning cold and scaly and silvery and blue beneath the crack of moonlight that spilled from behind the cloud cover.

I looked at the blood and chunks of flesh that covered my skin and my clothes. Some of the water-women ran and dove back into the river. I scanned the water's edge for Amber. He held a water-woman in his arms and another stood behind him rubbing his back. The one in front took hold of his hand and led him deeper into the water.

I ducked from the flurry of bullets I expected to buzz by our ears like mosquitoes. Todd and the White Gorilla stalked toward me. I crouched to the ground with my hands covering my head. When they were upon me, they stopped and hovered. I watched their work boots, afraid to look into their faces.

Todd and the White Gorilla stepped over me, mumbling apologies. They stumbled toward the river and its bounty of naked women.

As grateful as I was for their mesmerism, it also saddened me. That was to be my fate, my thoughtless death march to a land under the water.

I rose to my feet and ran to water's edge where Amber stood. I snatched at him and held him down. He screamed and cried, cursing and threatening me with great violence. I knew it was just a matter of endurance. When the island sank back into the depths of the river, he'd regain a certain sanity. His water-women didn't fight — that is not how they did things. They blew kisses and walked out into the river until their heads were fully submerged.

As for Todd and the White Gorilla, water-women gazed into their eyes, laughing playful laughs and twisting their naked hips. It was a beautiful invitation to a drowning and they accepted, holding tight to the women as they led them to the bottom of the river.

For Amber, the sinking of the island was the worst part; he twisted, thrashed, and screamed. But when it was over, when that island was again tucked beneath gentle currents, Amber grew calm and docile. He lay on his back atop the wet soil with his hands on his face.

Take me home, he said. I need to go home.

I looked off into the distance at the glowing town and I realized that Amber and I would never again be allowed there. He moved his hands from his face and it was as blank and innocent as a newborn baby's. His voice sounded simple and soft. He was my responsibility now and I had no idea where we would go. All I could be certain of was that part of him was now submerged somewhere within his depths and would never surface again.

Art by Kaysha Siemens

EACH PART WITHOUT MERCY
MEG JAYANTH

1746
Madras, India

The British give different words for everything. Thanthai's kallu kada is called a "Liquor Shop," and the padaneera drunk by the cup is called "palm wine," which Thanthai says makes it taste better on their foreign tongues. But there are some soldiers that come in and bang their hands on the counter and ask for "a shot of kallu, fellow, quickly" and Thanthai serves them the sourest kallu from under the counter. It gets sourer with each day, until it transubstantiates into unsellable vinegar. The workers would have thrown the tumbler back in Thanthai's face, but the British soldiers knock back peg after peg, their faces twisting and throats working, congratulating each other with slaps on the back. Thanthai says that they're after the authentic local experience, and it only gratifies them when the local experience turns out to be absolutely disgusting.

***

Thanthai isn't actually Cani's real thanthai. Everybody knows, though he pretends to be deaf whenever anyone says anything, and mute whenever she tries to ask him about it. Mama, on the other hand, becomes at first very Catholic, then very Konkani, and starts threatening to try to teach her Konkani even though nobody in Madras speaks it. "Then you can learn Portuguese," Mama suggests with airy certainty. "O que voce acha, senhora?"

Mama's face changes when she speaks Portuguese, an unfamiliar light reshaping the planes of her cheekbones and jaw. Her voice is rich and somehow yearning over the syllables, as if she'd like to hungrily swallow them back down again.

"I don't want to learn Portuguese." Cani turns away quickly.

Mama sighs and holds up her hands, "Que pena," she says lightly. "What a shame." And that should be the end of it, except Mama's dark eyes watch her intently as she leaves the room, and for days after. Cani doesn't ask her about her real thanthai again.

***

The cannon fire from the French ships besieging Madras lets up during the night, and the residents of Black Town throng around the narrow wall that encloses White Town and Fort St. George. Old mamis wearing braids of

63

jasmine flattened and crushed by the activity of the day, children clutching onto saris or chasing each other through the lamplit alleys, men of all classes talking and shouting. An aunty from down the street is screaming over a small body wrapped in bloodied white muslin.

The iron gates to White Town are firmly barricaded. Thanthai does a brisk trade in kallu, even to some of the hard-faced mamis who usually do nothing but complain about their drunk husbands and sons.

The French fleet is shrouded in thick black smoke that rolls over the fort from the river. Most of the shot was aimed at White Town's fortifications, but the French guns aren't particularly accurate, especially when fired from aboard ship. Black Town has no walls or barricades, and so bears the brunt of the assault.

Cani's eyes slide towards the bloodied bundle in her neighbour-aunty's arms. Mama catches the direction of her gaze and pulls her close, against the soft silk of her sari and the familiar scratchiness of the zari border, printing stylized mangoes and peacock-eye patterns into her cheek. "My darling Canimozhi," she whispers absently, lifting her head and glaring in the direction of the besieging fleet. "Maybe we should all learn French instead."

***

Cani dreams of the river turned to clear glittering glass, with the French ships frozen in the solid water. The froth around the hull shines sharply, slicing the hands and feet of sailors who try to drop from the rigging. The glass is cool under her belly as she watches the fish trapped under the surface like flies preserved in amber. She laughs and peers down even deeper where iridescent-scaled fish pool around the heads of peacocks, and elephants are stopped in the act of kicking up silt from the river bottom as they make their watery journey inland. Tigers perch on riverbed rocks, unfurling chiffon fins as delicate as dragonfly wings behind them in the water.

She takes a breath and wills the water to liquefy below the surface, leaving a thin layer to support her body and trap the ships. The wind picks up, carrying with it salt from the sea, whipping her loose hair into swirling loops as below her the glass cracks and runs, melting into currents speckled with bright wriggling fish. One of the tigers unfreezes mid-leap, body continuing to twist and stretch as it sinks its claws into an elephant calf's back and rips.

Blood ribbons into the water, dark and clotted, and the calf screams like her neighbour-aunty as the tiger uses a beat of its powerful fins to claw it again.

She watches, hands clenching into fists, but does not will the blood away.

***

She wakes to the sound of the temple bell, ringing for morning puja. Thanthai kisses them both before slipping away to temple; the gates to White Town are still sealed shut because of the siege, so Cani decides to stay and keep Mama company. Mama, of course, prays at St. Andrew's rather than St.

Mary's, which is where the British factors and their bell-sleeved, stiff-bodied memsahibs worship. Mama says that there is a big difference between an Anglican and a Catholic, as big as the difference between a Jain and a Brahmin, but Cani doesn't think they can be all that different – the Christians all pray in White Town, after all.

Mama looks around at their single-room home attached to the back of the kallu kada and sighs heavily, at a loss for how to fill her day without trading figures from Pondicherry and Goa and Bengal arranged in long columns. Cani feels briefly guilty that she ever wished for the gates to White Town to be mysteriously locked, for Mama to have to stay at home instead of going to clerk for the British governor. Thanthai pretends not to hear, but Cani has listened to the customers talk about people who *choose* who work for the British, calling them bootlickers and traitors and – even whores. They say that about her mama and make veiled references to Cani's green eyes and foreign features, half-damning and half-sympathetic. If Mama didn't work at the fort, they'd stop. Cani is sure of it.

The bombardment begins at 7 a.m. sharp. A few men and women, freshly bathed and dressed for prayer, duck into the shop for cover. The men give each other self-satisfied smiles when they realise their good fortune in landing up at the kallu kada, while the women look around avidly. The shop is magnificent. Rows and rows of gleaming bottles on shelves, painstakingly washed out in the river, polished by hand and then refilled; above the bar hangs a large painting of King George II with his legs on show and wearing more gold than a Brahmin lady at a wedding, as Thanthai likes to say. Thanthai's quite the painter; Mama brought him the oils and thick paper as a present last summer and he laboured away by moonlight behind the shop for weeks before allowing them to see his masterpiece.

Mama had rolled her eyes. "How nice. Even *we* are painting their pink faces now," she grumbled. But the painting had gone up, enjoying pride of place.

"You know the British. One look at the King and all they want to do is drink, isn't it, Cani my daughter?" Thanthai had said, winking. Mama kept glaring and so he heaved a sigh, gave her a kiss, and whispered, "All I want is a peaceful life, Nataline, just a peaceful life."

Cani grabs for Mama's long blue nightdress as another cannon strikes nearby, rattling all the bottles on the walls and perhaps even the teeth in her head. "Thanthai hasn't come back yet."

"Shh, anjinho, don't worry. Now, look at all these people in the shop. Don't you think your papa would like it if we sold them some drinks?" Mama's face is smooth and unworried, her voice teasing. Cani unclenches her hands and nods.

As they go to take orders, one of the men starts telling the tale of the besieged Queen Meenakshi of Madurai; it's a perennial Madrasi favourite, and Cani lingers to hear it again. "The wise Queen Meenakshi took the throne of Madurai when her husband died with no heir, but one of her husband's relations started plotting rebellion. Both appealed to their liege-lord, the Nawab of the Carnatic. The foolish nawab sent his advisor Chanda Sahib to settle the dispute." The man pauses for effect, and Mama dutifully contributes a disapproving noise from across the room. "Yes, my friends," he agrees sorrowfully. "Chanda swore on the Qur'an to keep Meenakshi on her throne, and together they ousted the usurper. But after the rebels were scattered, Chanda Sahib betrayed the queen!"

Cani gasps in shock, carried along by the story, and one of the neighbour-ladies cries "Shame, shame!" Mama hands the storyteller a generous shot to wet his throat, and he gulps it down before continuing with renewed vigour. "The faithless Chanda imprisoned the queen in her own palace. The blasphemer had sworn his loyalty – not on the Qur'an, but on a brick wrapped in glittering paper!" Cani leans closer as the storyteller lowers his voice. "But Meenakshi would not treat with the invader. She threw herself from a tower rather than submit, and so we remember her today: a Nayak queen, honourable to the end!"

Everyone quietens unexpectedly. But Cani is thinking of Queen Meenakshi at the top of the tower, leaning out of a stone-clad window and looking down at the ground far below her. "What happened to Chanda Sahib?" she asks.

The storyteller turns toward her with a patronising smile and then Cani is knocked to the floor in a wave of sound and light so thick that it feels like a physical force.

Glass shatters on the shelves. Sharply alcoholic shards pelt her back and scatter across the floor like chittering insects. The packed mud floor heaves and bucks, copper bowls ring and clatter; somewhere in the distance it sounds like many people are screaming. Cani feels a tug under her shoulders as she's pulled upright and her eyes slowly focus through the slick smoke: it is Mama's face, close to hers. Her mouth is working but instead of words Cani hears a loud, heavy hum like water rushing downriver. Mama looks frightened. There is blood on her chin, and her right hand is wrapped up in a length of cleaning cloth.

The sounds coalesce into her name: *Cani,* Mama says, shaking her and making the humming worse. "Anjinho, meu coração." Her words bleed into each other, water pouring out from a glass onto her face. The shop, the magnificent shop is littered with aunties lying on the ground and some men staggering around and big long pieces of glass like glittering swords, and George II has a cannonball embedded through his glorious head.

"The King," Cani coughs out. Mama starts to cry. "The King has no head."

***

Thanthai appears just in time to watch the British soldiers desert their posts to loot the kallu kada, drawn by the unmistakable stench of alcohol flowing out into the streets. He hugs Cani and Mama too hard and pulls them back when one of the officers arrives to shout at his men. The French ships are still firing their cannon, but the soldiers ignore the siege and their red-faced officer to drink alcohol straight from the bottle. "At least the shop didn't catch fire," Thanthai says fervently. "Thank Ishvara, both of you are alive."

And then the doctor peels back the last wrapping around Mama's hand and Cani throws up all over Thanthai's feet. Her Mama's right hand is a mass of blood and flesh, shredded by the glass.

"You are lucky," the doctor tells her. "You won't lose any fingers."

"I'm a clerk," Mama tells him angrily, with a rasp in her voice. "Don't you understand, you fool? This is my *writing* hand."

***

Cani dreams her frozen-river dream again, only this time all the fish are shaped like liquor bottles, and the screaming calf has mama's dark, thick-lashed eyes and bleeds indigo ink instead of blood. The French sailors impale themselves endlessly on the sharp ice of the river as she pulls the tiger away and wills the blood back into the calf.

She is concentrating so hard that she does not notice the interloper to her dream until he clears his throat and asks "Ninna hesaru enu, magale?" in what is clearly meant to be a kindly tone.

Cani starts at the unfamiliar language, and scrambles up to her knees before turning. A man in embroidered silks and a turban edged with extravagant strings of pearls is standing on the glass-river a few feet away from her, looking at her river-scene with a curious expression. Cani did not dream him; she has never seen such rich apparel in her waking life.

He offers her a smile. "Malayalam ariyamo? Paire endah, kutty?" These words sound a little more familiar, but still unintelligible. Cani crosses her arms and wills her hair into a severe oiled plait. He sighs. "Tumhara naam kya hai, beti?"

Cani glares at him, but is caught entirely off guard when he starts forward and seizes her chin. He tilts up her face and chuckles in understanding. "Oh, you are foreign!" he announces in English, and Cani pushes him away.

"I'm *Tamil*!" she shouts, and stamps her foot. The glass cracks with a sound like cannonshot and breaks into jagged spikes as her body rises up until she's hovering a foot in the air; the man collapses into the sharded water as her skin darkens a shade, then another until her hands are a glorious coal-black relieved only by her shining pink nails.

The interloper pulls himself onto an ice-floe, and squeezes out his salwar half-heartedly. "Yes, yes madam, you are Tamil only," he agrees with a choking laugh. "You are finished with anger, no? We can talk a little bit?" He looks down at his waterlogged clothes with palpable sadness, and raises his eyes heavenward.

Unnerved by his calm, Cani wills the glass-river whole before setting her feet down on its once again smooth surface. The colour leaches from her skin slowly as she lightens to her natural brown. Her eyes, she knows, are fading from rich brown to her normal, hated, *foreign* pale green.

"Your dreams are very bright, very clear," he compliments. "Good control. What is your name, magale?"

"What's yours?" she challenges, squaring her shoulders.

"You are a very interesting child!" He laughs, not at all angrily. "My name is Prabhu. I am sa-ilu to Muhammad Anwaruddin, Nawab of the Carnatic."

Cani wrinkles her forehead. "What is a sa-ilu?"

"I am a dream-walker – that is how I am to be talking to you now, while your body is sleeping in Madras." Prabhu looks suddenly sheepish. "You *are* in Madras, no, madam?"

"My thanthai owns the liquor shop." Her breath hitches as her dream flickers into broken bottles and smoke-damaged walls.

"Do you know Nicholas Morse?" He mangles the name, but Cani nods.

"He is the governor. Mama works for him."

"You know anything about this fellow?"

"Of course!" Cani tosses her head; Mama had gossiped about him with her friends many times, and Cani had made sure to overhear. "He likes Bengali sweets; he has them imported at the Crown's expense from Fort St. David in Calcutta. And," she added, "Mama says that he spends more nights with the gardener than with his wife."

Prabhu looks thoughtful. "You are a most useful little madam!" He clearly spots an oncoming eruption and quickly adds, "I am not saying you are too little, don't be angry, please, madam!" Cani tries not to smile. "Now, I must go make a visit to Mr. Morse's dream – but I will find you tomorrow. I think we will have a very interesting conversation, no?"

Perhaps it is his smile, or some sudden leaping fear that she can barely name, that makes tears spring into her eyes. "You won't come," she says, turning away. "You are lying to me because I am only a child."

"What is your name, magale?" he asks peaceably.

"Canimozhi Theruvil," she says imperiously, though she is unable to stop herself from adding, "Cani. Canimozhi is a mami name."

"I will see you tomorrow, Cani," Prabhu promises with a wink. He dives into the glassy surface of the river and disappears entirely.

***

The next day Governor Morse surrenders to Admiral La Bourdonnais. Cani wonders what Prabhu said to him in the dream, to make him give up so quickly. French troops take over White Town but mostly leave Black Town alone. "For now," Mama says darkly to their neighbours, who have come over to gossip and help clear the shop. "I do not like the new governor, Dupleix." Thanthai attempts to lighten the grim atmosphere by humming a song as he works, but the skin around his eyes is taut with worry.

As Cani is sweeping the floor, Mama turns to her and says, "I want my ashes to be scattered in the Ganga when I die."

Cani thinks that she has perhaps missed some vital portion of the conversation, and tries to look wise, but Mama doesn't seem very convinced.

"I do not want all of this funeral nonsense. People coming to the house, looking at my body, being buried in the churchyard dirt. Don't let your papa bury me, Cani. I want to be burned and scattered."

"You're not dying, Mama," she manages to say, and Mama rolls her eyes.

"Not now. But I will someday, no? And your papa will let the priests bury me at St. Andrew's, he is not the kind of man to argue with a priest, even of a different religion. So you promise me, anjinho: cremate me like a Hindu." Mama pauses, and then adds, "It's much more dignified."

"Mama–"

"Promise me, Cani."

Cani is saved from whatever answer was shaping itself in her mouth by the sound of Thanthai clearing his throat from the next room. "Nataline..." He trails off, and then clears his throat again. "There are some people here to see our daughter."

***

It is some relief to Cani that Prabhu is real. He looks exactly the same as he did in the dream, even down to his too-wide smile of greeting. There's a woman with him, wearing a delicate sari in ivory and lilac, draped in a strange style over her lush curves. Her eyes are arresting: large and expressive, limned in kohl. She is possibly the most beautiful woman that Cani has ever seen, even when she rolls her eyes

"She is even younger than you described, Prabhu," she sneers in lilting English, wrinkling her nose. "Close your mouth, child, you'll catch flies."

"Do not talk to my daughter in that fashion," Mama snaps curtly, her face drawing itself into the cool hauteur she uses to talk to drunken customers.

"Munira," Prabhu remonstrates, wincing. "I am sorry, madams, sir. I am Prabhu, sa-ilu to the court of Muhammad Anwaruddin, Nawab of the Carnatic. This is Munira Begum, sa-ilu to Alivardhi Khan, Nawab of Bengal. We are here to talk about your daughter."

Thanthai sucks in a breath, and pulls her back toward him. "You are–" He fumbles for a moment, searching for the English word; Mama has been teaching him English since they were married, but he is still not fluent. "Sorcerers."

"We are *dream-walkers*," Munira demurs. "We – Allah forgive me, what does it matter? Yes, you could call us sorcerers."

Prabhu gives Munira a pleading look. "Canimozhi has a gift. We would like to train her."

"She is – like you?" Mama's voice stutters, and Cani doesn't quite dare to look at her.

"No." Prabhu shakes his head. "She is not a dream-walker, but she has talent. Her dreams burn brightly. She could have a great position in the nawab's court."

Mama turns to her, smiling over clenched teeth. "Cani, meu coração. Go make us some tea."

***

The water takes forever to boil, and her hands seem to belong to some-one else as she sets out the tumblers. The door isn't particularly thick; one more step, and she'd be able to hear the low-voiced conversation in the shop. She grits her teeth, and takes the step. She can see just a sliver of Munira's face through the opening.

"She is clearly a bright girl," Munira offers, with a sharp little smile. "What prospects do bright girls of her background have here?" Mama says something indistinct, and Munira laughs quietly. "Come now, the girl has such a distinctive set of Portuguese eyes."

There's the sound of a stool turning over; to Cani's infinite surprise it's Thanthai that speaks, his voice hard and too loud for politeness: "She is *our daughter.*"

Prabhu breaks the pooling silence. "Of course, sir. We did not come here to insult you."

"It would be insulting to pretend!" Munira's voice, now, addressing Mama. "She will never have an easy life, will she, Cani-ki-ma? Prabhu and I do not care about her background, but your neighbours care, don't they?" Her voice becomes softer, more contemplative. "Now, money will help society overlook many flaws. But you have no money. A shop, perhaps – but, alas," her bangles clink together, and Cani imagines that she is gesturing to the ruin around her. "But then, maybe a position? Connections can be of value – you may have had those amongst the British officials, but as of this morning Madras is a French town. I know Marquis Dupleix; he will not take on a fe-male clerk, even if you do regain the ability to write."

"Things may change. Cani is not even eleven," Mama interjects.

"And what will she be at twenty? A clerk to a man who is not even half as clever, if she's lucky? A wife to a tolerant husband?" Munira's voice cracks harshly, and Cani is certain that the dark-voiced woman means her to hear this, means the words to rend at her ears – she is obscurely glad that she can't see Munira's lovely, savage face. "Perhaps you can go ask the foreigners for help. Go back to Pangim and beg the girl's father to take her."

Mama raises up her face from her hands to say, very clearly, "He's dead," and the water for the tea boils over the lip of the pan and sloshes all over the floor. Cani turns her head to look stupidly at the frothing pan. She should do something about it; wrap her hands in a towel, take the pan off the fire before the water dampens the wood. But she doesn't move.

***

When at last she comes back into the room, her face is carefully blank but she has no tea. Nobody seems to notice. Munira is perched on the shop's stool like an impossibly lovely rani; Cani's mother looks thin and worn in comparison. Cani finds herself feverish with hatred, wanting to pull the lovely smile from Munira's face with her hands and stamp it underneath her feet.

"There you are," Munira says. "Now, Mrs. Theruvil–"

Cani clenches her fists and says, "Be quiet, Munira." Only, instead of say-ing it calmly, she shouts it so loud that everyone in the room turns to look at her. Cani feels her cheeks flush. "Just – stop," she bites out, hands shaking.

Prabhu stands up in a flash of bright silks. "Little madam," he begins soothingly, but Cani is not to be reasoned with. She feels hot and wild and powerful.

"Shut up, all of you." Her vision is blurry; Thanthai's concerned face and Mama's churn together. She sits down on the floor, and to her surprise no one speaks. "You have money, don't you?" The silence persists, and Cani glances up at Prabhu, who nods once. She holds his gaze. "I want you to give my parents money. Enough money to rebuild the shop, to pay for a doctor for Mama's hand." Something bitter and mean makes her add, "Just one of the rings on your fingers would probably be enough."

Prabhu exchanges a look with Munira. "Yes," he agrees. "We can pay."

Thanthai's expression drops, and then he comes and settles on the floor next to her. There is something in his face Cani cannot put a name to, but it makes her limbs feel heavy. He reaches out a hand tentatively, and strokes her hair. She starts to cry under his gentle ministration and he whispers her name. She stops sobbing all at once, and his hands tighten in her hair.

"Don't go, my daughter." His voice is a plea rather than a command, as if he somehow knows that right now, she cannot be commanded.

She places her hand on his lined cheek. "I want to go with them, Thanthai," she tells him in Tamil, meeting his eyes. "I am going."

It's simple enough after that: she doesn't have many clothes, and she leaves her one doll behind on her pallet. Mama makes everyone tea, finally, and Munira makes pleasant small talk with the room at large until Cani is ready. Thanthai hugs her and talks too much as the time comes to part, but Mama stays back, unnaturally quiet until Cani approaches her.

She has no idea what Mama thinks; her face is unreadable, even as she bends down to give her a kiss on the cheek. "Don't come back, anjinho," she whispers into Cani's hair, so quietly that her voice is the merest suggestion. "Don't look back."

***

Prabhu and Munira have an oxcart waiting at the crossroads down the street; Cani climbs on and they begin their journey to Mysore in jostling silence for half an hour, maybe forty minutes before Munira turns toward her.

"Do you know what purdah is, child?" she asks, and Cani shakes her head. "Why would you? You're not Muslim, or well-born. I was kept separate from men from the moment of my birth, only attended to by women, only allowed to glimpse the wider world through shutters and veils. I was told that it would be haram, a sin, to look upon the face of a man who wasn't husband or brother. I was seventeen before I looked a man in the eyes, and do you know what happened?"

Cani shakes her head, even more confused by Prabhu's long-suffering look.

Munira leans closer: "Absolutely nothing!" She begins to laugh uproariously. "Nothing at all. Don't worry, child. You'll understand what I mean soon enough."

***

They make camp in the dark; Cani moves to help the driver and attendant, but Prabhu pulls her back. "You're not a servant, magale," he tells her kindly, before pulling a small glass vial from his robes. The liquid within glints unnaturally green in the darkness, and Cani suppresses a shiver. "Besides, we have work to begin."

They usher her into Munira's tent, and tell her to lie upon the cushions. The sheets are made of cotton colour-blocked with vegetable dyes, finer than anything she has lain upon before. She looks up at Munira and Prabhu, and sees herself as they must see her: scrupulously clean, at mama's insistence, but somehow rough and mean and small. She feels unpleasantly like a little girl as Prabhu opens the vial, and tilts her head back to spill a droplet of the green tincture on her tongue.

"This will help you sleep," he whispers, as he lays her head down. "You will soon be trained to sleep at will, but for now, this will help. Sleep and dream, madam, sleep and dream brightly."

The tincture is viscously bitter, coating the inside her of her mouth and spreading through her limbs until she wakes in a dream sheened a sepulchrous green. To her surprise, she has not conjured up her home, but rather the temple courtyard thick with the smells of burning camphor and tulsi. The temple floor creaks and that's when Cani stumbles to the side and realises that her dream-temple is a vast ship, floating on a churning verdant river of leaves and grass.

The sound of clapping makes her turn sharply, but doesn't quite wipe the joy from her face; Prabhu and Munira are standing on the wood floor of her frigate-temple, looking around with some interest. Prabhu is crowing exuberantly. "See, Munira, I told you she had power!"

"She still has much to learn," Munira says primly, but Cani catches her slanting a calculating look in her direction.

Prabhu ignores Munira to bestow a genial smile upon Cani. "Most dream unknowingly – they would not even know if we entered their dream. That is why I was so surprised that you saw me, when I stumbled into your glass-river dream."

"Can I..." She stops, and turns away from Munira. "Can I enter other people's dreams, like you?"

"No, magale," Prabhu shakes his head. "You dream stable, strong dreams – you are a conduit to the dream world. We sa-ilu rely on people like you to help us safely access the dreaming, and guide us home. You are having a rare gift, madam."

Munira yawns exaggeratedly. "It is time I returned to my own duties. Alivardi's planning to ambush some Maratha raiders tomorrow. I promised him I would... disturb their sleep tonight." She flashes them both an unpleasant smile.

Prabhu returns the gesture sincerely, even bowing slightly. "I thank you for coming, Munira. I did not want to arrive at the girl's house without a woman present. It would have been – untoward."

Cani raises an eyebrow at that – Munira had hardly charmed her parents – but then again, Thanthai would probably have thrown out a lone middle-aged man who came to their house and asked to speak to his daughter.

"You owe me a favour, Prabhu, and don't think I won't collect," she warns, opening the iron temple gate and disappearing as she walks through it. Cani's dream feels somehow lighter with her departure.

Prabhu watches the swinging gate for few long moments before shaking his head as if to clear it. "Now, madam." He tilts his head towards her. "Let us begin."

***

Prabhu teaches her to stretch the boundaries of her dream by slow degrees on their long unfurling journey to Mysore. The first night she is only able to paint in thanthai's liquor shop, but a few weeks into their journey she is able to build up all of Black Town and then more, farther, a dream that encompasses White Town and the glistening, gleaming river rushing away across the plain and pulling at the very edge of her consciousness as it goes.

By the evenings her mind already feels hammered thin with their cart-jolted lessons in history and courtly etiquette, but then she slips into dream and Prabhu asks for more. Her mind convulses and writhes and spreads and she populates the streets of Madras with much-hated mamis and the baker's boy down the street with the shy smile and the street-sweepers and vegetable sellers and smell of sizzling mustard from their neighbour's in the early morning and even La Bourdonnais on the French flagship, watching her dream-town with his brass-handled telescope hung with a glittering chain.

She tries to imagine Mama in their room, but there is something wrong with the way her starched second-best work sari drapes against her waist, something not quite right with how her hands move as she rolls chapatis on the mat, how her eyelashes catch the flour in the air. Cani changes her, cautiously at first, but then more desperately, trying to recall exactly how her lips stretched, just so, and as she shifts and pulls on those delicate details the edges of her dream begin curling up like blackened paper; the river boils to dust, the ships capsize, and the trees all turn to mice running in screaming circles but Mama's face still isn't quite right—

"Cani," Prabhu interrupts urgently, voice shaking. "Focus, madam! Keep your dream stable!"

She turns her head and all the walls turn transparent; the perspective buckles and heaves, and she is looking down at Madras through the lens of a telescope perched on the back of an enormous, jewel-beaked eagle. Prabhu pulls himself up from one of the eagle's talons and clutches her around the waist, muttering a prayer to Shiva and Saraswati. "O, whatever god is listening," he continues his litany somewhat blasphemously, "please save me from overenthusiastic little ladies!" He peers over her shoulder, and she follows his gaze: her carefully constructed Madras is a ruin.

Cani wonders whether Prabhu is afraid of heights, and pulls at the eagle's neck: it wheels in a wide arc in the cloud-stippled sky and Prabhu's prayers intensify. He manages to save enough breath to mutter, "We will try again tomorrow night," before his nerve breaks. "Now, can we please come to... ground level? The eagle has a hungry look in his eye, and people always tell me I have a mouse-like aspect."

Instead, Cani urges her eagle on faster, plucking its feathers absently and tossing them at the boiling, rupturing buildings of her city. She watches as the feathers explode like cannonballs in the noonday sun, and only lands when all of Black Town is flattened.

***

When they reach Mysore, Cani is presented at the weekly durbar of the Nawab of the Carnatic, Muhammad Anwaruddin. "I am not nervous," she says, as they wait to be announced.

Prabhu smothers his laugh with a cough. "Imagine it is a dream," he advises. "Imagine that you are someone else."

Cani asks, "Is he a good man?" Later she cannot remember whether Prabhu said "Oh yes," or perhaps, "He is my nawab," or perhaps "Who are we to judge those set above us by god?"

The nawab is a large man, perfumed heavily with rose attar and oudh, smiling vaguely at her before greeting Prabhu with unconcealed enthusiasm. They leave Cani with a group of young noble girls and retire to one of the inner rooms for a private conversation. Cani is teaching the girls Tamil swearwords when Prabhu returns.

"You did well, Cani," he tells her as they walk to their lodgings. "The nawab was greatly impressed."

The nawab's favour translates to beautifully appointed rooms near the palace and a generous monthly stipend on top of gifts of jewels and embroidered silk saris and gold. It is not long before Cani has as many rings as Prabhu, glittering dangerously on her fingers. It is a year before she automatically dreams herself into the silks and jewels of her new office.

***

"Why did you help the French take Madras, Prabhu?" Cani asks one day, trying to keep her dream stable as he destroys pieces of it with a sword; he has been testing her ability to keep her dreams steady, even under direct assault. He slits the throat of a tiger she conjures; it roars and bleeds brass clockwork pieces and scraps of yellow silk. He is sweating, and her dream barely wavers as she knits the tigers back to wholeness.

One of them gets past his guard and swipes at him; Cani disintegrates the tiger's claws before it rips out Prabhu's throat and he gives her a grateful look before letting his sword drop. "The British were supporting my nawab's rival, and the French promised they would give Madras to us after they took it," he admits, breathing heavily. That did not happen; Thanthai's letters are

74

full of complaints about Governor Dupleix's heavy-handedness. "The French betrayed the nawab."

Cani's lips twist. "Foreigners never keep their word," she says bitterly. Prabhu reaches out to touch her shoulder, but she shies away. She ignores the sadness that flits across his face; she is not a child any more.

***

Cani is fifteen when she kisses a boy for the first time; despite her years in Mysore she has only the rudiments of the local language, and so she does not understand what he whispers as he clutches her shoulders. His hand is up her blouse when the nawab's guards find her in the alley behind his parents' chai kada; they throw him to the ground without much ceremony and escort her back to her lodgings.

"You have terrible timing," she tells Prabhu irately, readjusting her sari.

Prabhu looks pained. "I have need of you, madam," he says, and hands her a French matchlock rifle.

Her annoyance drains away; she has never held such a weapon before. Prabhu demonstrates how to disassemble it, making her feel the weight and shape of each part until she knows its innards more intimately than she knows herself. Then he asks her to dream each piece, teaching her about metals and chemistry and physics all shaped like a weapon. She keeps dreaming the pieces into perfect shapes, but lighter than air; they float and playfully dodge Prabhu's hands as he tries to assemble them, and when he fires the bullets they spray out in a soft cloud of poppies and gold.

"No," he tells her patiently. "You must dream the rifle cruel. You must dream it bloodthirsty and vengeful. You must dream each part without mercy."

Cani unspins the rifle in his hands and the pieces clatter to the floor. "Why do you need a dream-rifle?"

"Please do not question me now," he pleads, kneading his temples, and Cani notices how much older and thinner he looks.

"Do you..." She hesitates, before crossing her arms. "Do you have children, Prabhu?"

He looks surprised at her change of subject. "I do," he says slowly. "A boy and a girl, close to your age. They are with their mother."

"Why haven't I met them?"

Prabhu looks stricken. "I – do not see them much, magale." He uses the term of endearment without thinking; he has not called her anything but her name in some years. "I am not a very good father."

Cani resolutely does not think of Thanthai, who has never worn gold turban pins or fought clockwork tigers in the dreaming. She does not think of Thanthai's hands as he paints, his terrible jokes, his little warm winks when Mama shouts at both of them. She does not think of him so hard that her dream begins to fracture into jagged, blackened pieces. She wakes to Prabhu's concerned face with the taste of ashes and shame in her mouth. Her dream hasn't collapsed since she was a little girl in an ox-cart on the road to Mysore.

***

Prabhu knocks on her door a few days later, and seems gratifyingly surprised when she invites him into her room. He trails his fingers along her embroidered silk canopy and looks discomfited by her dressing table crowded with kohl and henna and perfumes. At length, he says, "I should tell you why I want you to dream a rifle, Cani. You are not a weapon, to be mutely wielded." He pulls at the folds of his turban. "Do you know the name Chanda Sahib?"

"The man who betrayed Queen Meenakshi," she says, trying not to think of the last time she had heard the story. Her hands clench on her cotton bedspread.

Prabhu looks surprised before his face smooths in understanding. "Ah yes," he jokes weakly. "You are Tamil. I remember well."

"He was the nawab's advisor," Cani adds remorselessly, and the momentary lightness leaves Prabhu's features.

"He was once, but no more. Now he is our enemy. Dupleix has paid a ransom to release him from prison, and he is raising an army against the nawab with the backing of the French." Prabhu places his hand on Cani's shoulder. "The nawab has given me orders to kill him in the dream, and I must obey. No, Cani – I *wish* to obey." His eyes light. "This is why I need your dream-rifle."

Cani measures the drunken stories of the kallu kada with the weight of the rifle's pieces. Her fingernails dig into her palm. "Go into his dream first," she says, finally. "Without any weapon. Tell me honestly what kind of man he is. You can tell that from a dream, can't you? Isn't that your power – to see what someone really, truly is?" Prabhu nods. "So look, and tell me what you see." Cani adds, "I will trust you," and Prabhu nods again, slowly: it is a warning, as well as a promise.

***

Prabhu returns from Chanda Sahib's dream somehow reduced, his skin seeming to fit less firmly against his bones. He tells her what he saw as Cani spins him a soothing landscape: ektara players plucking gentle melodies in the shade of a banyan tree some cool autumn evening. His hands clench and unclench around hers and he whispers that Chanda Sahib dreams of white marble palaces with spires chased with gold, and queens beautiful and damned, breaking into dust and bright feathers under his fists, poisoning themselves endlessly, and pressing kisses full of fearful promise into the side of his neck. He dreams of land pulled around his celestial body like a cloak, each clasp a grove of coconut trees, rivers wound around his head for a turban. "The nawab is right," he whispers to her as his body regains itself inside her dream. "A man who dreams so imperiously is to be feared."

Cani believes him.

***

76

She dreams of her parents' house, and in that comfort assembles a rifle of perfect purpose: each part is unconditional and sure, each mechanism gleaming like a hand covered in jewelled rings, thrumming with the desire for blood. Prabhu watches her in silent agitation, but when she presses her creation into his hands he calms. He fires it at the painting of George II that hangs above the bar and it disintegrates into strips of canvas and wood.

She feels a hot prickling behind her eyes, but does not cry. "Be careful, Prabhu," she says instead, and he smiles too widely at her, like the first time they met.

"Thank you," he says, bowing to her so deeply that his head nearly brushes the ground. "This is a weapon of unsurpassed beauty. I will use it well."

Cani's dream shivers as Prabhu fits his hands around the trigger, but it does not break apart. He opens the front door of the kada, and disappears as it slams shut.

***

He does not return that night, and Cani knows he is dead. Dreamwalkers are vulnerable in the dreaming; that is why they need conduits like her. Each unfamiliar dreamscape is a risk. She does not think about her rifle in Chanda Sahib's hands, shooting bullets of lead instead of poppy-petals at Prabhu's head.

The next night she dreams of Queen Meenakshi standing in front of the enormous white pillars of the Nayak palace of Tirumalai, lit into gleaming magnificence by the sun. Cani cannot be sure whether she is dreaming of a real palace, or a kind of palatial afterlife. Meenakshi turns her face toward Cani and opens her mouth but her lips and tongue and throat are all blistered with pearls; she cannot speak.

There were some men at the kallu kada that told a different tale of Meenakshi: that she was not usurped by a political ally, but rather that she let Chanda Sahib into Tirumalai as a lover, and that she killed herself out of heartsickness at his betrayal. Cani does not believe this story. The Queen in her dreams climbs the window of her tower-prison slowly, and when she throws herself from the highest window her face is not twisted with grief but bright with rage; she is a weapon of silk and flesh. Her surrender is an act of war.

***

The next morning Mysore is an unfamiliar city: there is a rumour that Chanda Sahib is marching toward them with fifteen thousand horse-mounted men, and there is so much confusion and fear that Cani barely manages to cross the streets to the Nawab's palace. She is waiting for an audience in the antechamber when Munira saunters in, looking as irritable and lovely as the day Cani met her.

"I'm here to collect that favour," Munira says, and Cani smooths the pleats of her sari with a hand heavy with jewelled rings, and reminds herself that she is no longer a child.

"Honoured sa-ilu," she says silkily, dipping her body down in the correct courtly greeting. "I am not to be collected, by you or anyone else."

Munira inclines her head slightly, an opponent acknowledging another across a battlefield. "Then what are you doing here, waiting to offer yourself to Prabhu's nawab?"

Cani feels that tightening behind her eyes again; it would be so easy to cry, but she has not cried in a very long while. "You serve a nawab yourself," she says harshly.

"No," Munira's voice is oddly gentle. "I am of his court, but I do not *serve* him like Prabhu served his nawab. The kingdoms of nawabs are waking things, their borders are drawn in land and blood. They are powerful, perhaps, but they must follow the rules of the waking. We–" Munira gestures between them. "Cani, *we* are creatures of the dream. In the dream there are no borders unless we make them, no wars unless we choose to wage them." She laughs. "There is no purdah unless we wish to enforce it."

"It is not so simple for me. I am not a dream-walker like you, Munira."

"Perhaps not, Cani," she allows. "But do you wish to be like Prabhu? He sacrificed his life for his nawab's ambitions. Is that what you desire for yourself?"

Two spear-wielding guards open the heavy carved-mahogany doors to the durbar-hall; a court official approaches Cani from within. "Canimozhi Theruvil," he rasps nervously, not meeting her eyes. "The most benevolent and auspicious Nawab Muhammad Anwaruddin awaits your presence."

"Yes," agrees Munira acidly. "I am sure he does."

"You would use me too, Munira," Cani says, ignoring the official.

"Of course I will," she says. "But I am offering you a choice."

Cani lets out a breath. "I will never make another dream-weapon."

To her surprise, Munira shrugs. "Good. We are not weapons, to be used so carelessly."

The silk-clad official clears his throat. "Madam. The nawab expects you."

Cani looks at him and thinks about her parents; she is still young enough to go back to Madras. To let them hold her and love her and find her a husband. To have children and will herself to dream of only simple things. She could sell her jewels and silks and build from them a good life. She could even dream of the games of queens some nights, and wake to small and comfortable contentment.

Cani thinks of her mother saying *do not look back*, and turns to Munira as she says to the official, "Tell him that I serve him no longer."

***

Cani dreams that night of forests full of snake-trees and beaches sanded white with powdered skulls and a horizon that snatches itself away as she reaches out to grasp it. She dreams of a night sky full of stars that arrange themselves in the shape of Mama's face. She dreams that she is Queen

Meenakshi, climbing a tower to reach the window at the top and as she throws herself from the battlements she wakes, cool and light and almost unbodied, ready to be free.

Art by Daria Khvostova

THE WITCH OF TARUP
CLAIRE HUMPHREY

1886
Tarup, Denmark

Every town has its witch, or so the Midsummer Ballad says, but I had only lived in Tarup a fortnight and I did not know who the witch might be.

I asked Bjørn first, but the right side of his face was stiff like wax from his apoplexy, and his reply came out mostly in spittle. I placed a piece of chalk in his hand, as I had tried doing these several days since he began to sit up again, but as before, he could only make it glance across the slate before his hand spasmed and the chalk fell to the floor. His voice went on in a mumbling moan.

I wiped his face dry with my apron and said, "My husband, are you distressed because you are ill, or hungry, or because you do not like what I ask?"

He beat his hand upon the slate. I found his bowl and began feeding him spoonfuls of øllebrød, which was all he could eat now, morning and night.

"You have not had much time to know me yet," I told him, "but I would not look for a witch unless I had great need."

Bjørn jerked his face away, causing øllebrød to run down his cheek.

"If you have had enough to eat," I said, "I will go out."

He beat his hand upon the side of his chair.

"We have run out of beer," I said, and he stopped beating.

Mads Olesen was just coming up to the mill, a bushel of potatoes in his arms. "No wind," he reported, as if I could not see perfectly well the unmoving branches of the oak tree, as if I could not hear perfectly well the stillness of the mill's sails.

I gave him a sack from our dwindling flour supply in exchange for the potatoes, and asked if he would sit with Bjørn for an hour.

"My Farmor, when she was sick," he said, "she always liked me to sing to her."

"By all means sing to Bjørn," I said. "I am sure it will gladden his heart." I was sure of no such thing. We had known each other a matter of weeks before the apoplexy struck Bjørn. I was already unsure how his face looked with both sides alive.

Before I left, I filled a basket with eggs. The smell of the chickens, straw and shit and warm feathers, reminded me of the farm in Allerup, where I was born. One of my brothers held it now. Until I met Bjørn, I had been resigned to living out my days there, tending my brother's livestock and serving my brother's wife and reading novels in secret.

"Dagny Jorgensdatter," I said aloud, to reassure myself, "you are never

81

going back to Allerup." And I threw a scarf over my shoulders and a bonnet on my head, and went instead down the hill to the village.

Hans Fisker's wife, Maren Knudsdatter, was feeding her goslings, four of them, nested in boxes in her kitchen. She had a coffee pot just beginning to spit on the stove. "Dagny Møller," she said, without smiling. "I see you have eggs for me. I suppose you would like some herring in exchange."

I had not yet figured whether she disliked me in particular or disliked people in general, but either way, I did not intend to leave without a chat, and since the coffee was ready, she could not very well get rid of me. She poured coffee for each of us, and we pulled up stools close to the hearth and kilted up our skirts to warm our legs.

"And how is Bjørn?" she said.

"He is angry with me," I said, "because I told him I was going to look for a witch."

"A witch," she echoed, still with those flat brows. "You told Bjørn you were going to look for a witch."

"Allerup has two."

"Allerup has a Grundtviger parish leader who teaches girls to defy their families," Maren said. "All manner of things can be found in Allerup."

"I live in Tarup now," I said, "and I need a witch."

"I have lived in Tarup all my life, and I am a good Christian," Maren said. "I do not know such things as witchcraft."

I drank my coffee in silence then, from a blue and white cup small enough to hide in my fist. It was very good coffee.

Maren wrapped up the herring and I gave her the eggs.

"Kirsten Larsdatter could weave you a new scarf, if you wanted one," Maren said.

"I have a scarf. Bjørn gave me this one when we were wed." It was a fine one, bordered with tassels; much finer than anything I could buy for myself with the mill becalmed and my husband ill.

Maren looked away, up at the sky, well-bred enough to make it look as if she was not rolling her eyes. "Kirsten Larsdatter cannot walk about, and she would welcome a visit."

***

Kirsten Larsdatter lived in a small house, by herself. I did not know if she was a widow or if she had never married. Today, her front windows were open to the cool spring breeze and I could hear the hush and clack of her loom as I approached.

The sound stopped when I knocked, and then I heard the clatter of Kirsten taking up her crutches and making her way toward the door.

"Dagny Møller!" she said. "Come in and have some coffee."

"Thank you, but I have just had some coffee with–"

"Nonsense, nonsense! I have the pot all ready to go." I watched her drag her reluctant legs over to the stove.

I set my basket of herring beside the door and examined Kirsten's loom.

She was making a table-runner for someone, with red and yellow stripes. She had been lamed by a childhood illness, I had heard, and so she spent all her youth perfecting her weaving and sewing, and was known far outside Tarup for the fineness of her work.

"And how is Bjørn?" she said, with the same flat look I'd just seen on Maren Knudsdatter's face. I began to think I had seen it on the faces of all the people of Tarup when they asked after my husband.

"He is angry with me," I said, just as before, "because I told him I was going to look for a witch."

Kirsten Larsdatter laboriously poured coffee, leaning on one crutch, and handed me the cup: even tinier than Maren's, and the coffee was stronger, earthy and rich. I held her cup while she settled into her chair and leaned her crutch against the arm, and then I passed it over.

"A witch," she said. "You told Bjørn you were going to look for a witch."

"Am I to have this same conversation with every woman in the village?" I asked.

Kirsten cradled her cup in both hands and looked at me square. Her grizzled hair was pinned back but a few strands lifted in the breeze from the open window.

"You might have it with every woman in the village, and man too," she said. "In Tarup, we do not take quickly to outsiders."

I set my cup on her hearth with a click. "I am not an outsider. I am the wife of Bjørn Møller."

"Ask your husband where you may find a witch, then."

"I did," I said. "And I am sure he would tell me, if he could speak. He wants the wind even more than I do."

Kirsten Larsdatter sighed heavily, and leaned far over to set her cup beside mine. "You want a witch to raise a wind."

"Just enough to turn the sails of the mill, before all of our grain succumbs to rot or rats."

She looked me in the face again. "I am not the one you need to beg," she said.

"Ah!" I said. "I thought Maren Knudsdatter was hinting to me that you were the witch."

"That sounds exactly like Maren Knudsdatter," Kirsten said, "but I am not the witch."

I set my elbows on my knees and sighed down at the hearth. "Do you know who is?"

She sighed, too. "It is not for me to say. But I have something else that will help. My Farfar had an apoplexy when I was a girl, and though he could not speak or write, he could tap his hand, and we made a board of letters for him to tap upon, to spell out what he would say to us."

I felt very low that I had not thought of such a thing, and very grateful that she had.

She smiled, and squeezed my elbow. "Go and see," she said.

***

I walked back up to the mill with my basket full of herring and a jug of beer from Christian Brygger. I paused before the door to look at our oak tree: even this far into spring, it was leafless, the buds still brown and hard, barely green-tipped.

Inside, Mads Olesen was not singing, but was combing Bjørn's hair. "He did not like my singing, but he likes this," Mads explained.

I thought he was not wrong: Bjørn was not banging his fist on anything, at least.

I sent Mads on his way with a fresh loaf of the bread I'd baked that morning, I put the herrings and the beer in the icebox, and I sat down with Bjørn by the hearth.

"Kirsten Larsdatter gave me an idea," I told him.

I wrote out all the letters on the slate. Bjørn breathed harshly through his mouth, the coals in the stove settled now and then, and the chalk squeaked, and I could hear everything too easily in the quiet of the windless weather, without the sweep of the mill's sails above.

When I was done I held up the board. "Can you point to the letters of your name?"

Bjørn extended his trembling left hand toward the board. The index finger smudged over the B, and continued.

When he had spelled it out, he lifted his chalk-smudged fingertip and pointed it toward me, and I saw the lines deepen and lift around his good eye, as if he would smile.

***

The next days were quiet. The wind did not rise, and the oak tree did not come into leaf, but the sun shone and the other trees greened and the chicks grew strong enough to peck in the yard. Bjørn's old dog limbered up in the warmer air and ran about nosing at everything. I traded out some of our dwindling flour; I baked some and traded the bread; I gave some grain to Christian Brygger for beer.

Each morning after I had washed Bjørn and helped him out of bed and given him his øllebrød, he would tap upon the slate and I would come to him and watch him spell out the day's business.

Some of it was needless. I chided him for telling me to do the washing, for, I said, why get a wife if he did not trust her to do the washing? But some of it was needful, such as parts of the mill that might need oiling, or the instruction to send to Odense to cancel the next month's order of flour sacks.

I had Doctor Henriksen back again, and he let more blood and pronounced Bjørn better healed than he expected. As I dug in Bjørn's moneybox for the kroner to pay his fee, my fingers scraped bare wood at the bottom.

When Doctor Henriksen had left, I came to Bjørn and showed him. "We cannot keep on this way," I said. "We need the mill working again. We need this calm to break. And if it does not, we need to think about what I can do for hire."

He tapped on his thigh, his sign for wanting his slate. I brought it to him and he spelled out, "Wind."

"I know we need wind, husband. That is why I asked you for the witch, earlier, but I did not want to bring it up again since it angered you."

"Me," he said.

I did not know what he meant. I looked at his face, which wore the half-vacant, half-pained expression it almost always wore.

"Me. Witch," his finger spelled.

I caught his hand in mine. I knelt on the hearth before him and looked up at his eyes, the one that followed me and the one that did not seem to see.

"You are the witch?" I said, to be sure. His chalky fingertip tapped against my palm. He shut his good eye.

"Then teach me," I said. "Teach me to raise the wind."

***

I went down the hill to visit Kirsten Larsdatter, as I had been doing many days lately. Through her window I heard the rhythm of her loom and the aimless sweet mutters of her geese.

"I know now," I called through her window. "I have learned what you could not tell me."

The loom stopped and Kirsten crutched to the window. "Bjørn told you?"

"With his slate," I said.

"Finally," she said. "It is clear to me that he chose you well, even though I was surprised at first."

"So was I," I admitted, for Bjørn was past the age when most men marry, and he was thought to be particular, and a particular man did not usually favour a plain woman past her best years, especially one who had given up churchgoing. "But now I think he is not sorry."

I let myself in through her door and tucked up my skirts to tend her fire; she could do it herself, but she had to pull a chair over and bend deep, and it hurt her legs and back, whereas for me it was a moment's work.

"I already owe you more favours than I can count," I said, "and I have come to ask another. I need a blue scarf, of fine wool, such as I know you have made."

"Must it be blue?" she said. "For I have a red one I made for a customer in Odense who has not yet paid."

"Bjørn says it must be blue."

"Then give me a week," Kirsten said.

"I will give you all the money I have left," I said. "It is to make the wind return."

"Then give me two days, and help me smooth things over with Agneta Blok when I do not have her dress done in the time I promised."

I helped Kirsten select the wool from her stores. I lingered long enough to make her a pot of coffee and set it on the tiny table nearest her loom, and I refilled her lamps with oil and set them close too. Then I went back up to the mill to wait.

***

The scarf was very fine, so fine it caught on the rough skin of my hands. As Bjørn had instructed, I teased out strand after strand of the blue wool, snipping them to the length of my arm, and tucking them into my bodice. It seemed a pity after all the work Kirsten had put into it.

When I thought I had enough, I touched what was left of the scarf to my cheek. It felt like a blanket for a baby.

"Dagny Møller," I said to myself, "you are not going to have a baby. You are not even going to have the mill for long unless you get this done."

I was standing on the walkway that stretched around the middle of the mill like a belt around the waist of a stout woman. Before his apoplexy, in the first days of the calm, Bjørn had positioned the sails at rest, in an evenly-balanced X. Now I reached out with a broom-handled hook and dragged the left-hand sail down straight.

Mads Olesen had helped me carry Bjørn and his chair outside, and the two of them waited in the yard below.

I wrapped the shortened scarf around my neck. I had taken off my apron and vest, tucked up my skirt more than was proper, and removed my shoes and stockings. Now I took hold of an upper rung of the sail, and stepped my bare feet onto the bottom one, and prayed that the wind would not rise just now.

I climbed up and up, right to the top rung, where the sail narrowed and the spine of it joined the central rotor. Right hand for the work, left hand to hold: Bjørn had spelled out the rule three times over, but it still felt precarious to have only my left hand clutching the rung while my right searched out a thread from the tangle of blue wool tucked in my bodice.

Bjørn had made me repeat the words of the spell thrice, too. I said them now over the thread, touched it to my lips, touched the scarf there too, and tied the thread to the top rung of the sail to which I clung.

Going down was very slow. Every rung needed a thread, every thread needed the words. I paused once to look down at Bjørn and Mads in the yard; their pale upturned faces looked blank and blurry from here, their eyes dark blots.

I reached the bottom of the sail and stood again on the walkway. It had felt high and narrow before, but compared to the sail it was solid as an oak. I turned and waved down to Bjørn.

Mads shouted up, after a moment, "He wants to know if you remember the words!"

I shouted them down.

"He says that is right!"

"Of course it is right!" I said back, but only under my breath.

I reached up with the broom-handled hook again and dragged the next sail down. As the first one swung up, I could barely see the blue threads upon it, even against the white sail.

I climbed again, all the way up to the heart, and began tying and speaking and tying and speaking, working my way back down.

When I finished this sail, I looked down into the yard again and saw I had an audience: Maren Knudsdatter, looking cross, with her arms folded.

"You should not have your poor husband out of doors!" Maren called.

"He is directing me," I said.

"He is an invalid!" she said. "He belongs in his bed!"

"He is teaching me to bring the wind," I said. "And I do not care what you think about witchery – without the wind we will starve."

"How can he teach you witchery when he cannot even speak?" Maren demanded.

"Mads, tell her," I said, reaching up and out again for the next sail.

I did not listen further, but I heard Mads talking excitedly, and even a rumbling groan from Bjørn. I climbed up until their voices were lost in the creak of the oaken sail-frame and the rustle of my skirts against the canvas.

When I finished this sail, Maren was gone. Mads and Bjørn remained. I could not tell, from this height, whether Bjørn looked pale.

"If you must go in, you must go in," I said. "I can finish alone."

Silence for a minute.

"Bjørn says you are a very fine wife and you will not finish alone while he has breath in him," Mads called up.

I did not think Bjørn had had time to spell out all of that, but I thanked him anyway, and pulled down the last sail.

***

The trampled earth of the yard stretched impossibly deep and wide beneath my feet. I clawed my toes into it like the chickens did.

The legs of Bjørn's chair had sunk in a little, too, but he still sat, alone and triumphant; it seemed Mads had gone home for his dinner. I came to Bjørn and knelt on the ground.

"Dagny," he said. His tongue sounded thick and spittle bubbled at the righthand corner of his mouth, but it was my name, nevertheless.

I grinned up at him, and unwound the tattered scarf from about my neck.

I placed one end of it into his hand, and he closed his fingers over it. I took the middle of the scarf and folded it, looped it around, knotted it tight. I set my lips against the softness and said the words Bjørn had taught me.

When I looked up, his good eye was crinkled at the corner.

"Do we wait for morning?" I said, for the sun was westering now, the days still short.

Bjørn shook his head. It was not just a palsied motion on his neck.

I hauled in a breath and took his good hand in my free one. "Are you ready?"

He nodded. He nodded, and I stroked the back of his neck the way you do with a horse who has been strong and brave, before I realized what I did, and took my hand back.

We held the frayed scarf, one to each end. I said the last of the words, which were very simple.

I pulled my end of the scarf. The knot slipped free.

A frozen minute. The earth was cold under my knees.

Bjørn's eyelids drooped, especially the right. His hand trembled a little; I could see the fabric of the scarf rippling in the sunset light.

A lock of my hair stirred, very lightly, against my cheek.

Up above, the sails of the mill began to ripple, too. I could hear the canvas as it filled taut. I could hear the slow sweep and creak as the arms began to turn.

I kissed Bjørn full on his mouth, and on the palms of each of his hands.

***

The mill turned day and night for a fortnight. We made up for all of the lost time and more. Mads moved his things up to our house and brought his brother with him, and still I had to bring another young man over from Langeskov to keep up with all the milling.

Bjørn grew stronger. He formed more and more words with his lips and tongue, and set aside the slate except for when he was very tired. He learned again how to chew meat, so that he might vary his diet of øllebrød. I invited Kirsten Larsdatter up to teach Bjørn how to walk with a crutch. His right foot dragged so that I had to stitch a leather patch over his toe, but his left was sound enough to bear him a few steps at a time around the house and yard, although he could not walk into the village or climb the heights of the mill.

The blue wool threads slipped free from the sails: I found a few of them snarled in the bushes here and there. But the wind did not cease for many days, and when it did, it was only a short calm, as happens in all seasons.

I watched the oak-buds finally break open into sprays of painful green. I watched the leaves grow, tender and wet at first, but darker and thicker and stronger by the day.

I pointed them out to Bjørn one evening, as we took our coffee by the open door, feeling the breeze of summer lift our clothes.

"The oak tree is like our family," he said. His words were still thick and stumbling. Others could not always understand, but I could. "Last to bear leaves."

"Our family has not borne any leaves at all yet, my husband," I said.

"It will," he said.

And sure enough, in the next winter, we turned the sails of the mill so that the uppermost was just coming on vertical, which meant celebration, and I was delivered of a son.

We called him Hjalmar Egekvist, which means oak-twig. Kirsten Larsdatter stood as his godmother so that he could be baptized. He was a small baby, slight-boned, but long, and I thought he would grow up tall.

"I cannot see what may come for him," Bjørn said, over his cradle. "My witch-sight is not what it was."

"He will take over the mill when he is grown," I said.

"I hope I will live to see it," said Bjørn.

"Maybe he will be a witch," Kirsten said, "for he was born of a witch and a witchwife."

"Hjalmar, no," I said, "but perhaps his children, or theirs." As I spoke the words I knew them for truth, and by this, I knew that our dreams of a moment ago did not hold that same truth, and would not come to pass.

The knowledge ran over me like cold wind called from over the sea. I reached across the cradle and gripped Bjørn's hand, and then I gripped Kirsten's hand too. We sat in a circle around the cradle, the three of us, all the family little Hjalmar had: each of us frail and growing older, here for such a short time.

Then the fire settled within the stove, and I shook my head, and sighed. For Hjalmar would have all manner of things I could not see, just as I had things my own parents had never imagined. No, this feeling I had was not for him, but for me, for my own little family, and I held tight against the time when I would have to let them go.

Art by Daria Khvostova

MARIGOLDS
L.S. JOHNSON

1775
Paris, France

1.

This room is the universe. This bed the earth, the ceiling the sky. Somewhere in the plaster heavens above me are the clear brushstrokes that will flare like sunlight when I will them into being.

When *I* will them.

I watch Maurepas enter the room, framed by my knees. He is plump and old, like the others that come to us, ministers and directors, princes and counts. Smelling of cognac and roasted birdflesh, their doughy skin scored by silks and velvets cut for younger bodies. He strips now, this minister, and when the last piece of cloth is discarded he is just another old man.

All their power is stolen, Mémé says. *Even that of kings: they steal their power, and as such it can be stolen back. Why should they have so much and we so little? Do we not come into the world the same, and leave it the same? What does anyone truly possess, save the body she is born with?*

Our bodies and their power, the only true power in the world.

Or so Mémé says, and we are supposed to believe.

Maurepas watches the blood between my legs. Already his lips have parted, his face become damp with sweat; the air between us crackles. Is it already beginning? Do they all yield so easily? These men who rule France, rule it with pen and paper and sword and shot, all paying in coin and dissipation to taste me.

Mémé teaches us that the spasms we feel are not pain; they are *hunger*. Every wrenching ache is not some ancient curse; it is *anticipation*. Our bodies are doing what they were made to do: open completely, the better to impose our will upon the universe.

I feel his energy flow into me, stoking my own fire. His mouth between my legs, tasting me before he rises over me, his lips wet. I close my eyes; I cannot bear to look at him. *It smells like marigolds*, they tell each other in the salon, smirking like naughty boys. Thinking they are taking from us, gaining a few extra years, a last rally of youth. When instead it is we who take from them, we take their power and their vigor, we take and we take and we take—

Somewhere inside me I am crying out *Isabella*—

I open my eyes and set the swirling heavens alight in a glorious golden rush.

We are remaking the world.

Or so Mémé says, and we are supposed to believe.

***

As Maurepas leaves he kisses me, his mouth sloppy and redolent. "I feel alive again," he whispers in my ear. "Like I was twenty years younger. Marvelous, Claire, simply marvelous... "

I hate this time, after, when he is once more just a debauched minister and I his whore. Yet I cannot bring myself to tell him the truth: he has gained nothing. If anything he looks older, older and tired. How can they delude themselves, that a taste of my blood is the elixir they crave? Do they honestly believe they are the first to try, that no one has dared to taste a woman's courses before?

Or perhaps this too is part of what we create, when we make the symbol appear on our ceilings: this irrational belief in their own renewal.

I wash my face and my mouth, wash between my legs, and bind myself in fresh linen. Only when I feel clean do I creep, barefoot, into the hall. The air is hot and thick; everywhere I hear sighs, panting cries, the grunting of the men. I was lucky tonight: Maurepas is a quick one. Some of the others will be at it till dawn.

A quick one, and I was already on the brink before he arrived, as we are told to be. *You must feel pleasure, real pleasure, or it will not happen,* Mémé had said. *I make them wait before going to you, so as to give you time. Bring yourself as close to the moment as possible.* From a box she had pulled out objects, feathers and patches of soft fur and ivory carved to look like a man's organ, all while I blushed and squirmed. *Imagine you are with a lover, or would you prefer one of these? You can try anything you fancy. Or is there something else you like? Louisa, peasant girl that she was, used to use marrows, and Aimée has a little embroidered pillow, very firm...*

But I have no need of toys, or imaginary lovers. All I need is to envision the door across from mine, and what lies behind it, and what might happen should it one day open for me.

Isabella's door.

I crouch before it now, humble with longing. I know every inch of its surface, every whorl of the grain. The key is always in her lock so I can only listen. The space between door and floor glows brightly; Turgot likes to see her and I cannot blame him, were it myself I would fill her room with candles, to see every inch of her—

She mewls like a kitten, gasping and crying theatrically, and I grin at the parquet. Poor old baron. He probably thinks himself a great lover; he is always preening when he leaves.

But then her noises change.

I press my ear to the door. My hand drifts between my legs yet again; every sound of flesh against flesh leaves me breathless. I can even *smell* her, not marigolds but something sweet and tangy and peppered all at once, like the rush of air on a spring morning, everything blooming and blossoming—

When at last she cries out I shudder in turn. A moment later Turgot makes a barking cry that trails off into a pathetic bout of coughing. *Isabella.*

When her door finally opens I am back in my room, watching through the keyhole as the fat ass laps at her neck, then gropes between her legs one last time. Shoving his red-tipped fingers in his mouth all at once, like a child.

Isabella watches him go – and then she looks at my door. Does she know I'm watching? Is she truly looking, or is she merely lost in blissful recollections of the Baron de Laune's gouty mass?

I dare not move, I cannot even breathe, until she closes her door once more. The hall silent and dark now. Lifeless.

***

What does Isabella imagine, while she waits for Turgot to arrive?

2.

"...Maurepas," Mémé recites, sliding her finger down the page of the ledger spread open on her lap. So many names and only eight of us, have there really been so many? "Sartine. Vergennes. Diderot. Forbonnais. Malesherbes. Albert." She smiles down at the page. "And of course Turgot..."

We all look at Isabella, who blushes. She is Turgot's favorite, which makes her Mémé's favorite. Bread at more than three *sous* a pound, the prices driving people to protest – you can see the joy in Mémé's gaunt little face when Turgot arrives. The tangible result of all our perverse couplings. He comes now in a plain carriage, to avoid the crowds that each month are becoming a little more violent, a little less reasonable.

Not that reason ever had a place in this.

Mémé counts out our money, each coin washed clean. It's more than any other brothel in Paris, even the finer ones. But I barely glance at the coins in my hand; I no longer study Mémé's odd ageless face, her hands at once lined and strong; I no longer wonder at the strange circular scoring on her floor, how every room is arranged so the beds point west. All I can think on is her desk, where she draws the symbols and hands them over one by one, almost careless in her gestures. Nothing more than circles and lines and curves, the whole twisted so as to seem a knot; yet each time it is a different symbol, never quite the same. Each time too we must paint it on another's ceiling. We never see what is on our own.

Isabella balancing on my bed that first night, frowning at the slip of paper in her hand, the brush in her other dripping that queer cloudy liquid, and the straining arch of her bare leg–

Somehow the symbols and our blood make things happen. Sometimes Mémé has us paint them even when we are not bleeding, but in the moment they merely brighten a little, there is no blinding flash. *Without our blood, all we can do is nudge matters along,* she explained. *But when our blood comes: that is our time. Our ancestors knew this; they secluded their women when the moon waxed, lest they inadvertently ruin the crops, or kill a man*

93

through lovemaking. Only I learned to control our power through the sigils. With a clear sigil before us, a powerful man to take from, and our blood flowing? That is when we can lay our hands upon the tiller of the world, and change its course for good.

Save that I no longer want to go where Mémé says, if ever I did. I no longer care about Paris, or bread, or power. The only world I want to make is one where Isabella holds out her hand to me as she did the first day I saw her, except this time she doesn't let go, she instead draws me close and presses her lips to mine—

All I need is the right symbol, the right *sigil* as Mémé says, only I do not know how to make them.

Not yet.

***

Our week may be done, but we cannot relax; we still have the rest of the month to survive. There is our own bread to earn, the shopping to do. We change the lantern outside from red glass to clear; we dress plainly to run our errands, our hair tucked into mobcaps and worn muslin aprons over our skirts.

We go out in the world, and see what we have wrought.

We go in threes, three and three and then a pair with Mémé. She takes whoever she feels needs encouragement, the better to exhort them at length. *This is not for our own gain, this is for everyone, for France herself. I have seen them at their estates. I have watched them dance and screw, drunk on their own gluttony, while children die of starvation at their gates. It is not right, it is not right. But we have the power to change this – the power and the understanding.*

Today, however, there is no Mémé and her philosophizing; today there is only Isabella at my side. Aimée too, but she stops to peer in every shop window, she dawdles and hurries after us and dawdles again. She has kept her little *mouche* on, the red drop below her lip that we all wear during that week, the mark of our specialty; she only tossed her head at Isabella's tut-tutting. Men eye her as they pass – after so many months word is getting around – they eye her and she simpers and flirts, loving the attention.

I try my best to ignore her, to imagine that it is only Isabella and me. Our list in her careful print: soap, pigeons for our supper, more cognac for the gentlemen. Her arm in mine, her laughter sweet in my ear. Would that it could last forever.

Aimée draws close to us, peering over Isabella's shoulder and giggling. "Does your wild girl even know what cognac is?"

"Aimée," Isabella scolds, but says nothing more.

But it is true: I was a wild thing when Isabella found me. Digging through the garbage at the waterfront for anything I might eat or barter, begging in the Marais, hand to mouth and day to day, unable to think on anything save making it through one more night...

Your wild girl. Wild with despair, wild with hope, at the sight of Isabel-

94

la's beckoning hand. Her hair perfectly curled and pinned and powdered, her dress so creamy and bright it seemed to glow against the filth of the street. The shimmer of her décolletage, her lips rouged scarlet, and just beneath that single red drop.

I took her hand and I looked into her brown eyes and I thought, *I will follow you anywhere.*

And then I realized: I was making a *choice*. For the first time in my life I was *choosing* my fate.

No one else could have brought me to this. No one else could make me part my legs for these men.

As soon as Isabella took my hand, I would have followed her to hell.

***

Our own neighborhood is as peaceful as on any day, but as we draw near the market the mood turns ugly. Everywhere voices thick with discontent. Hats are pulled low, hands raised over mouths as people mutter to each other. There is even an outright duel in an alley, despite the laws: swords flashing, the young men furious as they lunge at each other, scrabbling for purchase on the slop-covered cobblestones. Barefoot, lean children run past us, tormenting a mangy cat. Half-lidded eyes running over us. The very air making my stomach churn.

I clutch at Isabella's arm, pressing close to her. "Never fear," she says. "They cannot harm us."

But she is only parroting what Mémé tells us, that our safety is part of the sigils. *You enact not only the great change but your place in it as well.* Yet who decides what our place is, other than Mémé? Who knows what she really puts in her drawings, what retribution they might invoke?

My only hope is that she would protect Isabella, for Isabella has Turgot.

The market, at least, is its usual chaotic maze of long, low tables overflowing with wares: vegetables, meats, raw fish stinking atop the shredded pages of gazettes; scraps of fabrics and old clothes that the young women crowd around, hoping for some pricey bit of lace; pots and pans and tools, rusted but serviceable or new and gleaming. I can sense, behind us, Aimée's head darting from side to side. This is where Mémé found her, a clerk's daughter trying to make herself appear something more. She had lost her virtue to a butcher's agent, she was desperate for a man with clean hands; her last customer was Malesherbes, which means she has not come far at all.

As we move deeper into the market the sunlight disappears. I look up, thinking perhaps a storm is coming, but it is only the shadow of the pillory. Three bodies are silhouetted within, slumped in their stocks. The stone front of the tower is smeared with rotting foodstuffs; a man offers us some bruised fruits, would us ladies like to throw one?

Aimée reaches for his basket but Isabella grabs her arm. "Leave them be," she says, her voice low.

"It's just a bit of fun—"

"Leave them be," Isabella repeats, and for the first time I hear anger in her voice. "There but for the grace of God, Aimée."

"As if we're like them," Aimée says, her cheeks flushing. "Soon enough it will be your precious Turgot up there, or hanging from–"

Isabella shakes her hard, cutting her off. "For God's sake," she hisses. "What if someone hears? There are spies everywhere, you'll get us all arrested."

"Not you," Aimée retorts. "Never her precious Isabella. Take care," she adds to me, "this one will do anything Mémé asks, even if it means ratting on you."

At her words Isabella recoils, as if Aimee had struck her. "I would never," she says, a tremor in her voice. "I would *never*." She looks at me and I see her eyes are full; before I can speak she looks away again. "Forget the vegetables," she says to the ground. "Let's just go back."

But I cannot move. The tremulous *never*. The anger in her voice, her anger and her *tears*. Always she had seemed to believe wholeheartedly in Mémé's scheme–

"Isabella," I say. A dozen half-formed phrases tangling in my mind.

At the far end of the market a group of men suddenly appears, causing a murmur to run through the crowd. Conversations die away as everyone turns. Each man is spattered with powder–

No, not powder. *Flour.*

"Fifteen sous a loaf!"

The roar comes from somewhere in their group; it is picked up at once, the call echoing through the market, deep and furious.

Isabella grabs my hand.

Fifteen sous!

At once the space around us fills with bodies, male and female, old and young, pressing against us. They wave spoons and knives, sticks and hammers.

Fifteen sous!

We are being pushed forward, carried along in the crowd. Behind us Aimée whispers, "What should we–" But Isabella hushes her, a single hiss, her hand rigid around mine.

An older man climbs onto one of the tables, calling out for us to stop; another climbs beside him and with a polite smile punches him in the head, knocking him into the crowd that swarms over him without a glance.

Isabella twists beside me; a hand is pulling at her skirts, she pushes it away. Another chuckle, somewhere in back–

And then Aimée is gone.

I start to turn, to go after her, but Isabella pulls me close. Hands are groping me, I cannot tell who is touching me. My foot catches on a body, a woman huddled on the ground, covering her child as the mob tramples thoughtlessly over her.

The mob swells, pushing towards the rue de la Petite Truanderie. We keep our arms wrapped around each other; Isabella is stepping to the left at every opportunity and I do the same. Throughout, she keeps her head raised, keeps looking ahead, and I do the same.

I will follow you anywhere.

We round the corner, still side-stepping left. We are nearly at the edge of the crowd now. Above the rumbling of voices I hear a high-pitched shrieking and I think *Aimée!* But I see now it is a horse at the intersection; the people have rolled the carriage and they are swarming over it with sticks and clubs and both horse and driver are screaming for mercy beneath the blows. Fruit tumbles from the cart, crushed into the ground by the unseeing feet of the mob. Just a farmer and his animal, and what in God's name do they have to do with the price of bread?

What is Mémé creating, that would make people act so?

I look at Isabella and her eyes are red, her lips trembling; still she keeps her head up, keeps wiggling free of the pawing hands, keeps moving to the left as best she can.

At last the mob halts before a building. The people press together, some rising on tiptoe to see what is happening. They are looting a bakery, flinging loaves through the smashed windows, passing sacks of flour out hand over hand only to see them torn apart, releasing white clouds into the air, turning the looters to ghosts.

"I cannot help it! I don't decide the prices!" the baker bellows from the floor above, his voice echoing in the street. "Go attack Turgot, go to Versailles, they are selling the very grain from our fields to line their own pockets!"

The mob roars back, a bestial sound. Isabella seizes the corner of a building, dragging us bodily forward. Across the street is the rue Mondétour and a hint of open space around the bend–

And then I smell the fire.

The flames fill the ground-floor windows, licking up the walls, smoke billowing into the street. A woman screams from somewhere within, screams and screams, and a ripple of mocking laughter runs through the crowd. Now they begin throwing things back into the bakery: rags, trash, whatever is to hand and might burn.

A little boy appears above the heads, balancing on a man's shoulder, and begins to sing:

Panis angelicus
fit panis hominum
Dat panis coelicus
figuris terminum
O res mirabilis!
Manducat Dominum
Pauper, servus et humilis

And just then, listening to his sweet soprano and the screams of the people dying – just for a moment, the world flashes terrifyingly golden.

It is *happening*.

Isabella pulls me across the street and around the bend, so fast I nearly lose my pattens as we hurry back to the safety of the brothel.

***

"Creation," Mémé tells us that night, "is always violent: look at how babies come into the world, how plants rip their seed-shells apart, how birds hack and bite their way free of the egg. Is it no wonder that the mobs tear apart the bakeries, that they burn houses regardless of who might be within? They too are trying to wrest power from those who have it. They simply don't know a better way."

And what might they do to us, I want to ask, *if they knew you thought fit to starve them for your own schemes, using perversion and witchcraft?*

Outside there is still so much noise. Scattered cheers and shouts, the spatter of pistol shots – there were militia on the streets, Louisa reported breathlessly, there was talk of adding gibbets to the Place de Grève.

Aimee's room is dark and silent. I can still hear the screaming, can still smell the fire in my hair.

What have we done?

3.

It is nearly our week again when Mémé finally goes out. To look for custom, or so she says. She goes to the Opéra and the Comédie, salons and supper-parties, with blood-red mouth and crimson gown and one of us in tow: a sample. She lets the men boast about their connections, their power, their proximity to the king's ear – and when she thinks she has found a suitable candidate she takes him to a room or her coach, the better to be fawned over.

And you know who does all the work, Aimée had confided in me, *while she gets away with a few kisses.*

Aimée...

I wait until the brothel is quiet, save for a trio of young noblemen who came to the door with a fat purse and a great deal of wine. We drew lots for them, the other girls salivating at the money, and I pretended to be disappointed, but wasn't it a sign? Their loud voices covering my noises as I tiptoe into Mémé's room and go to her little desk.

The drawers are locked. And if I try to break them open, and am caught...

I search the rest of her room, looking for a key, trying to think on what to do. Love letters at her bedside, from men – perhaps she has done a little more than kissing. At first her bookshelves seem mostly libertine novels, but when I open one up a pamphlet falls out, a tract on grain. More pamphlets and broadsheets are wedged between the books, many of their authors' names familiar.

There is nothing, however, to explain the sigils.

And then I open her commode.

It is filled with shreds of paper, smelling of urine, but I can see the marks clear enough. Letters, stretched and cramped, twisted and combined.

The sigils are words, their letters layered over each other to form one shape.

I can make out a few of them, words like *King* and *People*. Numbers too: *60 livres* – that is what some say is the price of flour now. *4 sous*. *Lenoir* – he replaced Sartine as the head of police, only to be fired in turn.

Wincing, I reach in and push the pieces around. *Burn. Gallows. Turgot. Aimée.*

I stare at her name, the pale ink lines smudging and blurring. To what end? To save her? Or to be rid of her?

She had always been a little crude, a little boastful. Never a favorite.

Who among us had made her name glow?

Voices in the hall. Quickly I close the commode, wincing at the smell on my fingers. But as I hurry back to my room, I start to feel a nervous excitement in my belly.

I can make a sigil. Not for myself, I cannot paint my own ceiling, she would suspect me at once.

But I can make a sigil for Isabella.

***

To love me. To run away with me to the ends of the earth. To feel the same wet desire that I do, to want to taste me as I long to taste her.

To stop Mémé's madness. To make us all safe from that mindless rage.

To love me.

Long into the night I stare at the blank page, I start to write words and stop again. If it takes eight of us just to raise the price of bread, what can I do, alone?

Is it not enough, to simply want to love?

But I think of that mob, and how it would feel to be battered by their clubs and their fists, or helplessly burning as they feed the fire.

I write, then, before I can rethink it, printing the letters atop each other, over and over on scraps of paper until at last I have a drawing that looks like Mémé's.

I tear up the other papers and I lay them in my chamber pot and cover them with my own waters. I will slop them out later, in the far corner of the yard, where the muck gathers just before the drains.

And then I lie in bed, staring at my sigil. *My will.* Staring at the intersection of lines, the moonlight streaming in. *My will upon the universe.* Already my body feels full and heavy. *Isabella.* It is *happening.* My hand between my legs, stroking, rubbing. *My will.* Watching the lines, the paper lit by moonlight as I hold it above my head–

I cry aloud as the sigil flares white, so bright as to blind me, my whole body arching off the bed. Never have I. Never. So much bliss.

The paper on the bed. My palm streaked with rust. Only the fat moon as witness.

Waxing gibbous, Mémé would say.

Almost time.

***

99

I am cramping as I dress, breathing through gritted teeth as I wiggle into my gauzy petticoat and draw on my red-clocked stockings, securing them with red ribbons. My feet in slippers. Only then do I lace up the ridiculous stays that stop just below my breasts.

In Mémé's room she is handing out the buckets, their brushes swinging gaily inside. That strange cloudy liquid, what is it? Where does it come from? The smell like burying your nose in dirty clothing, sweat and piss and something deeper—

I think of last night, washing my hand after, and I blush. Like *that* smell.

One by one Mémé hands over the slips of paper, pairing us with a flick of her wrist. "Sophie, for Marie. Jeanne, for Catherine. Isabella, for Claire."

My stomach drops. If Isabella paints my ceiling, how can I paint hers?

To wait another month—

"Catherine, for Louisa. Marie, for Isabella."

I grab the slip instinctively, snatching it from Mémé's hand. Marie looks surprised, and then she smirks at me. "Claire wants to paint herself in Turgot's place," she says slyly, and the others laugh.

"Bite your tongue," I mutter. "I – I thought she said Claire." More giggling.

I have not let go of the paper.

Mémé studies me for a long moment. "It is... unusual," she finally says. "Two marking sigils for each other – but perhaps it will intensify the results?" She nods at the slip in my hand. "Claire, for Isabella. This might be a special night indeed."

***

Isabella's room smells of her: her odors lie across every surface like dust, and they rise as I move through the space, clinging to me in turn. Her few dresses, the Bible on her nightstand – how is it that she has such a thing, Mémé will not permit so much as a rosary in our rooms.

There but for the grace of God.

I kick off my slippers and climb onto her bed. I paint in quick, strong strokes, I have memorized every line and curve, I know them by heart. For it is my heart I am painting, the picture of my love, the shape of my hope.

Our hand upon the tiller of the world. Or so Mémé said, and I pretended to believe.

And what do I believe now?

I am just finishing when Isabella comes in, surprising me; the brush falls from my hand to her bed, the liquid quickly spreading on the coverlet. At once I snatch it up, not sure where to look, my face burning.

"I didn't mean to startle you," she says.

Still I cannot think. I stumble off her bed. I am trying to gather up the coverlet and keep the bucket and brush to hand, great armfuls of cloth and the bucket swinging wildly. Mémé's slip flutters from my hand to land in the bucket, soaking into the residue. I am scarlet, my ears on fire.

Isabella takes the coverlet from me, wadding it into a ball and shoving it under her bed. And then just stays kneeling on the floor, one hand on my ankle as if to keep me in place.

"Claire," she whispers. "Oh, Claire, they just came..."

I put the bucket down and kneel beside her, carefully putting my hand on her face. Her soft cheek in my palm; I nearly sob aloud, I am so overcome. Still I draw her face towards mine. Her eyes are full.

"Policemen. I heard Mémé speaking with them. About Aimée." Her tears spilling into my hand. "They found her in the Seine, they say she was not, she was not *whole*..."

I hug her tightly, feeling her body shudder against mine as she cries, rubbing her back through the thin silk of her negligee. And if my sigil doesn't work, if she is next to disappear into the crowd, never to come back whole?

"Oh, Claire, Claire," she whispers into my neck. "What if we're making things worse, so much worse?"

"We are making things worse," I say fiercely. "This whole business is madness." Then, in a rush, "If I could get enough money, for us to leave–"

There is a knock on the door, then it swings open. "Mémé's changed the lantern to red," Marie says. "And Turgot is already here. You'll just have to wait your turn, Claire," she adds, sniggering.

Isabella pulls away from me, wiping at her face; when she looks at me again I see not only sorrow and fear in her eyes but a hint of something else, something hard. "I will come to you after," she says.

I will come to you. She has never spoken so before, she has never held me save after my first night. She had come to me after the man left, saying nothing, just holding me until I fell asleep.

I will come to you I will come to you I will come to you

All I can think, as I hurry back to my own room and quickly rouge my face, douse all but a few candles, arrange myself on the bed – all I can think is that something happened, last night. I had made the sigil glow, truly glow, without the energy of a man.

Yet Isabella's words, and all they imply – that wasn't what I had written at all.

***

I change the sheets after Vergennes leaves, I open the window to the fresh night air. I wash and I comb my hair and I put on my softest, prettiest shift.

But Isabella never comes.

***

It is early when the knocking rouses me from an uneasy sleep. I think *Isabella*, but instead it is Catherine, looking nervous.

"They brought in emergency flour last night," she says. "The price of bread has dropped to three *sous* four *deniers* and the people are cheering Louis. Mémé is furious, she thinks one of us changed their thing." She shrugs,

101

but keeps her eyes lowered. "More likely we just missed a line. Anyway, she wants us to show her what we painted, and to talk to each of us."

As she speaks I feel my stomach disappear. I cannot remember what Mémé gave me, I had been far too intent on getting my own sigil right. I manage a nod, but as soon as Catherine leaves I drop before my dressing-table, trembling.

I do not fear for myself. What can she do to me in the end? Beat me, turn me out. If she denounces me to the police she risks herself; if she throws me out I know better how to survive now.

But I know she will never let me see Isabella again.

I make myself dress, swallowing my sobs. Halfway down the stairs I remember: the paper had fallen in the bucket, it might still be there—

But when I hurry to the closet, I find only clean, dry buckets, neatly stacked for next month.

And when I step back into the hall Mémé is standing in her open doorway. She beckons to me, her strange smooth face expressionless. Her long thin hand, beckoning, as Isabella had beckoned all those months ago.

My choice.

As I enter the room she shuts and locks the door behind us. Isabella is sitting on Mémé's bed and she will not meet my eyes.

"Sit at the desk, Claire," Mémé says.

There is a piece of paper, a pen, an inkwell. The chair creaks beneath me as I sit down. My hands on the polished wood surface. All the drawers are unlocked now, but what does it matter anymore?

"I want you to draw, as best you remember, what you painted on Isabella's ceiling."

In my mind's eye I can see the sigil flaring into life. The pen and ink sit there, waiting to be used.

"And thus hath the candle sing'd the moth." Mémé sighs the words out as the bed creaks beneath her weight. "Claire, Claire. I have never before taken a girl I did not choose myself, but Isabella is special to me. Now I can see I made a mistake."

She strokes Isabella's head. Isabella still won't look at me.

"We are so close, Claire." She takes Isabella's hand and presses it into her own lap. "So close to an uprising that will change all our lives. But I cannot have less than eight each month. Did I not take Aimee's place myself last night, so we could be eight? So we might finish what we began?" She takes a breath. "Yet now, because of you, we were not eight. Because of you, we may lose all that we have worked for. What did you paint on her ceiling?"

"I cannot remember," I say, hoping against hope it sounds like the truth.

Mémé's foot taps on the floor, the tempo increasing with each passing moment—

And then she seizes Isabella by the throat with one hand, a knife in her other, pulling her close and driving the point into Isabella's cheek, just below her eye. Blood wells around the blade and Isabella shrieks in fright, making me cry "No!"

"Draw it," Mémé says calmly. "Draw it or I will cut her face and she will spend the rest of her days servicing men at the quays. Draw it."

"You wouldn't hurt her." I nearly stutter in my panic. "You need her, you need her for Turgot."

"What do I care about Turgot if we fail? And if I am to replace one, I can as easily replace two." She digs the blade deeper and Isabella starts sobbing. "Draw it!"

Choking on my tears, I shove the pen in the ink and draw as fast as I can. The point digging and scratching, the ink splattering. Isabella crying behind me, *oh my love—*

"There," I yell, holding up the paper, smeared and blotched. "That's what I drew! And it didn't work because it's all a ploy, to make us do what other whores won't. We haven't made anything happen, we've changed nothing!"

Mémé shoves Isabella aside and lunges forward, seizing my arm and spinning me face-first onto the floor. Her knee pinning my back, her hand on my neck; she presses down, crushing my face against the wood.

"We'll see what I can change," she cries furiously. "Let's see if I can change *your* world, eh? Yours and hers and anyone else you have turned with your deceit."

I buck and kick but I cannot dislodge her, something in my nose is cracking and I cannot breathe and I can feel her tensing against my back—

There is a rush of air, a sickening thud, and her weight disappears. I look over my shoulder to see Mémé fallen on her side; I turn over completely and Isabella is holding the poker in her hand, its tip darkly wet. It takes me a moment to realize she is trembling everywhere, her face pale save for the scabbing blood on her cheek.

Mémé's body is still.

I start to crawl towards Mémé. If she is dead it will be the gallows for us both...

"No," Isabella says hoarsely. "Don't touch her."

I get to my feet, my head throbbing, my nose hot and tender. "We need to get away." I sound as if I am speaking through a tube. "There may be money in her desk."

Isabella only stands there, shaking, her eyes darting from Mémé to me and back again. Carefully I take the poker from her hands, not daring to touch the gouge on her cheek.

Behind us Mémé makes a gurgling sound; we both jump. Still she lies unmoving.

"I'm so sorry," Isabella whispers then.

"For what? She would have killed us both."

"For bringing you here." She is crying again. "I — I changed your sigil. Claire! I changed your sigil. Only I could not find the words to confess it, she was enraged, it frightened me. But it was me, it was me, I figured out how she made them and I changed yours."

I can only gape at her.

"I changed your sigil," she repeats more slowly. "I couldn't bear it any more, watching them go to you, knowing I did this to you. You were just so beautiful that day, so beautiful and sad, and I thought I could help you, give you some, some food, money, I don't know. And then Mémé thought... well." She wipes at her eyes, takes a shuddering breath. "I made it say you would leave Paris, leave and be happy and never again have to do *this*."

"But I changed yours," I say, stupidly.

Isabella falls silent.

"I changed yours. It wasn't that I couldn't remember hers. What I showed her was what I painted. That's why I took the slip from Marie, to be the one to paint your ceiling."

"What did you change it to?" she whispers, her voice nearly inaudible.

"That something would stop her, and you would be safe." I am weeping now, my breath catching in my swollen nostrils. "I know – I know you don't love me, not as I love you, but that day, all the violence and Aimée... it wasn't right that we were making things so terrible. And I thought I could at least free you from her, I could make you safe..."

At once she is in my arms.

5.

There is little here save for rocky beach and scrub to the front, grass and stunted pines behind. The cottage was once the residence of an elderly fisherman – *a hermit*, the villagers tell us, shaking their heads that anyone would want such a decrepit property, only that tiny garden and a barn they wouldn't keep the devil in.

It suits us perfectly.

Every day we listen to the surf; every night we study the fields of stars. We have turned our bed to the east, to face the dawn.

We ordered marigold seeds, giggling together like naughty little girls.

Did the sigils really work? I still cannot say for certain. I had wanted Isabella safe, Mémé stopped, but I had imagined it would come in the form of police, not our own hands. I do know that there were no more mobs after that day, or so we read in the gazettes after; we were away on the first coach. The fishermen here tell us that a tiller takes a light hand; perhaps Mémé tried too hard, demanding instead of asking, pushing instead of letting events unfold in their time.

Isabella's body next to mine, embracing me. Her hand sliding over me, inside me. And then rising up again to draw the sigil on my face, lazy strokes of her thumb, the easy slide of her fingertips.

Kissing me, everywhere but where she traced the sigil. Drawing my legs between hers, pressing us together. Her thigh between, her heat against my skin. My mouth dropping to her neck, her breasts, and we are rocking and sliding and then she suddenly cries out, staring into my face, her own suffused with love and I love and oh the light–

We do not demand; we ask. We do not plot; we suggest. No hunger, no suffering, no murderous rage. Just the slightest touch on the tiller, turning the world towards something a little kinder, a little sweeter, a little more like love.

Art by GMB Chomichuk

DIYU
ROBERT WILLIAM IVENIUK

1883
Hell's Gate, Fraser Canyon
British Columbia, Canada

My ears rang as dynamite shattered stone. Rocks flew from the blast zone. My eyes followed the wire that vanished into the dust-cloud billowing out of the hole. Releasing the detonator's plunger, I stood. I lifted my goggles, praising Buddha under bated breath.

Six fellows neared the opening with picks and shovels. I heard the banter of Mandarin as they entered. "Keep your eyes up," one warned his brothers. "Who knows how stable it is here." I seized the wire and dragged it over. Wrapping the cord around my arm and lifting the detonator, I watched them dig through the rubble.

Then I remembered I had to go.

Sprinting ahead, I chased down a supply wagon, jumped into the back and held on tight. Cold winds bit the Fraser Canyon. Morning sunlight crept over the horizon. Orange blades stabbed through the sky, illuminating the trees and cliffs. Light danced along the river beyond. We neared the edge. I watched the torrent rage, shivered, and missed home.

Before too long, we reached the bottom. Pines guarded the old railway town, dotting the rolling hills around it. Workers toiled by the roads. Wagons and horsemen passed. Two railcars sat on tracks we had already laid out. Men cleaned the railcars' sides; others lazily smoked near them. I leapt out and headed to my supervisor's cabin. Lamplight flickered behind the windows. I stepped through the front door.

Five whites sat around a hardwood desk, consulting piles of documents and a large map. One ran fingers through his thinning hair and sneered my way. A portly man sat on the right, cane on his lap as he glossed over a page. The project overseer, Mister Bunting, raised a hand and silenced a bearded man on his left. His niece Olivia, slender with tied-back brown hair, hungrily read a leather-bound book beside him. Boredom crossed her face. No doubt her visit to the countryside was not as she had expected.

"There he is," Mister Bunting declared, standing and straightening his lapels in a bid to look official. Fading blonde hair gripped his scalp. His belly pressed against his shirt. A smile nothing short of venomous covered his face. "How's it coming?"

"Fine, yes." Colleagues who had been in Canada longer than I, and some genial whites, had taught me key phrases and words. Sadly, my comprehension was better than my speaking ability, which was better than my laughable reading level. "We make another two metre. Cleaning up is now."

"What's his name, again?" The sneering man aimed his chin at me. "Wushu or something, right?"

Mister Bunting turned his hand over. "Introduce yourself, lad."

Showing respect, I lowered my head. "Wu Xiao-Li."

"Gesundheit," someone joked. Leering grins wide, the men laughed, nudging each other. Olivia hardly moved, but sighed heavily, annoyed. I kept my peace and let them finish.

A wave of Mister Bunting's arm and his cohorts fell quiet. He bent down and produced a set of rolled-up papers. "Now, listen." Mister Bunting put the papers in front of me, speaking as though addressing a child. "I want *you*. To take-ee *this*. To *Benny*. *Benny*, all right?"

"Yes, Mister Bunting." He meant my foreman.

His smile again. "Good boy, Charlie."

I took the papers. "Xiao-Li."

"Yes." Bunting nodded condescendingly. "Yes. *Charlie*. That's your *name*."

I hid my frustration. "I take to Benny."

"Make him roll over next," the portly man guffawed. Another round of raucous laughter. I left, anger nipping at my heels.

***

I found Benny in the centre of town, dragging a man out of a latrine. Three of his thugs had pulled the poor soul from his business and brought him into the street, trousers still around his knees. I tried not to stare at his shame as the men held him down. One hooligan gripped a long broomstick eagerly. A crowd gathered; Chinese and whites alike stopped to watch the half-nude man forced onto his knees. I put myself behind Fat Leung, a fellow whose girth kept me well-hidden.

Benny glared down at his captive joylessly. A wide-brimmed sunhat sat on his head, his pristine suit pants and vest woven from high-quality cotton. In his hand was a gold-plated pocket watch. His thumb tapped its side impatiently. I was told that Benny once went by Bai Wei, but changed his name when he started moving up in the ranks. Reminding him of his old name often resulted in beatings. Then again, Benny's name was synonymous with pain.

"Wing," he addressed the half-nude man in Mandarin, "would you like to explain where you were this morning?"

Now I recognized my colleague. Wing's stringy hair covered his gaunt, unshaven face. Too scared to speak, he stumbled around his words incoherently. Benny lost his patience. "Well! It seems you were out looking for your tongue. Open his mouth! Let's see if it's still there!"

"Please, sir!" Wing cried. Struggling, he freed himself from the men's grips and shuffled forward on his knees, hands clasped. "I had an upset stomach when I woke up! It's the food, sir! Last night's meat was rancid!"

Benny faced the crowd. Shocked looks circulated. "Your colleagues seem healthy."

"Then it was something else!" Rubbing his hands, Wing kowtowed before the foreman, head to the ground. "I just couldn't work with my bowels rebelling against me! Please, sir, I'm sorry! *I'm sorry!*"

"You think you can squat on the job when we have a whole mountain to tear down?" Benny snapped his fingers at his flunkies. "Beat some sense into him."

As Wing wailed in protest, Benny's heavies fell on him. The man with the broomstick dealt terrible blows against his bare legs and backside. Cackling, his companions' fists pounded against my friend's torso and face. Turning, Benny barked at the onlookers in English: "Back to work!"

Everyone scattered. Some left at a leisurely pace. Others skipped away like scolded children. Fat Leung waddled off, wiping sweat off his ham-like face. I remained, watching the thugs beat Wing into a stupor. I felt my chest tightening. The foreman saw me.

"Wu Xiao-Li." He approached, pocketing his watch. "Now *there's* a worker. We'll have the tunnel finished by the end of the week at the rate you're going."

I tried not to look at Wing. The men broke away from him and came to Benny's side. Wing whimpered and rolled onto his back, straining to pull his pants up. Welts formed on his bottom.

I produced the papers. "These are from Mister Bunting."

Benny snatched them and read them over. He was an educated man, having taught himself English and reached a level far above us all. This advantage netted him the comfortable foreman position he enjoyed far too much.

"New blasting orders," he mused aloud, folding the papers and pocketing them. "We're to widen the tunnel, bring it a little closer to the river's edge." Benny put his hands together and cocked a stare at me. "Perhaps so future travellers can enjoy the view. Do *you* enjoy the view, Wu?"

I nodded. "I just wish this place had a better name. 'Hell's Gate,' I heard people calling it."

"They can call it whatever they like," Benny spat. Behind him, Wing was trying to stand. His legs wobbled under his weight. "It's a popular fishing site. Perhaps you can catch us dinner."

"I'm not a fisherman."

"I bet you never worked a detonator before, either."

Flashes of my past danced before me. Rain hitting old stone steps. The smell of incense. The ringing of prayer bells.

Hair like silk.

I coughed. "Very true, sir."

"Meet me at the pass in an hour. Get Wing to a doctor first," Benny turned to Wing, who had finally maintained a semblance of balance. "Maybe we should dynamite a latrine for him." Benny and his thugs laughed and sauntered off.

I went to Wing, supporting him on my shoulder. He whimpered all the way to the doctor's office.

***

Soon enough, I was back at the work site. Some of my fellows were on break, resting in whatever shade was available. Others, out of fear of their superior and his goons, worked harder than before, speedily shovelling rocks out of the chasm.

The ridge, tufts of grass growing along its top, towered over us and the river. A great shadow stretched across the valley. Sun-bleached rock led up the side. Overhead, four birds sailed and dove over the hill.

I stood with my foreman, who took time to regard the scene. Benny sniffed. "Reminds you of the Dalian coast, doesn't it?"

I shrugged. "I've never been. Have you?"

"My father was born there. He brought me to the coast every summer. Even after he died, my mother and I kept visiting it, just to smell the sea air. As if doing so somehow kept him alive."

"He must have meant a lot to you."

Bitter silence. Scowling, Benny waved vaguely at the mountain's base. "Place some sticks there. And be quick about it. Bunting's taking more photographs today." He turned on a heel and left.

I groaned. Mister Bunting hired a man to take photographs every other week: of the men at work, of the site's progress, and more importantly, of himself. It was during those times that Mister Bunting would stop everything and get a photograph taken of him shovelling dirt, driving a spike, reading at a desk, or standing beside the river. Word around the camp was that he sent them to his family out east for some private collection they loved showing off. His good niece, in fact, was to accompany the latest set's delivery and ensure its arrival at their door.

His narcissism was not my concern, however. I had work to do.

I returned to the supply wagon we had ridden up in, gesturing to some explosives an older fellow drank next to. He regarded me briefly then reached in and tossed my supplies to the ground before returning to his flask. I took them and left. To keep my spirits up, I hummed a song from my old life.

***

I was checking the wires on the dynamite sticks when Bunting arrived. The process was delicate and needed my full concentration. Imagine my surprise when I heard him cry out: "Move it, boys! Charlie, are you done?!"

I snapped out of my trance and finished quickly. I turned and bowed. Bunting neared, rubbing his hands and grinning smugly. With him came the photographer and Benny's thugs. Frustrated young Olivia was in tow, gripping the front of her skirt.

Past them, I saw a frail-looking figure bringing up the rear. It was Wing, face twisted in agony as he carried a fat camera and tripod on his back.

The sight of it was too shameful. I jogged to Wing and made a motion at him. "Here, I help," I muttered in English.

"Good show!" Bunting beamed, snapping his fingers at the photographer. "Take the shot just as the dynamite goes. We'll do another of us at the crater."

"Oh, Uncle Neil, must we?" Olivia pleaded, gazing out at the rows of trees beyond, "I so was hoping to take a carriage ride through the woods."

"They're no place for a lady," he scolded her. "It's best you stay where it's safe."

"Uncle Neil–"

"None of that, now. Come, let me look you over. This must be *perfect*."

As they bickered, I set up the tripod with Wing. "What are you doing?" I asked in Mandarin, spreading the device's legs.

My friend shuddered. "Benny's fiends came by the doctor's office. Dragged me out and made me carry this."

"How do you feel?"

"How do you think?"

I met his eyes and saw misery. Sighing, I barely had the chance to answer when I heard Bunting call my 'name.' "Charlie, move it! The photographer's gotta do his job!"

I apologized and stepped back; Benny's widest goon pushed Wing aside. The photographer positioned himself. Lifting the tarp from the tripod, he stepped in front, raising the switch. Before him, Mister Bunting stretched his fingers and set them on the plunger. Olivia folded her arms and waited. He hesitated. Sweat rolled down his cheeks. His niece huffed. Breathing deep, he pressed down.

An earth-shattering eruption. Stone flew and clouds rose from the blast-site. Light flashed across the valley as the photographer's shot snapped.

Low rumbles sounded.

Rose.

Fissures spread across the ground and up the cliff. Cracks opened wide, swallowing the land. I fell backwards. Around me, men dropped what they were carrying and ran for safety. Their equipment vanished behind them. An unlucky few tumbled into the earth's gaping maw. I watched in horror as the cracks spread toward us. Bunting and his cronies fled the scene, hoping to outrun the coming disaster.

Wing tripped and fell flat against the ground.

I froze then. Stared at his prone body. Watched him turn over and cry out as the ground swallowed itself. A swelling in my chest made its way down to my legs.

I ran. Someone was calling out. I shut them out. Suddenly, I saw Olivia by my side, skirt hiked as she rushed alongside me. Just as the ground gave out beneath Wing, we shot forward, seizing an arm each. Our bodies lurched and hit the earth. Muscle and bone stretched. Pain ran through me. Wing cried out. Olivia jerked, tugging at his sleeve.

Beneath us, more earth gave way.

We dropped, skidding down the side. Tumbling into darkness.

***

You should leave. They're going to notice you're gone.

A voice from long ago brought me back to life, words echoing in my mind as my eyes opened. I pulled myself up from stone. Fire burned up my side. Arms and body aching, I propped myself against a wall and gripped my head. Eyes adjusted to the black. Faint light spilled from above. Darkness covered everything below me. I pulled my hand off my temple. Blood stained the palm.

Shadows shifted near me. I ran to them, seized shoulders amidst the rubble and pulled my friend into the light. I leaned him against the chasm wall. Crimson ran down his face. Beside us, Olivia coughed and staggered to her feet.

Wing's eyes fluttered open and he moaned at me. "Did we die?" I shook my head. My friend groaned in disappointment.

We looked up together. Steep rock towered over us. Midday sun bled into the pit. Shapes moved overhead. Shadows danced along the wall. Someone called down to us in Mandarin.

I called back: "We're here!"

"Is that Xiao-Li?" a man cried. "Hang on! We're sending men down soon! Just stay still and don't go near that thing!"

I did not understand. "What thing?!"

"Don't you see?!" A faint gesture waved at a sight unseen. "Look!" Cautiously, Wing, Olivia, and I followed his arm. Olivia gasped, clutching my arm.

For a moment, I thought we were gazing upon a train carriage. However, it was far too large to be anything of the sort. Its grey body was almost as tall as the wall behind us. Sunlight reflected off its metal skin. Three great cylinders fitted into its side. A pointed head stabbed into darkened earth. Its massive, rectangular backside loomed behind it.

A gash sat between two of the side-drums.

Wing's breathing grew heavy. I felt Olivia trembling. "What is that?" she wheezed. "Are you seeing that, Mister Charlie?"

"Yes, miss," I assured her. My eyes traced up the iron mystery and I wished I knew what it was.

***

We were out of the pit before too long. Rope-ladders fell over the walls and men scrambled down to collect us. Some of our rescuers stopped to observe the massive machine. Two whites stood in the middle of the cavern openly contemplating an investigation as I was carried to the surface.

By the next day, the doctor had finished patching me up, saying I was fit return to work. The aches and pains I felt told another story. Poor Wing was in sadder shape than I, Fat Leung told me that morning, but he was still "expected to recover soon." I shuddered at the thought.

As I was being released, Benny arrived. He wore grey and fiddled with the stopwatch in his hands. "It seems young Olivia was impressed with you and your fellow's bravery," Benny said as the doctor finished changing my bandages. "She's insisting that we increase your pay by ten cents."

"How generous." I smiled at the thought. "Please, tell her that I—"

"Will not receive a penny." He glowered at me. "Your callous rigging nearly cost that girl her life. If she died, we'd *all* have suffered for it."

"I was following orders."

"At the cost of your discretion."

"You never said how much to put down. I didn't expect us to blast open an old cave. Or unearth that *thing*." I rotated my arm limply. "What did we find, anyway?"

My foreman stared at me, his face dire. "I'm not sure. The side of the cave nearest to the river has track marks along its bottom, as though it crashed inside and caused a cave-in ages ago."

"It's a vehicle?"

Benny and I headed for the front doors. "It has no wheels to speak of, but we suspect those cylinders are engines of some kind. Since it does not look fit for moving in water, it's likely to be a dirigible."

"From where?"

"No idea. Bunting sent people down there this morning to inspect it. Sent the photographer to take some more pictures, too. One man came back an hour ago." He breathed deep, "He found bodies inside."

That struck me. "There are people in there?"

"He did not describe them as such." Benny's eyes grew distant. "He said that they were tall, taller than any of us, and human-like, but..." He stared into the distance, looking lost. "Their hands and skin were as serpents' scales with wide, toothless mouths. They were slumped over some desk by a window at the machine's front."

Monsters. Possibilities ran through my mind as I followed Benny into the street. The obvious one was that these were men fleeing Diyu, Buddha's earth prison for the most wretched of souls. It was a feared place where dreadful King Yanluo Wang and his underworld wardens tormented those unforgivable ones that were not yet allowed to be reborn. Perhaps these men had escaped the gaze of their wardens, constructed a ship out of unused torture instruments, and then sailed to Earth on cursed winds. Speaking my mind thusly would elicit scepticism from my foreman, who had long abandoned his patience for the immaterial.

Wind blew up from the river, tickling my wounds as we walked down the road. Benny continued, "Bunting's sent a telegram to the Geological Survey of Canada, hoping we can get it put up in a museum or taken apart." We rounded a corner and neared the centre of town. "Either way, it's out of our hands now."

A wagon had parked along the main road. People stopped to watch as men's bodies were thrown to the ground, wrapped in white cloth. Some were unwrapped, or had the material around their heads pulled by coroners or co-workers. I noticed something among the corpses, a troubling fact I could not ignore.

My foreman was saying something, but I cut him off. "Where are the dead?"

Still walking, Benny regarded me strangely, "What?"

"Where are *our* dead?" I pointed to the row of bodies.

Benny cleared his throat, "Bunting says to leave them for now."

"*Leave* them!" I cried, running to his front, "How could he —?!"

He pressed a hand against my chest, stopping. "I'm talking to him about arranging something. For now. Well. 'They're already buried, so why bother,' he said."

Shock beat at my chest. Benny saw my surprise and sighed. "Xiao-Li, I don't care for it either, but I can't move them without Bunting's approval, and right now he's more concerned about moving Olivia to—"

"No."

Benny's face tightened. "I'm sorry?"

This would not do. Silence would not help me. I pointed in the direction of the site. "We need to gather them and have them properly buried. At the very least, we should pray for them." He said nothing. I continued: "Sir, it's important that we do! So that when they're—"

"Xiao-Li, how long have you been working here?"

I hesitated. "Since the autumn, sir."

"I see. What did you do before coming to Canada?"

My heart crawled into my throat. I thought of sweeping the monastery's steps. The morning mantra recitations. Pilgrimages into town for Ghost Day celebrations.

Her hand on my arm as we walked along the river.

"Nothing, sir."

"Is that so? You did *nothing* back home?"

My words turned to dust in my mouth.

"You did *nothing* and you think you're in a position to make demands?" Veins in Benny's neck and along his forehead throbbed. "I *crawled* to get where I am now. I *fought* to put myself above you *ingrates* so I didn't have to shovel another damned thing. Who the hell are you, Xiao-Li? What *nothing* did you *do*? Were you a potter? A noble?" He put his face close to mine. "A *killer*? We don't know, do we? You've never *said*, *ever*, and all you *do* here is rig dynamite and *eat*. So, *Mister Nothing*, what gives you *any* kind of authority *over me?*"

A weak noise came from my throat.

Benny's face gained a sinister sense of serenity. "Let me explain something, Wu Xiao-Li. So long as I am foreman, *you* do as *I* say. *I* tell you where the dynamite goes, *I* tell you what to eat and when, *and*—"

A cry from afar.

Halting, Benny and I heard men howling across the canyon. Without a moment's hesitation, we ran, leaving the argument where it was. Benny took a horse from a white that had just dismounted it. He saddled up, jabbering at the man in English, and rode off. I followed, calling after him. No response. Not even a glance back as his steed scaled the slope.

Reason said to run back and find a cellar to hide in. However, faith said to push onward. Undoubtedly, something else had fled the cave: another evil escaping Diyu. Something only a man of my station could deal with. I remembered some banishment rites and hoped they would do, for the sake of both the dead and the living. I had to move.

A quick scan of the town found a man loading a six-shooter into his belt while setting his boot into a steed's stirrup. I rushed to him. In broken English, I hurriedly begged him to take me. The white cast a glimpse at the chaos ahead and lifted himself onto his mount. Then, reaching down, he seized me and tossed my body over the backside of his horse as though I were a potato sack. We rode towards the screams.

I struggled to hold onto the rider's saddle. Each bucking of the stallion made my injuries sing and threatened to cast me to the ground.

Men were panicking around me when we stopped. One poor soul had fainted around his fellows. Four fled downhill on foot. The rider dismounted and loosed his pistol. I dropped, aching all over as I staggered onward. Benny was shaking someone and screaming at him in English. Their conversation was too fast for me.

Men stood by the hell-ship's pit. I went to them, approaching the edge. Hesitatingly, I looked down. Lantern light split the darkness below, revealing rocky floors and scattered tools. The photographer's camera lay in shambles. One side of the ship had been pried open, as though giant hands had parted the steel.

Amid the stone was the distinct sheen of fresh blood.

***

News of the murders spread like fire. Men were found shredded, cleaved in two or pulled apart. A lone survivor, Bunting's photographer, uttered something unintelligible before bleeding out. Witnesses around the hole claimed they saw a terrible shape bolt out of the dirigible at blinding speed and vanish into the woods. We were not safe. Wagons were loaded immediately, with most of the townsfolk swiftly evacuated to the next town over.

Olivia asked to see me before she was evacuated with Bunting's peers. Head bandaged and hobbling, she took my hand and led me to her carriage. I saw the look Mister Bunting gave as we walked together. His shock at our friendliness was a welcome surprise.

"I do hope you'll be alright, Mister Charlie." Olivia pawed my shoulder. "This business with monsters and dirigibles is too much for anyone to bear, I fear."

"Yes, miss."

She smiled my way. "When this is over, do come with my uncle to Ottawa. I would have you help with my gardens."

"Gardens?"

"Your hands, Mister Charlie." She took one and examined it. "They're too delicate for a man's. Hard labour is not for you, I can tell." Her grip was soft. The slimness of her fingers made me nostalgic.

I withdrew my hand slowly, bowing my head. "I do my best."

One last smile.

I watched her leave. As the carriage rounded a bend, and as the grinding of its wheels grew distant, I prayed for her health.

***

Night fell. Half of us stayed behind to search for the killer. Benny oversaw the mission, bent on bringing the fiend to justice. Mister Bunting, furious at the death of his photographer, interrogated my colleagues for answers. Men patrolled the grounds with lanterns. Some whites bore pistols and rifles. My fellows were forced to arm themselves with shovels, sledgehammers, and hatchets. I saw Fat Leung pacing around with a meat cleaver. He looked like he knew how to use it.

I, meanwhile, sat by the pit. It was clear our attackers were more tortured souls come to haunt the living. Hands rubbing together, I hummed all of the necessary mantras. Among my prayers, I begged Yanluo Wang to send his wardens to protect us should our weapons fail.

"I never knew you were a praying man," someone said. I turned to see Wing. He was bandaged tightly, white cloth wrapped around his neck, head, and leg.

Finishing my chant, I rose and made for him. We headed for the town slowly. A quartet of men were nearing the pit, passing us as we chatted. "In Buddha's words are truth. Hopefully, mine will reach the right ears."

Wing looked to the woods beside us. A thick patch of trees and shrubs choked a path over the hills. "Can you really keep faith here?"

"Life is suffering, Wing. The path to Nirvana frees us from it."

"I'd sooner be free now," he sighed. "What are we doing here, Xiao-Li? Why are we so far from home?"

"We came in search of work. We were promised a dollar a day and a chance to settle in the new world."

"*We* were. What about you?"

I hesitated, "I had to leave China."

"Are you a criminal?"

"Not really."

"'Not really'? You're not filling me with confidence right now."

"I broke a law." I glanced at my hands idly. "Not one a policeman or dignitary would care about, but I had to be punished just the same."

My friend shook his head. "You're strange."

"I just try not to focus on who I was. I'd rather work on who I want to be."

"So you think suffering out here with us will help you on your way?"

"Wing, we are born to suffer."

I looked to the lights about town, stared out at them and the way they danced like the stars overhead. "From our first meal to our last piss, we suffer. Not only because of the harshness of existence, but also because of what we do to ourselves. We are all so fragile and yet the walls we built around ourselves are so high. Look at Bunting and Benny. They put themselves above us while we writhe in the mud for their satisfaction. That is because they are taught that suffering is integral to progress. And it is, but only progress in the realm material."

Wing raised an eyebrow, "So you follow Buddha to create progress for your soul."

I remembered her breath against my face. "I try to. More than ever. In his words, I find peace. In peace, I find progress, and I hope that when my time comes, I will be put in a better place."

A faint laugh. In Wing's face, I saw the beginnings of a grin. "Xiao-Li. You truly—"

Then his head was gone.

A black shape swept through the air, snapped out of the trees and then back again. Blood specked my face. Wing's headless body went limp and dropped.

Men screamed around me. Gunshots fired and bodies scrambled, weapons raised. I stared down at his corpse. At his blood. My thoughts fell away. Fear took hold. I stumbled backwards, words caught in my throat. Invisible weights gripped my legs. Lurching, numb, I made for the town. The world tilted with each step.

***

Fat fingers slapped my cheek. I snapped awake and re-entered the world. Cleaver in hand, Fat Leung gripped my shoulder, saying something. Men rushed past, hollering. In front, Bunting was panicking, pointing at the path leading out of town. Benny shouted orders at someone. His thugs paled at the sight of me. Thoughts returned to my mind. Sound came next.

"I said get to the goddamn wagons!" Bunting cried, scrambling my way. "Escort me! I'll raise your pay, gladly!"

"We need to stand our ground!" Benny bellowed, loading a pistol.

Bunting kicked dirt in his direction. "*You* can stand your ground!" He clapped his hands in front of my face. "Charlie! Charlie, snap out of it! Help me get my bags!"

All at once, my blood boiled. Red mist came over me. Suddenly I began to hate the mere sight of him.

"Charlie!" Bunting lost patience. "Wake up, you *dolt*! Wakey-wakey! We *go*! We *go*, right, Charlie?! *Charlie!*"

I had enough. Teeth grating, I rushed at Bunting, growling and falling on him. My hands grabbed his throat. I shook and choked him with all my might. Amid my fellows' shouts and Bunting's gagging protests, I screamed, over and over again:

"XIAO-LI! I AM XIAO-LI! SAY IT! *SAY IT! XIAO! LI!*"

I meant to rip him apart. Bunting's face grew wild with shock. Two sets of hands took my arms and pulled me from him. Like an animal, I thrashed in their grip.

Something flew out from the darkness. I awakened from my murder-

117

trance and was dropped. I thought it was the same force that claimed Wing. I was wrong. The bloodied carcass of a horse flew past and struck one of the workers behind me. Great slash-marks lined its side. Its neck was twisted backwards.

A shape moved out of the corner of my eye, snapping forward. Veering, it encircled the camp. With it came a horrible screech. Shots rang. Benny opened fire as the shape shredded through the cliff's edge. It sprang at us. Entering the lamplight, I saw a mass of black, dark orange, and pale yellow rip through the town centre. An unlucky marksman vanished under the mysterious missile as it fired into the surrounding darkness again. A horrible *crunch* followed.

Then, silence. The men formed a clumsy half-circle, facing the woods where the thing hid. Bunting propped himself on one of Benny's thugs and got to his feet. He held his throat and stared at me hatefully.

A rustling. Rising, I looked round, trying to find its source. It seemed to come from everywhere. Suddenly, a voice:

"Hear me!" It came as a scratching, scraping cacophony, melding over what was very clearly Mandarin. "Which of you is patriarch here?! Speak! I have need of you!"

Confusion took my colleagues. "What's he saying?!" Bunting wheezed.

Gun cocked, Benny put his hand out. "I'll translate."

"Christ!" a white yelped. "First moon-man we meet and he speaks goddamn Chinese!"

"Shut *up*," Benny growled. Stepping forward, he switched to Mandarin. "Right, whoever this is—"

"We would know your name!" I called, cutting off Benny.

"Are you the patriarch?" hissed the voice.

I ignored my foreman's stare and pressed on. "Please, we need to know who this is!"

"For what reason?"

"So I can help you!" I explained. "I know I have done wrong by Buddha! I know I strayed from the path, but please!" My arms went up. "Let me send you on, so your soul can be cleansed!"

A horrible trilling. "Soul! You think I am some *living dead* walking the land again? Oh, my sweet bumpkin. There are worlds so far beyond your star that your primate brains would shatter at the truth."

"Then who is this?!" Benny knocked me aside and aimed the pistol at the dark. "*Tell us what the hell you are!*"

A thoughtful hiss: "Shurach Ul Urana of the Bendrax Cluster, Seventh Brother of Kalkak Ul Kraien. Does that mean anything to you?"

No colleague of mine went by any of those names. Mister Bunting shook his head. Benny continued with the translation. "Not at all."

The thing's horrible trilling sounded across the camp. "Wonderful," said the creature. His voice had become serene, jovial. Just then, I realized that he had laughed.

"What are you?" Benny asked.

"Assassin," he declared, almost giddily. "Hired blade of the Akarcza

Hidden. The product of four long years of biomoulding. Reborn as the finest weapon you could imagine. A hundred lives claimed in my time before my capture. If not for you curious lot, I'd still be in that ship."

Doing his best to translate, Benny explained to our supervisor and white fellows what was said. We watched their eyes bulge and their bodies shake. His words came as a mystery to me. I did not know what biomoulding was, but it sounded horrible. My foreman called out, "What do you want?!"

"I *need* you," our hunter declared from his hiding spot, "to repair that ship. It was my prison vessel, collecting me from my trial and transporting me to the Cortze Nebula Penitentiary. The engines failed and my wardens put me in stasis, no doubt sounding some beacon before we crashed. I mean to leave here before reinforcements arrive. Now, bring your engineers—"

Benny made a sweeping gesture at the camp, "Men are *dead* because of you! You spent the night leaving us *terrorized!* If you need us so badly, *why are you killing us?*"

Silence. Not even one of its hisses. It seemed to contemplate Benny's words. Then, an answer: "I had been asleep for too long. I needed the exercise."

All colour fled Benny's face. I watched as he weakly translated our hunter's words for the whites. Mister Bunting looked to us imploringly.

Benny declared in English: "We might want to run."

Suddenly, a granary erupted. A force ripped through the back and out the front door. Splinters and flecks of grain covered the grass. Then, the front half and part of the roof burst.

From the wreckage came a horrible sight. A hunched, man-like body sat on a sextet of crab's legs. Bloodied pincers pushed aside the remains of the door and a long, barbed tail snapped at the machinery behind it. A mouth sat in its chest; in it was my friend's bloodied head. Wing's lips and jaws flapped mindlessly as the devil's torso-fangs pressed against his cheeks. On its broad, muscular shoulders sat a smooth head with dead black eyes. A set of mandibles twitched at us.

"Run, then," the horror from beyond Heaven hissed in English. "Go on and run. I am ever so bored."

The others opened fire. Bullets ricocheted off of its inhuman body. It shielded its face. Then, it crouched. A hum. Springing forward, its body spun in midair and ripped through the crowd. Men scattered, shooting at where it was and where it might go. Rogue shots clipped other gunmen or hit the sides of buildings.

I fled. One of Benny's thugs set Mister Bunting over his shoulder and ran. I saw the one who had beaten Wing with a broomstick; he burst, stray limbs scattering across the ground. Bodies flew. A snap of the twisting shape sent Fat Leung flying into the woods. Eight of us ran to the last wagon. Two horses, scared and baying, stood tied to a tree near where the last wagon and pair of stallions lay in pieces.

The thug and Bunting took the front. Benny and I climbed into the back with the rest. Stumbling, I tripped and fell face-first into a pile of supplies. I heard reins snapping. Horses neighed, and hooves thundered. I got up and looked back. A smattering of men neared, trying to wave us down. Their forms vanished over the hills as we sped off.

Around me, we contemplated our fate. We knew how fast the beast could move. It was only a matter of time before it caught up. I looked down, moving my hands through the pile of tools at our disposal.

I found three bundles of dynamite and a plunger.

"We'll reach the bridge soon!" Benny shouted. "We might be able to lose him at–" He stopped. A cautious smile crossed his face as he watched my fingers tie several dynamite sticks together. "Good man, Xiao-Li! We throw those at him lit, and–"

"Leave me behind."

My fellows looked at me strangely. Blinking hard, Benny leaned in. I fixed the cords to the base of the plunger as I spoke. "That thing, that creature enjoys murder. It's not chasing us because it's busy killing everyone back in town. When it's done, I'll wait for it, and when it comes near–"

"You'll blow yourself up?" Benny slapped his forehead. "You don't even know if that'll be enough!"

"We're out of options."

I saw my foreman shaking his head. "What's gotten into you? What on earth –?"

"I was a monk." I gripped two handfuls of dynamite, putting them under my arms. "I lived in a temple outside of Chengdu, spending my days memorizing the sutras and freeing myself of earthly wants."

"You–" Benny's eyes went wild. My fellows looked as surprised; one removed his cap. Our two white colleagues just looked lost. "You're a damned *priest?* Then, when you wanted to see our dead–"

"I wanted to see them off. However, I'm not sure what spirits would hear me. I..." I stammered as I remembered her. Long black hair held together with a comb. Slim features, wide eyes. Skin smooth as paper. She never gave me her real name. It was different each time we met. "I was with a woman, you see."

"You weren't allowed to be with her."

"No," I shuddered at a terrible sound in the distance. "The high priest sent me out into the world to learn Buddha's path again. I thought that if I punished myself, toiled and raised funds for the temple, then Heaven would be kinder to me." I looked back. "Now I see that my redemption lies beyond. And if I can take that creature with me, I can avenge Wing's death and the deaths of everyone else."

I trailed off. Suddenly, I wondered what I believed.

Hooves beat against wood. I looked behind us to see the grass give way and become the pine bridge built before I arrived. Below us ran the raging current of the river.

"Do you miss your father?"

"What?" Benny shook his head.

"You never answered me. Back at the cliffs, before Bunting and Olivia came." I didn't know why that thought came to mind. Yet I asked again: "Do you miss him?"

I looked at him. He drew breath. Lips tight, he nodded sharply.

That was all I needed.

I leapt out of the wagon and hit the middle of the bridge. Groaning, I rose and set the dynamite in front of me, fitting sticks into the cracks.

I had finished rolling out the wires when the beast appeared. It stood at the other end of the bridge, stained with blood. Red rolled from its shell and dripped, forming pools at its horrible feet. Wing's head was gone. I didn't care why. Slowly, the thing advanced.

"Hello again," it hissed, almost giddily. "So that wasn't you I flattened back there. I wondered why he wasn't trying to exorcise me."

Saying nothing, I raised the detonator to my chest. One hand held it up; the other rested on the plunger. His top head tilted at me, "Oh? Is this a standoff?" That horrible laugh once again. "I don't suppose you're mad about your friend. So sorry, but his head was just the right size. Not that I need it now. My—"

"Let's get this over with."

It stopped. The beast lowered his top head and chortled. "Brave."

A flash. All at once, the creature sped my way. Wood ripped beneath its frame as it soared across the bridge. I seized up. Waited for half a second. Then, as I saw the bend of a claw heading for my face, I pressed down.

Fire ripped through the bridge and erupted underneath the monster. I heard roaring agony. The limb snapped forward and knocked me aside. I dropped. Twisting round, I looked up. The monster's body had been ripped by the explosion. Bits of leg and carapace fell from the bridge. White blood dripped from above. Shurach's trilling howl sounded as he hit the side of the bridge and rolled off.

I hit the water and praised Buddha.

Art by Nilah Magruder

COLLECTED LIKENESSES
JAMEY HATLEY

1913
Harlem, New York

The kindly way to feel separating is to have a space between.
This shows a likeness.
— Gertrude Stein, "Roast Beef" from Tender Buttons

1.

Before your grandmother was Clementine, she had a Houma lover called Jacques who would pilot a pirogue up the river to court her before her owners ran him off. Your grandmother had a lover called Honor on the plantation. "Him was the best thief. He always found me what I need." They married her to a man called James. There were others where the language is tricky. Master. Uncle. Emancipator. Cousin. Owner. Sister. Mistress.

"Master August, though, him teach me to cut a figure. I was at a fine family in Louisiana. Rich like will never be seen again. Master August come from Europe, over the sea. He cut figures of my people and I picked it right up. How I loved to cut. How I miss it," she says.

2.

You, too, love sharp things. Long, slender hatpins tipped with opal or quince feathers. Buttery leather shoes with pointed toes. Fish that can only be consumed by an eager tongue searching for pin bones. Needles that can free an ingrown hair, mend flesh, or stab. Prick, blister, choke. A threat sidled up next to such delicious beauty.

3.

Before your grandmother's hands twisted like roots through stone, before she was your grandmother (great? great-great? great-great-great?), before she came to live in this tiny, hot room that you share with her, sleeping at her feet, your grandmother could sew. She could look at a garment and gauge what the inside was like. Could cut her own patterns. Cipher the amount of yardage it would take to complete at different levels of quality that she made up herself and charged accordingly for: A *Passable* would look like the thing, but skimp in every possible way from fabric to fabrication. A *Copy* would get

123

you a garment indistinguishable from the model if you could obtain the exact materials. A *Clementine* would be the garment with her improvements and enhancements. A *Clementine* would be better than the original, what the garment really wanted to be. A *Clementine* would be worthy of her name.

Clementines were the gift from the Master at Christmastime. Always a joy. Always a delight. She was made to the pattern of her owners, but when it is time to cut her own figure in the world, she names herself Clementine after one of the few sweet things she's known.

4.

Your younger cousins do not know this. They do not care. They have never had and never will have a *Clementine*. They call her your spooky old slave in the attic. This is how you learn to trip and bite and scratch and pinch and fight even when they are kin. Especially when they are kin. This is how you learn to keep silent. This is how you learn to hide.

5.

You use your sharpest scissors to clip your Grannie's nails like she taught you. Her hands gnarled and tight. You let the hardened yellowed crescents fall into your free hand. Her eyes are an ancient, rheumy blue, rimmed with white like moons. She watches you cut and file and shape.

"Catch all them trimmings up and the dust, too. Put it in yond' fire and burn it up," she says.

6.

Once your Grannie is in the bed and it is clear that she will not get back up, she calls you to her, pulls you down to her, and her breath is Dr. Tichenor's and Garrett's snuff. "I'll never finish all this work," she says. The doctors don't know what is killing her, but time itself is enough of an answer at almost ninety. Some days her breath is almost gone. Other times her papery skin is covered with a web of blue bruises. Spasms. "I want this done cold. On purpose. Not fickle. You're my blessing, my waited-for one. It must be you," she says.

7.

Grannie's quilt eats her fever and is bitter with her sweat and dying. She pats one of the quilt pieces. You have seen it thousands of times without ever really registering it. It was navy once, not quite square, nubby and rough. Only with your hands on it do you realize that it is also a pocket. A safe. A hiding place.

"Save this piece. I didn't run. I should have. My color was a caution, but I should have took my chance. I didn't, though. I waited and waited until the law forced them to let me go," she says.

You take your tiniest, sharpest seam rippers and cut thread after thread along the perimeter of the square. The pouch pulls free from its moorings. The other side looks obscenely rich compared to the part that has been exposed for several generations. For the first time you see the grubby constellation spring forth from the rough cloth. There are embroidered stars on the front of the pouch. You hold the tiny sky in your open palm.

Open the seven pearly buttons hidden in their placket. Your inheritance. Your legacy.

8.

"Are you ready?"

9.

Gingerly, you pinch the tiny people out. These little cut-figure people — some fabric, some paper — came out of slavery with her. Were emancipated with her. Some are cut from newsprint, already crumbling; one gentleman in a top hat is cut from onionskin transparent and luminous as a star. Many are cut from thick buttery writing paper, cotton-laid with the watermark of an eagle with an A on its chest. These figures are cut so the watermark lies at the heart of the figure. You line them up into a parade, a march.

"These your family folk?" you ask your Grannie.

"Some directly so, yes. Others, no. We all bound up together by blood, though. Kin all the same."

"Why don't you put them up?"

"These ain't toys, child. This not for play. Not for show, either. Every single figure a life. A true likeness. If you can't treat them as such, then I'll just take them to my grave."

"No, Grannie. I want to help."

"Then pick you one out." She spreads the little people out across the table. There were men and women represented of all ages.

"How do I know which one?"

"The figure will tell you."

You hover your hands over the figures like the preacher does over the collection plate at church. The figures seem to be calling out to be chosen, to be picked by your eager fingers. You feel them tingle and ache a bit. You squeeze your eyes shut and lean into the ache of your fingers pointing you to something fertile and alive. Your fingers are divining: water, lightning, gold, life. Your eyes fly open and without even reaching your figure is in your hand. One of the fancy ladies with a parasol on a stroll. She seems to bow a bit to you. She is pretty and light.

"Who is this, Grannie?" you ask. She lifts up in the bed. Motions you closer.

"My second Mistress in slaverytime. I give her younguns my milk from my breast. She give me to her brother as a Christmas present." You turn away. You flush as you recall the taunt. *Your slave in the attic.*

Your fingers start to close, to crush the likeness into a ball.

"Not like that," your grandmother cautions. "This kind of work, some want to do quick. Fire. Crushed glass. Poison. You get one tree that way. I want a forest. I'm not still here from being hasty. Think on it. " Your Grannie leans back against the pillows. Watches. Waits. For you.

10.

You open your hand and stare at the likeness. The figure has changed. Now the little woman looks haughty, eager and greedy. You settle the likeness into a little brass dish. You strike a match. Watching it burn, you feel a surge like running down a steep hill. You feel a spark with each bit of destruction that builds into an explosion.

Your Grannie yelps and grabs her arm. There is an angry mark that wasn't there before.

"What happened? Did I hurt you?" you ask.

"Look," she says.

You watch the burn go through phases like a moon. From new wound, to blister, to scab, to gone.

"Every likeness a life," she tells you again, and you start to understand.

"Do it hurt them too, Grannie?"

"This work is a revealing. Both sides. Ain't no hiding place in it. Strike a match to a likeness, you feel the burnt. Cut one and you bleed. Drown it and you fight to breathe. This little I take is a willing price for what they pay on the other end."

"They still alive, Grannie? These folks that hurt you."

"Some live. Some be gone. If they already gone, this'll find the next in line."

Every likeness a life. Every likeness a wound. Every likeness a debt.

When you destroy a likeness, you only feel a shadow of your Grannie's pain. An echo. You feel the quick sting of a slap, a burn, a cut, a disavowal, the tenderness of a bruise already fading. The two of you hold the hurt together.

She is fading, your Grannie. You try to make her rest between likenesses; you try to take more of the revealing as you watch her get weaker and weaker, still. It won't be long now. As she fades, you bloom. Each new destruction of a likeness is another settled debt: you are fulfilling her true legacy. This is the last, genuine Clementine, balancing the record book of her life. Collecting payment for her wounds.

How could your Grannie bear it? And then bear it again?

How can you?

11.

You try your hand at cutting figures. Your hands so gifted to the work of sharp things, but no matter how you try, you cannot master a true likeness.

You fail.

12.

As soon as your Grannie is buried, your family puts you out. They send you to a distant cousin who runs a very elegant house in the city. You have never been away from home. You have never lived among white folk.

You have never been in such a house. The walls soar way above your head, blue like a sky. A crystal chandelier breaks the light into a thousand pieces that are reflected in mirrors. And the light, such light! Gas lamps, candlelight, and a whole wall of windows swathed in heavy silk drapes.

The lady of the house takes pity on your situation and gives you a bed and a uniform and a meager salary. The uniform must always be on if you are "in service." You are always in some kind of service under this roof.

It is almost Christmas when you arrive, so until she decides what to do with you, the lady of the house has you prepare for the holiday season. You polish and shine all the woodwork, dust every single knick-knack and object. She gives you white gloves and a feather duster to attend to the artwork.

Over the sideboard, right at eye level, is a long gilt frame. Inside of the frame there is a series of figures cut of black paper. Six in total. A background of this very parlor has been sketched in behind them. The likenesses captured are so fluid, so intimate, that you expect them to chat, or raise their paper pipes to smoke or order you to clean their shapes in a more suitable way, but they stay almost still, almost fixed under your gaze.

"These are very, very delicate," the lady of the house says. "Silhouettes cut by the European artist Mister Auguste Edouart on his tour of these United States." She looks to her bored teenage daughter, who is waiting for her piano teacher to arrive.

Your Grannie's figures were not all of heavy black paper. They were not behind glass. She did not have to tell you that they were "very, very delicate." Your Grannie's likenesses were cut from whatever she could get her hands on.

When the lady of the house leaves you to your cleaning, the daughter stands at your side.

"With them being black like that, that lady could be you," the daughter says. You start to hate her a bit more. She is about your age, you guess, and has taken you as her personal servant whenever you are not in service to her mother.

You lean in toward the figures, searching for Mister August's signature. Your Grannie's Master August.

"I hate all these dead people on the walls, watching my every move. At least these don't stare," she says.

Her hand flutters at her jaw line, ruddy with pimples. "I saw you lance my sister's boil. Can you help my complexion? I have my own pocket money if you can keep a secret."

You can keep secrets.

13.

You had to.

When the men (and boys) of the house start to corner you, you borrow a bigger uniform and keep your hair covered. You are always busy, in a rush to somewhere with witnesses. There is no hiding place for live-ins.

You are your mother's outside child. The whispers are not even whispers about your ruined mother. The secrets not even secrets. Adults speak freely around you because you know how to disappear. Your mother disappeared. Your father died. Becoming invisible runs in the family line. You try to make yourself invisible before they can force you to disappear.

14.

Your cousin is gray around the edges. She is tall and almost glamorous. Almost. A pinched look of bitterness has settled into her features and makes her look sterner and older than she is.

You ask your cousin how to leave this very elegant house. Your cousin tells you that you will never get set for day work. That you will be destroyed without a home, a family to take you in. She tells you stories about all of the live-ins who left and came crawling back. She spits the names of the ruined ones as a warning: Gladys. Morease. Mary Francis. Eloise. Hortense. Ruby.

"I will not speak a word on your behalf to return if you leave this household," your cousin says. She taps her hand over her heart as she says this. A pledge. A promise. A hope. A worry that is something a little less than a blessing. Her fingertips break loose from the pledge and tug nervously at her stiff, high collar. Her eyes rim with tears.

15.

The string of ruined women's names is a map. When you quietly ask about the ruined women, bit by bit you find your way. Miss Gladys gives leads for houses where the menfolk will mostly leave you be. Miss Morease helps you enroll in the penny-saver at her church. Miss Mary Francis loans you her map of the city. Miss Eloise promises to make your first day work uniforms. Miss Hortense teaches you to roll a cigarette and drink corn whiskey. Miss Ruby runs the boarding house where all these ruined women once lived.

"Get yourself set," Miss Ruby says, "then come see me."

So you bide your time at that terrible, grand house. To get set, you must learn to speak and keep quiet. You save every penny back. You make yourself useful to your household and to their guests. On your day off, even though your legs shake, you ride the streetcar up and down to learn the city.

You keep stashing your pennies. You do complexion work on the sly for your employer's spoiled friends. You let your stomach grumble when you pass the people selling food in the street. Slowly your money grows. *This is a day's wages. This is a week.* You mark the stations on the jars. *This is a month. Six months. A year. Set.*

16.

When you are set, you start day work like everyone else with housekeeping and laundry, but soon, much of your money comes from skin work. You hone the profile with creams and tonics, and you are known for your extractions. You have a whole arsenal of sharps: tweezers with and without a slant, needles run through the blue of a flame before they free ingrown hairs, sewing tools repurposed for the job. You use the tools of your trade to poke and prod the face, tighten the skin. Your best tools are your sharpened fingernails, wrapped in cotton to press up long-submerged sins.

You blame their favorite food or drink or cosmetic or habit for their imperfections. You frown and tell them to abstain from what they love best. This is the first deprivation that some of them have ever known. How they thank you for this punishment. How they admire the longing they feel for their vices denied.

How they ooh and aaah over the pain you inflict. They come to crave the ecstasy of the release you provide as you squeeze out the blackheads, lance the boils of pus and blood, and steam the whiteheads up to ooze. They crave the sting and burn of the astringents and tonics you slap into their skin. They feel pure and regal. Saintly.

You wear a white work dress for skin work. When Miss Eloise measures you for this dress, you weep from missing your Grannie. The white uniform lets them know that to clean this type of dirt costs more than to scrub a floor. You always leave a bit of blemish behind. You make your work *almost* perfect. Close to perfect. And wait for time to do the rest.

17.

In the basement at Miss Ruby's there is an illegal club where the musicians and dancing girls come to be themselves when they are finished with white people. One night she tells you your cousin's story. For a few weeks not so many years ago, your almost glamorous cousin left her very elegant house. She did not get herself set first. She did not save up the cash, make the contacts, or learn the city by streetcar on her day off. She met a man right there in the basement club who promised to marry her. She waited for three days for him to return.

"He was a wonderfully terrible man," Ruby says.

18.

You and the other girls eat breakfast together and share chores around Miss Ruby's place. You make the coffee and fill the cups.

"Do this in remembrance of me," Sally says and holds her coffee cup up for a toast.

"What?" You ask.

"That's what the old lady said in my dream," Sally says.

"What old lady?" you ask. Sally yawns. She is no good before coffee.

"The one with the stars on her dress," Sally says.

Sally has the new girl position near the drafty window. You loaned her your Grannie's quilt.

You realize it has been months since you destroyed a likeness. You are busy – keeping your room paid for, learning new dances, and work, work, work. You haven't actually stopped, you tell yourself, only put it off.

Later, when you're alone, you check on the likenesses and they are silent, haughty as ever. You take out a likeness from the group, a man in a cape. You hold him on your palm, ponder a suitable destruction. You glance at your Grannie's quilt on Sally's bed. You flush with the duty of what she's asked you to do, the slow destruction of the flesh of those who sinned against her.

You want to snatch the quilt off Sally's bed, to climb under it and dream. Instead you pack the likeness away. You borrow one of Sally's dresses without permission. You line your eyes and rouge your cheeks. You spray perfume on the nape of your neck and head downstairs to sweat and dance.

19.

You plan to tend to a likeness on the next day off, but now that you do day work, you work every single day that you can. Your nights belong to your lover, who is full of laughter, song, and a tenderness you have never known.

Your Grannie comes to you in the night and shows you her scars. She is naked, but you do not look away. She hands you a likeness of herself. When you wake up you look and look for it and sob when you realize that the likeness and your Grannie only exist in the land of dreams.

20.

Your lover gets you to pose for a photograph in front of the club where he works as a back-up piano player and bartender. You tell him to keep his money. You tell him that your hair isn't right, you have on the wrong dress, but he insists. He wraps his arm around you and he is Jacques, Honor, James, and Master August.

The photo comes back a few weeks later. Your lover shows you how the cardboard back folds out to make a little frame. He stands it up on your little dresser. In the photo, the wind has lifted the hem of your skirt. He holds on to his hat. Together, you lean against the wind.

"You two make a fine pair," Sally says when you show her the photograph. "In fact, you favor. He could be your kin."

This is the only likeness you have of yourself.

21.

You have been dealing with a likeness. With the finest pumice stone you could find, you have been slowly eroding the figure cut from heavy white stock. The likeness that you are working is stubborn. You wonder where this woman in the fancy gown is, whether she shrieks when her skin rips, or does she whimper? Which of your Grannie's scars does she place her name to? Would she even know? The tendering lasts longer and longer.

Your skin is chafed and raw from it. You are trying to get ready for work, to get into your clothes before the flash of tendering can be seen. You have been careful with the likeness, working on the parts of it that would be under your clothes.

"What's troubling your back?" asks Sally.

"Maybe my new soap is vexing me," you say.

"Be careful your complexion folk don't see that," Sally says.

22.

Your lover is singing softly:

I'm going home on the morning train
I'm going home on the morning train

He has taken ill. The doctor has been no use. He can barely put on clothes. His skin is irritated. Every touch pains him. His back. *Your back.* His arm. *Your arm.* His face. His lovely, lovely face. *Your face.* You make compresses with gauze soaked in chamomile and sage tea. You beg ice chips from the iceman.

"Thank you, thank you," he says burning with fever.

"Tell me, lover," you beg, "where are your people from?"

Even without the fever he could not answer you. He was put out. Abandoned. Bastard.

Like you.

We're all bound up together.

You are feverish with knowing. You search your lover's face for your Grannie's, for some feature of the likeness, but you have pumiced it into a dark, ragged shape. You remember the burn on your Grannie's arm, her wince, her shout. You imagine a bright red thread stitched from you to your Grannie, see it tremble as you set that likeness against the flame for the first time. You follow the thread from you to your lover as he trembles in bed.

Each likeness a life.

23.

You lock the likenesses away. You stow them in a box at the top of the closet. Under your bed. On a bright, cold morning you take them to the river to tumble them all away and yourself, too. The likenesses shift and writhe in your pocket. You feel an invisible web of ropes tighten and tighten around you, cutting off your breath. Long dormant, they have grown powerful, greedy since your Grannie came to trouble Sally's sleep. You turn and run back to your room. The likenesses settle.

You pumice away a little more of the likeness and can breathe again even as the welts on your back start to weep.

Your Grannie endured the wounds of her bondage. She carried them into freedom. She refused to forget. She took her payment. She demands you remember. The work is yours now. It has claimed you.

You gaze down at your lover, sleeping with his mouth open just so. He burns with fever still. You burn with fever, too.

Later, he calls to you: "Lover, lover, come here and let me look on you."

You approach his side and settle next to the bed.

"I'm here," you say. His eyes are rimmed red. His skin raw and ragged. He opens and closes his eyes, searching for you. Your fingers ache with need. The likeness is just an arm's length away on the dresser, telegraphing a wild heat.

"Bring our picture from over yonder. Come look at us together, pretty and strong," your lover says.

You hold the picture up close to his face. You hide your own face behind the cardboard frame. You won't look at the photograph. Your lover's fevered eyes tell you what you already know. *In fact, you favor. He could be your kin.* His eyes, gone pale with fever, search for you — on the photograph, all around this tiny room. *If they already gone, this'll find the next in line.*

The likeness shimmers in your hand before you remember grabbing it; you take the pumice to the likeness and scrub. The woman in the dress is almost gone, chafed beyond recognition. It will be delicious to finish it off, a deep breath of air after almost drowning.

You are almost gone.

Past the wreckage of pulp and your trembling hand, your lover trembles.

The thread tugs you between your Grannie and your lover. The thread tightens, soon to break.

Art by Eric Orchard

ANGELA AND THE SCAR
MICHAEL JANAIRO

April 1900
Ilocos Norte Province, Philippines

She padded barefoot and silent in the early morning darkness – long before any rooster's first crow – across the nipa hut's floor. Snores rumbled out from the older couple in the neighboring hut, and Angela didn't want to wake them and give the woman she called Auntie Dungo anything more to gossip about.

She gathered things that had been her father's, things she had saved without her mother knowing. From her small, wooden chest, she took out a threadbare cotton shirt, hole-ridden trousers, and a beaten, floppy-brimmed hat – the clothes her father used to wear while working the tobacco fields. From a spot hidden behind her books, she grabbed the same sheathed bolo knife that had been found on his body after a failed rebellion four years before.

She wore the shirt inside out, cinched the trousers with a bit of rope, and tied the leather straps of the sheathed bolo around her waist. She drank some water from a jar, filled a canteen, and slung it over her shoulder.

From a basket, she clasped the last three eggs, cracked them open one by one, and sucked out the yolks and whites. That was all her mother had left her the morning before, when she took all their chickens to the market outside town. Her mother hadn't returned. Angela had no brothers or sisters; her grandparents, like her father, were dead.

She rolled up the frayed pant legs, set the hat over the uneven tufts on her freshly shorn head, and crept through her empty home, down the stairs and through the barangay. By starlight, she walked footpaths that skirted fields of sweetly ripe tobacco plants, rose between rice paddy terraces alive with chirping insects and croaking frogs, and climbed into the hills, where light breezes let faint traces of sea-salt air mix with the rich dryness of fallen leaves from balete trees.

The day's first light cast a blue-green glow as she walked the forest edge. Long, ropy tendrils wound round wide trunks or hung lazily from muscular branches, as if they had always been there and always would. She kept walking until she smelled cigar smoke. She planted her feet and they sank into the cool, soft soil. She called, "Buenos días, Señor!"

A cough from high in the tree turned into thunderous laughter. A booming voice said, "Angela! You've come back!"

Leaves rustled and branches creaked as her kapfre descended. He didn't climb with slow and deliberate pauses to doublecheck footholds and handholds like a human would. Instead, he glided through leaves, branches, and limbs, leaving them swaying behind him. His body seemed to flicker and change, one moment, part giant; the next, part tree. She thought it magic and smiled with delight, despite her situation, to see him standing before her.

He clutched a lit cigar in one meaty hand. He wore baggy pale cotton pants torn at the cuffs, a dingy white shirt, and a dark vest with deep pockets stuffed with cigars and who knew what else. A smile spread across his bearded, weather-beaten face, a vigorous light shining in his deep black eyes. He doffed his hat, bent his back in an awkward bow, and then, straightening, lifted his brows and widened his eyes as if to make his lined face as open as possible. "You've come to live with me forever?" He sucked deeply on his cigar and exhaled a long, white stream. "Together, we will live atop the trees and watch over the forest." He took another puff and smiled.

Angela's smile waned. Even though she felt comforted by his routine words, she knew she couldn't give her usual reply. "I can't go with you; my mama needs me," she said as usual. Then she added: "You see, there's a war going on and my mama hasn't come home."

"Hmm," he said, brows tight. He scratched his beard, leaned against the tree trunk and again said, "Hmm."

Usually, their banter would lead to stories, riddles, and jokes. They only stopped when they heard voices of others, most often rice farmers in the fields below. At that moment, his eyes would turn into Os of surprise and he'd smile at her, wink, and disappear back up into the trees.

He puffed on his cigar for a while before saying: "War? What's that? Some kind of game?"

"You don't know?" she said, unable to hide her surprise or the whine in her voice. She realized her mistake, confusing an ancient forest spirit for a human adult. "It's not a game. It's–" she didn't know what to say next as words crashed into her mind: *Yanqui, Peninsulare, Illustrado, Insurrecto, Spain, America, colonialism, empire, occupation, benevolent assimilation, nationalism, patriotism, Philippines, freedom, rebel, guerrilla, revolution.* She knew these words were important, but they stood for things she didn't quite comprehend. She said, "War is when strangers come with guns and your father is killed and your mother disappears."

"Hmm," he said again, and he coughed. Clouds of smoke spewed from his mouth. He poked at them with a lazy index finger. "I've no mother or father, so maybe I need not worry about this war."

"But," she said, her voice rising. "This is serious."

He snapped his fingers, and his eyes brightened. "Angela, you must stay with me. I will make a home for you in the trees, and we can stay away from war."

"Mama needs me."

"Hmm." A mischievous half-grin bloomed on his face. "How can you know if she's disappeared?"

"She might come back," she said. "You disappear all the time; you always come back."

"Ha! Ha!" He said: "I do not disappear, Angela. I hide!"

"This isn't a game!" She frowned. "Maybe Mama is hiding, hiding from men with guns. I have to find her."

"I've an idea," he said. "I'll give you a riddle, and if you don't get it, then you must come live with me forever. Deal?"

"And if I do get it?"

"I will help you find Mama!"

She said, "It's a deal."

He shoved his cigar in his mouth and rubbed his giant hands together. "What moves over all the earth, is heard everywhere, but never seen?"

She closed her eyes and thought of owls hooting unseen at night. Then she thought of the creak of wood planks in the hut at night. How many times had she heard that? How many times had she thought it was her father returning home? Her mother said wood "talked" as the weather changed, but she liked to think it was her father's spirit come to watch over his little girl because he loved her so very much. She had her answer. She opened her eyes.

Her kapfre said, "Well?"

She said, "A ghost!"

"A ghost? Ha! No!" Quicker than she thought possible, he scooped her up in one arm and climbed smoothly and magically to the top of the tree. He set her on one of his broad shoulders. They swayed a bit. "Here is where you and I will sit and smoke forever." He didn't sit. He said, "Do you want to know the answer to the riddle?"

"I'd like another guess."

"No, no, no. That wasn't the deal. But here's the answer." He grasped her two legs with one hand to hold her in place. He jumped straight up.

They rose. She clutched his straggly hair. The air rushed against her face and swooshed into her ear. She shouted into the breeze: "The wind! It's the wind!"

He laughed. They continued to rise. Even though she gave him the answer, their ascent didn't stop. She had no idea when it would stop. The morning's full light revealed to her the vast expanse of forest; it went on and on and on; and that, too, frightened her. She couldn't see the paths she had taken that morning, the paths that defined her world. They were too small and hidden away to be of notice from this height. How tiny she felt; and still they continued to rise.

Then something changed. She felt her kapfre's shoulder muscles tighten. His laughter ebbed. It was replaced by a gruff shout: "What? What?" He thrust an angry finger toward an area where the lush green of the forest was injured by a long, deep scar.

"What? What?" He pointed in another direction, to the right of the scar, where farther in the distance a steady column of white smoke rose from the trees.

"What? What?" he said again, harsh and angry.

They fell, gently and slowly, his bare feet landing firmly on a branch atop a tree.

"What? What?" he asked, a piercing heat in his eyes aimed at her, as if he blamed her. "My trees? Disappeared? What?"

"Don't blame me," she said, but she couldn't help thinking that the fires were cook fires and that her mother was there preparing food. Or maybe that was only a fantasy created by her hunger and the dizzying heights she had climbed. She said, "That's war."

"No!"

"Yes, in your forest."

"Men with guns took my trees?"

"Not men," she said. "Yanquis."

"Yanquis? What's that?"

"Bad men."

"I don't like bad men."

"I know," she said. "But I can help you."

"You?" he said. "Help me?"

"You take me to the smoke, and I'll find out who it is. If it is Yanquis, then we play tricks on them to make them leave."

"Yes! Yes!" he said. "Let's go make them leave! Let's go now!"

"First, you must answer my riddle. If you get it right, then I'll help you."

"Hmm," he said. "A riddle is it? And if I get it wrong?"

"Then you must help me find Mama. Deal?"

"Deal," he said.

She thought for a moment, then said: "I wear a crown, but I am not a king; I just crow like one."

"Ha! Ha!" he said. "Easy! You've used that one before! You're talking about a rooster!"

"Very wise, Señor," she said. "Now I will help you."

He sucked on his cigar, now wedged between his lips, smoke pouring from him. "Ha! Ha! Let's go!"

***

Treetops shook as they sailed across the forest. The giant leapt from tree to tree, his feet barely touching a branch as he landed and pushed off again. They rose and fell as if riding waves, carried at treeswift speed, the forest canopy a blur below.

The sound of human voices brought her kapfre to a stop. They swayed on a tall, thin branch. With cigar still lit between his lips, he said, "Hmm." Leaves whispered in their wake.

She knew he wouldn't want to get close to other people, but she was still surprised when she saw him smile and wink, and then, in less than a blink, she found herself standing alone in the dense shade of the forest, her bare feet awkwardly atop an array of twisted roots. She whispered, "Señor Kapfre? You'll wait here?"

His only reply was a fresh waft of cigar smoke. Then she smelled the mouthwatering aromas of cook-fire smoke. She again heard voices, but they were too distant to make out. She crept toward them, staying low, her eyes on her feet and the uneven roots, so she wouldn't trip as she got closer to spy on these trespassers.

138

After a few steps, a man's voice shouted: "*Tigil!*"

She stopped and looked up.

An unshaven man holding a rifle across his body – one hand on the stock at his waist, the other on the barrel near his shoulder – blocked her way. He wore a loose cotton shirt, dark woolen trousers, and brown boots. His black, sweat-matted hair stuck to his tan forehead. He said, "Where you going with that bolo... boy?"

He spoke neither Spanish nor her native tongue, Ilocano, but Tagalog, a language from the south, from Manila. She knew enough to understand his words, but she wasn't sure why he smirked when he said "boy." Did he think she was a boy and was commenting on her youth? Or did he know she was really a girl?

She stood, rested a hand on her bolo knife's handle and said in Ilocano: "I'm here to keep the war out of my kapfre's forest."

"Kapfre?" He looked left and then right in a pantomime of a search. He shrugged. "And you're what? His bodyguard? Is he shy?"

She didn't like this man.

He rested the butt of his gun on the ground: "Tell me something, little man. Kapfre are magical, right? But all they do is sit around, smoke cigars, and play pranks? I mean, come on, doesn't that sound like something that came out of a lazy person's daydream?"

She narrowed her eyes.

The man with the gun said, "Your kapfre is a superstition, little man. But war? That's real. It's been real for years. And it's fought by men. So why don't you and your kapfre run along home." He pointed his chin to the forest behind her to send her on her way.

She didn't move. She said, "I'm not afraid of you."

"You're certainly a bold one."

"And you're a stupid Tagalog!" she said. "My kapfre showed me the smoke of your cook fires. He brought me here to check it out. Don't you think Yanquis can see the smoke, too?" She watched the smirking twinkle in his eyes fade into something hard and calculating.

But then, just as quickly, his expression changed: his brows lifted, his eyes widened, his mouth opened as if in wonder. He said, "Maybe you can help us. That is a fine looking bolo you have. May I see it?"

Disarmed by his sudden friendliness, she unsheathed the bolo and handed it to him.

"Oh, this is very nice," he said. He swung his rifle around so it hung by a leather strap on his shoulder. He examined the knife some more with both hands. "Solid. Good craftsmanship." He held the knife in one hand and, with the other, he reached around her and seized the back of her shirt. "Now, you will come with me." He pushed her onto a narrow path, released her shirt with a shove and said, "Keep walking, boy."

***

Thin, haggard men shuffled about or slumped against tree trunks or lay on the bare ground. Their vacant eyes stared at things she couldn't see. She saw bandages made of torn, filthy rags wrapped around heads, necks, shoulders, arms, torsos, legs. Here and there, small tents had been set up. From those came cries and wails of men in pain. Their air reeked of sweat and blood and something dark and pungent. She scrunched up her nose to stop it from penetrating her.

The soldier said, "Keep going, boy."

They walked beyond the wounded and dying, though a dense part of the forest and into a second clearing, where horses stood tied together. One rose taller than the rest, a stallion with such a deep, black coat and glossy mane that she couldn't stop herself from gaping.

"That," the soldier said, "is Father Aglipay's. And that is where you'll meet him."

She turned from the horse to see a large tent in the line of shade between forest and clearing. A cloud of uncertainty settled around her. Had the soldier said "father," as in a priest? He didn't mean a priest was leading this band of rebels?

The soldier said, "Tell me your name."

"My name is An" – she paused and decided to be the boy he thought she was – "Angelo Silang."

They stopped outside the heavy canvas tent, where the soldier spoke quickly in Tagalog to a guard. The guard stepped inside, and the soldier turned to her. "Don't be afraid," the soldier said. "Just tell Father what you told me."

She nodded, even as her confusion solidified with his saying "father" again. Priests, she knew, couldn't be trusted. They either came from Spain or sided with Spain, and then sided with Yanquis. Could this priest and these Tagalogs be on the side of the Yanquis and against the Filipinos? She reached for the comforting wood of her bolo handle, but of course it wasn't there.

The guard stepped out of the tent and held the flap open.

Inside, the warm, dim-lit space smelled like church. A dish of incense smoldered in a corner. Deeper inside, men hunched over a table. One was saying, "...surely, if our information is correct, that would be the only route."

Another said, "Thus making this the spot" – the table thunked as if hit by a fist – "to ambush them."

More men spoke, their voices rising over and through one another. One of the men turned from the table and looked at her.

She gasped.

The man's unruly hair stood tangled and unwashed above a high forehead and wide face. Uneven stubble littered his cheeks and neck. But what shocked her was his long, black cassock with a square of white collar showing, a wooden cross suspended by a chain around his neck. He had stern eyes and a serious mouth. His voice seemed to bark when he said, "Private?"

"Father," the soldier said, shoving her forward and knocking the floppy hat off her head. "This boy, Angelo Silang, claims a kapfre showed him our cook-fires."

The priest stepped forward and smiled at her.

140

All she could think to do was to follow tradition by taking the priest's hand, kissing the back of it, and raising it to her forehead.

The priest made the sign of the cross over her and, while still mumbling a prayer in Latin, rested a large hand on the tufts of hair on her head. The touch felt warm but only for a second.

The priest said, "Now, tell me child, is this true?"

"Sí, Padre," she said.

He nodded with downturned lips. He looked over her head then and said, "Private, please tell the cooks to douse the fires."

"Yes, sir." The soldier left, and he still had her bolo.

The priest picked up her hat and handed it to her. He said, "Your kapfre doesn't want war, I assume. Nobody wants war. But we are in a difficult situation, with our leader, General Aguinaldo, on the run."

She felt a bead of sweat roll down her forehead and drip to the ground. He seemed to be waiting for a response, but she had only ever said, "Sí, Padre," to the village priest, the one priest she knew. But this man had said the right thing. She knew the name General Aguinaldo. She had also heard adults call him Presidente Aguinaldo. He was the Tagalog man who led the rebels against the Spanish and now against the Yanquis.

The priest said, "Kapfre are known to be tricksters, my child. So how do you know your kapfre isn't tricking you?"

"I don't know," she said. "But I am wearing my shirt inside-out."

He laughed – "Ha! Ha!" – with deep, unexpected joy that reminded her of her kapfre. His laughter silenced the men at the table. "I see, yes, your shirt is to trick the trickster. Ha! And your hair, too. Did you chop it off to trick your trickster, my dear?"

She said, "My mother cut off my hair before she went to the market and disappeared. She did it in case Yanquis came to my barangay, so they would think I was a boy."

The men at the table stopped moving. Lines of pained worry spread across the priest's face. For a moment, it seemed as if no one in the tent was even breathing.

The priest nodded. He said, "My child. My child." He shook his head. "Now, if I showed you a map, could you tell me where you saw your kapfre?"

She said, "Sí, Padre."

He set a hand on her shoulder and led her to the table. The men stepped aside. Stretched over the entire surface was a map unlike any she had ever seen. She understood what was land and what was sea, but she didn't understand the dizzying array of squiggly, uneven circles within circles all over the land. Maps she had seen had squiggly lines to represent paths and roads that linked church, market, barangays, towns, and fields. It took her a long time to find her barangay, Torre, but she eventually found it after spotting the nearby barangays of Salugan and Lioes. From there, she traced her path through the tobacco fields and rice paddies and up into the forest. She tapped her index finger on that area. "This is where my kapfre lives."

Some of the men whispered, but the priest said, "I see. So how did you make it all the way from here to here?" He traced his finger from where she had pointed to a spot in the forest much farther north and inland than she expected, even beyond a big town – Batac – where she had never been.

"My kapfre brought me," she said. "Because we saw white smoke, and I didn't want to go to the scar."

The priest asked, "Scar?"

She nodded. "The place where all the trees were cut down."

"Can you point that out, too?" the priest asked.

She screwed up her eyes as she recalled seeing the scar and the smoke. The scar had been closer and to the left of the smoke, meaning on the map it was closer to the big town. With her finger, she circled a large area south of the town. "I think, maybe, around here."

The men drew closer, murmuring. She could feel the heat of their bodies and smell their sweat and cigarette smoke. In the murmurs, she heard the word *Yanqui* a few times.

"Thank you, my child," the priest said. He turned to the men. "Gentlemen, young Angela here has brought us useful information, but I don't think it changes our mission. Except now we know we are in a kapfre's forest, so you must order your men to wear their shirts inside out. That way, we won't be tricked. Dismissed."

"You." The soldier from before was back. He scowled as he spit out her real name, "Angela," letting her know he hadn't liked being lied to. Still, he returned her bolo to her and led her back outside and onto a different path. She saw his shirt was now inside out. They passed through some trees and into another clearing, which was rich with the scent of cook-fire smoke.

The soldier said, "I must return to my post, but Father wants you to–"

He may have kept talking, but she stopped listening once she saw a woman take a wet sheet from a basket, plant her feet a little more than shoulder-width apart and flick the sheet into the air with such swift force it unfurled with a snap and came to a rest neatly on a rope tied between two trees. She knew those moves.

***

"Mama!" she cried, running toward the washerwoman.

The woman stood and turned. Her long, dark skirt was wet, and brown stains – blood? – spotted her blouse, the one with the wide, elegant sleeves she wore on market days. She fell to her knees and opened wide her arms.

Angela ran into them, hugged her mother and breathed in her mother's rich, familiar scent, a musky combination of sweat and clean that Angela equated with strength. She said, "Mama, I found you! My kapfre helped me find you!"

Her mother pulled back and ran her eyes over her daughter, from floppy hat to soil-encrusted toes. "You silly girl." Her mother smiled then looked up at someone behind Angela.

"Excuse me, Doña Brigida," the soldier said. "Is she your child?"

"Yes," she said. "My Angela."

"Well, you should be proud. She made quite an impression on Father

Aglipay. Now, if you'll excuse me."

"Thank you," her mother said.

The soldier nodded to her and Angela and walked away.

Brigida said, "Did you eat the eggs I left? Even so, you must be hungry." She took Anegela's hand and walked her to a place not far away, where enormous kettles sat over the smoldering remains of once-strong fires. Men and women guarded the pots of cooked rice, dried fish, and water. Brigida got Angela a bowl of rice topped with dried fish.

Angela brought the bowl to her lips and scooped the food into her mouth with her fingers, barely chewing as she swallowed. She washed it down with water from her canteen.

Brigida said, "Now tell me what's going on."

They sat together on the ground and Angela recounted her morning. At times, she felt like she rambled and confused some events, but her mother didn't interrupt. Angela finished by asking, "What happend to you?"

Brigida told her a story about taking the chickens to the market, only to find that no one was there. Father Agliplay and his men had stormed the Yanqui garrison in town. So residents stayed at home, and market-sellers fled into the fields and forest. The Yanquis, though, with their rifles, repelled the attack. Brigida arrived to see countless men — men who worked the tobacco fields, fished the sea, or grew rice in the terraces — limp out of town, wounded and in desperate need of care. So she went with them, helping those she could as they retreated into the hills.

She said, "Listen carefully, Angela: Father Aglipay is a charismatic man, but he should be leading prayers, not battles. They think they have God on their side, even if they don't have enough rifles. Now he says he believes your kapfre story?" She shook her head. "Angela, dear, it is not safe here. You must go home."

"But Mama, I can help." As she said these words, she felt like the young girl she was, powerless and afraid.

"I know, of course, but you see Father Aglipay has angered the Yanquis. They want to get him, so being here is not safe. Our tiny barangay? They do not care about it. You can go home, cook rice, and eat. You can even buy some chicken or fish from Auntie Dungo. Do not ask for it; buy it. Money is hidden in a wooden box inside the rice jar. If you leave now, you will be home long before dark. You must go, my sweet, sweet Angela."

They embraced again, quicker this time.

Her mother wrapped more rice and dried fish in leaves and gave it to Angela. Then she straightened out her hat, the shoulder strap of her canteen, and the leather belt that held the bolo in its sheath at her waist. "Look at you, my little soldier. You came to rescue me, and my heart feels rescued, my strong warrior."

Angela slid the food into a pocket. Together, they walked through the encampment, as men with shirts on inside-out hurried to and fro.

***

Alone in the forest, Angela stopped walking when she smelled cigar smoke. "Señor Kapfre?"

He laughed low and deep. The tree shook. Leaves rustled. Then there he stood, a giant with a lit cigar clamped between his lips, one eye squinting to keep out smoke.

"Angela, you have to see this." He scooped her up again and set her on his shoulder. Together, they seemed to levitate to the top of the tree, where they swayed without falling. He pointed with pursed lips to a rolling cloud of smoke in the distance.

She asked, "Another fire?"

In response, he leapt from tree to tree to get closer. The air whooshed about her ears until they stopped atop a tree that stood high on a hill and afforded them a clearer view of the rolling clouds. It was dust kicked up from the march of men, mules and horses on a dirt road.

"Is this war?" he asked.

She didn't say anything at first. She saw two men on horseback, wide-brimmed hats shielding their faces, brass buttons glinting in the late-morning sun. With their straight backs, they appeared taller than any Filipino she had ever seen. Behind them, through the dust, she saw mules laden with canvas sacks and wooden boxes being led by men on foot in white shirt-sleeves, wide suspenders and dark trousers tucked into high, leather boots.

She said, "Those are Yanquis."

"In my forest?"

She remembered the map. "I think they're bringing supplies to the Yanquis who cut down your trees."

"My trees?" He sighed, weary and ancient. He looked away from the Yanquis, his deep eyes dark and contemplative.

She followed his gaze to the scar cut into his forest. She hadn't realized how close they were to it, or how wide it was, or how deeply it penetrated the woods. The Yanquis would soon march past a dark, narrow track that led into the scar, which was pockmarked by the stumps of once-magnificent balete trees. She now knew that these Yanquis were the next mission, the ambush. But the Yanquis carried rifles. Every one of them. She had seen very few rifles among Father's men. Most wielded spears or bolo knives like the one at her side.

She said, "We must do something."

"We?" her kapfre said.

She sighed. "You. You must trick them. Make them get lost in the scar."

He laughed with a depth she had never heard before, a low chuckle mixed with a thin, echoing wheeze. It shot a dark tingle of fear up her spine that spread across the back of her neck. The chill deepened when she realized she, too, was laughing: "*Heh, heh, heh.*"

Her kapfre raised his hands to his mouth and made a knocking noise, like a woodpecker at work. Then he lifted his hands in the air and waved them in circles. A gust of strong wind blew down the road, clearing the dust long enough for her to see the paleness of the skin on the Yanquis' faces. The wind kicked up, and the Yanquis raised their hands to screen their eyes.

Her kapfre's hands kept moving. Leaves rustled and the impossible happened: the trees danced. High branches twirled in air like dancers' hands, while the trees swayed and sashayed in quick, short, rhythmic steps, changing the shape of the forest.

The wind settled. What was once road was now forest; the once-narrow track now a wide road leading into the scar. The forest all around had become thicker, darker and seemingly impenetrable, as if all the trees had crowded together to see what would happen next.

She said, "You did it!" She wrapped her thin arms around the kapfre's thick neck, feeling the scratches from his bristly beard and inhaling cigar smoke and something deeper, a wild-animal scent.

"So I did." He nodded.

She released him. "Now we have to go back, back to the rebels."

He didn't answer right away; she saw something different in his eyes, a more-intense light but also a new kind of weariness, or maybe even pain. Had his magic worn him out?

She said, "Señor, are you all right?"

His eyes stayed on the Yanqui horse riders as they wiped wind-blown dust from their eyes. He said, "We can't miss the best part: when they realize they are lost."

"Por favor?"

He looked from the approaching men and mules to her. A sadness lingered in his gaze.

She said, "Please?"

This time, he smiled and said, "Hold on!" He shoved his cigar back between his lips and leapt backward with such force and speed that she shrieked as she wrapped her arms tight around his neck again. The air roared in her ears, and she lost all focus on what was tree, earth, and sky. She tried to speak, but gusts filled her mouth and silenced her. Then everything stopped. He smiled, winked and – in a blink – she found herself standing on tree roots again.

She shouted up to him: "Wait for me!"

He responded with a cloud of cigar smoke.

***

"You again?" The soldier from before stood there again, rifle at the ready.

"They're going the wrong way," she said.

He said, "What?"

She dodged around him and ran back along the path that led past the wounded men in one clearing and into the second. This time, though, the clearing was filled with men standing with spears or bolos in hand, waiting. A handful of men sat atop horses. She caught a flash of black of Father Agliplay's cassock and horse. She ran toward him, ignoring the men who called out "Hey!" or "What are you doing?" or "Stop!"

She shouted, "Padre! Padre!"

The priest looked down at her. His placid face showed no recognition at first, then his eyes widened. His horse whinnied and pulled, but the priest reined it in. He said, "To what do I owe the pleasure, young lady?"

She paused. She felt small, looking up at the priest on his horse. She shouted: "You won't find the Yanquis where you expect!"

"What?"

She repeated herself, this time louder. The priest's horse even turned its massive head in her direction. She said, "¡Hola, Señor caballo!'

The priest said, "Your kapfre said this?"

"I saw them myself," she shouted, wishing her kapfre would just show up and explain it all. She noticed the dark skin of the priest's neck in the spot where the white of his collar should've been. She didn't see the buttons of his cassock or his cross. He wore his vestments inside out.

She said, "I can point on the map. They aren't on the road anymore."

The priest just stared at her.

She aimed her mouth toward the treetops and shouted, "Señor Kapfre!"

Then she heard her mother. "Angela?"

The girl spun around. A crowd of silent, grim-faced men holding blades stared at her.

"Angela?" Brigida called again and then once more before she pushed through the men and stood there, shorter than the men, but with lips pressed tight together, brows furrowed, the skin on her face red.

Angela felt the heat of her mother's anger as she hovered over her.

"I told you to go home."

"Mama..." Angela began.

"These men," Brigida said, gesturing with laundry-wet arms to those around her, "don't need you in the way."

"But..." She looked around, watched a dirty, calloused hand tightening its grip on a bolo handle, then loosening it and tightening it again. She thought of her father and how these men were ready to die.

Her mother knelt before her, wrapped her in her wet arms and whispered, "You silly, silly girl."

She held her mother tight. Tears welled in her eyes. This felt more real to her than anything at all. Had everything been some kind of mad dream? What if her kapfre had never been real at all? She wanted to stay in her mother's embrace.

A rider galloped into the clearing, shouting, "Padre! Padre! The Yanquis aren't there!"

The priest slid gracefully from his saddle and said, "Please excuse me, Mama." He set his hand behind Angela's back. "Now, child, you will show me on the map." They quick-stepped into the tent, where she told him and the other men all she had seen.

***

She watched from her kapfre's shoulder high in a tree as Yanquis shouted at the animals and each other with harsh, angry voices, and stubborn mules brayed and cried and stood their ground. Some Yanquis even whipped the mules to get them to turn around, while other men and mules continued to march forward, tripping and stumbling over roots and stumps.

Even though she knew what Father Aglipay and his men were going to do, she still gasped as they stepped out of the dark forest and into the clearing. The change from their non-presence to presence was so sudden and so complete that they seemed to appear as if peeled from the bark of tree trunks.

Some Yanquis gasped, too. Others let out startled moans. Some stepped back from the forest's edge. Most went silent. None raised a weapon. None had time. In an instant, the tall, well-armed Yanquis had become surrounded, trapped by a group of rebels in tattered clothes wielding farm and fishing tools.

The most startling image of all, though, was of Father Aglipay astride his huge, black horse. With sword pointed, he slow-walked his mount toward a Yanqui officer. The blade extending from his arm was pointed like an accusatory finger.

The Yanqui showed neither fear nor surprise. Instead, he kept his cold, hard eyes on the approaching blade as he took one hand off his reins and lifted a whistle to his lips. He blew three shrill blasts. The Yanquis quieted; some of the mules still brayed, though most – no longer being herded – had quieted, too.

The Yanqui said something to the priest.

Father responded with a shout: "Viva la Independencia Filipina!"

A deafening roar rose up from the rebels. They took the Yanquis' rifles, whips, pistols, bayonets and swords. The exhausted, defeated Yanquis didn't raise a hand.

The Filipinos shouted and cheered again.

A warmth spread through her body.

"Ha! Ha!" her kapfre laughed. "Got them!"

Again, the kapfre called to the trees, waved his hands, and rustled up a strong, swift breeze. The men in the scar – Yanquis and Filipinos alike – covered their eyes at the sudden swirls of twigs, leaves, and dust. They didn't see the trees dancing again as they opened a path back to the encampment. When the wind calmed, Father Agiplay shouted his orders and led men, mules and prisoners through the just-created track.

Her kapfre said, "Look, my Angela! The war is leaving our forest."

She smiled.

"Now we can live in peace, yes? Ha! Ha!"

The thrilling charge of victory filled her with a heady lightness. Even she couldn't believe what had just happened, what she had done.

Her kapfre couldn't contain his delight. A giddy laughter spread through him; his entire body quaked. He said, "Now I will make a home for you in the trees!"

"Oh, Señor," she said. "You know I must return to my mama."

He frowned and his shoulders drooped into a slouch. In that gesture, she saw this magical creature as nothing more than a spoiled boy.

"I belong with my mama, with my people."

He didn't say anything for a while. He closed his eyes, and his breathing slowed and deepened. Though she had once taken comfort in his deep, steady breaths, and even though his silence seemed petulant, she couldn't help but feel a wave of heartbreaking sadness.

He opened his ancient eyes and stared at her.

She saw something unexpected beyond the reflection of herself staring at him, a flicker of light and mirth.

She had never felt so important or so complete. Then he smiled and winked and she was left standing at the base of a balete tree, a fresh breeze scented by the sweet familiarity of cigar smoke nudging her away, back toward her mother.

Art by Sasha Gallagher

THE COLTS
BENJAMIN PARZYBOK

1514
Hungary

It was a warm April Saturday. We sat on the top rail of a fence overlooking the king's pasture, where the new colts were trying out their legs. Andrzej, Istvan, and I were dead veterans of the kuruc revolt (or was it the kuruc crusades?), buried a week or so earlier, risen up only recently.

"Do you think the brown will live the season?" I asked.

"No," Istvan spat and left an earthy-red stain on the grass. "Its knees — *no* — too weak. It has the fever."

In a vague gesture, Andrzej held his big hand out toward it and paused, as if searching for the perfect word. How it makes one's heart tender, to see such fragile things. "*Gar*," he said finally.

We watched the filly in silence as it struggled to its knees. One leg collapsed under it and it went to the ground, panting. It made me sad, to watch it struggle so.

I wanted the horse to live. I felt like I had a stake in it. She was a soft thing and I was half-tempted to walk out and bring her to her feet. But we'd learned we had an effect on animals. Best to keep my distance, for her sake.

"That new girl," I said. "She's a master with the sick horses. Like witchcraft. She'll come."

"*No*," Istvan said, and then said it again. "She won't be able to do anything for it."

We sat and watched a bit more and I thought of Anelie, my sister-in-law. Though I was unsure what relation she was to me now.

She would be at home in the village, mourning, perhaps mourning me. The longing to see her burned in me like some unnatural flame. They had taken my niece and nephew, burned my brother at the stake after his conversion, and my father had followed my mother into the grave, his heart unable to take the blows dealt it.

Anelie was the only family I had left, and she and I had taken refuge in each other. The memory of a single night was wedged in me still, like a chunk of stone in my chest.

The field had greened seemingly overnight. When I'd died, the world had been brown with the remnants of winter, and now in this strange return it too was reborn into spring.

To my right Andrzej began humming György's battle march, and we all joined in:

Over the fields
They're ours again!
Through the woods
We claim as ours!
Castles we storm
Throw the devils out!
Kuruc come see
Your shining country!

It was about here I realized I was the only one really singing the words. Istvan sang: *No the fields, no no!* And Andrzej, with his wonderfully deep singing voice, sang what sounded like: *rah gna gra, gah nu rah!* I began to lower my voice, conscious of the racket we were making and a little embarrassed for them, and they elbowed me to keep going. I redoubled my efforts but then stared into the grass afterwards, unsure of what to say. We awkwardly chose separate areas of the field to study. My friends, they were not well.

After a while Istvan cleared his throat and said "Oh *no*," and Andrzej pointed across the field and made a soft sound, like the monkey I'd seen in Transylvania.

The horse trainers were coming in. Too far away to worry about much, but I noted the gleam of armor. One of them was not a kuruc. We watched him eagerly.

I patted each of their knees – not liking much the way my hands looked, to be honest, so pale they were nearly blue, the wounds I'd been given there unhealed – and moved to the opposite side of the fence. When we were settled Andrzej grunted in a soft, thoughtful way and I understood what he meant. If there was eating to be had, a nobleman would make a fitting target.

It came to me with suddenness what we were. I'd spent near my whole life, twenty-four years, in the smith trade, under tutelage of my father, but in the last year I'd been so many different things I could hardly keep track. Soldier, rebel, consort, criminal, martyr, and now? A hunter.

We'd been soldiers together. Recruited to fight in the crusades against Islam, us kurucs, farmers and workers of Hungary. What did we know about swords? (As the son of a blacksmith I'd held a lot more swords than most. Against a wooden post I was deadly.) For that matter, what did we care about Islam?

None of us wanted to go. But the nobles' men circled on their horses, with threats and harassment. It was hardly like any of us could get out of it. Andrzej was whipped; my father's hand was broken in trying to stop them. After Istvan refused the first time, his wife, Erzsébet, was taken and he never saw her again.

"*No*," Istvan said. He sighed heavily and stared at the grass between his legs.

Out in the field the noble dismounted and approached a stallion, whose bridle was held by a kuruc.

"Shouldn't have armor on," Istvan said, "not to break it."

The horse breakers were probably all dead, I thought.

The noble tried a running leap but the horse deftly sidestepped and the momentum of the man took him to the ground. Andrzej chuckled appreciatively at the folly and we all sat up a bit straighter, feeling a maddening hunger inside us.

"We make a bet," Istvan said. "For your finger." He pointed into the field.

"Whether he rides?" I said.

"No. He does not ride."

"You bet that he cannot ride, and I'm to bet that he can?" I sighed and stared down at my wretched-looking fingers. This was certainly my own doing. In a moment of marvel at our weird condition earlier I'd bet Istvan a finger, and upon having won it, I pulled it off with a satisfying pop, to our mutual horror. I'd held it in my hand, wondering what one ought to do with such a prize. He asked for it back, and I agreed with relief. He spent some time pushing it here and there on his knuckle in an attempt to reattach it. *"No, no, no,"* he'd said with each attempt, as if going through a checklist of possible locations it might fit. He kept the thing in his pocket now.

The honorable thing to do was to take the same bet.

With misgivings, I held up my pinky. "We bet on this one. We'll give him until the sun reaches there." I pointed. "If I win, I ask a favor concerning..." I didn't finish. He knew what I asked. He considered for a moment and then nodded. I had gone on about it at length, and they had seen me tortuously scrawl out the letter to Anelie in my crude writing, asking after their opinions on phrasing until they'd tired of me. "We have a bet?"

"No," he said and stared at me.

I tried to understand his objection. Had he not just suggested the bet? "By no, you mean actually to say yes?"

He nodded and I could see it pained him. Out of old habit we looked down at our hands as if preparing to shake, but neither of us really cared to. It seemed a habit that belonged to the living.

The knight was patiently attended to by his servants. In the air, I got a whiff of them. Meat. And though we were far, I suspected I knew who he was. My father and I often took special requests from the lords. A hundred candelabra, three hundred hooks for the hanging of what I wasn't sure, chains of a certain style. Armor, weapons, and devices of torture; dark, evil things we could hardly refuse to make, or we risked having them applied to us.

General György Dózsa would have enjoyed watching the knight lose against the stallion. He was appointed to lead us kurucs in our new crusade against the Ottomans, but when they armed us with so little, and with no provisions, and harassed our families and took our lands, and we began to starve before we'd even left, György's temper flamed hot, and his temper was to be feared. He raged against the nobles, asking for their help, telling them they were sending us to our death. Finally, in a speech to his army I hope to never forget, he suggested that perhaps the enemy was not Islam, but here in front of us. For all who heard, it would have been hard to argue otherwise if a grain of sense he had in him. And so we warred against our own country, for the farmer and the kitchen maid, for the horse trainer and the stone mason. We rose up nearly a hundred thousand strong. Granted, we were inexperienced, but we were successful at first. Under György's leadership we took half of Hungary back.

We rose up together, and now some of us had risen up again. I wondered if György was among us. Revenge would have mattered greatly to him. Honestly – and I tried to push the images from my mind – I'm not sure there would have been enough left of him after what they did to him: forcing him naked onto a smoldering throne, crowning him with a molten crown, in his hands a burning scepter. When his flesh was cooked, the nobles brought in a few soldiers they'd starved, to eat of him while he still lived or else be cut to pieces themselves.

I spent a moment with my own hunger. Out afield, the nobleman's brain made a few more poor decisions. We were patient. We had all the time on Earth.

I whispered "*Yes*" in Istvan's direction and then pretended to stare deep into the field, as if the word had materialized out there.

"*No!*" Istvan said, and slammed his fist into the ground.

"*Yes*," I whispered again and Andrzej gave a chuckle, watching our friend glare. With my brother's young children I had been a terrible tease, they who had held on to such tiny and powerful opinions. While they slept, I had told them, the grass became the bearded face of a giant, the huts warts upon his face. And he roamed about the land eating stars from the sky. The youngest had lapsed into a comatose stare and the oldest screamed an ecstatic "*No!*" with such persuasion that I had to reassure my sister-in-law. It was best, now, not to think of them, my niece and nephew, but it was difficult not to.

"I have to go. I have to see Anelie," I said, feeling in my chest a terrible pull. I stood and started toward the village, but Andrzej ran after me and caught hold of my arm and held me in place. I tried to jerk away but he was strong. We stared at each other and I could see he felt sorry for me. He pointed out into the field, and I saw our prey there and remembered and hung my head.

We settled back into the grass to watch. The knight fell from the horse again in a loud clatter and for a moment did not move. After another try he gave up and let one of his peasants continue on with the work. Istvan and I immediately fell into debate about what that meant for our bet.

Our conversation got heated. Me arguing my defense: he had time yet! Istvan growling *No*, and reaching for my finger. Before long we looked up to see we'd been noticed.

The knight mounted his own steed and began to trot toward us in a wary fashion, his bow at ready.

Per our plan, Istvan and Andrzej hid, and I walked toward the forest, glancing backwards to see him coming on. He was shouting at me to stop. The smell of the living grew strong as he approached, and I was hungry for it.

When he was 20 yards away, I loped. I felt a punch to my rear that sent me sprawling forward into the grass. I turned to rise but had trouble, my movement constricted by the arrow embedded in my right buttock. I was shot! The knight's horse reared over the top of me and through his visor I saw the look of horror on the man's face. He drew his sword and dismounted and raised it over his head. I turned aside just as it came down and scrabbled toward him, and then Istvan and Andrzej were on him, pulling him to the ground. He began to scream in a way we later tried to imitate, as if it were the funniest of jokes. There was so little time between screams that he exhausted all the air in his lungs and the screams piled on top of each other in a hoarse syncopation. Meanwhile, his horse bolted and I concerned myself with the arrow.

It caused no feeling. It seems absurd to say that I miss pain. I experienced more than enough of it in my life, especially at the end. But still: what clearer sign of living is pain? Now there was an arrow in my rear and it was an impediment to sitting, nothing more. I couldn't loose it from the flesh, so I borrowed the knight's sword and sawed the shaft short and joined the others.

They had removed his armor and were having a go at him. I stared at his face. "Is it him?" I said. But I couldn't get either of their attention. They all looked like torturers in the end, and there had been many.

We were quiet for a while after Istvan removed the skull cap. The peasants, so recently from the wrong side of the war themselves, did not come looking for their noble, whom they'd surely seen fall.

After a long while, Andrzej looked up from the handful of brain meat in his hand. "*Gnar*," he uttered. It was profoundly said. I nodded and Istvan agreed *No*. Surveying what we'd done, the fallen knight before us. His skull opened. In our hands this. "Look at who we are!" Andrzej meant, and "Look at what we've done! Our enemy here slain, dressed full for battle." And but "Oh God, what have we done?" And "How is *this* so enjoyable?"

"*Nar*," I replied in kind, and smiled. A grotesque sight, I'm sure.

But after a few more moments, an unbidden and lovely image of Anelie came into my mind again, how I'd seen her once with her head on her pillow, the soft arc of her naked shoulder, the childhood scar along her calf that made me love her so. And I saw myself through her eyes: ravaged and bent over and gnawing on a dead body, and the horror of her witnessing my state caused me to leap up and fall backward into the grass. I shoved my face down into the weeds there and moaned. She would be repulsed by me. She would loathe what I'd become. I would starve myself. I would do anything.

But after some moments of this show I felt a hand on each of my ankles, and my friends pulled me back. Andrezj motioned to the knight's leg and showed me there was a bit of brain they'd saved, considerate friends. And I was so hungry.

***

When we'd finished, Istvan pointed at my finger.

"Sorry, my friend," I said. "We did not give him a chance to settle our bet."

"*No*," Istvan said, and gestured for it.

I turned to Andrzej, who had reclined into the grass and had a peaceful,

155

dazed look in his eyes. "Andrzej, you must settle this."

He waved lazily at us, indicating he was above such petty wagers. But we were insistent and camped over him, waiting for his decision. Finally, with his great furry fist he indicated to us how the knight had ridden after all, albeit on his own horse.

I suddenly had a memory of this man, my friend Andrzej. In battle he bore a great double-sided axe. A poor pig farmer transformed into a giant who reigned over the field. A man who, when asked, always used to be ready with a line of wisdom, and many had sought him out for it. When the king's troops finally got the better of us, he did not run like the others but stood against them like a boulder in a stream and fought.

"A good point!" I said. "The knight rode!"

"No. That's not what – no!" Istvan kicked the fallen knight's booted foot. After a while, he thoughtfully replaced his own worn shoes with the knight's boots and it seemed like such a good idea that Andrzej and I followed suit. At the end of it, our appearance had improved, though that's not saying much. The knight, it should be said, looked a bit poorly, naked and eaten of, his armor scattered about him like the shell of an egg.

Then we were back to a sort of beginning, though much livened-up. What to do with ourselves? There were the colts to watch. There was Anelie to think on. There was a hunger we knew would rise again within us. We lay in the grass and stared deep into the blue sky.

The thoughts that tinkered away in my brain seemed some weird residue of the living that had leaked from my friends. A leftover artifact. I feared it was only a matter of time before these thoughts were replaced by some single track of my own, a bit of repetition my brain could not jar itself away from.

I had to go see Anelie.

What haunted her, surely, were her dead. It seemed only moments ago that we had kissed, she and I, in the wake of the destruction of everything. When we were the last survivors of our kin, my brother long dead, both of our families done in by the war. I'd stood as a soldier in her house before the last battle, and she'd taken me into her bed and we had cried there and more. After, when I fought, when I was captured and cut, when I saw György die, inside of me a fountain gushed. What haunts the dead is the living.

"Come on," I said suddenly.

We walked over the hill, wary as we went to keep from view, and then down into the valley where the village lay.

When we got near town, we detoured by the cemetery. My grave was there and there was something in me that felt a little fondness for it. It was a comfort. We followed Andrzej until he stopped at another grave and went to his knees in front of it. It was György Dózsa's. It was undisturbed still, and so we knew he was taking the long rest. Andrzej made a hollow sob-like sound and then went quiet. I plucked a handful of grass and leaned it against the humble stone. Istvan said "No." Our bodies had been thrown in the river – General Dózsa's too – but the villagers recovered them and gave us proper burials.

Before he died, I remember the calm in Dózsa's eyes. How he spoke in a voice that did not show the pain. He told his tormentors, with us there to witness, that each rebellion they crushed would rise again, and again, until the nobles were driven from the land. At the time it seemed a far-fetched thing to say.

We would do right by him, even if we ate them one by one.

***

We waited in the cemetery until dark. In the pocket of the noble's cloak I found a gold piece. A pocket! What an odd invention. Made for those who have need of carrying things about. I took to flipping the coin and Istvan and Andrzej stood looking on in stony amazement, all of us eager to see which side would come up. Tails, heads, heads, heads, heads, tails. Who decided these things?

For Anelie I would be like an angel, vengeful and terrible. Except, I thought, looking down again at my awful hands, very much different. I wanted to see her.

In town we ambled from shadow to shadow. The village was reduced, what with so many martyrs having floated in its river. What could I buy with a gold coin? The only thing I wanted was Anelie's happiness. Our happiness together.

We hovered about outside her hut. It was quiet, but there was a dim light within. Through the small windowpane my brother had installed before the poverty, I saw her sitting. She stared toward me, which gave me a start. She could not see me for the reflection on the glass.

From tucked inside my clothes, against my dead skin, I pulled the letter I'd written her. If Istvan delivered it, he would give weight to it, as she had known him living too. I could not bear to have her see me. I unfolded it and stared at the scrawl. She could not read, but she would find someone who could, and in that there was a complication too. My hands shook as I held it, and then I felt the weight of a hand on each of my shoulders.

No, Istvan said softly. Andrzej shook his head and squeezed my shoulder, and then held out his hand for the note.

I clutched it fiercely and pushed them back and we scuffled there. I would not hunger for her, I would not! We were all we had left, each other. But they finally got through to me. She did not have me. I was not myself. They were right. It was a fantasy.

To give the letter up was a terrible pain, like nothing I remembered at my tormentor's hands, a scooping out from inside me, and for a moment I had trouble standing. Andrzej put the letter in his own pocket. They were right, wise friends. The living do not wish to hear from the dead, not like this.

Instead I stared at her through the window, and Andrzej and Istvan came to the glass and looked in too. Her head was free of its scarf, and her hair pooled on her shoulders. I could see the enchanting outline of her bosom under her linen smock. In her hand she held my nephew's cap. I moaned softly, unable to keep the sound within me. Andrzej put his big paw on my shoulder, and we stayed like that, looking in, me murmuring, until she finally must

157

have heard something and looked toward us with alarm.

I hastily leaned the gold coin against the window sill, and then we bolted, loping through the streets. I was only vaguely aware of the sound that seemed to be issuing from me.

When we got back to the cemetery I ferociously clawed my way back into my own grave, Istvan standing over me saying "No, no." I could hear them about up there for some time as I lay down there in the dark, the earth pressed in comfortingly against me.

I had always believed that what I feared most about death was that I would not hear how the story ended. How my kin fared. But in the end, perhaps it is not worth knowing these things. Perhaps the best tales are only half-told. I wished my tale had ended when I'd fibbed to my niece and nephew, myself eaten up by a grass-faced giant. Or when Anelie had pulled me into her bedroom, resting her lips against my neck, already wet with her tears.

But after a long while of sorting myself out, I hungered more and was a little bored and decided to come out. They were glad to see me, in the dim light before dawn. Istvan, with a surprising quickness, snatched my left wrist and held it up for inspection. My ring finger was missing! I stared at my hand with horror. The clawing scrabble down to my grave had been hard work, and I suspected it had become dislodged somehow. I kicked around in the dirt looking for it, but found nothing but worms.

"No," Istvan said, and by that it was quite obvious what he meant: "Yes! Yes, we are brothers in arms! We are united! Yes!" He held his hand up next to mine, and I heard Andrzej's low chuckle in the background.

"All right," I said, but the words didn't sound right in my mouth. "Come on."

It would be dawn soon. We turned and headed back toward the castle. When the sun came up, the colts would run in the field again, and we wanted to be there to watch.

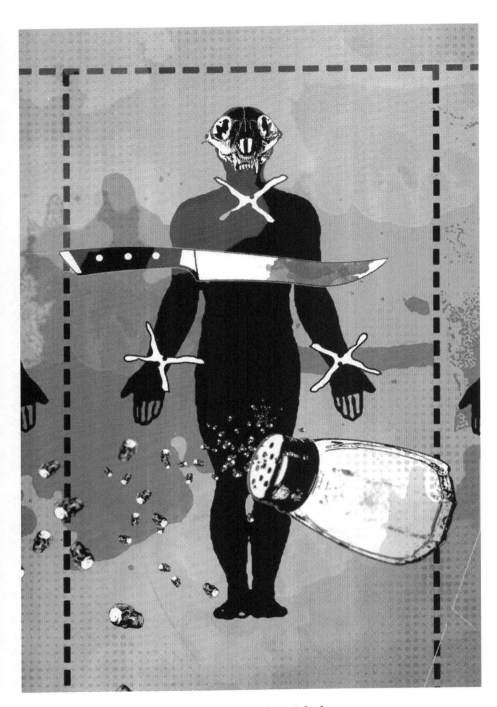

Art by GMB Chomichuk

NINE
KIMA JONES

1902
Phoenix, Arizona

Friday

Tanner named the motel Star Motel because calling the place North Star Motel would've been asking for it. Colored folks recognized that "star" and the little lights Jessie insisted they burn in the windows. Most of their customers were hungry, travel-weary young men who did not believe the VACANCY sign as they approached the motel and did not believe that Tanner, round as a dishpan, wide as the door, was its owner. None of them had the nerve to ask her if she was a man or a woman, but she saw their longways looks anytime she entered a room. They never stayed more than a night or two and spent most of that time asleep. Tanner checked them in at $1.25 a night on weekdays and $2.00 on weekends. She never shamed anyone for not having the full fee and would accept three quarters and a "thank you kindly."

"Get up, Tanner, sounds like the iceman is here. Last time he didn't ring the bell and most of the ice melted all over the porch. We don't have money to waste, and I can't stretch half a block of ice for a whole week." Jessie was sitting up in bed, her breasts and collarbone soaking in the day's first light. "I said go on and get the ice. The Campbells are checking out this morning, and Flo needs to get breakfast out to them by nine."

"If you run me out this bed one more time, woman, you're going to know it."

"Ain't nobody running you, just go get the ice. You can come back to bed after. Oh, and feed Rinny!"

Tanner knew Jessie was lying, but she got out of the bed anyway. By the time Tanner got the ice into the icebox and came back to their bedroom, Jessie would be halfway dressed, talking about the ledgers and dividing the day's work between them. Best to go get the ice and start the day.

The ice was melting when Tanner reached the porch, but not enough to make Jessie have a fit. The iceman slipped everybody's blocks into their iceboxes. Except for colored people. He left their ice sitting outside, anywhere, in dirt or sand or on a dusty porch. Tanner poured hot water down the block and quickly lifted it inside of the wooden box. Didn't make no sense to tip the iceman but Jessie tipped him every delivery. "He don't have to come out here, Tanner. Ain't like we can leave to go into town and get it," she would say.

Tanner headed back into the house and to the bedroom she shared with Jessie. "Mr. Campbell say what time they'd be heading out?" Jessie stood

161

wearing a white blouse and ankle length skirt, her brown leather ankle boo-
ties tied tightly. "He wants an early start on the road. Almost fifteen hundred
miles between here and Seattle. He thinks they could be there by this time
tomorrow."

Tanner grunted. Could be. She'd tried to talk some sense into Mr. Campbell the night before, but he was determined to make it his way. Tanner
thought it would be better for them to stop somewhere in California for a few
days and then head back to the road. Maybe leave his wife and newborn in
San Francisco for a week or two and then send for them later. But Campbell
wouldn't hear of it. Said he was driving straight through, driving even if his
eyeballs went bloodshot and burst through his head. "Give me the rundown,
baby," Tanner said to Jessie as she pulled her work trousers over her belly
and bent to cuff them.

"Did you feed Rinny?"

"Yes, I fed Rinny, now give me the rundown."

"Well, Campbell's checking out this morning. That'll leave us empty for
the weekend, which is good because we're sure to fill up the singles." Tanner
nodded. Single people always ran off the job on Fridays, soon as the boss paid
them. By Monday morning they were long gone and so far on their way north
or west it didn't make sense to send Klan after their families. They were just
gone. "Flo is getting started on the weekend menu, and I'm waiting for a cigarette delivery and the bread delivery. Me and Flo will get the parlor ready for
this evening. I'll air out the singles and Newt will sweep them. All you need to
do is change the oil on the Campbells' car and check the tires and whatnot.
Maybe wash down the sides of the house."

The house was peach-colored with a brown roof and sat a quarter of a
mile from the highway. Travellers could see the Star's marquee from the road
whether on foot or automobile. The marquee was its own detached, two-
pronged structure painted in mint green and white and lit up every night at
9:00 p.m. The house's front room served as the motel's lobby, stripped of all
furniture save an upright and uncomfortable sofa, two wing chairs, a wall
clock, and a small lobby desk with a silver bell. Tanner kept a wide black
leather barstool behind the desk to sit on when her knee acted up. All other
times, she preferred to greet her guests standing. The single rooms stood in a
row of six to the left of the house. The doubles, another six, off to the right.
The only formal place to stay for colored folks headed west on the lonely, desert highway.

It was Flo who came up with the idea of having jook nights on Fridays
for the locals and travelers alike. Black folks were starting to stay in Phoenix
to make a home and needed a place to go on the weekends. Friday nights at
the Star Motel were for card playing, thigh slapping, and smoky mingling.
Tanner hated the idea at first. She needed to keep her family safe and didn't
want all of colored Phoenix in their parlor room on Friday nights, but the
women were lonely. Flo complained of never having company and Jessie did-
n't have to open her mouth for Tanner to know she was cross about it all.

Flo was one of Tanner's first guests. Flo arrived with a belly brimming
over its due date. Tanner knew the kinds of things that would make a woman

run, pregnant and all, out of the swamps of Florida. They never spoke about it or how Flo found the place. She was flat out with her intentions when she checked in that night. "I can cook. If you let me stay on until my baby big enough, I'll be your cook. I used to cook lunches for the orange pickers and deliver them in my truck. I can cook anything, and I can kill anything." After Flora went into labor, she named the boy Newt, half because Tanner slipped on birth water running over trying to catch him out of the birth canal and half because he kind of looked like one.

Jook night at Star Motel started at 9, but folks trickled in around 10:30. It gave Flora and Jessie time to change, time to tuck Newt in, time to perfume behind the neck, time to cast their muscled legs in nylon. The women always wore all black, including Tanner. That was the rule, everybody in something bright. Other rule was no outside food and no outside liquor. Tanner played the doorman and Jessie worked the bar. Flo managed the kitchen, bringing plates out to the cards players and collecting tips in her bosom. Flo wore a deep, matte red lipstick but kept her fingernails short and bare. "Can't cook with that shit on my hands," she'd say and wink at whatever woman was questioning her manicure. The manicure-questioning woman always knew Flo's reputation: she could outlast a man, she took her time, she could cook, and she didn't lie. Flo was thickset, with an impressively square jaw and roundish eyes. She openly bedded other women; the few nights a month she spent with Tanner were in one of the single rooms.

Tanner stood at the front door of the house, on the porch, collecting the dollar fee it cost to get in. "Order your plates with Flo," she said, "All plates from Miss Flora. All booze from Jessie." The parlor was lit just enough to see a card hand but barely enough to see if you were putting your fork in meat or vegetables. As soon as the brass band started up, Jessie rattled her tambourine. She bounced it off of her hip and then smacked it into her open hand. Her feet moved in time, and her hair wagged back and forth on her head with every tambourine slap. They would bring in an easy three or four hundred dollars between the food and hooch and card games. They split the income evenly and saved for their future plans. Jessie was going to Los Angeles, Miss Flora was sending Newt to Howard, and Tanner would open another motel.

Hours of dancing passed on top of hours of drinking and the night wound down. Couples were filing out on foot, holding each other up. Tanner walked over to each spades and craps table and announced that it was closing time in ten minutes. "Last bets for the night. Make them count." A hand reached out for Tanner's and caught her at the wrist. Tanner looked down at her hand and over to the arm holding hers. "Can I help you with something, sir?" She was used to the belligerent drunk from time to time and escorted them to the front yard to sober up. Come morning, they'd be gone and ashamed. This man's front tooth was as gold as his watch, and he smiled big as payday, not a whiff of alcohol on him. His suit was a butter yellow and his white shoes were unscuffed. There was no dust on them either. He was a good foot and a half taller than Tanner and his reach, she estimated, twice that of hers. "I think maybe you can help me, ma'am. I'm looking for a missing person. Any information you could fetch me would sure be a nice gesture on the part of you and yours. Name is Tanner Harris, wanted dead or alive. Ring any bells for you ma'am?" The man's grin faded as he whispered through his teeth, "Maybe you want to be clearing the party on out of here so we can settle this. You got a debt to pay, girl."

Flora, never missing a thing, hit the lights. "All right now, y'all heard Tanner. Jook's closed. Next week, same time, same place." She moved from table to table pointing folks to the way out. Some of the drunk ones begged a dance from her, and she chided them, "Go on, now. Go on, I said." The last patrons bid farewell to Jessie and promised to be back. Jessie thanked them for coming and walked them to the front porch. Tanner stayed in the parlor with the gold-toothed man. When Jessie returned to the parlor, Flora headed in a quick scramble for the kitchen door. "Come on over here and take a seat," the gold-toothed man said. He kept his hand wrapped tightly around Tanner's wrist and had a smile on his face as she sat. Flora returned to the parlor with a gun pointed at the back of her head. The man had not come alone. His companion was thin, with a face slender as toilet plumbing. He wiped his mouth with the back of his hand and nudged Flora forward with the gun. "This one here was reaching for this gun, boss." The gold-toothed man looked over at Flora and smiled at Tanner. "Tanner love a talented woman, don't you Tanner? I'll be damned. I come to talk to you and your girlfriend here want to shoot me down."

The gold-toothed man let go of Tanner's wrist and draped an arm around her shoulders. Tanner looked over to Flo, but she ignored the gaze. Flo pushed back on the mouth of the gun, putting weight on her captor's arm. Jessie was still sitting at a table, weaponless and remote. Jessie was good at disappearing inside of herself. The gold-toothed man cleared his throat, making a show of himself. "Seems to me like we have us a problem here. See, I only need Tanner, but it don't seem like you girls gonna let me leave here with what I need. Second problem is I know either one or two of you bitches helped this fat nigger kill off all my brothers. I'm no adding man, but that's simple enough math to me." Droplets of sweat populated his upper lip as he talked. "Except Maud can count and do. Eight dead boys divided by three living niggers ain't enough change at all."

"Speak plain, if you come to speak. Kill if you come to kill," Jessie blurted at the man.

"I'll be damned, Tanner. I thought that other one was a robust woman, but this one here, this one got some nerve, don't she?" The man turned his full attention to Jessie. "You want it plain, country girl? I'll give it to you plain, baby. Name's Glenn, Maud's baby boy, and I come to collect this here debt. You see, girl, dead don't scare Maud because Maud been dead, but she lonely something awful. Now Tanner here, and you bitches, the two of you, end up killing every messenger she sends. That ain't right. Maud took her time when she made her sons. Took her time when she found Tanner, too. You know what taking time is, country girl? Let me spell it out for you. Eight niggers minus three niggers is five and you going to pay that five out in lifetimes. With Maud. Maud'll like you. She'll like your big girlfriend over there, too."

"I never did nothing to Maud," Jessie said.

"You call killing eight grown children nothing? If that's nothing, I sure would like to see what you call something," Glenn said.

"Maud's the one doing it. She already done cursed us. Why she keep sending her sons to kill us?"

"That don't have much to do with me. I come for Tanner, and I come for Tanner's women keep helping Tanner. That's all."

Peanuts shot into the air like fireworks following a parade. Flora had picked up a tray full of them and smashed it against the head of her captor. His face burned down to the bone and revealed rat's teeth. Jessie ran toward Flora, and Tanner booted Maud's boy with the flat of her shoe. "Salt, Jessie, salt!" Tanner screamed out. Jessie hit Flora's captor with another tray of bar nuts. Flora held the man's head and snapping jaw in the crook of her arm as Jessie threw every salty thing she could find. The man's arms and legs flailed about. He snapped his jaw at Jessie's torso until he melted into the creases of Flora's black dress, blue and red clumps of him exploding down her front, into her patent heels. The women were so busy they didn't hear the shot. Didn't see Glenn's body slumped at Tanner's feet or see the blood trickling from his nose and into the wood floor.

"Flora, how'd you know that wasn't no real man?"

"When I went into the kitchen to get the gun, he was eating Rinny."

"Eating him?"

"That's what I said."

"The dog?"

"Only one, unless you know another."

Saturday

Tanner looked at the dead man on the floor, turning the bottle opener over in her hands. She listened to Jessie opening then slamming drawers for a sheet to wrap the body in and knew that, even in distress, Jessie would not waste a good sheet on a dead man. Tanner listened to the sound of the whiskey cabinet's old latch and heard the shuffle of glasses sliding onto the bar. Jessie poured faster than usual and Tanner half-smiled when she gulped. Tanner liked to see Jessie throw her head back and down a drink. Jessie was no wine woman. "Want one?" Jessie asked. Tanner looked at the dead man again, figuring out how long it would take to strip him down, bleed him and bury him. "Set me up," she whispered back, letting the back of her shaved head cool on the wall behind her.

Jessie came from behind the bar holding Tanner's drink in her right hand and a ragged sheet draped across her left arm. Her hair, usually mussed about her shoulders, was braided into a single rope, doubled over itself and secured with a rubber band. "You can't keep killing these boys and expecting they won't come back bigger and badder," Jessie said. His was the ninth body on the floor in almost five years.

"You'd think they'd stop coming after me by now, Jessie. I'm trying to live good on this place here. I didn't send for them, they come for me. You'd think Maud'd be tired of sending her boys to slaughter by now." Tanner held the drink in hand but didn't sip from it. Maud only had nine boys, just nine of them. If she could get this one buried by nightfall, she would be rid of Maud for good. "We need to get a move on it, baby. You know sundown comes quicker than a fly to shit."

Jessie fixed the sheet around the dead man's body, tucking its ends beneath him. She stood up to get salt and licorice root for his ears and mouth and backside. "He's stinking already. We got to plug him up."

"Can't plug him until he's bled through and through," Tanner said. "This ain't a time to be skipping steps. You know the way it's got to be done."

Jessie stared at Tanner as if to cut her down. "I didn't leave Georgia to get caught up in this mess you got yourself into with Maud. And now I'm trapped, just like Flo and just like Newt. You got me here plugging up dead bodies because you couldn't tell your last woman goodbye the right way. Now I'll never get to California. It ain't no more safe for me here in Phoenix burying Maud's sons than it was in Georgia. At least in Georgia I could walk off the land when I wanted to."

Tanner didn't shush her. Didn't make sense to. It was all true. Tanner left Maud one morning without so much as packing a bag. She left on foot, the weight of travel and her body at times too much for her knee. She stopped every few days in a field or under a tree to wash herself and rest up. Sometimes she found a rabbit, other times she ate nothing. She laid her suit out in the sun to dry and napped, naked, through afternoons too hot to travel. She chewed leaves of mint and packed them under her arms to keep her dry. When she could hop a train car she did and shared liquor with the men aboard. Men with names like Willie and Richard and Bartholomew and with pasts as unspeakable as her own. Most of them were going north or west. Most of them had left women behind, too. And kids to send back for. No one was lucky enough to ride one train all the way out, but no one was willing to hop off before getting into Arkansas. Some piled out in northern Texas and others in New Mexico. None of the men bothered her because none of them knew she was a woman. Her breasts were no larger than the chest of a very stout man. She wore her hair shaved close to her scalp and carried a handkerchief to wipe sweat from it. She kept a pair of socks stuffed down her shorts and listened as the other men chortled through stories of close encounters with another man's wife. She told her own stories of being ran out of a house and marked for death. When she spoke, the gap between her two front teeth seemed to grow and swallow her audience. The soft flap of gum that hung there was the most delicate thing about her. By the time she walked from New Mexico to Phoenix, her knee had doubled in size and her cane was about ready to give up the ghost. She settled on a little abandoned ranch and in a year converted it into a motel for colored people traveling west. Out of the south, Lord knows.

It took Maud almost as long to find her and send the first boy. That first one wasn't sent over to kill Tanner so much as he was sent to tie her there. Maud's juju kept Tanner bound to the place. She could go anywhere on the property, but she could not leave. The first time Tanner tried to leave the motel, she learned what it was to die and come back. The juju allowed her to walk off but every step took a little bit of her life force from her. Walking off the motel property meant dying. She couldn't leave if she wanted to and, by extension, anyone she loved couldn't leave either. That meant Jessie. It meant Flora. It meant Newt. Maud was holding them hostage until she was ready for them all. Most Tanner could do, the most she asked her family to do, was make the best life they could. "Ain't no such thing as life with both feet tied," Jessie would say, "no such thing."

Flo came down the stairs with Newt in hand, not bothering to shield the child's eyes in any way. "The two of you can keep the hollering down because some of us need to sleep before folks start ringing on the bell tonight," Flo said, stepping over the dead man. "What's taking y'all so long to get this one in the ground? He the last one, ain't he?" Jessie waited for Tanner to answer and continued to work on the body.

"Well Miss Flora, we need to get him outside and my knee is in no good condition today. Can't bleed him in here, on the wood floor, but Jessie done washed him down with turpentine soap. If you could help get the body out back, I'd be mighty obliged, ma'am." Tanner's grin spread across her face when she said ma'am and tipped her head toward Flo.

Flora kicked up at Tanner, "Just shut the hell up and get the hell on before I change my damn mind. Least you could do is grab the stretcher out the back for me and Jessie, or we got to do that too?"

Newt ran from his mother's side to follow behind Tanner and held the screen door open as Tanner came up the back steps with the canvas and wooden pole contraption. Tanner held out her hand to the boy, and he slapped her five. "Thought I told you not to come out on this back porch without any shoes on, boy. I gotta start repeating myself around here?"

"No, Uncle Tanner," Newt said, running through the parlor, over the dead body and into the coat closet for his shoes.

Flo rolled the dead man on his side and slipped a new ragged sheet halfway under his body, then turned him back toward her so Jessie could get to the other side. With the sheet in place, they slid the body onto the stretcher and out into the yard. They left him atop a butcher block table like they had with his brothers. Tanner walked over with her knife in hand and made incisions in his neck, groin, and armpits. Newt placed buckets around the table where Tanner had made the cuts. They sat around the dead man and said nothing, Jessie sometimes looking at Tanner, Tanner sometimes looking at Jessie. "Maybe the bottom of his feet too. This is taking too long," Jessie said and Tanner walked over, knife and cane in hand, and bored a hole through the dead man's arch.

"Ain't nobody had breakfast yet," Flo said, "no more courting the dead until we all eat. C'mon, Newt."

Newt looked over to Tanner and waited for her to get up. "Mama said let's eat, Uncle Tanner."

Tanner smiled at the boy. "Tell Auntie Jessie that your mama said come and eat. I don't think Auntie Jessie wants to come in the house. What you think, Newt?"

Newt shrugged his shoulders and smiled at Jessie. "Better come and eat before Mama gets mad at you, Aunt Jessie." Newt pulled Jessie up off the ground playfully, making a show of his little muscles until Jessie laughed.

The three of them walked into the house as Flo set the table. "About time. Thought the dead man got up and walked away with all of you."

Sunday

They got on good together, but Tanner never wanted any juju, not even for her knee. Most Maud could do was offer a poultice of steamed herbs or strong tea. Wasn't church that kept Tanner away from juju. Maud thought maybe she was raised in the Christian way, but that wasn't it, wasn't it at all. It scared her. Tanner was plain scared of juju. Scared of going to bed with a locked knee and waking up to throw out her cane. Scared of having split teeth then the next minute all the spaces gone. Scared to know the hair on her head didn't gray as long as she was with Maud, and her skin didn't grow slack. Because Maud told Tanner that the only reason why her knee still hurt was so she wouldn't have to hear no mess about juju, because she told Tanner that as long as she lived so would Tanner, Tanner walked down the road. Because Tanner wanted a natural death, she kept walking. Carried a little salt with her for all she learned and kept on walking.

"I think the best thing to do is send Newt on up the road," Tanner said to the women. "If he drops, one of us can go fetch him. If the juju is broke for sure, he'll make it past the general store. Then we'll know for sure." All four of them were up early. "If one of you go out, I'm not sure I could get you back to the house before the juju took your soul altogether. If I go out, the two of you can't drag me back, and I'm dead for sure. Best thing is to send our boy because he's light enough to run with. Plus somebody has to perform the rites over Glenn."

Jessie looked at Flora and so did Tanner. Newt was everybody's child, but he was Flo's boy. She would have to make the say. "Newt big enough to walk down the highway by himself. He's been wanting to since he started walking," Flo said, not trying to conceal her smile. "This going to be the first time he walked down the road. Four years old and the boy never walked down the road leading to his own house."

Newt made it a quarter of a mile off the grounds before his calves lost their way and he slipped into the couch grass. Tanner stood watching, the NO VACANCY sign alit behind her like a solitary headlight. Tanner, leading her body with her left foot and then stepping with her right foot, walked out toward the boy. Every step was lighter than the last, the marrow in her bones being pulled away from her heart and out of her skin. It did not hurt, this dying, it was more like wrestling a witch off your back – involuntary paralysis of body but total control of mind. When she reached Newt he was supine, tufts of couch grass in his hands. He was holding on. Tanner dragged Newt back to the motel by his left leg, her cane eating through the soil. She left his body at the bottom of the porch steps, having dragged it as far as she could before collapsing just steps away.

"Why didn't Newt make it, Flo?" Jessie asked. Her eyes were tired but no water fell from them. "This was supposed to be all over, but it ain't. We going to die here and Maud coming to collect our souls." The two women were crouched over the bodies of Newt and Tanner, pressing cold rags against their foreheads.

"I don't know what's doing, Jessie, but we need to get to that grave and move that man on to where he got to go next." Flo looked down at her child, his loose pants and plaid buttoned shirt, his eyes flickering every few minutes. The blood running from his nose. He was fighting it. Soon his heart would start beating again and his color would return. Harder for children to come back from the dead after their soul's been snatched from them. First time Miss Flora tried to leave the grounds, it felt like a pebble found its way into her shoe, snaked up her leg, and then went straight through her lungs. Wasn't so much pain as it was surprise. Like someone snatched a piece of fruit from a tree inside her and kept snatching and snatching and instead of taking the last piece of fruit or letting it drop to the ground for harvest, they stood on their tiptoes, opened their mouth to the branch and ate her seed and stem and all. Even after she came out of it and understood she couldn't leave the grounds, Flo would still try every now and again, checking her shoe for the elusive pebble when she came to.

"I don't understand why we have to ask a dead man to move on," Jessie said. "Every time Maud sends one of her boys out here I end up standing up for them in her place. Don't make no kind of sense."

"What don't make sense is that they can come back. That don't make sense. Feels like sense to make sure a dead man is really dead to me."

Jessie thought on it. "Well what if somebody pulls up for a room and sees the two of them spread out here like this?"

"Nobody stopping for a room with two dead-looking niggers out front. Let's go." Flo and Jessie walked around to the back of the motel where hours before they threw a warm body into a new grave. They held hands and repeated the same words at the same time again and again. *Leave from here. It's safe to go. Leave from here. It's safe to go. Leave from here. It's safe to go.* Their clasped hands looked like prayer, but their heads weren't bowed and neither dared to close their eyes.

Tanner ascended the porch steps as the women returned. She opened her mouth to greet them, but her voice had not returned from the other side of life. Miss Flora bent down to scoop up Newt's body, his bare feet dirtying the front of her trousers. She cradled his neck with her right hand and kissed his small face. "I better get you washed and put to bed, little baby," she said into her son's neck. Jessie rubbed Newt's back as soon as Miss Flora got him close enough to touch. Tanner watched the boy's dangling feet and thought of him as an infant, before he could walk. "We thought we lost you, boy, out there in that couch grass like that. C'mon back and come see us. We waiting for you, hear me Newt? Mama here. Auntie Jessie here. Uncle Tanner right here. We'll be right here when you wake up."

Tanner stuck her free hand into Jessie's hair, her other hand gripped around the porch railing. She massaged Jessie's scalp while looking out to the road at passing cars. "Nobody dying just yet. We gotta get this place ready for guests. No bookings since the Campbells left." The three of them had scrubbed the parlor shortly after they took Glenn out to bleed him, so that was one less thing to be done, but there was still food to be made, linens to take out, and the porch needed mopping with boiled water and salt.

Miss Flora headed upstairs with Newt, while Tanner went to the backyard after the mop bucket and Jessie moved pots and pans around in the kitchen. Today was the largest supper day of the week. Folks expected a family meal on a Sunday evening. Even the man who grew up eating nothing except corn mush and butter expected a decent Sunday dinner on a Sunday afternoon. Jessie stacked her ingredients all over the countertop, opening a cabinet door and reaching for everything by memory; Flora kept a well-run kitchen with everything in its place. Jessie rubbed birds down with salt, paprika, sage, and black pepper and stuck white onions, garlic, and several carrots into the hole where their hearts used to beat.

Flo came downstairs and washed her hands so she could help Jessie. "Where's Tanner?"

Jessie kept her hands and eyes on the dough she was kneading, "Tanner mopping the front down with saltwater. How's Newt? Sleep yet?"

"Newt's fine. I rubbed him all over with rum and laid him on his side until his nose stops bleeding."

"What nose-bleeding you talking about, Miss Flora?" Tanner asked, coming into the kitchen for more water. "Newt ain't been having nosebleeds."

"I thought it might be peculiar but then I figured he was having a tough time getting back from the other side. No fever, no sweats, but his nose is bleeding."

"Out the nose, huh?"

"Where else you bleed from, Tanner? Yes, out his nose."

"Let's all go check him. Jessie wash your hands good and grab the salt."

Jessie and Flo turned to Tanner with widened eyes but nothing to say. Flo retraced the morning in her head: the four of them up early, deciding to send Newt down the road, feeling happy, Newt laid out in the couch grass, Tanner gone to get him, Tanner's cane tip covered in dust, Newt's skinny feet, Newt in the bathtub cradled in her arm the way she used to nurse him. His heartbeat returned, shallow. Nothing was different about the boy except the blood coming from his nose. And who doesn't bleed a little coming back to life?

Tanner wiped her brow with the back of her hand and wiped the sweat from it on her pant leg. "I used to know a boy whose nose bled all the time. Boy was bumped up and bruised up all over his body. Lost a tooth and bled for two gotdamn weeks. Couldn't go to school, couldn't go out to play. Those kids with it bad like that don't live past eleven, twelve."

"With what, Tanner?" Jessie asked.

"Doctors called it hemophilia. I known it to be called bleeding. Just bleeding."

"Bleeding? I never heard of no children bleeding, Tanner, where you get this mess from?" Jessie demanded.

Miss Flora interrupted Jessie's question, her arms folded. "But what happened to the boy? What happened to the little boy you knew?"

"He died, Miss Flora, he died and every time he died, his mama brought him right back." Tanner didn't wait for her women to piece the puzzle of it together. "Glenn was Maud's favorite boy. And her last."

Jessie grabbed onto Tanner and Flo just stared. "You trying to tell me there's a haint in my boy, Tanner? You trying to tell me the boy upstairs ain't my own? Like I didn't spend the last half hour washing his ass, you going to tell me that ain't Newt up there?"

"Miss Flora, I'm not saying you wrong, I'm saying we should go check. Can we go check on the boy?"

"You want to go check on my boy with salt in your hands? That's what you want to do?"

"I'm afraid so, Miss Flora."

"Jess, you hear this woman? This woman climb in your bed and mines the same and now she talking about killing my son."

"I ain't talking about killing, Flo, I said let's check him."

"Checking sounding a lot like killing. Ain't nobody killing my child but me. You got that? Only shot'll be fired is mine."

Tanner opened Newt's bedroom door and found the boy sitting up in bed putting on his shoes, trickles of blood hanging from his nostrils. Jessie and Flo flanked Tanner's sides, Jessie with a fistful of salt, Flo carrying a musket.

"Glenn, you got to leave this place," Tanner said. The boy did not look up from lacing his shoes. "I said Glenn, you got to leave this place now."

The boy looked at the trio, stood and walked toward them. "That's exactly what I intend to do, Uncle Tanner. I'm going to bring this body back to Maud like she told me."

"What you say, haint?" Flora screamed at the boy, aiming the gun off-center.

Newt began to laugh. "So it is in life, so it is in death. Heard something you didn't like, woman? I can't call her Uncle Tanner no more? You didn't like that?" The boy put one hand on his hip and continued, "Maud found a way to settle this here debt of Tanner's. Nine sons for one. Nine boys for one boy. That's the new math. All my brothers and me for Newt."

Miss Flora let off a shot over the child's shoulder. "You ain't leaving here with my boy, haint."

"I don't think you got much of a choice, Flora, seeing as your boy is dead. He died out there in the couch grass this morning. I'm just wearing him. He died a *natural death*. Tanner is a fan of that, those natural deaths. Your boy gone on, girl. You and your friend sent his soul off mighty right this morning. He dancing right now with the little colored niggers on the colored side of heaven. How you like that?"

The man-boy passed between Jessie and Tanner. Neither of them moved to stop him. The man-boy called out over his shoulder as he marched down the steps, "Your debt is clear. Nine sons and one son paid in full." Then he twisted the door handle, walked off the porch, made it past the quarter of a mile mark where Newt had dropped dead that very morning, and kept on going.

Miss Flora laid out on the floor like a pile of dirty clothes. Tanner sat on Newt's bed. Jessie went downstairs first, salt in fist. The sun was high. She closed the front door hard, turned the VACANCY sign on and stood at the lobby desk, waiting.

Art by Janet Chui

THE HEART AND THE FEATHER
CHRISTINA LYNCH

1589
Innsbruck, Austria

Crouching behind a lilac bush, I remove my jewelry, my stiff brocade dress, my farthingale and undergarments. I untie the ribbon garters and remove my hose. I run my hands over my body, feeling it finally free. Without those constricting little shoes, my feet sink into the earth's embrace.

"Anubis," I say. "I am here."

I enter the dense forest. It is massive, and very dark. I can hear movement in the trees. The archduke has stocked the hundred acres with animals from all over – deer, stags, wolves, boar, birds, bats, snakes. Somewhere out there is a camel, I've heard. But that is not what I seek tonight.

When I am far enough from the castle, I climb a tree and drop over the wall of the hunting preserve into the fields below. I felt safe with the animals in the forest, but now I do not. The howling has started, and I must go before they breach the walls.

***

My father was a gift to King Henri II of France. I believe it was on the occasion of Henri's twenty-first birthday, which would have made it March 31, 1540. Though he was the second son, Henri had become the Dauphin after his elder brother dropped dead four years earlier from drinking a cold glass of water following a vigorous game of tennis. (The poor nobleman who gave him the water was literally torn apart by horses on suspicion of having poisoned the heir.) At the time of the birthday I speak of, Henri had already been married for seven years to Catherine de Medici, and had a lover, Diane de Poitier, twenty years his senior.

I like to imagine the scene: it's a big party. People in velvet and the finest brocade are milling about, drinking wine. There are pipers, and drummers, and a tambourine with ribbons. Henri has typically French eyes: dark, hooded, slightly derisive, atop a long aquiline nose made for sneering. The royal pate sports a plumed *chapeau*.

Henri is fond of dogs and loves hunting, so when Diane comes towards him with a wriggling, hairy object wrapped in a blanket in her arms, he assumes it's a puppy. His wife, Catherine, watches in annoyance – she loathes her husband's mistress and, after his death, will banish the woman. Diane sets the bundle down on the table and removes the blanket.

The crowd gasps. Laughter ceases. The drummer stops drumming. Catherine de Medici wrinkles her nose in horror, backs away, and looks like she's going to faint. She makes the sign of the cross.

Standing there is a small child, about three years old. He is naked, and not naked. He is completely covered in hair. The hair is fine, silky and black, but coarser and straighter on his face. Monkeys are a popular pet in court circles, and the child appears somewhat familiarly simian to the party guests, but the dark eyes peering out from the thick hair covering the entire face, and the way the hair there sticks out a bit, like the beard on a terrier, make him more resemble a cat or a dog. He is different from any other child only in that he is furred, and yet that makes him so unbelievably strange that no one can do anything but stare.

Diane reaches out and prods the child, who bows and says, "Happy birthday," in a high-pitched little whisper.

"It has been baptized," says Diane cautiously, suddenly not sure of the success of her gift.

No one says anything, and the child looks around the room and begins to whimper.

It is a cry of profound loneliness, and it spurs Henri out of his trance.

"Amazing," he says. "Take it to..." he says, pausing. The kennels? The servants' quarters? A barber? A priest? For certainly the poor child is cursed, baptism or not.

"My tailor," he says at last. "And have proper clothes made for him."

That animal cry that pierced Henri's royal heart was, I believe, my father's one and only lapse in dignity. In his every word, gesture and action, my father strove to be utterly and unmistakably human, as if any and all animal instincts that lay within him had been pushed out through his skin, leaving nothing beneath but noble Catholic soul. All who met him believed him punished by God, but my father never showed himself to be guilty, merely gracefully accepting of his burden.

My father was given a room on the top floor of the palace, under the eaves, which he shared with a dwarf named Coco. He was not unhappy at the French court, even though he was the king's property, with exactly the same status as the paintings and chairs and draperies that filled the king's palaces, and the birds and beasts that stocked his private zoo. He had been sold to a ship captain at age two, and then sold by the ship captain to an exotic animal dealer. My father did not remember his parents or anything about his early childhood, though he remembered the animal dealer's cruelty, and the peacocks and leopards he was caged alongside. He also remembered having rocks thrown at him.

He always told those who asked that he was born on Tenerife, one of the Canary Islands belonging to Spain off the coast of Morocco, though I suspect that that may have been a fiction created by the animal dealer because Gran Canary has been known since ancient times as the "Island of the Dogs." It is written that there was an Egyptian cult of Anubis, the jackal-faced god, on the island, but such things were not mentioned with regard to my father, as he had been duly baptized and regularly took communion.

My father was not one to rail against his strange fate; he knew that things could have been much worse for him: quite likely, he could have met his destiny in a pit with a lion or a bear, or had his eyes clawed out by falcons. At the court of the King of France, he did not lack for food or clothing, and it appeared not to trouble him that Catherine de Medici asked that he wear a handkerchief over his face as he roamed the palace.

Henri would occasionally demand that my father be brought into his presence. He would make my father recite poetry in Latin, then ask him to remove his coat and doublet, and stand naked atop a thin-legged table. Henri would walk around my father, staring in amazement and shaking his head.

"Your mother lay with a dog, you think?" King Henri would ask my father. My father would shrug. "Or a wolf. Or perhaps there is a curse on your family for some reason?"

This question was never answered to anyone's satisfaction. There were people, and there were animals, that was how God made the world, but no matter how much he strove to stay on one side of that line my father seemed to bridge the gap in a way that made everyone uncomfortable. For what if there were no line at all?

***

The breeze ruffles my fur, making my skin tingle. In my whole life, this is the longest I have ever been naked. I have been taught in church that it's a sin to admire your own body, to take pleasure in it. I have been taught at home to keep as much of my body as possible hidden at all times. When my mother saw my breasts emerging from my girlish chest last year, she shook her head, told me I looked like the archduke's spaniel, and laced my dress more tightly. Now I rub the hair where it has been compressed by the dress and the hose, and feel it spring up under my touch. My mother is wrong. My hair is not coarse like a dog's — it's more like petting a rabbit.

I run along the banks of a river, staying in the darkness, not making a sound. My dark fur conceals me, allows me to slip through the shadows.

I venture across the fields to a place where my instinct tells me to wait.

I sit in silence, feeling my breath quiet, hearing my heart beat in my ears. What I am doing is madness — no one knows I am out here, and no one will come to my rescue. I am a fourteen-year-old girl, alone, hunting a wolf. Children have been disappearing; the villagers are frightened. Large tracks in the soft earth, body parts gnawed, white bones splintered. Normally a pack of men would set out lighthearted on this chase, with packs of dogs and brazen horns, singing songs of the chase. The archduke himself might join them, offering a cask of wine to the man whose arrow brought the beast down. But the local people do not believe that a normal wolf is the cause of these deaths. They believe that a werewolf is on the loose.

Naturally, my family has fallen under suspicion.

***

When my father was fourteen, King Henri studied his genitals intently, using a walking stick with a golden lion on the top to move the penis from side to side to see what lay underneath. "I have a lovely terrier bitch I think you would enjoy," he said at last. "I am very curious what the puppies will look like."

My father politely thanked him for the offer, but said that he would prefer a wife he could converse with.

"So you think now," said Henri with a lifted eyebrow and a little laugh. He reached out and petted the hair on my father's forehead, which had to be kept trimmed and combed back with pomades so as not to obscure his vision. "Very well, I will find you a wife," he said, and left the room.

A couple of weeks later, my father was once again summoned to the king's chamber. There he found a young girl of five holding her mother's hand.

"Now we shall both have wives named Catherine," said the king.

The girl shrieked and my father saw the mother's face pale. "When she has come of age, she is yours," said the king grandly.

I was not born until twenty-three years later. My mother did not speak of such things, but I can only assume it took her some time to accept the king's choice of husband for her, and I would guess that my grandmother was slow to announce the arrival of her daughter's womanhood as well. But if it was the king's will, it was God's will.

I know that during her pregnancy my mother prayed every day, but that was nothing unusual for her. Many times I saw her lips move even while she was asleep. Despite her prayers, I was born with a light brown downy fur over my entire body. My father, the midwife, and my mother all crossed themselves at the sight of me.

"At least no one can claim you've cuckolded me," said my father to my mother grimly.

By the time I came along, my mother and father were quite fond of each other, and she would patiently sit and with an ivory comb remove the lice and fleas that often plagued him. Henri had died from wounds sustained during a joust in 1559, and when I was born my parents were living in Munich, the capital of the Kingdom of Bavaria and part of the Holy Roman Empire, Catherine de Medici having given my father away to her cousin by marriage Margaret of Parma after Henri's death, and the ingrate Margaret having re-gifted my father to a German nobleman who was apparently quite the swordsman. The nobleman seemed frankly a little offended by the unusual *cadeau*, and locked my father in the basement of his castle, leaving him to feed himself on any rats he could catch with his bare hands. My father preferred to starve, and was soon on the verge of death. My mother's appeals to the local priest fell on deaf ears, but she continued to appeal to God on an hourly basis. My parents rarely spoke of those days, and I sensed that even more terrible things had happened. But then the nobleman died suddenly, and apparently in debt, and my father became the property of a Bavarian hatmaker who set up our family in a room above his shop, where he charged people to climb up and stare at us.

It was an unusual way to grow up – with an audience, and often unpleasant to be interrupted in one's daily tasks by a steady stream of visitors, though far better than being locked in a dungeon, my mother pointed out whenever I complained. The shopkeeper would charge extra to let the gawkers touch my father.

"They are merely expressing their true awe," said my father. "If it is the truth, it should not pain us."

And yet, when visitors offered large sums to touch me, he always refused them.

My father was, as I have said, a man of great dignity, always dressed in a clean robe and with his hair neatly combed. He could read and write Latin, and would bow upon the arrival of visitors and introduce himself as Petrus Gonsalvus. He would offer to discuss Aristotle or recite Bible passages from memory while they stared, dumbstruck, then he would slowly, very slowly incline his head and let it be petted by farmwives smelling of the pigs they had brought to market, or by sticky-fingered boys who stole coins to gain entrance, and who tried to pluck out my father's hairs to sell as potion ingredients to local witches.

At first I was unaware of my difference, and would toddle forward smiling, to the gasps and shrieks of the paying customers. But that time of blissful innocence ended, and I became shy, hiding behind the curtains when I heard footsteps on the stairs.

As I grew older, it was harder to hide.

One day a fat man in tall black boots and a purple peaked hat nodded at me and asked, "How much to kiss it?"

My mother sewed a hood for me out of the tablecloth. In the summer it was unbearably hot underneath, and I felt faint with my own scent.

***

I sniff the breeze, watch the shadows in the trees. My heart is still beating quickly, and I am afraid, but I also feel more alive than I ever have. There is a part of me that does not want this night to end. But I must not forget my purpose, my family. I am out here to prove their innocence by losing mine. To save their lives, I am willing to risk mine. Or am I deluding myself? Is there another, darker reason I am here?

The longer I stare into the gloom, the more I can see, and hear. It is as if I am becoming my true self. I am a hunter, but of what? I am certain that what I will find is a normal hungry wolf, but I am holding wolfsbane from the castle garden just in case, and a silver dagger I lifted from the display of arms in the hallway. The archduke's books were not clear on how to kill a werewolf.

My father did not wish to have more children. When I asked my mother why she had become pregnant again, she obliquely cursed her "animal urges." I had never thought of my mother as an animal and was confused. Father and Mother educated me and my siblings, two more of whom shared my father's hirsutism, to emulate his calm and dignified ways, to be charming and polite, hold our heads up, to speak well and wittily of the matters of the day, to be nicely scented and groomed at all times. We were vegetarians so that no one need ever see us tearing flesh with our teeth and draw conclusions. My mother even arranged through Margaret of Parma to have my portrait painted by Lavinia Fontana, a lovely young Bolognese artist of great skill. I am wearing full court dress, complete with stiff white ruff, pearl headdress, and necklace with omnipresent cross, and my expression is that of distant serenity, as if my fur only heightens my holiness. Though my name is painted into the corner, I have heard that the painting is displayed under a card that reads "Monkey Child."

When I was six and very angry over a seed cake stolen from me by my little brother, I snarled and barked, and it was the only time my father struck me. "Never," he said, returning to his calm demeanor. "Never," he whispered.

I believe my father felt his life, all of our lives, depended on this maintenance of humanity in the face of constant insult and indignity. Witch trials were all the rage those days. All anyone could speak of in the terrible summer of 1587 was Walpurga Hausmannin's confession under torture that she had drunk the blood of more than forty babies at the behest of the devil. She was paraded through the packed streets of Dillingen an der Donau, where one by one her breasts and hands were torn off until at last she was burned to death to the raucous cheers of thousands.

I was twelve years old that summer, and my parents were already talking about whether I might be safer in a convent. We were still the property of the Bavarian hatmaker, and he was making noises about spinning us children off into a satellite act that would tour Europe in a wagon. My father was not an idiot, and was trying to work with the man to ensure a protected future for us all, together, rather than rebelling. How could he rebel? He was the hatmaker's property, and so were we. We could run, but there was nowhere to escape to. Our hair could be trimmed, razored even, but it would always grow back. We required the protection of powerful, educated people who thought of us as scientific curiosities, something to collect and marvel at like narwhal horns and two-headed calves and delicate coral figurines. Superstitious, ignorant country folk saw only the devil's hand on our flesh, and wolf's blood in our veins.

Word of our family's extraordinary charms reached the ears of Archduke Ferdinand II of Tyrol. The canny hatmaker asked an astronomical price for all of us, and Ferdinand paid. My mother said her prayers were answered, though I would guess that was only partly true.

I vomited many times on the narrow winding road to Schloss Ambras. Our whole family was filled with fear. We kept the drapes on the carriage closed so as not to attract attention in the villages we passed through. When we did have to descend, to stretch our legs and answer nature's call, we did so in remote areas, keeping our faces hidden even from curious livestock so as not to be blamed for causing them to abort their young.

Ambras, to our enormous relief, was a marvelous place. High stone walls and iron gates concealed a huge castle with red and white striped shutters and crenellated towers, surrounded by low buildings to store the archduke's collections. I set out to explore every inch of the castle and quickly found a secret passageway that I told no one in my family about – a secret is a kind of treasure, isn't it? There was a grotto, and a labyrinth, and a hunting preserve. We met a man shaped like a shrimp who lived in the castle, and a giant named Salvatore, and too many dwarves to count.

The archduke, it turned out, was an eccentric collector with a large *wunderkammer*, and beside his corals and his jewels and his paintings and clocks and sculptures, he had jars of babies with one eye in the middle of their foreheads, and conjoined twins dead in their mother's womb. I tried not to stare.

We were surprised to learn that the archduke did not plan to display us for the public – he measured us, studied us, made notations in his notebooks. He seemed fascinated by us, but always treated us with dignity. I found him kind, despite his many questions and his habit of collecting our bodily effluvia. His second wife prepared medicines for us from herbs she grew in her garden, and prayed for us all the time. They say his first wife, who died not long ago, was a good witch, and that she planted the herbs.

Though my parents pressed me to practice my dancing, gossip, games, and music, I preferred to hide myself away in the archduke's library, which he allowed me to investigate. I was supposed to be reading poetry, and learning to tat lace, so that I might in my turn entertain and unnerve the nobility in their drawing rooms and palaces as my monstrous father had, but I was more interested in the archduke's stash of alchemical tomes.

Reading those heavy leatherbound books with their pages of symbols and strange drawings, I learned about antisyzygy, the union of opposites. That is what alchemy seemed to me to be focused on, the marriage of sun and moon, man and woman, God and the devil, in a great alchemical wedding in which truth is revealed. Was I, I wondered, the result of someone's spell, an attempt to unite animal and human?

The books were filled with potions and incantations and rites to call out the angels and also demons. In his laboratory at the top of the castle I discovered the archduke had many strange powders and tinctures in tiny, labeled jars: bezoars, unicorn horn, dragon scales. I examined the jars for boiling, and a small oven, and many vials and vessels for purification and distillation.

From the archduke's books I also learned about Anubis and his connection to the Island of the Dogs where my father was assumed to have been born. Anubis, also called Hermanubis by the Greeks, who merged his legend with that of their own Hermes, was an ancient Egyptian god of the dead, specifically of the passage to the afterlife. The archduke, whispers in the castle said, was trying to bridge that gap, to speak to his late first wife. The job of Anubis, I read, was to remove your heart and weigh it against a feather to see which contained more truth. If it was your heart, you went on to a happy afterlife. If it was the feather...

Anything seemed possible at Ambras, a place of experimentation and curiosity and acceptance.

It felt like we had landed in Eden.

But then we heard the howling.

***

Tonight, as the moon passed behind a cloud, I crawled out my window onto a small ledge and made my way into the adjacent chamber, and then through a tiny door behind a tapestry into the secret passageway, down a small flight of stairs, and out into the garden. I quickly slipped away past the topiaries and the maze and the grotto into the hunting preserve below. As I removed my clothing and hid it under the lilac bush, I could hear the drums, and the chanting for blood. I could not see the anxious faces of the archduke's guards, but I imagined them as sweat- and soot-streaked, wild-eyed, and at the breaking point.

Now the night is still. I do not even hear an owl, or a nightingale. It is as if the whole world is holding its breath, as I am.

I wonder if I am indeed a daughter not of my father, but of Anubis. For several months now, I have had the urge to to bite something. I want to feel my animal self, not hide it. I have dreams, dark dreams of flesh and fire and pleasure.

I hear footsteps, and a faint crying. I crouch, suddenly afraid. This is not a feverish dream. I am awake.

***

This morning my mother woke me at dawn, fear in her eyes, and told me to dress.

"What is it?" I asked.

For several days, I had smelled smoke in the air and heard shouting in the distance. The few servants who came from the village, usually friendly folk, avoided me and my family. I felt as if they had seen my dreams, seen what I longed to be. Could other people see what was inside your head, inside your heart? Or only God?

"Greta," I finally said to one of the housemaids whom I usually embroidered with. "What is the matter?"

She averted her eyes. "Several children have gone missing," she said. "And yesterday one of them was found."

"What happened?" I asked, my stomach tightening.

"The flesh was torn from the poor child's thighs." She began to weep.

"A wolf, then," I said, patting her hand, which she quickly withdrew. "The men will hunt the animal. The archduke has a fine set of dogs. Last year he himself took down a bear."

She said nothing, her lips pressed together.

Generally the wolves that inhabit the wooded areas of the surrounding forests prefer to keep their distance from humans, but young males do occasionally come down from the mountains to prey on livestock or small children. They are quickly dispatched. I did not understand her agitation, the sense of foreboding that enveloped the castle.

After lunch my father gathered us in our chambers, his brow creased with worry.

"They believe it is a werewolf," he said.

We children and our mother stared at him in silence.

I knew the term, of course, but it had never been spoken aloud in our family. I had read that werewolves were men who, in exchange for doing the devil's work, were given the power to transform themselves into wolves. There had been trials over the years — a man in Bavaria confessed to eating several young women, and I had heard the kitchenmaids say that in recent months confessed werewolves had been tried and burned in Anjou and Valais.

"How do they know?" I asked my father.

"Some of the villagers say they saw someone..." He sighed, knitted his brows and began again. "The archduke is concerned for our safety. He asks that we stay in our chambers." The way he said it made it sound like it was the werewolf we had to fear.

My mother nodded and turned away, picked up her sewing, as did my little sister. "But," I said, "do they think it's one of us?"

My mother's eyes widened and she told me to be quiet.

After lunch I wanted to go down the hall to the archduke's library, to look at his books on witches and werewolves. But when I opened the door to our chamber, there was a guard outside. He was in armor and carrying a halberd. I knew him.

"Good day, Friedrich," I said as he blocked my exit.

He said nothing, just pushed me back inside and shut the door.

As darkness fell I heard shouting outside the walls of the castle grounds. I could smell smoke and hear the crackle of the flames.

"Bring him out," they yelled. "Bring us the werewolf."

A flaming branch sailed up past the window and illuminated my father's shadow against the stone wall of our chamber. He shrank back in fear. My father, whom the Italian naturalist Ulisse Aldrovandi traveled hundreds of miles to meet and whom he declared one of the great scientific marvels of the world. My father, who says the rosary every day. A stone smashed the window and the crowd cheered. They tried to launch a torch up, but it fell to the ground and set a small bush alight.

In the early evening the archduke's personal secretary came to us. "We are not certain we can hold off the mob," he said. "There is talk of moving you to another location."

"Is that... safe?" asked my father. I thought of how easily a carriage could be stopped, overturned, burned. Sending us out there was akin to sending us to our deaths.

The archduke himself did not come to see us. I chose to believe he was ashamed of his people, these ignorant mountain villagers. But perhaps he too was afraid of us.

The drums began. I heard my parents whispering. Another child had been found dead, half eaten. People from surrounding mountain towns had traveled here to witness the burning of my father alive. The archduke's promise to protect us was in doubt.

I saw in the moonlight that my mother was sitting in a corner of the sitting room, weeping silently. My father sat nearby, not touching her.

"Maybe I should go talk to them," he said. "They will see I am a man of God."

"Do you know what they did to Peter Stumpp of Bedburg?" my mother said.

I didn't, but I knew what they had done to Walpurga.

"The whole point of being a werewolf is transformation," my father said in exasperation. "If I had the power to be hairless, would I be this way?" The gesture he makes, throwing his hands up, makes my heart grow dry and light like a dead thing. My father hates himself. Does he hate me, too?

"Peter Stumpp was flayed alive on the wheel, and his daughters and his woman were raped and strangled," my mother whispered.

***

The grass rustles. I can smell the animal before I see him. He smells of death. A tall wolf, gray, with yellow eyes. It is only a wolf after all, as I expected. He is carrying an infant in his mouth, but gently, like a hunting dog with a bird. I imagine he has grabbed it from a nearby farm.

The wolf looks around and drops the baby, who is uninjured but too exhausted and frightened to do anything but stare with huge eyes.

I will kill the wolf, and save the baby, and the villagers will see that my father is innocent. Perhaps they will be ashamed, though I suspect not. My family will be safe, and we will be able to continue to live at Schloss Ambras, under the archduke's protection.

This year or the next, the archduke will choose a husband for me. Will my husband want me? Or will he be repulsed? Perhaps I will be sent to the palace of one of the archduke's family members in Vienna, or Prague. *What manners*, the people will say, staring in amazement as I pour tea, and dance a minuet. And think about ripping their throats out.

As I plan my attack, the wolf noses the infant until its bare neck is exposed. The infant is calm, just the way the rabbits are before the archuduke's hounds pounce. This is the moment of the pact, I think. The moment of connection, when one life is sacrificed to another.

I am about to launch myself at the wolf, but something stops me – as the wolf stares at the infant's neck, he begins to transform. His snout disappears, his claws retract. For a moment I stare in disbelief as he looks like me, like my father, like my little brother and sister. Then his fur disappears, replaced with smooth skin.

I suppress a gasp.

My mind leaps in excitement. For an instant, I almost forget about the baby, I am so fascinated. Who is this man? He is so free. It's awful and beautiful at the same time, this freedom he has. To be both man and animal. To choose.

The baby reaches up a tiny hand, waves it. The man pauses.

I will speak. I will ask him to spare the infant. I will rebalance him, be the voice of our human side. Restore the man/animal equilibrium. In exchange he will teach me how to live in freedom.

I could run away with this man, live in the shadows. There are woods, deep, dark woods we could flee to. Never be found. Live on rabbits, and mice. I could be free, with this man. I am reminded of my nakedness, of the pleasure I feel in being naked. I look at the man's naked body, watch the play of muscles under his skin. He is an animal, and I am an animal.

But we are also human. I will remind him of that. We do not eat our own.

The moon comes out from behind the cloud, and the man's face is illuminated.

It is the archduke.

I am all amazed, I almost stagger, swoon. The archduke, who studied the dark arts in order to bring his lost love back to life. The books, the potions, the spells... they are real. He has mastered the art of transformation, of unification. The marriage of two things. Alchemy. He is a man, and he is an animal.

I am about to step forward, to reveal myself to the archduke. Tell him that I too have dreamed of this, of blood and biting and of wildness... tell him I understand. That we are twin souls. Of course he will not kill the infant. He is the archduke. He is—

In that moment, I look again at the glint in his eyes. This is not a momentary impulse. I realize he has planned this, this murderous spree. I realize why he brought my father to Ambras. For this. To take the blame for this. When his animal side took over, someone would be blamed. Will be blamed.

He picks up the child and opens his mouth to tear out its throat. I see one tiny feather lift off from the archduke's lips and float away into the night air. He must have eaten a duck, too, in the farmyard.

The baby whimpers. It is, I think in that moment, the same cry my father uttered, standing on a table in France. My father, who believes that I am not an animal, but a lady.

My father is wrong. We are all animals.

I spring, and plunge the silver dagger into the archduke's back. I have not been trained in feats of strength, in swordsmanship or wrestling. I have been trained to dance and sew and laugh. To drink from delicate porcelain cups. But I am still strong, and my heart has the heavy weight of truth behind it, so the archduke's own silver knife goes deep into his flesh. I have helped the kitchen maids quarter pheasants many times, but now it is the ease with which the thin blade slips in that surprises me, and the warmth of the blood that covers my hand, its scarlet color, the color of royalty.

The archduke whirls, stares at me.

"You," he gasps, dropping to his knees.

"Yes, your grace, it is I, Maddalena Gonzales," I say, and despite my nakedness I give a polite little curtsy.

I snatch up the baby as the archduke groans, snarls, twitches in agony, paws at the blade but cannot reach it. Blood pools beneath him. His face pales and his lips form a grimace. His hands claw the dirt. I stare at the pool of blood, where the reflection of the moon appears. He twitches once more, then is still.

I scream, as loudly as I can. I place the baby down on a soft pile of leaves.

185

When I hear footsteps, I run. I can hear the shouts of the farmer and his wife discovering the baby, alive, and the archduke, dead. They will not be surprised to learn that the nobleman strayed to the side of the devil, I think. The whispers I took for idle gossip, for superstition, were true. It is I who was ignorant.

I return to the castle walls, make it over unseen, and dress myself once again under the lilac bush. I pull on the stifling hose, button the brocade dress. I stuff my feet back into the tiny shoes. The archduke's second wife, so pious like my father, will protect us for now. The public's need for blood has been sated. But we will be sold again, no doubt, now that the archduke is dead. We will be back on display somewhere, or hidden away.

We will continue to unnerve people, to remind them of the animal within. But it is not, I now know, the animal in us that we should fear.

Art by Eric Orchard

A SCORE OF ROSES
TROY L. WIGGINS

1870s
Memphis, Tennessee

I.

Sunshine flowed through the crowd, sliding between hooters and hungry-eyed applauders. A whiskey runner with a long, toothy scar down his neck poured up servings of burning moonshine at a row of nearby tables. The harsh, fruity scent of the liquor filled Sunshine's nose, luring her with its sweet poison.

She swayed up to the tables, lowered herself into a seat, and stretched out like a yawning cat. The runner regarded her with flat eyes. She nodded. Her hand landed softly on the thigh of the stony-faced man sitting next to her, and her lips quivered. The scent of rosewater wisped from her skin, cutting softly through the dense reek of smoke from hand-rolled cigarettes, black bodies, and day-old sweat.

"So tell me, baby, why's yo ears so pointed like that?"

Baby took a sip from his tin cup. "You wouldn't believe me if I told ya, so I ain't gonna tell ya."

His skin was black, like the dead time between new days. She reached out and traced along the curve of his ear with her finger. "They like knives. Like knives made'a skin and bone. You kin to the devil?"

"Devil don't exist, honey."

Sunshine pulled a pout. "C'mon, baby. Tell me somethin'. You sayin' things like that just make me more curious."

Baby turned to Sunshine and met her gaze. His face was angled, his chin tapered, and his eyes were thundercloud gray, full of lightning and storms. Sunshine scooted closer to him, and he smiled.

"So, you not gon' answer my question?"

"Nope."

"Fine then."

"I might answer another one of your questions, though, if you promise to smile again."

Sunshine fulfilled his request. "I ain't seen you round here before. Where you come from?"

Baby tapped his chin, considering. "You sho' do know how to ask the wrong questions. What am I supposed to say to that, huh?"

"Tell the truth. Shame the devil." Sunshine took a sip, stopped, slapped her thigh. "Oh shit, he ain't real. Forgot. 'Scuse me."

189

"Yo mouth gon' get you in a lot of trouble. Fine, you want truth, here it go: I come from the dirt."

"And I come from yo' neck bone. Gimme me some mo liquor, Jerry. And you, gimme some mo' answers."

"I tole you, I come from the dirt and live wit' the dirt, laugh wit' the dirt, love the dirt and everything that come to be because of it."

"You soundin' like one'a them big foot country boys that just learned the world was bigger than a fool's middle finger, baby."

He laughed, a *boom boom* from deep in his chest that sounded like a drumbeat delivered from the top of a mountain. "Maybe so."

Sunshine swished a swig of moonshine around in her mouth, swallowed it, and growled away the burn. "Yeah, you talkin' like a man who's fulla some good drink."

"I'm sober as a stone, honey."

Sunshine hooded her eyes and ran her tongue over her lips. The air seemed to clear. "Well, that just ain't no good. What's the point of sitting' up in a place like this and not drinkin' yo troubles down the river? Why'ont you just come on home wit' me and tell me some mo' stories about yo' dirt, then? I might even sing you one of my special songs."

Baby laughed again and drained his cup. "Now that don't sound like a bad idea a'tall."

II.

"Ah..." Baby gasped. "Sunshine..."

"Yeah, Baby," Sunshine growled, jerking her slick hips. Rosewater and musk hung heavy on the air. Her eyes glowed in the darkness.

"Ah–" Another jerk. A flash of dusky nipple. An umber thigh against onyx. A cresting moonbeam. "Ah – *a'lina suatha tautroga...*"

"Shit, Baby. What that mean?"

Baby's white smile split the night. "You owe me a song, honey," he gasped.

III.

She claimed that night was safer, so they met after sunset. She said that the riots had brought out the evil in everyone, especially those people that already had hatred in their hearts toward folks like them. Baby had rolled his eyes. Nobody knew who he was. Still, she'd said, better to stay on the side of skin. Baby looked out over the hard faces and noticed how many hands twitched inside of pockets, how many backs bent before pieced-together shanties. He snorted at the "safety."

A familiar itch tingled on the tips of his ears. It was time to leave, past time. He stayed anyway, standing in the lopsided shadow of an old wooden fort that still bore the stink of dying and despairing men, still wore smudged gunpowder on the gates, still muddied the dirt road before it with blood and sweat. He could hear the hoots of the men inside as they glimpsed brown thighs and were swayed by low-down song that reminded them of times before horrors.

Someone yanked on his ear, and he whipped around, growling murder. Only Sunshine was there, wearing an old housedress with faded pink flowers. Her skin and hair glowed. There was no dirt on her shoes. He removed his hat, held it to his chest. She smiled, and he forgot the stink of the outdoors, forgot the darkness.

"I ain't think you was gonna come," she murmured, sliding her arm into his. He looked down at his boots. They were dirty. He didn't care.

"Why wouldn't I come? I don't cut and run."

"Let's go downtown, baby."

"Thought it wasn't safe there. Besides, I like the trees over here. Ain't no trees or nothin' really alive downtown that's no different than what we can see here."

"You call this livin'?"

"Bein' in these walls y'all done made ain't livin' at all, but at least here there's more dirt, more trees and such."

"You and yo dirt. Fine then."

They walked. Different lives unfolded a million times in the span of a few minutes. Three boys played baseball on the next street over. One boy couldn't hit the ball and called for a change of rules. The other two yelled and screamed. Several men sat around a fire built in a low pit. The biggest of them stood backlit by flames, swinging his arms and building a tale out of yells and memories. The other men laughed as they passed a jug between them, looking around before they sipped. Ahead of them, two rickety houses made of discarded slats of wood nearly leaned on each other. Moans and creaking spilt into the street from them. Glass clattered and crashed. Someone defiled the name of God. Baby smelled blood, pulled Sunshine closer to him.

"They the same damn thing," she whispered. He pretended not to hear.

Violence faded from the air, along with the scent of blood and donkeys. Children ran flat-footed through the dirt. A red rosebush stood in muted bloom along the edge of the street, its flowers drooping. Baby led Sunshine to the bush. He knelt before it, reached inside of the leaves.

"Watch the thorns," she breathed.

"They won't hurt me." Baby grasped the stem of a flower the color of congealed blood, put it to his nose, and whispered. Beside him, Sunshine shuddered and wrapped her arms around herself.

When Baby stood, he held a bloom aflame with red and pink and orange. Gone was the rot.

"Something to be said about dirt." He handed her the flower. "Watch the thorns."

"You'd let 'em hurt me?"

"Naw. But you still oughta be careful."

Sunshine breathed in the flower's scent. A lavender light flashed in her eyes and disappeared.

"What's wrong?"

"My first husband died thinking that I had the devil in me, and couldn't

191

make chil'ren. Now I know that it was his fault, not mine."

Baby poked his lip out and stuck his hands deep in his pockets. He knew many words, but none of them would come. His ears burned. "What happened to yo first husband? How he die?"

"I got fire in me, just like he said. He couldn't deal wit it. My fire ate him from the inside out." Her eyes snapped back into focus and the curl returned to her lips. Baby thought for a moment that he could see the fire licking beneath her skin. He wanted to sear the tip of his tongue.

"But you ain't like him, is you? You ain't gon' die from my fire."

"Ain't no fire been able to kill me yet, and I been around a while."

She put the flower back to her nose. "What's yo real name, Baby?"

"You first."

He smiled when she slipped his arm back into hers. Before they could take a step, she made a small noise. He looked at her. She looked back, confused. "You know what I just thought of? We gon' need somewhere to live."

IV.

Sunshine's city was big in the center, with all the trappings of steel and mortar and slow rot. But the wild places lingered. They called to Baby, and he knew. He knew about the paths and straightaways because of the wild places. They were easy enough to find, dank and green and slick with pot-bellied copperheads full of field mice and baby catfish. He picked through them, mud streaking his boots and face and hands, and he didn't care because this was *good* mud, the kind of mud that you were supposed to wear.

The sun was high when he realized that he had gone too far, so he doubled back. Mud squelched beneath his boots and his ears still itched. A copse of trees stood at angles over a large dirt clearing. Beyond the trees, Baby could see a plot of muddy, loose land where someone was trying to force beans and hard turnips. He whispered to the vegetables struggling in the mud, to the lopsided trees, to the slumbering dirt. A breeze flipped through the grasses.

Baby nodded, sat cross-legged on the ground, and began to whisper. The winds picked up and the soil stirred beneath him. His whisper became a slow chant. He closed his eyes. For once, his ears didn't itch.

The ground rolled like boiling water. Trees popped and rent and cracked and moaned. His chant rose into song. Soil tumbled onto his head and shoulders. Something blocked the sun. Another something brushed gently against his cheek.

The house was a flat sort of yellow, with a low wooden porch that seemed to dive straight into the ground. The steps leading up to the porch rose from the earth, and the windows had no glass in them. The roof was long overlapping wooden slats covered by leaves and bark. All around the house was deep brown soil, ready for tilling and planting, and the sun shone strong, unblocked by leaves or branches. To either side of the steps, twin rosebushes bloomed.

Baby didn't brush the dirt off of his shoulders when he left the clearing.

V.

They named her Rana. Sunshine told Baby that it meant "rose," but she never told him the language that the word came from.

They had called in an old midwife from the city who wore a dress the color of burlap and square-toed boots as heavy as a stonemason's. Before she came into the house, she tossed salt on the doorstep. Baby bit his lip so hard that it nearly bled.

"No mens. Bad luck," the midwife said, waving her hand. "You need ta go on outside."

Rana came healthy and brown, with pink lips and shiny black hair that possessed an otherworldly sort of curl. Her ears swooped slightly upward, and when she opened her eyes, they were a little too lavender. The midwife threw more salt, and Baby threatened to throw her out.

"Y'all quit all this foolishness," Sunshine snapped at them. She sat up tall in the bed, framed by a halo of black hair. She studied the baby, wearing an unreadable look. The air was hot and heavy. Tiny motes of dust danced in the shafts of midday sun. The midwife gathered her things quietly.

"I never wanted a child," Sunshine said. When she looked up, she had no smile. "My husband always did, but never me. She look like you, Baby. She got your skin. Your ears too."

"Yeah, maybe so. Look like she got yo fire, though. And yo eyes."

The midwife covertly threw a bit of salt in the corner, prayed a quick prayer, and smudged oil that had been prayed over seven times on the door-frame. Then she left.

"Y'all know what this mean, don't you, Baby? I can't go sing at the joint no mo'," Sunshine said. Rana smiled and gurgled.

VI.

Rana heard her mother's feet scuffing on the earthen steps and she scrambled to open the door. Sunshine walked in and sat down heavily on a plush chair, the only bit of furniture in the large family room. She kicked off her tight work shoes. Sunshine's brown skin looked flat and gray, her lips and hair thin to breaking.

"I made a new friend today, Mama," Rana said. She slid a steel washbasin full of hot water across the floor. A few suds sloshed over the lip of the basin and onto the floor, where they were immediately soaked up.

Sunshine lifted her feet and slid them into the water. She sighed, smiled a tiny bit, and closed her eyes. A small breeze blew through the windows.

"I made a new friend today, Mama."

Sunshine opened one eye. "Really, flower? Tell me 'bout it."

"Well," Rana began, kneeling to rub Sunshine's aching feet, "I went down to the creek after school today, and I was playing in the water when this big ol' snake came up out the water and started talkin' to me. Her mouth wasn't movin', but I could hear her in my head. She said that normally she'd eat a l'il thang like me, but because I could hear what she was sayin' we could

193

be friends. We had us a good time catching frogs, and she even followed me back to the schoolhouse. But I had to make her go 'way when we got to school cuz I didn't wanna scare Missus Teacher."

"What I tell you about going down to that doggone creek? You supposed to stay at the schoolhouse and play wit' the rest of the chil'ren."

Rana studied the blue veins in her mother's legs. They looked like streets on the maps Rana had seen at school. She wondered where they led. "I know, Mama, but them chil'ren don't be wanting to talk to me."

"Not 'be wanting.' You know the right way."

"The children at the school don't wanna play wit' me. They say evil stuff bout me and talk 'bout my ears and say that my daddy must be the devil. Even the grown folk talk about me. They think I don't be hearing em."

Sunshine sighed. "Shoot, people 'round here talk about everybody. It's a wonder we all still got ears."

For a while, the only sound in the room was the soft splashing of water. Occasionally Sunshine would grunt when Rana rubbed a particularly tough knot of muscle.

"Mama, how come you don't sing no more?"

Sunshine jolted. "Huh? What?"

"How come you don't sing no more?"

"What you talkin' about, girl?"

Rana focused on her mother's legs. "When I was real little you used to sing and go out into the woods and stuff. Your voice was so nice. You remember? You used to sing me all kinds of songs."

"I ain't sang in a while, huh? Got nothin' to sing about, I guess." Sunshine sat up, flicked the end of her housedress. "I used to wear nice dresses, you know? Folks used to love to see me comin' and hate to see me comin' at the same damn time. And I used to sing for people, instead of cleanin' up after they asses. Well, I sang mostly for colored folks at the joint, but it was still good singin'. Every once in a while, a white man would come through. There was one white man, he loved my singin' so much he bought me a shiny blue dress wit' the earrings to match. I ain't seen that dress in years. Wasn't a man alive that could resist fallin' in love wit' me when I sang to him."

"I ain't no man, Mama, but I'd like to hear you sing a song. Like you used to."

Sunshine waved a hand. It was wrinkled and veiny. "Naw, girl. I doubt I even could sing now. My voice ain't what it was."

"I don't care, Mama. I just want you to sing. You used to look so happy when you was walkin' 'round and singin'."

"Humph," Sunshine said. "That's cuz I was happy, not dog-tired. I can't sing you nothin' like I used to. But I can teach you a song. That way you can start to singin' for yo'self. You probably got my voice."

Rana clapped her hands and threw droplets of water across the room. "Really, Mama? I'd love to learn one of yo songs!"

Sunshine sat up and leaned forward. The heavy lines in the creases of her mouth and eyes lightened a bit. "I'mma teach you a song that my mama taught me, long before we got to where we is now. This the kinda song that build a fire in you, and let you get that same kinda fire from whoever else you wanna get it from."

Rana scooted closer. "I'm listenin'."

Sunshine pulled her daughter into a hug. She whispered the words into Rana's ear, supported by a melody that seemed to be the heartbeat of the earth itself. The sky reddened a bit, and the wind stirred.

Rana clasped Sunshine's arm so hard that the flesh bruised. Her mother's skin was hot, so hot that it nearly burned her fingertips. The words were ancient and unfathomable, a story told in a language that had long since been forced beneath the earth.

But Rana understood it all.

As the last words slipped past Sunshine's lips, she sat back on the chair. Her skin was pink and her hair a bit more fluffy.

"You sing that one. You ain't even gotta sing it loud, just put it out in the world. Sing that one, and you'll get the exact person you need, l'il flower. You'll get em right when you need 'em." Sunshine swung her feet out of the tub, stood, and walked around, as if testing her new legs. "Only thing is, you gotta decide how long you gonna need em. Don't let the song tell you. Don't let them tell you. You decide."

Rana ran her fingers down her skinny brown arms. She could feel small flames blooming beneath her skin, following the trails of her fingertips.

"This world will try to put yo' fire out, flower," Sunshine said. She walked over to one of the windows and stared out into the woods. "This world will try an' beat you and tell you you ain't shit and treat you like the shit that you ain't. Don't let 'em take yo fire. Don't let 'em take it wit' nice words or wit' a knife to yo throat. Don't even let em get you by laying pretty tricks on you, unless you want them tricks. Even then, do everything in yo power to keep yo fire going. Fight for it. Steal it. Kill for it. You understand me?"

"Yes ma'am," Rana whispered. Her eyes flickered violet.

Sunshine ran a hand over Rana's curly black hair. "Lookin' like it's gonna be a good day, l'il flower. Yo daddy's around here somewhere. Go find him, and stay with him. I'll see y'all later."

"Yes ma'am," Rana whispered again, trying to bury herself in Sunshine's touch.

VII.

Baby was standing near the doorframe when Rana came home from school, muttering in a language that she only minimally understood. He took off his hat and scratched his head, then his pointed ears. Rana absently touched her own.

"What's wrong, daddy?"

"Hi, flower. Heard you comin' a while back. I can't seem to figure out what done happened to this doorframe. The wood is turnin' to dust and fallin' off in one spot, and no matter what I do to it, it won't stop."

"Might be time to replace it," she said, scooting past him and into the house. She dropped her schoolbooks and they thunked heavily against the dirt floor. Her father continued to poke at the doorframe.

"Might be, at that."

"At least the rosebushes still going," she said as she came back on the porch. She handed her father a cup of water and watched him pour a little bit of it onto the earth before he took a swallow.

"Yeah, that's a good thing. I thought they'd be dead by now. I ain't took care of the things in years."

"Ever since Mama left."

Baby grunted and sat down on the porch. Rana studied her father's jaw, his quick brown eyes, his curly black hair. He'd looked the same all of her life. He absently scratched his pointed ear again.

"Any luck finding work?"

"Nope. They don't want you to do what you can, they want you to do what they want you to do. They pickin' boys that they know, boys who beg and lick they ass. I ain't never been a man to – shit, 'scuse me, flower. Don't pay me no mind."

They sat in silence for another few minutes.

Rana was the first to speak. "You miss her?"

"I miss pieces of her. No, ain't no truth in that. Really, I miss how she used to be. I think... I think I played a big part in her leavin'. Yo mama was special. She used to get something special from me. I think I stopped giving it to her. And I think that I kept her from getting it from anywhere else."

"I think she chose that, Daddy. 'Let' wasn't a word Mama ever took to."

"She didn't. You right 'bout that."

Baby stood up, and Rana noticed for the first time how delicate her father was. His torso was lean and his arms were long and thin. He walked over to the rosebushes and picked the flower that sagged the most.

"She used to say yo' name was rose, that Rana meant rose. She never told me in what language, and I never figured it out. I believed her, though." He put the rose to his lips and whispered to it. All of the shadows dissolved into gray, all of the colors of the world seeped into that one flower, and for a few seconds, it shone brighter than the brightest star.

"You got a lot of yo' mama in you. But you got a lot of me too. We didn't call you flower for nothin'."

When she took the flower from him, she could feel the tiny pulse of life inside it.

"Like that flower, like me, you gon' endure. It's gon' hurt, but it's also gon' be your strength. Keep it close to you. Under ya heart if you can."

Rana nodded.

"You know, you look just like her. It hurt sometimes to see you walkin' round here. For a second, I see you doin' something and I think that you her, that she done come back." He stared off into the distance. "Sometimes... sometimes I think I feel her out there. I'll be out looking for some work and I'll feel a flash of heat nearby that remind me of her, almost like she standin' next to me. Then she – it's gone."

Rana reached out, paused, touched her father's shoulder. "It's OK, Daddy. It is."

He smiled. Wrinkles creased the corners of his eyes. "You done forgave me already?"

"Oh, Daddy," Rana said, pulling her father close. He smelled like the forest, like ancient soil and freshly fallen leaves. "Daddy, I forgave you as soon as Mama taught me my first song. I forgave her too. I got my own song now. I'm as good as Mama was. Better, even."

Their eyes met for a moment. Then Baby kissed Rana's cheek, stood, and walked into the house.

All the birds ceased singing for a moment. A strong wind blew, carrying the scent of fresh tree roots and ancient soil. The rosebushes shimmered, red and pink and purple. And Rana began to whisper her song.

Art by Kaysha Siemens

NEITHER WITCH NOR FAIRY
NGHI VO

1895
Belfast, Northern Ireland

As my brother read me the grisly tale from *The Irish Times*, I felt a stone in my belly. The stone had been there, sometimes smaller and sometimes larger, since I was very young, but finally, I thought I had a name for it.

"Read it again," I said insistently, and Paul looked at me warily.

"Now, Ned, keep calm, it's only a story about a foolish man and his poor wife. There's no need to go flying off."

"I'm not going to go flying off," I said through gritted teeth, but to please him, I sat down on the threadbare rug on the floor of the room we rented and worked my hands loose from their fists.

"Read it again," I said in what I hoped was a calm voice, and with another dubious look at me, Paul did as I asked.

Bridget Cleary was the wife of a cooper, stern and solemn-faced in the only picture of her that could be found. She fell sick after delivering eggs to a relative of her father's, or maybe she was roaming the fairy forts, and as she lay ill, her husband and her male kin took her for a changeling, a fairy thing left in the place of the woman Bridget. They asked her questions, they slapped her, they threw foaming piss at her face, and they threatened to set her on the grate because fire would force the fairy out. Despite all that, she was getting better when she sat with her friend and her cousins on the afternoon of March 15. Then her husband came in one final time, ranting about the fairy that sat where his wife should, and when a spark caught her chemise, he was quick to douse her with paraffin. That was the end of Bridget Cleary, and my brother folded the paper briskly, putting it all away.

"Poor woman," he said, lighting himself a cigarette. "Done in by superstitious fools who thought her strange for visiting the raths."

I looked at my hands, long and white and bony. Bridget had lived her married life in Ballyvadlea, not close to Clonmel where Paul and I grew up, but not far either, and we both knew the fairy forts as well as Bridget must have. The old people called them evil places, but they were thrilling things to us. We would dare each other to stay in the center of the great earthen rings as the sun slipped below the horizon, and we'd even stay past full dark sometimes, if we were feeling especially brave. I always made sure to be the last to leave and the first to suggest staying. It was far better to be thought too reckless than a coward.

"She must have been very brave," I muttered.

Paul frowned at me, and I could tell he couldn't see the bravery in being

199

burned to death at the hands of a madman. I couldn't find the words to tell him that if it were me in the bed and him screaming at me and telling me I was something foul, I might have said anything he wanted to make him stop.

***

Six days out of seven, Paul worked at a linen factory on Bedford Street, and he came home soaked to the skin from the wet spinning rooms. It was my job to take his clothes from him and drape them out the window to dry for morning. He would scrub his skin dry with a cloth and sit in his nightshirt by the hearth until he felt human again.

He would have a bite to eat, and then I would watch with envy as he painstakingly practiced the rolling clerk's hand, replicating as closely as he could the elegant script of the copybook he had bought. Reading and writing didn't come easy to him, but we could both see that they would in time. For me, the letters seemed to swim so that they traded places, the words as unreliable as a cross-eyed thief. I couldn't look at them very long without feeling that old spark of temper, and so I watched my brother copy the letters night by night, sweating as he tamed them to his hand and made their curves smooth and sleek. He meant to look for work as a clerk when he mastered them, and then he would never need to smell the factory's muddy, pulpy reek again.

Paul would work as long as he could, and then he would read from the paper that was passed around the rooming house, stumbling over some words but getting smoother every day.

That night, as he climbed into the single bed, I couldn't hold the question back.

"Do you think there was something to what he said?" I asked.

Paul looked at me quizzically as he slid under the covers.

"Who said?"

"Michael Cleary, that that was a changeling he burned and his Bridget would come back on a gray horse."

Paul paused for a long moment, and I could see it warring on his face. We were raised to call out a warning to the fairies when we threw out the wash water, but we had lived in Belfast for the past four years, since he was 15 and I was 11, come up from the country and terrified of everything from the factories belching smoke to the mass of people who surrounded us. People in Belfast had less use for the fairies than they had for the French, and they had no use for the French.

"Fairy or not," he said finally, "burning to death's a bad business, isn't it, Ned?"

***

When my brother slept, I slipped out the door, taking the big key off its hook and locking it securely behind me. He didn't like for me to roam through the night, but as he had told me the first night we spent in Belfast,

200

tucked into a pew at a boarding house that didn't even let you lie down, there was nothing he could do to stop me.

I knew the Belfast streets better by night than I did by day, and even if it was a city that spun around the factory whistles, there was life here after the darkness filled the streets.

It was a working town, not like London where we had heard that there was a musical hall for every night of the week, but there were still a few little places where you could see acrobats, mystics with snakes in their baskets, and the odd comic singer. One that I passed was just now emptying people into the street, causing a brief crush that made me anxious and nervy.

One couple, baby in arms, started at me and hurried away, and I winced. Sometimes I could look a fright when I wasn't paying attention, and I straightened up and ran a hurried hand through my hair to do a little better.

Distracted, I looked at the posters plastered to the theater's walls. They featured pretty young women, and a pair of boys who probably couldn't scratch together the cash to go in were standing close. The posters made them laugh and gesture, shaping fat bottoms and round bosoms with their hands, pretending to faint and paw, but there was something about the pictures that broke my heart. Those girls with the shape of their legs so clear, and the sweep of their dresses down to the very line of their nipples, they made me *want* so much that I was nearly sick, and I had to turn away.

I walked faster, as if I could outrun it, but in Bridget Cleary's fate, I could hear an echo of my own. I had a name for this wanting now, and the terror of it was twisting me up. I wondered where my parents' son really was, because despite what they had called me and despite how my face looked like Paul's, with its short nose and round blue eyes, I wasn't Ned. I wasn't *human*.

For the first time in months, the shadows of Belfast looked long and grasping rather than comforting, and I realized that I was practically running. That was a good way to get clopped about the head by a policeman, and so I made myself slow down.

As I walked I found myself thinking about the fairy forts that hid in the hills. Someone once tried to tell us that they were abandoned settlements of the old people who lived in Ireland long before, and it had made us all laugh. But before our people, and his old people, there were people before that too, weren't there?

My mother taught us about the fairies, and about how a bit of bread and a bit of salt in our pockets would keep us safe while we roamed, and how a small saucer of milk on the doorstep could buy some luck in a lean season. She taught it to us the same way that she taught us to sweep and to tell good eggs from bad, and we accepted it all as one and the same.

I was walking faster again, and I made myself slow down again.

I knew one man in Clonmel who had gone out into the fields and chased after a golden spark all night. In the morning, his bare feet were cut to ribbons on the quarry stones, and whether he was chasing a golden spark, a golden girl, or the lights at the bottom of a bottle, it was only by good luck and grace that he hadn't broken his neck.

I winged my shoulder on a man rushing by, and he spun me around with the force of it. For a moment, in the light of his lantern, I could see just the sharp planes of his face, no softness about it, and I had to stop myself from screaming because it looked so strange.

There was another girl I knew from the village, a girl about Paul's age. She and I had hated each other round and round, the way that two strange people will. It's like there is not enough love in the world to go around, and if you're odd, you have to fight for what you can get. She ran out on her folks one night, and they never saw her again, even though her family put notices in the paper for weeks after, telling her she could come home no matter what she found on the moors. Most people thought that she had taken off after a bad man or perhaps got done in by the bandits that haunt the roads, but her brother told me that they had found her dress folded up on a stump in the forest, as neat as it would be on her bed at home, and her shoes set next to it and filled with flowers.

The Belfast night was brighter than it should be. The moon was already set, but the stars, though dimmer than what I knew in Clonmel, were dropped like sparks on the sky. That was the wrong thing to think, because I imagined that like sparks, they would go out, leaving the heavens as cold as a dead hearth. Then I thought about them not going out, but being snuffed, one after another, and that made the hair on the back of my neck stand up.

I was running again, and the streets looked strange and dark to me. The thought struck me that it wasn't Belfast I was in at all, and that only made me run faster. The streets were crooked where I thought they were straight, and when I dashed by the window of a milliner's shop, I thought the wooden heads turned to follow my progress.

My breath was coming in dragonish plumes out of my mouth, and though I was dripping sweat, I knew how cold it was. It was almost spring, but people could die in the cold of Belfast's streets. The thought of myself as one of those frozen corpses made me want to laugh, and I bit my tongue because I thought that if I started I would never stop.

When I was small, I used to beg to play with my mother's china shepherdess, a pretty figure all smooth and cool. I was so careful, carrying her around in my hands, the one bit of finery my mother had from her mother, and I never broke it, either. That was my father, who saw me playing with her like I was her mother, and slapped her from my hands to shatter on the floor.

I almost brained myself on a hanging sign, but I saw just in time to duck my head and get a scrape on my temple. I left skin and some hair there, but I didn't look back. God almighty, but I wished I could tear more of myself off like that.

I was nine when I had my worst fit, right before Sunday mass. I was bare as an egg, and getting ready to put on my clothes, and I couldn't. I didn't want them, I never wanted them, and when I looked down at myself, naked and scrubbed, I made myself sick. I started to beat my body with my fists, and claw as well, and then I fell into a fever so high that my parents had the priest in. I remember Paul sitting by my side, holding my hand hard in his.

"Please don't take my brother," he said over and over again, but now I could see that they already had, perhaps long ago, and left me in his place.

I ran flat into a woman, her face tired and scared, and she stiff-armed me away from her with a curse.

Ned Graham wasn't me, had never been me, I knew that now. Maybe they had taken him from the cradle, or maybe it was when he played on the doorstep. Mother had looked away, and not ever noticed that her baby was gone and I left in his place.

I was wrong, I had been wrong my *entire life*, and finally, this skin was choking me. I needed out of it by water or by fire like poor Bridget Cleary, I must climb out of it, or I would die, I was sure of it.

I would be rid of it, and there would only be Paul to mourn the thing I left behind.

Paul...

As I thought of Paul, I skidded to a stop, and then my heart dropped down to my shoes, though not for a memory this time.

The banks of the river were high and sharp in the poorer areas of the town, and another step would have sent me right down into the frigid water. Some dirt crumbled from the edge in front of me, falling down twelve feet, and I breathed hard, imagining myself tumbling into the water, all my frantic thoughts quelled by the cold once and for all.

I might have done it after all, but I thought again of Paul, and then of something my mother had told us at the same time she showed us how to carry a bit of bread and salt in our pockets to bring us safely home.

I took a deep breath and stripped my coat away from my shoulders. It was damp with sweat, but I turned it inside out anyway, shoving my arms through the sleeves and noting in a numb way that it was grown too tight over the past year. I turned three times on my heel, and when I stopped, I could see with perfect clearness the two figures standing just a few paces away.

"So the child figured it out," the first said, shaking his head. He was taller than any man I had ever seen, and his skin was dark like an African sailor. In the starlight, which was surely brighter than it should have been, I could see the brown and withered leaves where his hair should be, and the glint of his eyes. He was dressed like a fine gentleman of the town, and in his hand, he carried a cane capped with the silver head of a cat.

"I do not know whether to be pleased or not," complained his companion. She was small and dainty, every inch a Belfast lady until you saw that she was bald underneath her hat. When she smiled, her teeth were as sharp as knife points. The hand that rested elegantly on her hip was the same as mine, but the other, held up as if to pluck lies from the air, was the paw of a fox.

"You did that to me," I snarled, turning like an animal brought to bay. Behind me was the river, and before me were two creatures I knew to be just as dangerous.

"We did," the dark gentleman said, inclining his head and making the leaves rustle. "But you stopped yourself. Why did you do that?"

I narrowed my eyes at his polite, curious question.

"Why didn't I throw myself into the water, you mean?" I asked sarcastically. "I suppose I thought it a bit chilly for a swim, didn't I?"

"No you didn't," the lady chimed in. "You thought it was just perfect."

"We could see it in your eyes before you left the theater," the gentleman added. "We thought, 'There's one who will leap and thank us.' Won't you do it now?"

I started to answer them, but then I stopped. They stood within in an arm's length of me. If they had wanted me in the water, they could have pushed, and if they were really disappointed with the game, they could have left. There was no reason they would stand around talking to me unless they were bound. No, there were rules to this, and it was all the better for them if they played them with people who were Belfast-born and didn't know the rules. Some city-raised might have turned away in anger and fear, breaking their spell and freeing them. I wasn't, though, and I started to smile.

"I've won, and you're sorry," I said. "You owe me a forfeit."

Their smiles froze on their faces, and I laughed out loud. I was right, and no matter how beautiful they were, now they looked like cats who had licked flypaper.

"Careful," the lady said coldly. "After your forfeit is done, we will still be here."

"I was ready to plunge into the water of the river," I retorted. "Tell me how afraid that makes me."

"Is that your forfeit?" the gentleman asked, and I thought he might have liked me a little, because otherwise he would have taken it as I said it.

"It's not." I hesitated, and then I simply shook my head. There was only one question that mattered when fairy gold turned to leaves in the morning and fairy girls turned to goats by midday.

"What am I?" I said, and I looked between the two of them, waiting for them to tell me for certain sure.

The gentleman raised his eyebrow, and shrugged, gesturing me to come closer. I don't like being so close to people who weren't Paul – that was why I was such a failure at the factories – and it seemed this distaste extended to fairies as well. Still, I did as he said, and when I stepped close, I could smell him. He bore a strange peppery scent with a note of metal to it, and I realized in my heart the way I had only realized before in my head that there was nothing human about him.

"Hmmm." He leaned in until the strange and alien scent of him filled my head, and when he stared into my eyes, I could see that his were simply black, no white, no color, nothing but bottomless black. I could feel the heat of his skin, and I flinched when his hand came close to my face, hovering by my cheek, but not touching.

The lady was somewhere behind me, and I could hear her dress rustling as she drew close. Her skirts brushed the backs of my legs, making me want to pull away, but then I would practically be in the man's arms, and suddenly, the thought of it terrified me, made my heart beat faster until I was sure I would be sick.

They never touched me, but their inspection took apart everything I was, and I knew how little that was. Having them so close was like having spiders crawling up my skin, and the moment I thought that, I knew that they knew how I felt, and even worse, that it pleased them just fine. I thought I would scream, and then they let me go, stepping back like they would from a horse they decided not to buy.

"You're monstrous," I whispered, wrapping my arms around my body. I could still feel spiders running up and down, and I wondered a little madly if they would ever stop.

"If you say so," the lady said politely. "Do you want your answer or no?"

I nodded mutely, my jaw clenched so tight I thought I would shatter my teeth. I wanted the answer. I had earned it, but more than that, I needed it.

"Very well. You were named Edward Graham, called Ned, and born to Matthew and Alice Graham on July 6th, in the year of your Lord 1880. You were born on the night of the new moon, which we call unlucky in my land, but is the best of luck in my companion's home."

"You are the great-great-great-grandchild of a man who was taken to my home and then walked back of his own accord, and you have something of his stubbornness and something of his faith, as well," the gentleman supplied.

"You are strong, but not as strong as you will be if you live your full span, and water pulls you close. If you die early, you will die of water." The lady pointed to the river behind me for illustration, and I could see too clearly that she was right.

"You're of the race of men, who are of the earth, and to earth you will return," finished the gentleman. "That is what you are."

"That's all?" I whispered. "That is all you have to say to me?"

"Did you expect to be the sleeping king awakened?" The gentleman tapped his foot impatiently, and I saw starlight bounce off the silver chasings of his boot.

"No... no... I... I thought I must be... like Bridget Cleary."

"That poor woman? That was a bad business," the lady tutted. "But you mustn't take it so close to heart, lass. She was no kin of yours."

I looked up, first startled by the similarity of her words to my brother's, and then I heard another word.

"Lass?"

She smiled tolerantly.

"Of course. A great big girl, if one who knows nothing of how to act or behave herself."

"I..." The stone in my belly swelled, heavy as granite, recognizing its name.

"There's another gift for you, then, if you did not know," the gentleman said, tipping his hat.

They both turned to go before I found my voice, and it was a thin, wailing thing.

"What am I supposed to do with that?"

When they stepped away, it was like a veil had dropped between us, and they lost their sharp edges. I saw the suggestion of stag horns above the lady's head, and the gentleman seemed even taller, tall enough to snatch down a star.

"Anything you want."

"Yes," agreed the lady. "Go to London and learn to dance, or run away to the Americas to seek your fortune. Find a child so you can be a mother, or shave your head and become a mendicant nun."

"Come with us," suggested the gentleman slyly. "Present yourself at court. The queen has a love for silly country girls who clomp and shout. Make a name for yourself, and come back in a hundred years, when Belfast might love you better."

For a moment, they sharpened, him reaching out his hand, her reaching out her fox's paw, and I lurched back with a cry.

The heel of my foot found no ground beneath it, and in a panic, I threw myself forward to avoid tumbling backwards into the river. I fell flat on my face on the cobbles, and when I looked up, the only thing left of the gentleman and the lady was the sound of their laughter.

I shuddered, and remembered that the friendly folk had never much cared whether the people they played with lived or died.

I wondered if I would be sorry for not reaching for them, and then thought of the man from Clonmel with his feet shredded to ribbons, and a dress folded neatly on a stump, and I didn't think I would.

I walked home slowly, following the path of the river but keeping a healthy space between myself and its banks. Soon the Albert Clock would chime five, and I would start rousing the people who paid me to make sure they made it to their factory jobs on time. I got a penny for every room I woke up, and God only knew that it wasn't much, but it helped.

I thought of Paul, and I thought of poor Bridget Cleary, too. They hadn't told me whether she was a witch or not, only that it was a bad business all around. It was, and my steps faltered as I imagined Paul screaming in my face, asking me the names of God and the saints, demanding to know where his brother had gone.

I also thought about Paul's clever hands and honest face, and how tightly he had held my hand when we came to Belfast, the dirt from our parents' graves still dusting our shoes.

They had said I could come back when Belfast loved me better, but I knew that it would not matter if Paul were not there to love me at all.

As I walked, I knew that the stone in my belly would always be there, though it seemed lesser now than it was before. I thought about Paul having a younger sister and not a younger brother, and it grew smaller still.

There was no boy I could imagine myself being, but I could see a girl. Not a witch or a fairy, but a great clomping girl, a wandering nun, a dancer, a dairy maid, or a flower seller.

A sister.

The sky grew light and lighter still, and though I knew that Belfast had not changed, and that I had not either, everything was different, and I was not afraid.

Art by Aaron Paquette

A DEEPER ECHO
DAVID JÓN FULLER

1919
Winnipeg, Manitoba, Canada

The smoky-grey dire wolf loped between darkened hulks of wooden box-cars on the sprawling CPR train yards of Winnipeg. The early June air was already warm and the sun had yet to rise. Warehouse doors clanged open at the looming Canadian Pacific station.

The wolf came to an abrupt halt, sniffing the air. The scent of human body odor grew stronger through the heady mix of diesel and tar stench. A faint smell of pines tinged with oil lingered beneath.

The wolf's stocky shoulders were as tall as the tops of the massive, grimy wheels, and he knew what would come next: a hostile shout, warning off strangers; or worse, a cry of alarm at the sight of a wolf the size of a bear. He'd been shot at enough in the war. Best to hurry, then. Thomas Greyeyes shivered his thick fur to adjust the army-issue satchel that hung beneath his torso.

Didn't matter if you were a veteran of kaa-kii-kichi-miikaating, the Great War; honest work was hard for a man to come by in 1919. And though Thomas had been making ends meet in the dwindling fur trade since being de-mobbed, that wasn't the reason he had come to Winnipeg. Here, white work-ers had shut down a city run into the ground by its white owners. The general strike would make it difficult to find who he was looking for.

Thomas slipped underneath the couplings between two cars. The grind-clap-grind of leather soles on hard-packed ground told him the man ap-proaching was used to being in charge.

He turned his snout down to the dark ties and crushed slate and called up the power to change from the earth below. The energy flowed, melting his fur back into bare skin and pulling his snout back into his human face, the rest of his body quickly shedding all traces of his lupine form. He shivered despite the warm air, squinting to the east where the sky brightened to or-ange. He strained to hear – with dull, human ears, now – the man's ap-proach, and scrambled to get dressed in the clothes carefully folded in his satchel.

He was just tying up his shoelaces when a gruff voice said, "Hey! This is private property!" A kerosene lamp glared across the space between the cars.

Thomas stood. At thirty-nine, his knees were starting to feel sore even after the rejuvenating fire of the change. He wore the same army-issue shirt, coat, and trousers he'd had when returning from the bloody fields of France, and the cap that bore the symbol of his battalion, the timber wolf. He'd since replaced the shoes and leather belt with his own. His hair was jet-black, his nose shaped in a proud hook like his father's, and his skin was just slightly darker than that of the white man who now faced him.

"Listen, chief: this is no hotel. Scram."

Thomas squinted in the harsh chemical light. "I couldn't find the room service bell anyway."

"Company boxcars are private too."

Thomas stepped away from the couplings. He threw his satchel over his shoulder so the Canadian Expeditionary Force sigil and the symbol of the 107th Battalion on his cap were plain in the lamplight. "Then it's a good thing I walked here."

"Where from?"

"Red Sucker Lake."

The CP man lowered his light. "Infantry?"

"That, and engineering."

The guard looked him up and down. Now was not the time to comment. If you looked too much like an out-of-work Indian they might even find an excuse to call the cops. Winnipeg's boom years still hadn't made it "the Chicago of the North," and the city seemed to take out its resentment on anyone who didn't look or sound Anglo enough.

The CP man chewed the inside of his lip. "Four hundred miles to come to the railyard? That's a long walk, chief."

Thomas took a deep breath. He could never be sure what would sting a white person as much as *chief*. Probably for the best. He put his hand into the ragged pocket of his coat and clenched his fingers for the hundredth time around the letter he'd received only a week ago. "Don't trust airplanes much."

The other snorted. "They have an airport up there already?"

Thomas allowed a slight smile. "Nope. That's why I don't trust 'em."

The CP man spat off to his left. "If you're not after work, what *are* you looking for?"

"A family named Fotheringham."

"What, the clothesmakers?"

Thomas shrugged. "Mrs. Alan Fotheringham?"

"Yeah, that's the one. But you won't have much luck at their shop. All closed up."

"The strike?"

The CP man nodded. "Mood's ugly in town, if you're just in from the north. First the war, then the 'flu, now the strike. Most of our mechanical department fellas walked off the job, but I'm still here. Police all got fired two weeks ago when they wouldn't sign away their right to a union, and now the city's got some 'special constables' running around. Big fight with them and the strikers the other day."

Thomas was used to dealing with the North West Mounted Police near his reserve – some of them honorable fellows – but he didn't know much about the city police. He wondered whether the Ukrainian wolf pack in the city's North End he'd heard about were mixed up in the strike. Best if he stayed out of their way, too. "That doesn't sound good."

The CP man put a hand up to the side of his mouth. "Bunch of thugs. Don't tell anyone I said that." He glanced to the brightening eastern sky. "Going to get worse before it gets better. Rail and post office the only things still going for sure."

"Maybe I'll try that shop. Do you know where it is?"

"It's probably locked up tight — but it's 'Ladies' Day' at the Soldiers' Parliament today."

"The what?"

"A lot of vets aren't for the strike, but the ones who are meet in Victoria Park. They'll probably come after you, too. Today they're letting the women run the show and make the speeches."

"Hm," said Thomas.

"Just about all the workers at Fotheringham's are women. All on strike."

Thomas took a deep breath. "They might know how to reach her, eh?"

The CP man shrugged.

"It's a start. Miigwetch."

"Beg pardon?"

Thomas had been up north long enough to have slipped into Island Lakes Dialect Ojibwe without thinking. "Thank you," he said.

The guard waved it off. "Now, I wouldn't stick around, if I were you. Boss doesn't like Indians."

Thomas clenched his jaws. The boss would probably like a wolf at his door even less. He turned in the direction of Main Street and left the CP man to his rounds. Though his infant granddaughter was safely hidden with relatives on the reserve, he needed to find this nice white woman who had made off with his children.

***

The Fotheringham shop was closed, all the windows shuttered. The stink of uncollected garbage muddled up the heavy air.

At Victoria Park, men in full suits mingled with women in dresses and hats. It might have almost seemed a picnic but for raised voices and pro-labor placards. Veterans hurried through the crowd in their olive uniforms. The newspapers Thomas had glanced through over lunch had made much of the "foreign" and "Bolshevik" supporters of the strike. But here, the accent that soared most often through the air was distinctly British, not Russian or Ukrainian. A funny kind of Bolshevism, Thomas thought.

One of the soldiers took a second glance at Thomas as he marched by and stopped. "The 107th?"

Thomas noted the other's rank and saluted. "Yes, sir. Corporal Thomas Greyeyes."

The lieutenant saluted back. "The Indian battalion. You did your country proud at Hill 70. Scared the Huns right down to their boots, I'm told."

Thomas didn't bother to correct him that half the 107th had been white. "Thank you, sir."

The officer extended his hand. "Lieutenant Alexander Mackenzie, Fort Garry Horse."

Thomas nodded. The dark circles beneath Mackenzie's eyes that matched those on Thomas's face spoke for them.

"I hope you're here to show your support," said Mackenzie.

"Actually, I'm looking for someone, sir."

"Eh? Who?"

"A Mrs. Alan Fotheringham. She sent me a letter about my children, but I don't have an address." He showed the letter to Mackenzie.

"This is to your wife."

Thomas clenched back a sob. "She died. Tuberculosis."

Mackenzie's face smoothed. "Terribly sorry to hear it. All we hear about is so many ravaged by the 'flu."

Thomas bit his tongue to keep from shouting. It might not have been Mackenzie's fault the reserves didn't have proper houses or enough doctors to treat the epidemic – but he still had no polite response.

Mackenzie handed the letter back to him. "I daresay some of Fotheringham's employees might be here today."

"Thank you," said Thomas.

"Why not stay for a while – right 'round here, where I can find you, and I'll see what I can do." He saluted, which Thomas echoed, and then marched off.

Stay for a while, thought Thomas, *so it seems you are standing with us.* A sea of soldiers and women surged around him.

The sun crept overhead as the leaders of the event took the stage, and Thomas threw himself back to memories that had kept him sane during the war: the pleasing, awkward weight of his newborn son when his wife first handed her to him, swaddled in cotton and rabbit fur. That memory seemed more distant now than the bite of his shoulder stock when he fired into the darkness from the trenches, and it echoed more deeply through him. His children grew whenever he returned from the trapline. They tottered on pudgy legs across the bare boards of the space that served as kitchen, dining room and bedroom, little moccasins slapping the wood with every uncertain step. Then they were gangly coyotes, eager to join him in the woods, listening to stories about the Creator, the animals, and man's place in the world – and especially, as his grandmother had told them to him, tales of the mahiinkan, the wolf. Those moments were a different world.

After three years in the service, he'd finally gotten to see his daughter and son again and they were strangers to him. Worse, since his son looked so much like Thomas's own mother – the same long face, high cheekbones – it seemed she looked at him through his son's eyes. The silence between Thomas and his children became stiff, uncomfortable. The way they avoided his eyes now didn't seem a mark of respect, but shame. Could they see the invisible hole in his chest, which ached when the whine of a mosquito triggered the memory of an incoming shell? The way he felt blown apart without so much as a scratch on him? His son and daughter had stood across the room from him, the gulf between them as wide as the Atlantic. He was back in Canada after years in France and Belgium but it was like coming to a new country again, one in which he no longer belonged.

When the speeches were done and the cheering crowd began to disperse, it was late afternoon and Thomas's uniform was damp with sweat. Lt. Mackenzie appeared again, as good as his word, with a woman in tow who gave Thomas directions to the Fotheringhams' home.

***

The western sky was fading to orange when Thomas found 96 Balmoral Street, a dark red house that towered above the elm saplings on the boulevard. The row of two-storey mansions faced across a grassy expanse where scaffolding and cranes loomed against the enormous new Legislative Building. *How many families could fit into just one of these places?* Thomas wondered. The house on the Red Sucker Lake reserve where he and his wife had lived – and where she had died – was little more than a shack.

Thomas steadied himself with a quivering hand on the rail and crept up the stairs to the gabled front porch. *They're my children*, he told himself. *They'll come.*

Inside, he heard voices, plates clanging together, suitcases dragged up stairs, and closets opened and shut, punctuated by hurried footsteps. He heard a woman's voice, calling instructions, the notes high, even shrill.

He knocked once on the solid-wood door. A small, white woman in a housemaid's uniform opened it and said, "Finally–" She cut herself off and stared at him.

He swallowed. "My name is Thomas Greyeyes. I came to get my children." He wanted to add, "Can I see them?" as he would with dealing with any white person of authority, but he bit the words back. They had taken his children away. He was through asking.

"I, that is, who are you?" said the woman. Her face was flushed and she seemed out of breath. A door slammed somewhere upstairs.

Thomas pulled the letter from his pocket and unfolded it. "Is this the home of the Fotheringhams?" He knew some white people didn't know whether to trust you unless you had a piece of paper or a document to prove what you were saying.

"Agnes!" came a woman's voice from the floor above. It echoed through the porcelain-tiled lobby.

The maid glanced at the letter in Thomas's hand and then over her shoulder. "Just a moment," she said, and closed the door.

He waited.

When the door reopened, the maid stood behind a taller woman wearing her chocolate-brown hair up and clothed in a peach and grey dress. Her eyes were green and dark and fixed on Thomas, glancing up and down before she spoke. "Can I help you?"

Thomas took a deep breath and spoke the way he used to with the Hudson Bay Company man when he wanted the best price for his fox and mink furs: polite and firm, no smile. "I've come for my children, Marie and John. I understand you took them from the school they were in, but now it's time for them to come home."

"Shall I call the police, ma'am?" said the maid.

The woman turned to her. "The police are still on strike, Agnes. It's the special constables now. But no. I see no need for that." She turned to Thomas. "Won't you come in? Perhaps we can discuss this to everyone's satisfaction."

Thomas didn't like the sound of that – he caught the hard tone in her voice – but he nodded and stepped in. The maid closed the door and locked it.

"See to the luggage, Agnes, and remind the children they're to make themselves presentable." Her voice trailed off. Agnes waited a beat and then scurried up the stairs.

"Please join me," the woman said. She gestured into a candlelit room off the main entrance. The air was hot and muggy. "I'm Gladys Fotheringham," she said, extending her hand.

Thomas shook it. Her skin was soft and smooth, no calluses. "Thomas Greyeyes."

The room's dark walls were lined with bookshelves. Two deep green wingback chairs flanked a massive fireplace. Mrs. Fotheringham gestured to one as she sat in the other. "Please have a seat." Thomas did. "I wish I could offer you some tea – do you drink tea? – but with the water pressure so low due to the strike, we've been running short. I'm sure you understand."

Thomas nodded. "I'd like to see my children."

Mrs. Fotheringham cleared her throat. "Yes, I understand. May I ask how you heard they were here? We had no idea how to reach you when we received word your wife had died."

The lump in Thomas's throat made his words thick. "I asked around." He swallowed hard. "I'd like to see them. They need to come home."

"When was the last time you saw them?" she asked, an edge to her voice.

"Wintertime. At Christmas."

"I see." She smoothed a crease in the lap of her dress. "I don't believe that school was a good place for them."

Thomas's heart began to pound. Was it really going to be this easy? "We've been trying to get them home for years," he said. "For good. But the priests and the government men say we can't, not even when I'm making good money. How did you come to take them here?"

Her smile was brittle. "My sister is a nun who teaches at the school." He face fell and she looked to the empty fireplace. "They had... an outbreak of tuberculosis."

Thomas didn't need the keen nose of a wolf to tell him her scent was off, and so was her story.

But the mention of the disease brought back the thought of his wife and a roaring filled his ears. He saw his wife Clara's face again, pale and still. He wiped a sweaty hand over his eyes. *Stop it. She's gone.*

Mrs. Fotheringham's voice slowly intruded. He'd missed what she had been saying. "–seemed for the best. We had made arrangements for them to have a tutor – as we would if we had children of our own – but recent events have made that difficult."

"What did you say?"

"We planned to continue their education. Of course, you may—"

Thomas gripped the wooden corners of his chair's arms and leaned forward. "What happened?"

Mrs. Fotheringham licked her lips. "Where?"

"At the school. They weren't happy about going there but they stopped talking about it, to us. We heard they were beaten if they spoke our language, or sang the songs we taught them. We saw the marks on my daughter's back. Now she won't show us. Me. She wouldn't let us see, the last time they came home."

"I'm sure I don't know anything about that."

Thomas surged to his feet. "You're lying!"

Mrs. Fotheringham shrank against the back of her chair. "Mr. Greyeyes, please—"

The clack-clack of shoes announced the arrival of the maid. "Ma'am?" she said sharply, darting her face into the room.

Mrs. Fotheringham waved her off without looking away from Thomas. "When visiting my sister there last month," Mrs. Fotheringham said in a low voice, "I could see the children were unhappy. Whether it's because they aren't used to a civilized education or due to something else, I could not tell. The sisters and the principal said they were doing their best to teach them. I offered to take some of them should the need arise. And when we got word—"

Thomas shook and spoke through his teeth. "They let a white woman walk in and take our children when she wants to, but not their own parents who have been trying to get them back for years?"

Mrs. Fotheringham's eyes glistened but her mouth was set in a straight line. "I am not in charge of the schools, Mr. Greyeyes."

He stalked to the door, reentering the electric glare of the lobby. "They're coming with me," he said over his shoulder.

"Wait—"

But Thomas was already heading up the stairs. "John! Marie! It's your—" his voice gave out suddenly when he saw their beautiful faces peering down the staircase from the second floor. He spread his arms even though his chest suddenly ached. "Niniichaanisak!" he said. They both flinched at the sound of his voice, throwing their hands up as if to ward off a blow. He hesitated.

"What is it?" he said.

Neither of them spoke. They looked older now, especially his daughter, even though she was the younger of the two. Something about her eyes — the deep brown in them used to sparkle, but now it just seemed dark and hollow.

Mrs. Fotheringham came to stand in the middle of the lobby, waiting silently below Thomas.

"Kipaapaa niin," he said. They flinched and turned their faces, taking a step back. "I am your father," he repeated. "I've come for you."

His son glanced down as if he could see through the floor to where Mrs. Fotheringham stood. Thomas knew that look: it was the same face a junior soldier made when he didn't know which commanding officer to listen to.

215

Thomas turned to Mrs. Fotheringham. "I'd like to speak to them alone."

"Children," called Mrs. Fotheringham, "show him to the room where your things are. But make sure you're all packed."

Marie looked at him, her head bowed, then turned and went through a door near the edge of the second-floor landing. John did the same. Thomas walked up the second set of stairs and followed his children in. He closed the door behind them.

The drapes were closed and only light in the room came from a kerosene lamp, its glass flute already blackened with soot. John and Marie huddled next to a dresser with its top drawer empty, a half-packed suitcase by their feet on the hardwood floor. The flame cast deep shadows up the sides of their faces as they stared at him.

It had been more than three years since the Indian Affairs agents had come with the representatives from the school to take away his children and many of the others on the reserve. Thomas's tongue felt thick with all the words left unspoken since then. They were strangers now, and yet so clearly descended from his people, and Clara's; his ancestors' voices seemed ready to burst forth from their mouths. But they had shied just now when he spoke in their native tongue. Clearly at the school they had been taught to keep those voices silent.

He pulled up a chair draped with unpacked clothing – there seemed to be mountains of it in the room, more than he and his family had ever owned – and sat, leaning forward as he had when they used to sit around the camp-fire. They stared mutely back at him. "I would like to invite you to come home." He tried to speak the way his grandmother would, not the demanding way that worked better with city-dwelling white folks.

He paused but the two barely breathed, their nostrils twitching.

"There are some things I would like to tell you–"

Marie jerked forward. "Why didn't you come to get us?"

"I was unable to leave when, when your mother died." It was only partly true, but there were only so many things he could tell them about at once.

"No, before!" she said, tears welling in her eyes. Her beautiful black hair, still cropped short the way the nuns had cut it, was a jagged raven's wing of shadow in the lamplight. "You never came! They said we'd never go home until we could learn to be good! Why didn't you come?"

"I was away–"

Marie interrupted again, her chin jutting forward in a way that made Thomas proud even as it frightened him. Here was the girl's spirit he remem-bered, but now it raged at him. "Why was that more important?"

John put his arm across her body, holding her back. "Marie–"

"No!"

Thomas put up his hands. "We tried, your mother and I. They said if we took you out without permission we would go to jail. We wrote letters, I worked to make more money, and then the war–"

John stepped forward. "It doesn't matter. Mrs. Fotheringham got us out."

For a second, Thomas's heart soared, but then he saw the unforgiving set of his son's jaw.

"She'll take us to their country house, she said. When the strike is over, we'll come back. Then they'll have us in a real school."

Thomas's throat was suddenly so dry he could barely speak. "You have a home already. I can take you back."

"No!" said Marie. "You can't make me be Indian!"

"But I—"

She shook her head and crumpled, pulling her fists up to cover her face and ears. "I don't want to go into the shed! Please!"

Thomas's heart pounded as he recognized the tone in her voice. That same terror ripped from his own throat when he would relive his friends being blown apart by shrapnel, the whistling shriek of an incoming shell —

But there she was, even as her brother held her tight to soothe the shudders that wracked her body. She had known horror while he was away.

Thomas lurched out of the chair and fell to his knees, crawling toward his children until he could wrap his long arms around their shivering backs.

John tried to throw his arms away, but Thomas hugged them tighter. "I know. I don't know what, but I know it. I know it."

"You can't," said John.

Thomas wanted to tell them, he knew what it was like to be sneered at for being Indian, how the white men in his unit had welcomed him the least and the last. How he'd had to go the extra mile, literally, in his recon duties, to prove himself. The only comments had been about how he was older than most of them; but the unspoken remarks were what lingered. *Indian. Illiterate. Savage.* His first sergeant had assumed Thomas could only read animal tracks, that he fed himself by hunting with a bow and arrow and wouldn't understand tire tread marks, boot prints, or the sound of German soldiers creeping through the muck of no-man's-land.

His daughter's words, *You can't make me be Indian*, dredged all that back up.

After long moments of sobbing, he quieted and their breathing became less ragged. He didn't know how long Mrs. Fotheringham would give them before coming to claim his children, but so far her footsteps still echoed only from the first floor.

"Niniichaanisak," he said, before switching to English, "you don't have to be anything but what you are. And you are beautiful. If you could see the way your ancestors' faces shine in yours, you would be proud. As I am of you. You are so strong. And we can be strong together, not pulled apart to be put into other people's places."

Marie looked up at him, her dark eyes hard and her cheeks glistening. "I can't go. They took my baby. They might do something."

Thomas glanced to the side; his hearing wasn't as good as when he was a wolf, and it had been worse since the thunder of the war, but he was pretty sure not even the maid was close enough to hear through the door. He dropped his voice to a whisper. "Pimaatisi giniichaanis. We hid her, your baby. Your mother and I. The teachers at the school think she died in the hospital, but we took her. She's with your uncle, now, back home."

"What?"

"Shh, shh, we had to keep it a secret. Until we could get you out. Both of you. Will you come?"

Marie's lip trembled and she made a choking sound.

John grabbed Thomas's upper arm. "Why didn't you tell us?"

"We were afraid, too."

The sound of an automobile growled and sputtered to a halt from the street out front. In the lobby downstairs, footsteps clattered across the tile floor.

"They were coming to take us in a car tonight," said John.

"You don't have to go," said Thomas. "You can come with me." He cracked a tiny smile. "But you'll have to walk."

His son and daughter shared a long look.

Thomas caressed their shoulders and backs roughly. "There is more power in you than they know. And there is something else I can share with you, when the time is right. Think of some of the stories we shared when you were little. You know the ones. The ones you wanted to be part of, about the mahiinkanak."

Slow remembrance of driven-out words crinkled Marie's brow. "The... the wolves."

Thomas nodded. "I couldn't tell you everything then, because sometimes a story has to be told at different times. But if you want to come with me, that story is waiting for you. You're already a part of it, and you cannot be made to feel less than human in it. I don't have a big house. Or much money. But I can give you that."

"Children!" called Agnes from the staircase landing. "Grab your things."

There were deep voices from the entrance downstairs and quick feet clattered up the staircase.

Thomas held his breath as his daughter and son broke their gaze and turned to look at him.

"We're coming," said John and Marie. Together they went to the door and opened it. Agnes stepped back, startled. "Are you ready?"

John raised his chin and looked at her, the spitting image of Clara's father facing down an Indian Affairs agent thirty years ago. Confusion pinched her face. John and Marie started down the stairs. Thomas turned to Agnes and said, "Goodbye," and followed his children.

Two men waited for them on the main floor. Their shirtsleeves were rolled up and each carried what looked like a section from a wagon-wheel spindle, long as a baseball bat. Their dark eyes locked on to Thomas as he stopped on the tiled lobby. He knew by the straight-backed air of authority coupled with the rounded shoulders: they saw themselves as above the law. Given their neckties, vests and matching trousers, he guessed these were two of the "special constables" who had replaced the police.

Mrs. Fotheringham's hand was still on the doorknob, and the two men brushed past her.

"This the one?" said the taller of the two, glaring at Thomas.

"There's no need for trouble," said Mrs. Fotherinham. "Thank you all the same, sirs." She threw a glance at Thomas, cutting around in front of the burly men. "I did not call these men here, I assure you. Agnes! Offer our guests some tea while I speak to Mr. Greyeyes."

The constable ignored her. "All right, chief, let's go."

"It's OK," Thomas said with a slight smile, "you can call me Corporal."

The shorter constable, whose face was dark with stubble, stepped forward and pulled a revolver from his pocket. "I don't take orders from savages. Push off!"

The taller constable grimaced at his partner. "What the hell are you doing? Think we can't handle this the old way?"

"After them Bolsheviks pushed us around Tuesday, the boss said we should let 'em know who's in charge. Well, this is it. Come on, chief. Outside."

"Gentlemen, please—" Mrs. Fotheringham said, holding out her hands.

"It's all right," Thomas said to her softly. "We were just leaving."

"What?" Mrs. Fotheringham's eyes flicked to Thomas's face and then to his children. "John? Marie? Is this true?"

"We're going," said John. "And no white man is going to stop us."

The constable cocked his gun. Thomas's pulse quickened. He knew how badly things could go and the sooner they were outside, the better, even if the constables followed them out. As a wolf, he'd have had no trouble; but there was no time to change. "No one asked you, kid," said the armed constable.

"Sir!" said Mrs. Fotheringham, her voice carrying a note of panic. "I must ask you to leave. This is not a police matter."

"We'll see about that," said the taller man. He pointed his great stick directly at Thomas's face. It brought back the image of a German rifle Thomas had stared down for a split second before ducking — one of the times as a wolf he had prowled too close to enemy lines and been spotted. That shot still rang in his ears, even though it had missed him. "You," said the constable. "Outside. The little brave and the little squaw can stay here."

Thomas fought to keep his mind clear. He couldn't afford a flashback to the war now. "It's fine," he said weakly, then repeated himself, more loudly, and added, "I'll go."

He stepped toward the constables, his hands up. They wouldn't know to make him put his hands behind his head like he'd done with POWs; these two didn't seem like veterans of anything but street brawls.

Mrs. Fotheringham moved as if to put her hand on his shoulder but the constables still had their weapons up and she hesitated. "Mr. Greyeyes, I do apologize. Please stay."

"It'll be better if I go," he said, looking the taller constable in the eye. Without rank insignia, it was hard to know which of them was boss, but when in doubt it was always best to take out the bigger opponent.

The tremors rippling through his body subsided and Thomas slowed his breathing. He'd come back later for his children. They'd wait for him, after he'd dealt with the constables. It was going to be all right.

Suddenly John leapt from the foot of the stairs, knocking Mrs. Fotheringham back as he grabbed for the constable's truncheon. "You can't take him!"

Thomas shouted "Don't!" as the other constable fired.

Thomas watched his son crumple and fall. Other soldiers who had come back with shell shock might collapse into a ball, covering their ears, or attack the source of the disruption. But for Thomas, much deeper instincts kicked in, twisted by the horrors of modern war. He changed.

His clothes bulged and ripped beneath hulking furry shoulders. The revolver thundered again in the small space, but Thomas was already lurching right at the smaller constable, pushing him down, and the shot went wide. Something hard crashed down on his back and head, again and again: the other constable's truncheon. But now his clothing hugged him in shreds. He was the mahiinkan.

The constable fired uselessly at the wall, unable to free his arm from Thomas's teeth; the sound brought back memories of the trenches. At any moment a shell would come screaming out of the sky and destroy them all.

He shook the man like a rabbit. Bone snapped, the constable yelled, and the weapon clattered away on the floor. Thomas wheeled to face the other, still raining blows down on him with wild shouts he could barely hear in the fading echo of the revolver shots. Turning his great lupine snout to the side, he seized the man's rib cage in his jaws and crushed it. The constable gasped and crumpled.

Mrs. Fotheringham screamed and ran back into the sitting room. Thomas was conscious of his son's body on the floor beneath them, unmoving, and using his massive neck muscles he hauled the constable away from him. The urge to tear the man to pieces gripped him, but Thomas paused. He sought the quiet he'd sometimes known in the boreal forest long ago, a deeper echo of who he was.

His daughter stood frozen, clutching the handrail, a look of horror twisting her mouth and eyes. The maid, Agnes, had disappeared upstairs – he heard her wailing. His son lay in a widening pool of blood near the body of the smaller constable whose arm Thomas had mangled.

He crossed the lobby in a single leap and pressed his paws on his son's still form. He reached deep with his mind, down through the earth, to pull up enough power to heal the damage in his son's chest, knit the sinews and flesh back together, and make it whole beneath the black pads of a dire wolf's paws.

Long moments passed. No one made a sound.

When it was done, he allowed the power within the earth, the Great Mother, to change him back into his human self, clothed now in the tatters of his uniform, kneeling with his hands pressed onto his son's back.

There was no movement. He crouched down, cursing his still-ringing ears, but when placing his head onto his son's back, he felt it: a heartbeat.

Sobs shuddered out of Thomas. His son lay motionless but alive, and the sounds around him came as if from miles away. Mrs. Fotheringham staggered past, making for the back of the house. She slammed the door behind her. Marie slumped down on the wood staircase. After a long moment, Thomas looked up at her.

"We need to bring you to your daughter," he said.

Marie shook her head, staring at her brother. "How?"

"Marie!" he said. "We must go. John will recover." He wrapped his arms around his son, pulling his body up off the blood-slick tiles. Usually, after the change, Thomas felt renewed, energized; but trying to heal another always drained him. Now he felt cold and tired in a way that took him back to the day after Vimy Ridge, a victory that did not mean the end of anything. There was only hope in a new beginning.

He stood, raising John in his arms as he had years earlier. "We named her Marion."

"Who?"

"Your daughter. Because she looks so much like you."

Marie put a hand on the dark wood banister and pulled herself up. "What will we do?"

Thomas took a deep breath, listening hard outside. He could drive, but he had no intention of stealing the constables' automobile. A borrowed boat, however, might be the best way out of the city.

"To the river bank. The Red flows north. Selkirk isn't that far, and I can get help there."

"Kipaapaa..." she said clumsily, wincing. *Father*.

"Shh." He kissed her forehead. "Your mother would be proud of you."

Together they bore John out the open front door, into the deep indigo of summer twilight.

Art by Jennifer Cruté

結草銜環
(KNOTTING GRASS, HOLDING RING)
KEN LIU

1645
Yangzhou, Jiangsu Province, China

The proprietor of the Three Moons Teahouse brought Green Siskin and Sparrow upstairs to a private suite, where six men were seated around the table.

Through the open window, Sparrow saw a gentle spring rain fall upon the bustling streets of Yangzhou, where laborers and soldiers rushed to reinforce the city walls. "That's a lovely waist," said the man seated at the head of the table as he contemplated Green Siskin. He was dressed in a brand-new-looking red battle cape, and Sparrow guessed that he was an army captain.

Green Siskin smiled seductively at him and glided gracefully to the silk-covered bench next to the window. While the captain continued to admire her form with drunken eyes, Green Siskin nodded at Sparrow, who hurried over with her pipa and then retreated to a corner of the suite, where she tried to make herself inconspicuous.

Two weeks ago, the last time she had gone with Green Siskin on a client visit, Green Siskin had complained to Big Sister Magpie:

The guests pay for a certain vision of class, not her muddy shoes and floor-scrubbing fingers constantly on display!

Sparrow's ears grew hot. Of all the girls at the Songbird Garden, Green Siskin was the meanest, and yet Sparrow also craved her affection the most.

Sparrow's stomach growled, and she stared at the rich spread on the table with longing: sugared lotus seeds, water chestnuts marinated in wine, salt-boiled peanuts, frozen sweet tofu, salted meat dumplings... Ever since the Manchus had laid siege to the city, most everyone at the Songbird Garden had been making do with small rations of plain porridge and moldy, pickled vegetables. What real food could be obtained was reserved for the leading girls like Green Siskin.

"Captain Li, a man of courage like you deserves the best girl the blue houses have to offer!" one of the other men — by his luxurious robe, a salt merchant — said as he refilled the captain's cup with wine.

"Master Wen speaks the truth. A brave man must be served by a great beauty!" added another.

A third piped up, "A girl like that is only barely adequate, considering your, uh..." He stuttered as he tried to find a new word of praise. "Courageous bravery," he finished lamely.

Listening to these men vying to flatter the officer, Sparrow wanted to laugh. She suspected that the soldiers commanded by Captain Li were quartered at the houses of the merchants, who were unhappy with the way the rowdy men made a mess of their beautiful mansions. They had pooled their money to hire Green Siskin, the most popular girl at the renowned Songbird Garden, to entertain Captain Li so that he would rein in his men.

"General Li," Green Siskin said, her voice as silky and melodious as her namesake, "Do you have a favorite tanci story?"

"That's *Cap*–" one of the man started to say, but he yelped as Wen stepped on his foot under the table.

"I guess I look like a general to her!" Captain Li laughed.

"Sometimes fools speak truths!" Wen said. "Maybe you'll be promoted after the Manchu barbarians cower before your might!"

Captain Li shook his head humbly, clearly enjoying himself. Sparrow marveled at Green Siskin's skill. Her "mistake" had done more to put Captain Li in a good mood than all the unimaginative, repetitious flattery from the five merchants.

Green Siskin was so clever, so pretty, so admired by all the clients. But Green Siskin had never had a kind word for Sparrow. Back when Sparrow was a little girl, Green Siskin had convinced Big Sister Magpie that there was no need to waste money and time to pretty Sparrow up. Best to just leave her feet unbound so that she could run up and down the stairs and perform menial tasks for the other girls.

"I'm just a rough soldier," Captain Li said. "I know nothing about tanci. Why don't you just tell a story you like?"

Green Siskin nodded and held up the pipa in her lap. "Since we're on the topic of generals and beauties, how about I entertain the honored guests with the tale of General Wei Ke and the concubine he saved?"

"Oh, this sounds like a good story," Captain Li said.

Green Siskin smiled and began to sing as she plucked a lively melody:

King, duke, general, minister of state,
Beggar, monk, thief, woman from a blue house,
Here's a tale your sad pity to arouse:
Who kens the ways of unknowable Fate?

She paused, cradled the pipa, and spoke, her voice and gestures animated:

"Let's go back to the days before the Emperors, when all the states were vying for dominance during the Spring and Autumn Period. When Minister Wei Chou of Jin was sorely ill, he summoned his son, Wei Ke, and said to him:

If I should die, my child,
Do not bury my favorite concubine with me.
Still young, with a heart mild,

She deserves to live out her days sitting by the sea.
"And Wei Ke, being an obedient son, said yes."

"Was the concubine as pretty as you?" interrupted Captain Li. "That ancient custom is a bit harsh, but if she was I'd certainly want her with me always." He laughed.

The other men joined in and all said they'd do the same.

Sparrow shuddered, thinking about being led into a dark tomb and then having the heavy stone doors shut and sealed behind her. The laughter of the men frightened her. *Good thing that Minister Wei was more kind-hearted than these men.*

"I'm but a lowly girl of the blue houses," said Green Siskin, her expression placid. "How dare I compare myself to a beloved concubine of the House of Wei?"

"Continue," said Captain Li, draining his cup. The merchants promptly fought over who got to refill it.

"Minister Wei's illness worsened. He summoned Wei Ke again, and said:
When I'm dead, my child, bury my favorite concubine with me.
For in my stone tomb I shall be lonely without her by my knee."

"Ah, I knew the old man would come to his senses," said Captain Li.

Sparrow shook her head. *Why did Green Siskin have to pick such a morbid story?*

Green Siskin continued as if he hadn't said anything. "But Wei Ke buried his father alone, and allowed the concubine to remarry."

"He disobeyed his father's wishes?" Captain Li's face, red from the alcohol, was incredulous.

"How unfilial!" said one of the merchants.

"A man lacking in virtue," assented another.

"A woman like me can't comment on virtue, of course," said Green Siskin, "Many in the State of Jin did criticize Wei Ke for his disobedience, but he was unperturbed. He said, 'When my father spoke to me the first time, he was still alert. But when he spoke to me the second time, he was so ill that he no longer knew what he was saying. I respected his true wishes. Virtue is a matter of many mouths, but what is right exists only in my heart.'"

"A pretty piece of sophistry." Captain Li humphed.

Green Siskin plucked a few notes, signaling a transition. "A few years later, the State of Qin invaded Jin, and Wei Ke was appointed commander-in-chief to defend his homeland. When the Qin and Jin armies met at Fushi, the Qin champion, a man by the name of Du Hui, challenged Wei Ke to single combat on the field.

"Now this Du Hui was a giant. He was eight feet tall and his eyes blazed like a demon's. His fists were the size of copper pots, and he wielded an axe that could lop off a horse's leg at a single stroke."

"Sounds like a copy of you, Captain Li," said one of the merchants.

"Don't you mean 'General Li'?" said another.

Captain Li waved impatiently at them to be quiet.

Green Siskin went on. "Wei Ke fought valiantly, but Du Hui was so fierce that Wei Ke's arms began to feel numb from fending off the heavy blows. He had to retreat, and Du Hui pursued closely.

"Soon, the two came to a hill covered in long grass. As the two ran up the hill, Du Hui stumbled. Seizing the opportunity, Wei Ke turned and engaged Du Hui again, and managed to behead him this time.

"After he had a moment to collect himself, Wei Ke saw that the grass around Du Hui's feet was all tangled and knotted, as though someone had set a trap. He looked up and saw a mongoose dashing away, fading into the sea of grass.

"That night, as General Wei Ke slept in his camp, he saw an old man in his dream.

" 'Who are you?' asked Wei Ke.

" 'I'm the dead father of your father's concubine. To thank you for sparing my daughter's life, I asked to return to this world as a mongoose to give you what little aid I could.'

Our every act has its echo in time,
Karma turns the wheel, be mindful of your climb."

Green Siskin strummed the pipa a few times to emphasize the end of her story.

Captain Li seemed to awaken from a dream himself. "A pretty tale well told."

Green Siskin smiled in thanks.

"Let's drink in memory of honorable General Wei Ke."

The merchants were about to join in with a chorus of how "General Li" was even more honorable when the proprietor of the Three Moons opened the private suite door and rushed to Captain Li's side to hand him a note.

"Official business," said Captain Li. "Gentlemen, I regret to say that I must leave immediately."

"But Captain, you've barely had time to sample the delights this girl has to offer," said one of the merchants, no doubt thinking of all the money they had spent to hire Green Siskin. Then he timidly added, "I hope it's not the Manchus doing more mischief?"

"Don't be alarmed," said Captain Li, as he made his way unsteadily to the door of the suite. "Yangzhou has already withstood their siege for seven days, and I don't think that barbarian brute Dodo has the stomach to stay here much longer. Grand Secretary Shi Kefa has pledged that as long as he remains alive, he will allow no harm to come to any citizen of Yangzhou. I pledge to all of you the same."

The captain disappeared down the stairs, and the merchants, after a moment of silence, began to fuss and complain.

"An uncultured man indeed," said one. "He didn't even know how to use the finger-cleaning bowl properly! I hope the Manchus go away soon so that we don't have to deal with these illiterate peasant soldiers any longer."

"Really, they're barely better than criminals," added another.

"Why would anyone join the army unless he had no other skills?" asked a third.

Impulsively, Sparrow said, "Captain Li is fighting to protect all of us. I think he's very brave even if he has rough manners."

The merchants seemed startled to realize she was still in the room.

"This must be a first," sneered Wen. "A whore is lecturing *me* about virtue and respect."

"Honored masters," said Green Siskin, "forgive the rash and ignorant girl. Women like us really can only admire virtue, of which we obviously possess none. But there is the little matter of the rest of my fee."

***

Sparrow, running besides the palanquin and struggling with the weight of Green Siskin's luggage, whispered at the palanquin's window. "Sorry! I just couldn't hold my tongue."

From within, Green Siskin lifted the curtain over the window and said curtly, "Don't worry about Big Sister Magpie. I'll deal with her."

Sparrow was relieved. Part of her job was to make sure the clients paid. Magpie believed the Songbird Garden needed to maintain a certain decorum, and so it was unseemly for the client to haggle with the girl they ordered directly. A servant like Sparrow, however, could threaten to make an embarrassing scene in front of a crowd, if necessary.

But after Sparrow's outburst, the annoyed merchants had insisted that they would not pay for a full day and night, and they were beyond caring about embarrassment at a time like this. It had taken Green Siskin a lot of work to soothe them and get paid for at least the day.

"Thanks," Sparrow said, out of breath. At moments like these she was glad that her feet were not bound. No one was going to carry her around; that was for sure.

"You'd probably mess up the explanation anyway," added Green Siskin, "and get us both in trouble."

Sparrow's face flushed. Every time she thought Green Siskin was softening towards her, she would say something to shatter that illusion. It was like she went out of her way to make sure Sparrow knew she didn't like her.

Still, she liked talking to the older girl, who always said things no one else would say. "Hey, Green Siskin," Sparrow whispered next to the window so that the palanquin carriers would not overhear, "can I ask you something?"

The curtain did not lift. "What is it?"

"Do you really think the Manchus will take Yangzhou?"

For a few moments, silence. Then: "You better hope not. Women generally don't fare well when cities fall, and women like us do especially poorly."

"Grand Secretary Shi Kefa promised we'd be safe though."

A cold chuckle. "Men make promises they break all the time. We were promised a full fee. Do you have it?"

Sparrow felt the light heft of the purse attached to her sash. *Why can't Green Siskin just say something to make me feel better?* "But there are so many soldiers in the city, and I saw them hauling those Western-style cannons through the streets the other day–"

"Do you think Yangzhou is better defended than Beijing?"

Sparrow had no response to this. The unimaginable had happened just last year, when the Manchus took Beijing and the Emperor had hanged himself. The new Ming Emperor was now hiding in Nanjing, across the Yangtze to the south. The Manchus had announced they were going to conquer all of China, and so far, no one had been able to stop them.

She changed the subject. "Do you really believe in Fate and... coming back after you're dead?"

"What are you talking about?"

"You know, like the tanci story you told today? How things will balance out and good deeds will be rewarded?"

"That's just a story."

"I know, but... there are so many people here, and most of them have never done anything really bad. They pray to their ancestors and Guanyin or Laojun or Christ. They've never had anything to do with the Manchus. Some deity, or maybe Fate, will surely protect them? Otherwise it would be so unfair."

Green Siskin sighed. "Don't be stupid. I was five years old when my father was exiled and I was sold. What did I have to do with my father's crimes? You were just a baby when those men stole you from your parents – you don't even know who they are or where they're from – and sold you to Magpie. What about life is fair?"

"Maybe not in this life, but like your story, there's a next life... you really don't believe in it?"

"Oh, I wouldn't mind coming back my next life as a real bird. I'd always have plenty to eat and I could fly away if things went wrong. But who can ever confirm that actually happens? What does it mean to 'believe' in something you can't see or touch? I believe in gold and jewels; I believe in making clients happy so they'll pay me more; I believe in saving up enough to buy myself from Magpie. Oh, never mind. You're wasting my time with this maudlin prattle–"

Just then one of the carriers stumbled and almost fell. He cursed.

Green Siskin stuck her head out. "What happened?"

Sparrow, crouching a few steps behind, said, "There's a swallow in the road. I think one of its wings is broken. The carrier almost stepped on it."

"Quick, bring it here."

Sparrow dropped the overnight case and the pipa, wrapped the swallow in a handkerchief, and carried it gingerly up to the palanquin. The bird's breast was heaving rapidly and its eyes appeared clouded over. It didn't struggle in Sparrow's hands.

"It probably doesn't have much time left," said Sparrow as she handed the bird over.

Green Siskin chewed her lip. "I wish we had something hearty to feed it with. Rice porridge isn't going to give it the strength it needs."

This was another thing about Green Siskin that puzzled Sparrow. As haughty and mean as she was, she couldn't bear to see an animal in pain. Not only did she never eat meat – she fended off Magpie, who fretted about her being too thin for the clients, by claiming to be a devout Buddhist, though Sparrow never saw Siskin pray to Guanyin – she also never allowed the other girls to kill a spider or fly while cleaning the house. And she had a habit of tending to injured cats, birds, even an occasional tradesman's workhorse, and nursing them back to health.

For someone who claimed to be only interested in making money for herself, this was a strange hobby.

But the worry in Green Siskin's eyes made Sparrow forget how haughty the older girl had been all day. She took out a packet she had been hiding under her sash.

"Maybe this will help."

Green Siskin opened the packet to reveal a few salted meat dumplings that Sparrow had secretly taken from the table while the merchants were arguing with Green Siskin about her fee. Sparrow had meant to save them for later, after everyone had gone to bed. Big Sister Magpie would surely whip her if she found out about the theft.

"I figure they're close enough to bugs and whatever else swallows eat. I don't really like these dumplings anyway." Strangely, sharing the food with Green Siskin made her feel better about having stolen it in the first place.

"Thank you," said Green Siskin, and the gentleness in her voice made Sparrow think she would do anything to hear it again.

***

The next afternoon remained drizzly. Sparrow was in the market trying to buy some outrageously priced food when the shouting began.

"They opened the gates—"

"—not reinforcements—"

Around Sparrow, all was confusion: men and women pushed and shoved in every direction, children cried, and a few riders on horses tried to make their way through the crowd, heedless of who might be trampled. Palanquins were dropped and vending carts broke against the surging crowd. The air suddenly smelled sweet and spicy as panicked feet crushed the spilled fruits and pastries.

"Isn't that Grand Secretary Shi Kefa?"

"He's trying to leave the city! He's running—"

Sparrow pulled on the sleeve of a young man next to her and shouted, "What happened?"

"The Manchus tricked the city gates open. Yangzhou is done for! Prince Dodo gave the order to slaughter the city."

"Slaughter the city! Why?"

"To make an example of us for the other Chinese cities! It's like killing a chicken to show a monkey what will happen if it doesn't obey."

He pulled his sleeve loose from Sparrow's grasp and disappeared into the chaotic crowd. In the distance, columns of smoke began to rise from the city walls.

Sparrow shoved her way through the crowd until she finally got out of the market. She ran until she was back at the Songbird Garden, where Big Sister Magpie and all the other girls were waiting in the front hall, anxiety on their faces.

"Is it true?" Big Sister Magpie asked.

Sparrow nodded. "They say that the city is going to be slaughtered." She felt dizzy. *I'm too young to die.*

Big Sister Magpie was calm. "Perhaps fate has doomed the Great Ming. If we scatter throughout the city, there's a chance some of us will make it. Those of you with rich clients who favor you, this is the time to make the most of them. Go to their houses and beg them to take you in, tell the men how much you love them and the wives how obedient you'll be. Leave everything behind and we'll consider your debt to me paid. If you survive this, you'll be free women. Go! There's no time to lose."

Some of the women began to make their way towards the front door. Others, especially younger girls like Sparrow who had no clients they could call on, huddled and cried.

"Stop," said Green Siskin. Her gaze on Big Sister Magpie was cold. "To survive something like this you need money, and you want to send all of us away so that you can keep the money all for yourself."

Big Sister Magpie's eyes were equally cold. "The money in this house all belongs to *me.*"

"That money we earned with our bodies," said Green Siskin. "I couldn't care less about the contracts right now. If you want to accuse me of being a thief, you're free to go to the yamen and file a petition."

The women near the door stopped and turned around. Slowly, the fear and uncertainty on their faces were replaced by the same cold, determined expression Green Siskin showed.

Big Sister Magpie, seeing she was outnumbered, softened her tone. "How about we split it half and half?"

Green Siskin chuckled mirthlessly. "I heard the cook and the footmen run away. You better hope they left us something in your money chest."

***

Green Siskin and Sparrow picked the narrowest streets and darkest alleys to avoid the crowds. From time to time, small groups of escaping Ming soldiers ran past, casting off their bloody helmets and armor in an attempt to blend into the civilian population.

"Magpie might have been selfish, but she was right about one thing," said Green Siskin, wiping the sweat from her forehead. "We *are* safer if we don't draw attention by flocking together." She stopped and held onto a wall for support. Green Siskin could only shuffle along slowly on her bound feet, and even half a li's walk was tiring her.

It doesn't help that she's still carrying that swallow in a basket, Sparrow thought.

"Go on by yourself," said Green Siskin. "Get to the temples by the canals. Perhaps the Manchus will respect the Buddha even if they don't respect anything else."

"I'm not leaving you."

Green Siskin chuckled. "Good, I see you have learned something after all. Well, I'm not Magpie. Here, I'll give you these." She took out her purse and emptied it in her palm: jewelry and some scattered silver – Big Sister Magpie's stash wasn't much after it was divided among all the women.

Green Siskin picked out a jade ring and put it on her finger. "I'm keeping this. My father gave me this before... I came here. When I'm worried, touching it makes me feel better." She held out half of the silver and the rest of the jewels for Sparrow. "Now, go."

Sparrow didn't take the offering. "You're clever and my chances are better if I stick with you."

"Ha! Foolish girl. Here's another lesson for you: never refuse money when it's offered." She dumped all the valuables back into her purse. The screams and hoofbeats seemed to get closer every minute. "We have to find somewhere to hide, like the cellar of a poor man's house. The mansions would draw too much attention."

They tried every house they passed, but no one would open the doors. Then they came to a house with its door ajar, but through it they could see two women dangling by their necks from the hall beams, and a man dead at their feet, a pool of blood around his neck and head.

Sparrow gasped, but Green Siskin stepped in without hesitation. After fretting for a moment, Sparrow stamped her foot and followed.

She saw Green Siskin staring at the wall, where two lines were written in large characters. The ink wasn't even dry.

Sparrow couldn't read the calligraphic script. "What does it say?"

"It's a poem about virtue and faith, and how the writer wishes he and his family could have served the Emperor better."

"Poor man."

"I pity his wives more. I'm not sure they would have hanged themselves if he didn't tell them to. *Virtue* and *chastity* indeed." She spat.

"Let's get out of here."

"No, this is the best place to hide. The Manchus will think everyone's dead. We should work over the place to make it look like it's been looted so there's even less reason to investigate closely."

"I should have guessed that you wouldn't be afraid of ghosts or want to respect the dead," muttered Sparrow. "You don't believe in *anything*."

"They did," said Green Siskin. "Fat lot of good it did them."

***

From the kitchen cellar, Sparrow and Green Siskin could only intermittently hear sounds from outside: screams as houses were broken into, shouting, running footsteps, and occasionally a loud crash. A ventilation slit near the ceiling gave them some light and brought the smell of smoke and ashes.

"They're setting fires," said Green Siskin. "A house probably burned down."

The rhythmic pounding of a horse's hoofs shook the cellar and made bits of earth fall.

"You think Big Sister Magpie is all right?" Sparrow asked.

"Who cares? She has to rely on her wits, the same as us. I have enough to worry about."

Sparrow was a bit disappointed by how cold Green Siskin sounded. Magpie was the closest thing she'd had to a mother.

"Might as well take a nap," said Green Siskin. "If they find us, being awake and being asleep won't make much of a difference." She cooed to the swallow in the basket, who seemed to be doing better.

By the time Sparrow woke up it was completely dark and totally silent.

"They're probably finished with this neighborhood," whispered Green Siskin. "The looting and raping here wouldn't be as good as in the merchants' quarter."

Sparrow licked her dry lips. "I'll go get us some water. It's easier with my feet."

"Come over here first," said Green Siskin.

Sparrow felt along the ground and crawled over. When she was close enough to feel Green Siskin's breath, she felt Green Siskin's hand grab her around the shoulder and wrestle her to the ground. As Green Siskin straddled her, Sparrow tried to cry out, but she felt Green Siskin's cold hand over her mouth.

"Shut up!" she hissed.

Sparrow was terrified and confused. *Has Green Siskin gone crazy?*

Then Green Siskin's hand was gone, and something cold, metallic, and sharp was placed against her face. She flinched and began to struggle.

Green Siskin leaned down until her hot breath was in Sparrow's face. "Hold still. I have to fix you before you go out."

Sparrow felt her scalp tighten as Green Siskin grabbed a fistful of her hair. Then the cold blade against her face went away and she heard a *snick*. Green Siskin had cut away a bunch of her hair.

Sparrow was proud of her thick hair and often thought of someday wearing it in the fashionable, elaborate double buns that the older girls at the Songbird Garden wore. She whimpered and bucked harder.

"You stupid girl," hissed Green Siskin. "If they see you from a distance and think you're a scrawny boy, they might not bother chasing you."

"But you still have your hair!"

"My looks are the last thing I have to protect me. I know what they want and I can give it to them in a way that hopefully won't get me killed. But you? You don't know anything."

Sparrow stopped struggling and cried silently as Green Siskin continued to cut away her hair by ragged handfuls.

"I can't run," Green Siskin whispered, and her touch on Sparrow's head was gentle. "But you still can. I know you always wanted to be like me, but you don't have the hard heart it takes to be me. It's why I kept Magpie from binding your feet. Being able to run is always better than having to stay and smile and offer yourself up.

"I won't blame you if you leave and don't come back."

Sparrow cried even harder.

***

Outside, it was raining harder. Some of the houses of the neighborhood still burned. Sparrow's heart beat faster and she felt lightheaded as she saw more than a dozen bodies scattered in the narrow, muddy street, the dark pools around them perhaps rainwater, or perhaps blood. The doors to all the houses were broken open.

She fought to calm herself. She had to be more like Green Siskin. *Focus on what cam be seen and touched. Water. There is no time to be afraid of ghosts.*

There was a well at the end of the street. She just had to get there and bring back a bowl.

Slowly, quietly, she made her way towards the well, imagining herself a mouse. There seemed to be no Manchus around but she couldn't be sure. The raindrops hissed as they fell into the fires and struck against the shingles on the houses still standing, making loud splashes that matched her racing heart. She opened her mouth to the sky and gratefully felt the wetness against her parched tongue.

Finally, she was at the well. She prayed that no one had jumped into it to commit suicide. The rain had quenched her thirst but Green Siskin still needed clean water.

She picked up the bucket on the rim and lowered it by the attached rope. She felt the bucket hit water and there didn't seem to be any resistance, such as from a floating body. *Good.*

She hauled the bucket up as fast as she could and the rippling water glistened in the faint, reddish light of the fires like liquefied gold. Now she just had to find something to carry the water back in...

"What do we have here?"

Sparrow felt herself being jerked up by the back of the neck of her robe and lifted off the ground. She kicked and screamed and was thrown down, the wind knocked out of her.

Two men were standing before her, dressed in the armor and colors of the Manchu Army. But they were both clearly Chinese, and by the accent of the one who had caught her, from up north. She had heard that the Manchus had many surrendered Chinese fighting for them.

"Thought we had cleared this street already," the man who had thrown Sparrow down said.

"Must have been hiding like a rat," said the other. "Think it's worth the time trying to get something out of him? Or should we just kill him and get back to camp?"

"This whole area is slim pickings. Just our luck to be assigned to a neighborhood with all the paupers."

One of the men unsheathed his sword.

Sparrow now wished she had taken the jewels Green Siskin had offered. She would at least have something to bargain with these men. But it was too late now for regret. She squeezed her eyes tightly shut.

"Masters," came a clear, warm voice that seemed to make the night less dark. "Do not frighten my servant."

The men turned around. Some paces away was a woman in a flowing silk dress. Even with the faint light from the fires, it was clear that she was uncommonly beautiful.

Sparrow was stunned. What was Green Siskin doing? She would have been safe had she remained in the cellar.

"A merchant's wife or daughter?" one of the men whispered to the other. Then he brandished his weapon and raised his voice. "Come over here and show us all the treasure you've hidden."

Green Siskin walked closer, her movements languid and graceful. "What more treasure do you need when you have this?" She spun in a circle when she was about five paces away. "I would think your commander would reward you handsomely if you brought me to him."

The two men looked at each other.

"She probably would be to Janggin Yelu's taste."

***

In the morning, the two soldiers marched Green Siskin and Sparrow through Yangzhou. By now they knew Sparrow was a girl, but they left her alone since Sparrow helped Green Siskin walk.

The streets were strewn with bodies. Blood mixing with puddles of water had created a shimmering sheen like a painter's palette. The smell of blood and smoke and human waste filled the air, a nauseating mix. Green Siskin and Sparrow's cloth shoes were soon soaked through with the bloody mixture. In some places the corpses were piled so thick that it was hard to find a path. They crossed a bridge over the canal and saw that the channel was almost filled with corpses, turning it into flat ground.

Sparrow felt numb. There was so much death around her that the bodies no longer felt real. She kept on expecting them to reveal themselves to be puppets or sit up and tell her they were just sleeping.

Green Siskin's bound feet must have hurt terribly from walking this far, but she clenched her teeth and said nothing as she leaned on Sparrow. From time to time, when she really needed to stop to rest, she would engage the two soldiers in conversation to keep their interest.

"Do the Manchu officers treat surrendered Chinese soldiers like you well?"

One of the men shrugged. "No worse than my old Ming officers. At least they pay me on time, and now I get to make a little extra from the loot."

"A soldier's life is never easy. Have they caught Grand Secretary Shi Kefa?"

"Yes. He wouldn't surrender though. Prince Dodo ordered him beheaded."

Sparrow decided to not mention how Shi Kefa had been seen trying to escape from the doomed city. Sometimes heroes were made as much by what was not said as by what was said.

Small groups of soldiers were conducting house-to-house searches for survivors. When any were found, they were made to retrieve all the valuables from the residence and present them before the soldiers killed them. Howls and screams filled the air.

They passed two Manchu soldiers herding a column of female captives, strung together by the neck like a strand of pearls. Their bound feet made progress through the muddy streets difficult, and they stumbled, fell, pulled others down, and struggled to get up. Their clothes were so filthy that it was impossible to tell what color they were. The two Manchu soldiers urged them on, slapping them with the flat of a sword or poking at them with the tip of a spear.

"Looks like we aren't the only ones who want to give our commanders a nice gift," joked one of Green Siskin's captors.

"None of them are as high quality as ours though," said his companion, eyeing Green Siskin with pride. Green Siskin smiled back at him.

A woman holding a baby fell and could not get up. She kept on slipping in the mud. The Manchu soldier at the head of the column cursed, came back, and took the howling baby out of the woman's arms and tossed it into the street. The mother cried and tried to crawl over to retrieve it, but the rope around her neck prevented her from getting too far.

A small detachment of Manchu soldiers on horses came thundering down the street. Green Siskin and Sparrow barely got out of the way in time. The iron-shod hoofs trampled over the bodies, temporarily animating the dead limbs. Abruptly, the baby's cries were silenced.

The mother screamed and lurched forward, pulling the other captives along. The Manchu soldier shouted and struck her with his spear a few times, but the mother seemed to not feel the blows and continued to make her way towards the dead baby. The other Manchu soldier came over and stabbed her through the heart. They loosened the rope from around her neck, left her body a few paces from her baby's tiny, lifeless corpse, and urged the other captives to keep on moving.

Sparrow's eyes grew searing hot. She wanted to run up to the Manchu soldier and scratch his eyes out and sink her teeth into the man's ear. She was no longer afraid. She understood how Grand Secretary Shi Kefa could suddenly find the courage to not surrender. *When you've been afraid for so long, fear stops mattering.* She wanted to do something, anything, to assuage the pure rage that filled her veins.

Green Siskin grabbed her hand and squeezed so hard that it hurt. She pulled Sparrow back and hissed in her ear, "There's nothing you can do for her and her baby now. You must watch out for yourself."

Sparrow hated Green Siskin then. Hated her with a passion that made it almost impossible to breathe. Green Siskin was a coward, a cold-blooded monster who only wanted to survive. What was the point of living if you had to endure images like that haunting you in your dreams through the rest of your life?

She bit down on Green Siskin's hand until she let go, and rushed at the Manchu soldiers.

Green Siskin turned to her two captors. "Get my maid back to me. Tie her up if you have to."

"Why?" one of the man asked. "If she wants to die, let her."

"I need her help with my dressing and preparations," said Green Siskin. "Your commander will surely prefer a good-looking gift to a poorly wrapped one, yes?"

The two men looked at each other and shrugged. One of them lumbered after Sparrow and easily brought her down. He gagged her, trussed her up, and carried her on his shoulder as they continued through the streets of Yangzhou. All around them was smoke, howling, and the stench of blood and death.

***

Finally, Green Siskin and Sparrow arrived at a mansion that had been turned into Janggin Yelu's temporary headquarters. They were locked into one of the side halls with a dozen other young women, most of them merchants' wives and daughters, who had been brought there as gifts for the commander.

Some of the women sat alone and stared sullenly at the ground; a few others hugged each other and wept; still others huddled and conversed. Green Siskin and Sparrow were in a corner by themselves. Snippets of the other women's conversations reached them.

"He stripped me right there in front of all those men... I wished there was a well to jump into..."

"—he cut him open right in front of my eyes. Look at my clothes. That's blood! Blood!"

"Why am I still alive? Three brothers, all their wives, mother, father, grandparents, six nephews and nieces – all gone..."

"Did you see a little boy about six with a jade tiger around his neck? Are you sure? I lost him around the canal crossing..."

Green Siskin untied Sparrow.

"Don't expect me to thank you for saving my life." Sparrow's voice was cold as ice. She moved away, sat down, put her head between her knees, and began to sob. The image of that dead baby and its brains splattering in the mud would not leave her.

Green Siskin sighed and did not come after her.

***

In the afternoon a Manchu commander came to the side hall. Most of the women shrank against the wall and avoided looking at him. A few began to cry. The commander frowned.

But Green Siskin strode up to him and gave a low curtsy. "Honored Prince Yelu, I presume?"

"You're a bold one," said the officer, who couldn't hide his smile.

Some tricks appear to work on all men, thought Sparrow. *Just how low will she stoop to save her own skin?*

"Tales of your valor and mercy have filled my ears like thunder."

"Ha! Not even a hint of a blush when you lie. I have a guess as to what kind of woman you are. But I'm tired of weeping girls, and even if your arms have cradled the heads of hundreds of men, you might still be more fun. All right, come with me." He turned to the soldiers behind him. "Distribute the rest of them to the soldiers, then get rid them after two days."

The comment sounded so casual that it took a few moments before the other women registered what it really meant. The wailing in the room redoubled.

"Honorable Prince," said Green Siskin. "Some of these girls are quite pretty. It would be such a waste to not taste them. Why not save them for a while and see if I can persuade them to be a bit more pliable?"

"Never!" one of the women shouted angrily. "You unchaste, shameful *thing*."

Sparrow saw that, although Green Siskin's voice was as sultry as before, the hem of her dress trembled. She held her hands together before her in a gesture of supplication, and she was twisting and playing with the jade ring on her right hand. Green Siskin was terrified.

"My orders are to cleanse the city," said Yelu. He hesitated. "I might get away with keeping you, but all these..."

Green Siskin's face registered shock. "Ah, forgive me. I did not realize that you had not the authority to delay the execution of these foolish girls. It's just that you seemed to me such a powerful prince."

"Never mind," said Yelu as he puffed out his chest. "Of course I can do whatever I want on the battlefield. I've decreed that these women are not to be killed, for now."

"Perhaps you and I can be better acquainted," said Green Siskin. "But first, let my maid help me wash up?"

Green Siskin beckoned at Sparrow. They locked gazes.

She could have hidden in that cellar and never made a peep. She could have held her tongue just now and let the women die.

After all this time, Green Siskin still carried the swallow in a basket on her arm.

Sparrow walked up to Green Siskin and curtsied.

***

Sparrow observed the guards outside the bedroom. They stood ramrod straight and kept their faces impassive, focusing their eyes on the ends of their noses. They seemed to not hear the sounds coming from within the bedroom at all.

A soldier rushed into the hallway from outside, and, before the guards at the door could warn him, he shouted at the closed door, "Janggin! We've caught a few rich ones!"

The bedroom fell silent. Then, a few giggles could be heard through the door. The new soldier, realizing his mistake, blushed.

A few moments later, Yelu and Green Siskin emerged from the bedroom. Green Siskin's robe had been hastily tied back together and the sash was not straight. She hung onto Yelu's arm, a lazy smile on her face, flushed and sweaty, as Yelu straightened his robe and cleared his throat a few times.

"Let's go see what you've found." He shook off Green Siskin's hands and walked out, and the guards followed.

As Sparrow came up to Green Siskin, the smile on her face fell off like a mask. Green Siskin looked weary and scared, and Sparrow suddenly realized how young she really was.

"You'll have to help me figure out which among those *chaste* women are at least somewhat pliable," Green Siskin said. "We've got to give Yelu something if the rest of them want to live. And the swallow?"

"I got the guards to give me some jerky to feed it. It's resting in our bedroom."

Green Siskin's face relaxed a little. "Let's go see who our brave commander caught this time."

The front hall was filled with tables laden with jewels, coins, silver, gold, silk dresses, and furs. A row of captives, by their looks scholars and merchants, knelt on the ground, watched over by pacing guards. They looked exhausted and dejected, some possibly injured.

"Janggin, these are among the wealthiest men of the city," said the Manchu soldier who had come for Yelu.

Green Siskin squealed in delight and pawed through the piles of silk dresses and the jewelry, trying out various bracelets and pearl necklaces. "Can I have this one? Oh, no, this one is even prettier!"

Yelu observed her indulgently.

"Do you think there's any more treasure to be found?" he asked the soldier.

"I think we've squeezed everything we can out of them."

One of the merchants looked contemptuously at Green Siskin and spat at her. "It is because of traitorous whores like you, devoid of virtue, that the Great Ming ended up like this. Look at you, clinging to the enemy like a vine. I would kill you myself if I had the chance."

Sparrow felt her face grow hot. She recognized the merchant. It was Wen, one of the five men who had hired Green Siskin to entertain Captain Li so that the soldiers wouldn't trash his house. That seemed like a lifetime ago.

But Green Siskin seemed to not hear him. She was utterly absorbed with comparing two dresses and trying to decide on one.

"Then kill them," Yelu said.

The merchants trembled like leaves in the wind, including Wen. But his face remained defiant.

"Prince Yelu," said Green Siskin, pouting. "Are you hiding the best jewels from me?"

"What are you talking about?"

"That man over there is famous for his wealth. I remember seeing his wife wearing a beautiful strand of pearls at the Spring Festival last year, each of which was the size of a longan fruit."

"Oh?" Yelu looked skeptical.

"I'm sure he's hiding it somewhere. If you kill him now, you won't get it." Green Siskin strode up to Wen. "I bet you're hiding it in your servants' quarters. You asked them to bury it in case you survive."

Sparrow saw that Wen looked bewildered. If Yelu could tell that Wen had no idea what was going on, Green Siskin's plan would be ruined.

She stepped up, and despite her racing heart, she added, "Yes, I bet that's it. I knew his servants, and I saw them acting all secretive the other day, before the city fell."

Yelu turned to Wen. "Is this true? There's more treasure hidden?"

Wen was about to deny it when Green Siskin locked gazes with him. "But you don't know exactly where your servants live, do you? You just know it's in that neighborhood packed with huts?"

Wen finally seemed to understand. "Yes. It's true. We all sent our most valuable treasures to be hidden with trusted servants. It might take time to find the hiding places since the servants have died."

"Then you'll have to lead my men to the right neighborhood and go through every house," Yelu said.

The merchants, escorted by the soldiers, left.

"Make sure you look thoroughly," Green Siskin shouted after them, "especially those houses that had been burned down. Dig deep!"

***

Green Siskin kept on insisting that there was more treasure to be found, and the expeditions with the merchants kept on turning up just enough additional valuables that Yelu was reluctant to kill the captives.

Sparrow tried to help Green Siskin with her lies as much as she could. But she fretted.

"If Yelu finds out that you're just making up stuff–"

"Then I die. That was always the most likely outcome." She fed the swallow another mouthful of chewed-up jerky. The bird was getting stronger, and now could hop around a bit.

"Do you want their gratitude? They don't even like you!"

Green Siskin laughed. "What good is their gratitude at a time like this? I don't much like them either – if I could, I'd try to save the poor instead. But I do enjoy their accusation that China fell because of women like me. I never knew I was so powerful!

"I'm sure he never thought that the disdain he and his friends showed for the army had anything to do with it. They cheated on their taxes and starved the funding for the army for decades, but now everything is going wrong because I'm unchaste. This kind of subtle reasoning is clearly beyond you and me, mere females."

Sparrow had no patience for Green Siskin's jokes. "Then why are you trying to save them? Is this about karma?"

"I told you, I don't believe in any of that."

"Then what–"

"I don't know anything about morals or virtues." Green Siskin spat the word *virtues* out like a curse. She checked herself and went on, calmly. "I don't care about the cosmic balance or the next life. I'm not brave or strong and I'm not trying to earn myself any respect. Someday they might tell stories about how brave Grand Secretary Shi Kefa was to have given his life for the city, but they'll never care about what women like us have done.

"But much as I want a heart of stone so that I can survive, my heart keeps on telling me what it thinks is *right*. Ah, sometimes it's so much trouble. Just look at how much work it is to keep you alive!

"Though I can ignore the precepts of dead Confucian sages and living hypocrites, I don't want to stop living the way *I* want.

"There's been too much killing, Sparrow. I want to foil Heaven's unfair plans in whatever way I can. It makes me happy to defy Fate, even if just a little bit."

***

On the seventh day after the fall of Yangzhou, Prince Dodo finally gave the order to stop the killings. Corpses in the streets and the canals, soaked in rainwater, had begun to rot, and there was some concern that soldiers might start to fall sick with the miasma and stench. The survivors and the monks were told to start cremating the bodies.

Smoke from the burning pyres filled the sky of Yangzhou. It was impossible to breathe.

Janggin Yelu gave his mistress permission to go outside the city for some fresh air. Escorted by a few Manchu soldiers, Green Siskin and Sparrow rode about ten li from the city, where a green valley between two hills offered some shelter from the suffocating smoke. The soldiers left to patrol the area, and Green Siskin and Sparrow took a walk in the sun. In consideration of Green Siskin's feet, the soldiers left them a horse.

Green Siskin and Sparrow released the swallow, now fully recovered, and watched the bird fly away.

"I never thanked you properly," said Sparrow. She paused, feeling that the words were inadequate. She had never studied the Classics. The prettiest words she knew were from Green Siskin's tanci. "If I could turn into a mongoose someday to knot the grass to help you, I would."

Green Siskin laughed. "I'm sure I can find a use for a grass-knotting mongoose."

"But I doubt those merchants will remember how they owe their lives to you," Sparrow said.

"I'm just grateful none of them have yet asked me to commit suicide to redeem my shame."

Sparrow and Green Siskin both chuckled bitterly.

Two men emerged from behind a clump of trees. They held rusty swords and wore bright blue scarves around their necks.

"Kneel, traitorous whore," one of them said.

Green Siskin looked at them. "You're the remnants of Grand Secretary

Shi's militia?"

The men nodded. "The only way you could have survived the massacre was by collaborating with the enemy."

"You've gotten it all wrong," Sparrow started to say. But Green Siskin shushed her.

"Don't," whispered Green Siskin, keeping her eyes on the men. "The Manchus will be back any minute. If Yelu thinks I've been playing him, everyone will die. Now get on the horse."

"I'm not leaving you."

Green Siskin's tone grew impatient. "Haven't you learned anything? In this world, virtue is worthless. I'm not trying to be a hero. I need you on the horse because you have unbound feet and can use the stirrups. I need to ride behind you and hold onto your waist so the horse can run rather than just walk. Get on there before they're too close!"

Sparrow obeyed, and the two men began to run towards them.

Green Siskin smiled at the two men. "I'm so glad two great heroes have arrived to rescue me."

"Your wiles won't work on us. We're here to carry out justice."

"Come on, get up here with me!" shouted Sparrow.

Green Siskin smiled up sadly at Sparrow.

"How am I supposed to get up there with these feet? Now go." She slapped the horse's rump and it leapt away. Sparrow screamed and it was all she could do to hold onto the reins.

Looking back, Sparrow saw the two men descend on Green Siskin, who remained standing very straight.

***

Sparrow and the Manchu patrol looked and looked, but Green Siskin's body was nowhere to be found.

Instead, in the clearing was a large flock of birds: swallows, sparrows, magpies, hwamei, orioles, black drongos, martins. They were all chirping, twittering, singing, and instead of a cacophony, what emerged was a song that Sparrow instantly recognized: Green Siskin's tanci melody.

A siskin flew out of the flock and landed on Sparrow's outstretched hand. Its back, instead of being a bright yellow, was a faint, jade-like green. In its beak it held a jade ring which it deposited in Sparrow's hand.

"Green Siskin, is that you?" Sparrow's vision blurred. Her throat was tight and she could speak no more.

The siskin hopped in her hand and chirped.

***

The Twisted Ladle was doing good business on this night. It was right after the harvest, when people's purses were full and limbs sore.

The little inn didn't have the kind of delicacies that the teahouses in the big cities served, but the laborers and laundresses and petty farmers and farming wives who filled its benches didn't care. Rice wine and sorghum mead flowed freely, and fried tripe came by the plateful. People said what was on their minds, instead of what they thought they ought to say, as was the wont with learned scholars and clever merchants.

But they were all quiet now, listening to the young tanci woman. She strummed her pipa:

I sing of great Yangzhou, the city of white salt,
Of wealth and fame, a thousand refined teahouses.
But one night they came, iron hooves to assault,
So starts the tale of a girl of the blue houses.

The singer-storyteller wasn't pretty, not exactly. Her face was too thin, with a delicate nose and quick eyes that reminded one of a bird. Her long, dark hair was cropped short, as though to remind her listeners that she was selling music and story, instead of something else that some men might have desired. She wore no makeup or jewelry, save for a jade ring on her right hand.

On her shoulder sat a green siskin, a lovely bird apparently trained to chirp and harmonize with the playing of the pipa.

"...then the invading army surrounded Yangzhou, like a stormy sea pounding against a rock..."

She clapped two bamboo sticks together to simulate the sound of horses' hooves. She dragged a rusty nail across an old gong to simulate the sound of armor grinding against armor.

Of course the young woman didn't call the invaders in her story "Manchus." It had been more than a decade since the Manchu conquest of China. The new dynasty claimed the Mandate of Heaven, and clever scholars came up with cloying tributes to the wisdom and strength of the Manchu sages.

Like all true stories, her story was set a long, long time ago.

" 'What does a lowly woman, a concubine, know of virtue?' asked the captain."

The little siskin fluttered from table to table, picking at melon seeds, and everyone marveled at its beauty.

In the same manner, as the young woman told the story, she hopped between voices and expressions. The audience was mesmerized.

"Green Siskin strode up to the soldiers and said, 'What treasure do you need?' "

They clenched their fists as they pictured the bodies in the streets. They cheered and laughed as Green Siskin tricked the invading commander. They spat and slapped the table in anger as the ignorant merchant condemned Green Siskin.

Hundreds of thousands died in six dark days.
A despised woman saved thirty-one.
Ever cunning, she sought no fame nor praise.
Defying fate, she did what could be done.

As far as most in the crowd were concerned, the Yangzhou Massacre never happened. Official histories were always composed by sealing away ghosts.

But the truth always lived on in song and story.
Masters and mistresses, this I know to be true:
There is no Heavenly ledger, no all-fair Judge.
Yet general, prostitute, merchant, or child,
The fate of this world each one of you can budge.
And the little siskin took off from the young woman's shoulder and circled around the room, chirping and singing, lifted up by the warm air, by the loud cheer that exploded from the crowd: free, free, free.

Art by Nilah Magruder

JOONI
KEMBA BANTON

1843
Jamaica

Jooni woke to darkness and a hammering like hard rain; the little hut shuddered violently, then quickly rattled to a stop. She bolted upright and listened. There was now only her own haggard breath and the chickens fussing in the back of the yard. Pictures from her dream gathered as she glanced wide-eyed around the hut. She felt for the machete beside her banana-leaf mat. All was still. Maybe it was the dream... maybe.

She lay back down on her mat, her heart beating like horses' hooves battering the earth, and watched the first light of dawn creep through the clumsy window.

Eyes closed now, pictures from her dream descended. Yaa – Jooni's mama – with scars and blood and empty eyes and buzzing flies around her wounds. The only way she ever came, to haunt her.

Was every morning going to always be like this one? Waking in a sweat after seeing Mama like that, or thinking she was still back there, before 1838 – before Jamaica gave its slaves their full freedom. Sticky, hot slaving fields. The sky a treacherous ceiling. All the buzzing and buzzing in her head. And Mama – Jooni's everything – gone. Really gone.

It was all settling into her chest now. She could feel it – her whole day was going to be colored by this dream. She could feel how it was knotting up her insides, making her mouth crimple. She held her belly. No vomiting today. *Let me be still today*. But as she said it, she felt it a false hope. The whole world was broken and falling to pieces. She'd never known another truth. Her mama had once said wherever hope was robbed, you turned your hand and fashioned it into existence. But Mama had been wrong about many things. Jooni clenched her teeth and tried to breathe deep. Then *clicketyclackety-clicketyclackety*, there it was again, and the hut rattled. The chickens squawked and clucked. Something was falling on the rooftop. Jooni jumped up with her machete, grabbed the hem of her gown, and flashed to her door. In the soft glow of the morning, milky stones lay scattered on the steps and across the ground. The same milky crystals that had fallen some days ago and which had melted and disappeared in the heat. A man in the village had said he'd heard of it, had said the words *ice* and *hail*. Hard water falling from the clouds. Jooni raised her chin and searched the sky suspiciously. The yard was silent.

Calabash gourds were neatly lined atop the short stone wall that surrounded the yard. Dead leaves were strewn across the ground. A rubbish heap lay at the back, full of banana skins, fat earth grubs, and mango seeds. Under an otaheite apple tree, laden with the pink-red fruit, small statues molded out of dark earth clay stood surrounded by a banquet of food and water and other bits of offerings. There was a barrel of rainwater and pans. All was quiet.

Jooni set her mouth in a mean line and sighed. She waited, checking her irritation. Some days ago, the breadfruit tree had come loose from the ground and leaned to one side, as if it were getting ready to fall. Stones from the low wall had mysteriously slipped out of place and thudded to the ground. And then there was the day the skin on her arms turned to charred flesh, the next moment gone. Just so. It had happened so quickly she wasn't sure she'd seen right. When it happened again the following day, fright bit her. She'd spent the afternoon sitting in a tub of herbs and rainwater, scrubbing and whimpering.

At first, Jooni thought it was a duppy spirit playing tricks on her, but she didn't think so anymore. This felt strange. Different. What in heaven's name could be happening? Jooni stood there in the doorway, counting her breaths. The shadowy hut behind her groaned.

This hut – her refuge – it made many noises, but had been built strong by the freed man that built it shortly after Jamaica had fully emancipated all its slaves five years ago: 1838. She always had to say the year to herself, as if these things – numbers – which Jooni had started learning to read, were magic, as if not saying them would render the freedom absent, hurl her back into that wretched time. As if that time could come into this one – and capture her. 1838. No – Massa Williams wouldn't catch her.

She'd found the hut about a year ago, abandoned there on the side of the hill above the village, See Them Come, called so because it was founded by ex-slaves who after Emancipation had seized the uninhabited land, and continued to come and come and come. The numbers had swollen to the hundreds.

Jooni had stumbled on the hut desperate and cross, needing to find a quiet place. She was eighteen, nineteen, or maybe twenty years old – she didn't know what year she was born, not that it mattered. She had found the hut and could feel its barren solitude in the planked walls and echoes. She felt the man and knew he was never coming back for it. Probably left the island with the waves of people that had taken off for Panama to work, or someplace else, shifting and shifting – like ghosts – needing to forget. Jooni had made the hut her home. Hers. Where nobody's eyes dug into her. Accusing. Judging. Like Tenan, who never failed to remind Jooni how much she owed. For keeping by her after Yaa had died, for minding her, for putting up with her. For risking her own livelihood, running from the plantation with her, like some runaway, hiding even though Emancipation had come already. Lord knows what Massa Williams would have done to Jooni for what she done. They hid, working on other estates before finally coming to See Them Come, when the threat of an enraged former Massa had shrunken and confined itself to the nerve and muscle of the body.

Now patches of the brightening sky shone through the trees and made lace patterns of leaves. Jooni continued to count the moments, still waiting.

Beyond the yard wall, one could see the sides of the hills. Below all of this, down the path, there was the village, which would be waking at this same hour. Further down, the snake-like path descended, opened out, and led abruptly to where there was glittering sand, a road going to town, almond trees, and the broad, broad sea. Men were already there now, pushing their boats into the water, hunting fish and crab, and anything else in the salty depths that could be eaten or sold. Jooni briefly recalled the sensation of that water flooding all the membranes in her face, her eyes, her nose, filling her throat — the time she had dunked herself in, thinking she would drown. And the sea had foamed and spat and heaved her back onto the shore. A distant memory the taste of salt. Grainy. Jooni leaned slightly and spat into the dirt outside the hut; she pulled the back of her hand across her lips.

A light breeze picked up some dried leaves and blew them across where the ice lay, still shining like small pieces of moon, starting to melt. Jooni did something like a sniffle, and still holding her machete, now glinting in the new morning light, she pulled back into the shadows of the hut and slammed the door.

***

Jooni's memories sometimes seemed to have a breath of their own — they were so alive. She could remember so vividly working alongside her mama and the other women on the plantation. Yaa's presence had been so formidable as she'd swung her cutlass with power and tireless rhythm, slicing through the cane stalks and making them tremble and drop to the ground. Jooni could see her clear clear — her handkerchiefed head, the sweat breaking loose over her skin, her cowrie shell necklace dangling from her neck like the one Jooni also wore.

Jooni had seen how the men and women looked up to the obeah woman, Yaa, feared her even. Depended on her to ease strife, stave off chaos, offer tiny fragments of hope. Yaa stuffed wounds with plant poultices, made concoctions of man piaba bush and devil's horsewhip. She made fetishes and talismans for small troubles, blessed new babies and guarded their huts from unseen evils, stood over the dying — and afterwards, placated their spirits. She stood ready to brave monsters sealed in myths, and the ones that walked in human form. It was Yaa who taught Jooni the power of incantation, had grabbed her cheeks and gazed into the child's eyes. She'd said, *Look at me, Jooni. Here. Say after me.* And Jooni followed: *I am not no slave. Never was. Never have been. Never will be. I am no slave to man, nor woman, nor beast. No slave to no mind, no thought, no feeling. I am like iron passing through fire. The sky, the plants, the sea. I am life and nothing will break me. So I think, so I speak — I am.* And Jooni would stare into Mama's eyes, deep as ocean, and say those words like a spell.

Yes. Mama was magic. And those who knew also knew to be silent about it, would never tell Massa more than he needed to know.

To young Jooni, Yaa might have been a god, indestructible. Sometimes on the plantation death seemed more certain than life, but she did not think

Mama could die. Could vaporize in a cloud of smoke.

But she had.

***

Inside the hut, the floor creaked and grunted with Jooni's rocking. She hugged her folded legs. And rocked. Back, forward, *swing*, back, forward, *swing*. Creak, groan. *Knock knock*. There. A sound she didn't make.

Jooni stopped. Reached with her ears. Searched with her senses. Hm. Nothing.

The hut had its own ways.

A rooster crowed from the backyard, a loud *err-ah-err-ah-errrrrr* that echoed into the morning. The rising sun began stealing through the window and touched Jooni's long face and deep cocoa skin and glistened off the fat dark beauty mole above her lip. It creeped across the floor and glided over a basket, two wicker chairs, and a small table.

Then Damba appeared. Jooni didn't move, she only watched him.

Sitting on one of the chairs in his oversized pants and torn shirt, swinging his small legs.

He didn't have his head.

A giggle escaped from a corner behind Jooni, childish and bouncy. Then Damba's headless body dissolved. Jooni managed a crooked smile at the empty wicker chair.

Damba – the only spirit she hadn't the will to turn away. She held him once and he'd felt like any other little boy, alive and in flesh, in two pieces, his body curled up in her lap, his head cradled in her arm - his face wet from crying. Feeling him suddenly so real, she had held him with everything inside her, not minding the blood.

Holding Damba had been healing. Jooni had never done that before with no other duppy. They mostly came silently demanding – sad, angry, lost – always asking, begging, needing. Leaving a cavern of hollowness behind each time.

Like a woman duppy that came one time with a tin mask trapped on her head, and who came for days appearing here, there, everywhere, while Jooni had tried not to look – busied herself with yard work, trying, trying hard not to feel, to not understand the inundation of voices in her head, speaking like a swarm of bees, to not heed the tightening pain in her chest, until Jooni one day threw down her pot and screamed, her beauty mole trembling, telling the duppy to go the bumbo to hell.

And it went away.

And left Jooni with a vacuum that made her bawl. And the memory of those eyes behind that tin mask – like mirrors; in them Jooni had seen a fracturing that nothing could fill, a fracturing crack-whipped into the mind. It hurt – oh god, it hurt. That duppy had come *needing* and Jooni had sent her away. Yaa would never have done that.

Ah sorry... Jooni had pleaded. *Ah sorry... you hear me?* But the duppy never came back no matter how Jooni had begged the air, cried into the ground, whispered into the grooves in her hut walls, *please please* – and when all that had failed, screamed again and kicked over the frail furniture, screaming for them all to leave her alone. There was no way to fix this broken, brittle world.

And now who's-it-what's-it was getting renk.

Throwing down icy stones on her.

Jooni got up. She was tired. Tired of the battling. Tired of sad stories and dogging memories. Tired of the stress, the strife. These damned, rotten ghosts with their sufferations, as if she didn't have enough of her own. Her own mother's spirit never even came back to her. Never, not even once. Ever. Why? Because she was gone. Really, really gone. Gone, gone.

She felt the urge to run to her statues – her beautiful statues she'd formed carefully from the dark earth clay and into shapes of people, for those too-sad sufferation times she couldn't hold or rock away. She wanted to run to them, feed them, bring them drink, and pretty flowers. Make more statues fashioned from clay.

But there was work, always work to do. The chickens needed care, the yard needed raking. With thoughts and memories flying wildly through her mind, Jooni quickly changed her clothes and decided to face the day.

***

Outside, the sun was already high. The ice had left small dark spots, now fading. She pretended not to notice, ignored the flip-flopping in her belly. Her off-white cotton dress, smeared with dirt stains, gathered at her waist and fell down in skirts to her shins, lightly brushing against her legs as she moved. The cool air breathed on her arms and kissed her scalp where her hair parted into bulbous plaits that curled stiffly under her jaw and down the nape of her neck.

The green things were humming now – a gently trilling, slightly buzzing synergy. Like the way the cane fields used to buzz when Jooni used to help Mama and the other women in the field gang. The whispering stalks sometimes spoke of effort, and tiny struggles, of the uncurling of leaves and the hunger for sun, great growth and quiet changes. Other times they whispered frenzy – of heavy, driving work, of blood spill and loss of innocence. In those times, the cane fields were unbearable to be in.

Jooni took the rake and walked round to the back; the chickens scattered out of her way and then trailed her footsteps. The big cock perched on the wall followed her with his head. She pulled the blankets of dead leaves across the ground, leaving shallow canals in the earth, and worked them into one pile; she would set it afire later. Now she would head down to sea to sell her mangoes. She scattered feed for the chicken, watching them nervously as they scrambled, cluck-cluck-clucking and pecking each other for space. The rooster flew off the wall to join the fussing, a blur of wings.

Jooni walked over to the water barrel to wash the dust and mess off her hands, and sprinkle her face. And that's when she saw it, in the pool of water like a mirror – holding the light of the sky and shadow shapes of hanging otaheite leaves – she swore she saw another face – her own face, yes, but with blistering scars and pock marks and with eyes so fiery. A face that glowered. Glowered at *her*? Jooni pulled back sharply, reaching up to her face fast, fast, running her fingers up her jaws, over her forehead, down her cheekbones and nose. Nothing. Skin smooth as garden egg.

Her heart flapping, she stepped towards the barrel once more, paused before looking in, and then regarded the still water. In the reflection, her face was soft and sheen from work, supple and long, haloed by thick, scalloped plaits. Her eyebrows now reflected her confusion.

She spun around, glancing across the yard uneasily. Where was her machete? Her fingers began to tremor. Then the leaning breadfruit tree leaned a little more, lifting earth and sending stones to rumble away. Jooni jumped for her mango basket and quickly fled the yard, hot and testy.

***

On the pathway, down the slope, Jooni balanced the basket on her head and moved swift-like, descending on See Them Come. She would rather not, but she had to pass it on the way to the sea. She stepped past the cabins and shacks on the outskirts of the village, built so rough and fast they seemed to perch precariously on the incline of the hill. Outside of them hung clothes on lines tied to trees.

Jooni wondered if Tenan was home today. Tenan kept her distance, but Jooni visited when she could tolerate it, trying to do her best to comfort an old woman. It was the least she could do.

But today – today was no day to deal with Tenan.

Living with Tenan had been like daily battle. To Tenan, Jooni was a sinner; she said all that seeing spirits and strange dreams and things were devil workings, that Jooni's strange customs were obeah. And she'd called a crowd of amen-sayers to come sanctify Jooni without knowing that was the worst thing she could have done.

It wasn't just the crowd that laid their hands on Jooni that drove her away, it was how bad she wanted to hurt Tenan when it was all over. She wanted to say something. *Fall. Break your hip, old witch.* And she had to fight to hold her lips, while her beauty mole shivered, else it would happen. It would happen, like the other times she'd spoke things and they'd happened. Like how she'd hurt Tenan before. Like what she did to Massa Williams' favorite horse. Told it to die. And it fell to the ground wheezing that same moment, the veins in its throat bulging. That's how Massa had found out she was just like her mama. No Emancipation was going to save Jooni's skin then. Yes, Jooni had to hold her lips.

But Tenan stood comfortable in what she knew, there with her hands on her hips, and she pushed up her chin and said, "Is what, you want do some more of you obeah on me? The only mother you have left?" And that did it. Jooni ran in shame.

Remembering all this now, Jooni kept on the path, checking the rising pressure in her chest. Mama had explained it all. Jooni could see her clear like yesterday, twirling round a piece of tall grass in the side of her mouth. Her skin, always shine and smooth and deep dark like the purple skin of starfruit. Touching her cowrie shell, Yaa had said, *Your Nana was just like me and you. We could call weself vision people, bush doctors, spirit people, obeah people, mayaal people. No matter the names, the power have the same source and people could use them power for good or wickedness. But you see, everything that backra white man see and don't understand, they say is evil. And obeah is one of we own word that them hear and feel them own fear, for them don't want to get struck down...*

Because of all that Yaa had said, Jooni had understood why Tenan had called her a sinner. And she understood why mayaal people had embraced the Christ man. She understood why the old masters had made practicing obeah punishable by flogging and even death. She recalled Lady Hyacinth, the old village mayaal woman, who had once caught Jooni's gaze, and winked, smiling her toothless grin. The village people respected Lady Hyacinth. What was the difference? The mayaal people held their mayaals, danced down the spirits, and served the people's ails and conflictions. And they kept their African gods and went on crusades against the wicked, which they now called obeah — lighting lamps and pinning down shadows. And they also invoked the power of the Christ man, because his too was a power, and also because mayaal people had to take note, they had to take note that white men still ran the place, Emancipation or none. They had to make themselves different from obeah, that name which was now drenched in stain as a dark art. That name which Jooni wanted nothing to do with, nor any other name. None of it. She didn't want her gifts. Yaa was dead.

Almost clear of the village now. Two villagers were still up ahead, talking under their breath. Sometimes Jooni didn't hear a thing of what people said. Didn't hear any of the sus, the bad talk. But sometimes the whisper came from far and registered loud in her head, like now: "See obeah woman a come deh. Mad she mad eenuh."

As they neared her, the women averted their eyes. Jooni continued to mind her manners.

From under her basket: "How you do today, Miz Sally? Miz Eliza?"

"Yes, yes, fine thank you, Jooni, good to see yuh!"

And they were behind her, hushed words reaching back to touch the edge of Jooni's ear. She shut them out.

***

The sun's rays struck the sandy road to town. It shone like gold. The sea ahead, beyond the road, looked like a water-field of buoying diamonds. Sellers called out their goods — the women with wide hips, the men skinny and quick-moving.

Jooni walked the road in the sun-hot: "Fruuuiiit! Mango a sell!" She walked against the traffic — a throng of donkey carts, wagons and horse-drawn carriages. "Sweet mango fi sweet you mouth!"

A carriage grumbled by and stopped, and a man's voice called out. Jooni ran with her basket, "Yes, sah," and pulled the basket off her head, keeping her eyes on the wheels as she waited.

"How much?" His British was cool and level – disinterested. He had not once looked out the carriage. This man was probably an estate owner, or one of the important Parliament men from town. The woman by his side, with brown ringlets hanging from the side of her bonnet, flapped her folding fan and kept her nose in the air.

"Five pence for a dozen mango, sah."

"Give it to me."

The man reached out a big purse for Jooni to put the mangoes in, but she froze. The hands. So familiar.

Her eyes crawled up the arms into the darkness of the carriage. She started to make out the face with thick sideburns and then the eyes. Green. And her heart started to pound now.

The man seemed only curious at first, but then the green eyes were showing something else. Recognition. They widened until, yes, she was sure, now there was fright. How strange.

The man snatched the purse quickly into the carriage and continued to stare wide-eyed, his hand over his mouth. And Jooni got ready to lash with her words if needed, remembering his horse. How quickly his horse had went down when she'd said the word. *Die.* How fast it happened. Yes, she was ready to lash if he dared to make a move. The sudden heat rising to her skin made her slightly dizzy, as her chest heaved with her heavy breathing. But Massa Williams suddenly stuttered to the driver to go – to go quickly. He started rubbing his temples. "Move!" he shouted. As the carriage lurched off, Jooni heard in a hateful whisper: "*Witch!*"

Jooni stood there her chest sounding like drums, and then out of the wind with a hint of the sea salt, biting, bitter, and snarling it echoed: *Witch!*

Her nostrils flaring, she grabbed up her basket. The blood was rushing in her ears. Her skin felt like it was on fire. She slowly crossed the road just missing a donkey and its wagon. *Do you know what it is we do to witches?* Jooni slammed her palms over her ears and stumbled. With a heart-wrenched cry, she turned on her heel, and ran. Fast, fast across the road and hot sand, to the broad, waiting sea, cotton dress flying in the wind, feeling her fingertips, her skin, burn and burn. At the sea front she fell into the sand. The wind whipped as the pink sun began to dip in the distance. The sea's powerful, crashing waves rose and slammed against the shore. Heat choked Jooni's throat. Her head buzzed, then *clickety clackety clickety clackety,* a sudden shower of stones from the sky. Ice. Hail. They pelted her and bounced off the ground. *Stop it!* she raged. And the rain of ice stopped suddenly. Oh god. It was so hot. This hell was so hot. Jooni got up and faced the sea. Thirsty beyond measure, she stumbled towards it.

Was my mama a witch? No. She was an obeah woman. And fearless. I can still see her clear clear sometimes. When she stood, she stood strong, hands on her hips looking out on the fields real quiet, like she listening. Waiting. At night, in the pitch-black of our slave hut, sometimes I would stir awake, and Mama is not beside me, she on the other side of the hut, though I can't see her, but I hearing her. And what I hearing is not only her voice, but other voice too, she talking to the spirit them.

Sometimes I stir at night and Mama not beside me but she not in the hut neither. She gone into the night. And I would be afraid if she didn't already done tell me. Say when she disappear is gone she gone go plan freedom. An I mustn't say a word. An when Mama say that is like she talking with the edge of a knife. But she know she could trus' me. And she was there by morning.

It was Sam Sharpe rebellion Mama was planning for — he who they call Daddy Sharpe. I didn't know it then, but I know now. The year we was in was 1831 they say and Daddy Sharpe who was a slave over in St. James parish was planning a peaceful protest, but his peaceful protest turned out nuthin' peaceful. It wasn't the first time slaves was plotting a chance for freedom... they see Daddy Sharpe protest as a chance.

And Mama she'd been communicating with other rebels on other estates, plotting and planning with them under Massa's nose.

All of them, they would get beaten or hung — except Mama.

Before Daddy Sharpe rebellion, Massa never knew Mama was a obeah woman. She was too much stealth for him. Too much stealth for the whole of them. But Massa was in the town and she hadn't known. He was returning when he received news from the horsemen riding quick in the wind, reporting how everything was chaos, that the slaves were setting crops aflame, attacking the great houses. Massa flew into a panic; he musta wonder if the uprising reach our estate yet, and he come to check, frantically searching the rooms of the great house and found his family dead, and beside each one's head a little bag. A obeah bag. And then he knew what was done...

Massa round up his men quick quick. I remember hearing him shouting in the night. I never hear his voice sound so before, like an animal inside him.

He didn't guess it was a woman. But him catch her. Him catch Mama. Him was screaming saying she was a witch. He ask if she know what it is they do to witches. Mama talk back, she say she not no witch, she a obeah woman. And Massa screamed so loud, it make my blood curdle. Like something great rising up out of him.

I remember that night like it was happening this very moment. When the flames lunged up into the black of the night, like the tongue of a great monstrous serpent, licking the sky. And I was screaming out my throat so til I feel like it was tearing, and I fighting to wriggle out my clothes and run into those flames — but they were holding me back — hands from everywhere holding me back.

Everything was so silent, silent as the sky. Silent as stone.

I couldn't hear no sound coming from the thrashing body strapped to the pole, nor even Tenan who was bawling like I never see her do before. I see Massa Williams on his horse, his face twist up like his whole world coming down in brimstone. His eyes — those green, green eyes... I see him open him mouth and shout to his men, and he take off into the night on his horse, *that same horse... and in his hand, a torch of fire.*

Was that really Mama's body burning there? I could feel the heat, like it was eating my own insides. Ohh I wanted to swallow that fire, oh lawd. But I just see Mama stop moving. And when I see that, like everything inside a me stop too and I feel the people them lifting me, and the flames disappearing from my sight, and all I see is the black, black sky full of stars. I stare at all them pretty sky lights. And I wonder as they was carrying me back to my lonely hut in the wretched night, I wonder how these gods Mama had always told me about, how they could possibly be up there.

Jooni sank down, down, down into the sea – under the skirts of the great ocean that had carried and birthed endless stories and claimed near as many souls – a water graveyard and a womb. Jooni struggled against the water claiming her lungs and fell still, no longer feeling her throat constrict. Water bubbled at her ears, a cocoon of sound. Had she died? Her eyes closed, she surrendered everything, let her body fall into the nothingness beneath. No more fire. The water was so cool. She descended and descended and descended into blue black and then felt the hands close around her throat. She opened her eyes and saw... was it herself? The long face and bulbous plaits, the big beauty mole, the thin frame in Jooni's own off-white cotton dress. Yes, it must be her – but wrecked and brutalized, with bruises, jagged wounds and pock marks all over her face and skin. Her teeth like small triangular razors, her eyes flashing icy fire. The reflection in the water barrel. Jooni but not Jooni. Some creature. It tightened its sharp claws around Jooni's neck, choking her in the depth of the sea. But Jooni felt no urge to resist, only looked into those icy eyes and saw everything in them, held before her like a mirror: a world of pain, falling and falling into pieces. Empty hearts, heavy hands, and snatches of Jooni's own haunting dreams. A lonely yard and a falling breadfruit tree. Lost mothers and fathers mourning babies. Grief-stricken wailing. Damba – headless. Statues to kiss and cradle and coo over, but so helpless and sad. The forgotten and untold – chained, roped, dogged, hunted, crucified. Yaa, burning in a master's hell eternally. Hopelessness. *All* hopelessness and despair. And then Jooni heard her own voice quiet and small. *That's not true.* The creature looked startled, its eyes widening, its own beauty-mole trembling. *It's not true* – Jooni's voice said again – *we not hopeless. There's more.*

The creature pulled back in rage; streams of bubbles burst from its mouth. It lurched for Jooni again, this time digging its claws into her shoulder and opened its jaws wide to bite, but it was too late. Jooni was already understanding. She slowly lifted her hand and placed it on the creature's face. Without any effort, she held it back; felt it writhing behind her palm. And suddenly remembering, she searched, searched inside until she found it. *I am not no slave.* Yes. This was true. *Never was. Never have been. Never will be. I am no slave to man, nor woman, nor beast. No slave to no mind, no thought, no feeling. I am like iron passing through fire. The sky, the plants, the sea. I am life and I will not be broken.* The creature continued to struggle against Jooni's gentle hand, now making tormented sounds. *So I think, so I speak — I am.* How did Jooni forget her own power? That her own thoughts could make skies fall. Could bend experience. Could paint and color what she saw. That her own words — *die* — could take life, and yes, could heal. Give salve to the broken? Her heart brimming, she lifted her other hand and placed it behind the creature's head, and slowly she pulled it in, pulled it into her bosom, and wrapped her arms around it and embraced it as it wailed and convulsed against her. Jooni felt a glowing light humming, spiraling, brightening inside her, until it reached the surface of her skin. It vibrated through the two of them until the creature vanished inside her and she was one again, there, hugging herself in the sea, radiating like a moon. And it was not her time to die.

She stretched her arms and uncurled her chest in the water and felt a current gently push against her back and come around her. The water cradled her and carried her to the surface where she broke air and suddenly gasped for breath. The sea frothed, heaved, and gently rolled Jooni onto the shore. The moon was full; it shone against the sand.

***

Days later, Lady Hyacinth stood in the clearing under the big tree in Jooni's yard, grinning her toothless grin. Candles surrounded them all, placed on the stone wall and on the ground, and on the shrine Jooni had made for Yaa, which she had surrounded with flowers, seashells, pebbles, bird feathers, a coconut, a fat mango, and a calabash full of water. There were candles and fresh flowers around the little earth clay statues too — candles and pretty, pink bougainvillea. In the flicker of light, under an evening sky, elder mayaal women were wetting the ground and praying. Lady Hyacinth stood before Jooni, holding a long stick. She placed the point down at the center of the clearing and held it there.

"Kongo!" Her voice, followed by the *boom boom* from the surrounding drummers, flew up into the trees, and she began to draw with the stick *ssshhhhh* across the ground.

"Nzambi, Nzambi, *awesome* creator god. Ay!" Hyacinth leaned suddenly to the side. She kept her grip on the stick. "Ancestaaaaars! Woy!" Hyacinth shouted again and leaned forward, and then began to sing, the drums beginning soft pounds, while Hyacinth sang raspy words in another tongue Jooni did not know and continued to draw *ssssshhhhh* across the ground completing a healing cross, a spirit cross, a cross with a circle around it. The women poured something over Jooni's head, wiping it down all over her body. And Jooni leaned and swirled, the drumbeats intoxicating her mind. Short breaths escaped from her mouth as her bare feet shuffled in the dirt making pathways. She smiled — yes, pathways. She dipped to the right, spun around, holding her skirt tail. Dipped to the left. Rolled her torso, the sounds of the drums opening up spaces in her body. They were coming. She turned and turned. She slipped her eyes open, drunken, and glimpsed them — spirits, in white, dark faces, hands and feet — patient, ready and waiting. And when she opened her eyes once more, she saw *her*, behind the clearing, standing near

255

the stone wall.

Like she always did when she used to look out over the cane fields. Yaa. Mama. She stood with her arms akimbo, her cowrie shell hanging from her neck, her handkerchief tied around her head. And her chin raised high, high, high. Warrior woman, obeah woman, healer woman. Staring into Jooni, her eyes like steel, and Jooni's chest was brimming – she started to laugh. And Yaa smiled. And Jooni was feeling something new, but not new. Something so passionate in her chest, strong in her blood. She reached up and touched her neck. Her cowrie. How did she forget? And Jooni moved her hands to her hips. Akimbo. And raised her head and stood there, holding her mother's gaze, raising her own chin high, high, high. And Yaa, still smiling, vanished into the darkness. But it was fine now. Because Jooni was ready now. And she was laughing. And her laughter was powerful.

Art by Kaysha Siemens

THERE WILL BE ONE
VACANT CHAIR
SARAH PINSKER

1862
Ohio

If we are indeed living in the eternal now that Julius once wrote of –
writes of – then the soldiers on the battlefields of Pennsylvania and Kentucky
and Virginia are away at war still, and they are being welcomed home, and
they are kissing their loved ones goodbye. Their families are waiting for them,
but they have not yet left. Levi and Julius are still fighting at the dinner table
over obscure theological points. My brothers always argued, though they were
grown men already when I was still a girl, grown men already when we fled
Hungary for Ohio.

The Sabbath is meant to be ushered in as a peaceful bride, but our Friday
night meals were often contentious. Papa and my brothers always returned
from synagogue arguing some Talmudic point or another. Julius was by far
the most devoted scholar of the three, but Levi was too stubborn ever to
acknowledge he was in the wrong. Their walk home took some time, due to
Julius's shortened leg, and we could hear their arguments from some blocks
down the otherwise quiet street. They would grow silent when Mama lit the
candles, and through the other blessings, then erupt into discord again as the
meal was served. Even after Levi married and moved three blocks away, this
was ever the pattern, only his children would wail when his voice rose, and
his wife, Hava, cowered at the far end of our expanded table.

Their greatest fight occurred in such a manner, though on an evening
when Julius did not attend synagogue with the others. Levi and another of
the local doctors had been charged with conducting military examinations all
that day, to determine whose petitions for exemption from the Union army
might be granted. Julius had insisted on walking there without aid of his
stick. He arrived back sweaty and spent, and closed himself into his room until we begged him to come out for the lighting of candles.

Julius fumed through dinner. He sat beside me, as always, and I could
see the fist he clenched in his lap. Levi, oblivious or simply uncaring, picked
the very subject he should have left alone. "I still don't understand why you
came in today, Julius. I didn't need to examine you to mark you for a disabil-
ity certificate."

Julius kept his eyes down and pushed the shlishkes around his plate. His
mouth was a tight line beneath his beard. Levi continued, "I would have

259

thought you would be grateful to me for getting you out of fighting. Now you can stay home with the women and your books."

Julius slammed his fist onto the table. A dumpling jumped from his plate, scattering breading across the tablecloth. "Do you really think I prefer not to fight? I came to you because I thought you would approve me. You're my brother. Approve me for something else, if not for fighting. I'll chaplain, or nurse. I don't want to stay home. Not again. Just me and the scrofulous and the rheumatic."

"You are rheumatic. And that leg of yours can't carry you across the house without a rest, let alone a battlefield," Levi said. "You are meant to stay home, brother, whether you want to or not."

I knew that Papa and Levi had fought in the war back in Hungary, but I had never considered that Julius might have wanted to do so. I didn't understand why he wanted to go. Unlike the family stories I had heard about revolution in Hungary, this new war of Southern rebellion didn't seem relevant to our situation. I wanted to ask why they were joining the fight, to understand, but it was not my place. I could inquire of Julius alone, later. He always answered my questions as if I had a right to ask them.

Julius made a strangled sound and pushed himself away from the table. In his head he must have strode from our small dining room, but in reality his progress was painfully slow.

Levi shook his head and spoke as if Julius were out of earshot. "I wish he could see that I've done him a kindness. He'd be just as useless in the army camps as he is here."

Julius halted, then turned. He took two dragging steps, then launched himself at Levi. He managed one punch at Levi's jaw, and then Levi was out of his chair too, twisting Julius's arm and kicking his good leg out from under him, forcing him to the ground. Our parents watched slack-jawed. Levi's son Izsak, now six, stood up in his chair and swung his own fists. Hava tugged the boy's sleeve until he sat down. His eyes followed his father, who now spoke in mocking tones.

"You had the element of surprise and you still couldn't best me. How would you fare against someone with a bayonet? You can't stand, you can't fight, and you can't run."

"Julius," our father finally interjected, as if Julius were still sitting at the table, and not pinned to the floor. "Levi is not saying you lack courage or conviction. Merely that someone in your condition does not meet the minimum medical standards. Come, you shouldn't be fighting on the Sabbath."

The only tool I had for bringing peace to the table was Julius's devotion to me. "Mama and I will feel better knowing you are here when the others are gone."

His voice did not relax, but it deflated. "As you wish, Frieda."

***

Levi and Papa both left in April of 1862. Levi, like most of our neighbors, mustered with the 199th Ohio Infantry. All of our community's young men went together, except for Julius. At least they could converse in a familiar language.

Papa would not have the comfort of known faces or language, though he spoke English better than the rest of us. He had been asked to doctor on one of the new steamboat hospitals traveling up and down the river with aid and supplies. Mama and Hava and Izsak and I waved from the yard until we could no longer see them. Julius stood with us for only a moment before returning to his books.

Papa wrote often, though his letters sometimes arrived out of order or in groups of two or three. He was on a ship with three other surgeons, a few medical students, and several volunteer nurses of varying experience. He said that he had petitioned the President on behalf of the Jewish soldiers to ask for Saturday as an alternate day of rest.

"Our boat is not intended to venture into battle. Most of our patients suffer with typhoid or measles, as those with wounds are tended by the field doctors. I have not heard from Levi, though I imagine that is his role. Have you had news from him?"

We had not. We knew he was alive only because Reuven Goldstein, now Sergeant Goldstein, wrote often to his wife. She shared parts of the letters with Hava, who shared the news with my parents and me.

If Hava was upset with her husband's failure to write, she didn't show it. "He must be very busy," she said. We sat in her small parlor, knitting socks for the soldiers of the 199th. Izsak battled imaginary forces under the legs of our chairs while the younger children napped.

"But the infantrymen write, and they must be even busier."

She smiled at me. She had a scar that twisted across her lips like a winding river. "Frieda, you really must learn to think before you ask. Are you trying to make me worry more? I'd rather worry less, given the choice."

I blushed. I kept hoping age would bring discretion, but that never yet seemed to be the case. "I just mean I think he should be writing to you."

"I agree, but that doesn't make it so." She pursed her lips and resumed her knitting. She had dropped a stitch somewhere along the way, but I pretended not to notice.

Hava and I knit and sewed for the soldiers until our knuckles swelled, but Mama built herself a different role. She canvassed our community — by which I mean the other Hungarian Jews, for she had no means of communicating with any others — to find out which women were struggling while they waited for their husbands to return. There were so many. We were lucky my father and brother were doctors. We had more than most.

"I have been in their place before, as a mother and a wife," Mama said, as we carried between us a full pot of sholet for a family from synagogue. The smells of the stew, bean and onion and smoked beef and paprika and garlic, all swirled around us. My mouth watered. Then a stronger wind blew up the street, so that we were forced to hold our headscarves on with our free hands. I wondered what it must be like for Mama to endure her husband's departure yet again.

For Hava and Mama, the cooking and canning and knitting served as a distraction. For me, it assuaged my guilt. Several girls my age had left with the soldiers, to serve as volunteer nurses or cooks or laundresses. I was too frightened. I told myself Mama and Hava needed my help with the four children and Julius to care for, and that my English was poor. As long as I kept busy, these reasons were excuse enough.

They weren't mere excuses, either. I had served as Julius's nurse for as long as I could remember, bringing him his meals and caring for him on his worst days, which outnumbered the good ones. My brother continued his self-designed studies as though there were no war. He usually confined himself to the traditional biblical texts and commentaries, but occasionally he ventured into more esoteric topics. He tested these on me before discussing them with the rabbi or Papa – not Papa now, of course.

"What are you reading today?" I asked when I entered, and he always told me, rather than telling me it was not for my mind, as Levi would do. I loved that he conversed with me as if my education were equal to his own.

"Have I told you about Rabbi Luria, Frieda?"

"No?" I attempted to sweep the cluttered floor of his room. We had long since converted the first floor parlor into a bedroom and study for Julius. It robbed us of any sort of sitting area beyond the dining room, but the stairs gave him too much difficulty even on his best days. Though I fussed about his mess, I loved the smells of leather and paper and ink that I associated with him.

He held up a thin volume. "Ha'ARI, they called him. The Lion. He was a mystic. His teachings lie outside of my ordinary scope of study, but I found a book by a descendent of one of his students. Fascinating ideas. He believed that when Adam's soul was created, so were all the other souls of the human race. Until the arrival of the Messiah, these same souls will continue to wander from one body to the next, even to animals, to objects."

"What an odd notion," I said. I looked around the room, imagining souls clinging to the narrow bed, the desk, the bookshelves.

"I've always thought myself to be a poor excuse for a man. A good scholar, but useless to you, useless to everyone. How can I be a righteous person?"

"You are a righteous person, Julius. I don't know anyone who is more pious. Not even the rabbi."

He tugged at his beard. "I'm incomplete. How much does it matter that I study if I can't do anything with my knowledge? But there's one more extension of this concept that has piqued my interest. Ibbur, impregnation of a body by a righteous soul. Perhaps if I strive to be better, body and soul, I can invite a righteous soul to possess me. Perhaps another soul can use me to complete its work."

"I'm trying to understand, Julius."

"As am I, Frieda. I'm afraid I have no further appetite for study today, though. I think I shall go for a swim in the creek."

"A what?" I heard him, but it made as little sense as his talk of possessed souls. "Do you even know how to swim?"

He pushed himself back from the table and put a ribbon into the volume he had been reading to mark the page. "I do, though I haven't done it in many years. I don't expect it will be difficult to pick up again."

I considered everything that might go wrong. Though the creek was a short walk from our home, even a short walk was an ordeal for Julius. He would be exhausted by the time he got there.

"Shall I accompany you?" I asked, assuming his answer to be yes.

He surprised me. "I prefer to go on my own."

"What if you're pulled too far downstream? You condemn me to worry."

"I understand your concern," he said, in a tone that said that he both understood it and chose to reject it. So unlike Julius. He usually went to great pains not to burden me.

I blocked the doorway with my body, my arms crossed over my chest, so that Julius knew he could not move me. I did not enjoy shaming him. Any other man could have displaced me with ease. We stood opposed for several long moments, and then his shoulders sagged.

"Very well," he said.

The woods that bordered our community were not deep. I had taken Izsak to gather berries along the edges, but had never ventured in before. Julius and I followed a narrow deer path between the trees and down to the creek. I had only ever seen the more civilized portions, closer to the town center. It was wider here, rougher. I found a stone to sit on, just off the path but in view of the water.

"Are you sure this is safe?" I asked.

Julius didn't answer. He was not self-conscious in front of me, for I was the one to bathe him whenever he took ill. He stripped naked and climbed down the bank. The creek lapped at his ankles as he waded in, then his knees, then his waist. His movement seemed less awkward in the water, and when he dove in, it was with surprising grace.

I spent an anxious afternoon watching as he expended himself. When we finally staggered back to the house he was too weak to even climb the front steps without my help. He was smiling, though. "I think I'm going to swim every day."

Julius put aside his books for the first time in his life, if only for a few hours. He started swimming in the creek every afternoon. I grew to trust that he was not going to drown himself, and no longer insisted on following him.

One day he took Papa's Hungarian saber off the wall. Nobody had ever taught him to wield it, and he looked terribly awkward even to my untrained eye.

"What are you doing?" I watched him shuffle back and forth on his uneven legs, struggling to hold the sword in a usable position.

"We need to be prepared if the rebels should appear in our town. Who would protect you?"

"Give me the sword and teach me to use it. Then I can protect myself."

He lowered the sword, then handed it to me. "I suppose you'd do just as good a job as I would."

I hated myself for having told the truth. I didn't see him pick up the sword again, though he continued swimming in the river daily. His arms and chest grew visibly stronger from the effort of dragging his weak legs through the current. In the mornings, when I brought his breakfast to him, I often caught him gritting his teeth at the pains he was trying to ignore. He stopped as soon as he noticed me watching.

"Have you encountered any other souls in your excursions?" I asked him.

He shook his head, refusing to be baited. "I can say only that I have found a sense of calm and strength in the water that is equaled only by a perfect thought. Both happen rarely, but I strive to achieve them with more regularity."

His answer was so earnest I could say nothing in response. I watched him as he continued to exhaust himself, body and mind, day after day, and week after week. If Papa had been home, I'm sure he would have talked to Julius about the dangers of his new hobby. If Levi had been home, he would have mocked Julius so comprehensively that Julius would have redoubled his efforts and dropped dead of the exertion. But all I could do was watch.

Summer turned into autumn. Letters from Papa said that he was forced to work on the New Year and the Day of Atonement, on the latter treating bloodied limbs with no food in his stomach, until he nearly collapsed. I tried to imagine being in a place with no Jews at all, where the rituals of the holy days were transformed into improvisations and compromises. I ached for him.

A heavy rain brought down all of the leaves on one October night, and then the temperature dropped, so that everywhere we walked we felt the crackle of frozen leaves beneath our feet. Julius gave up his swims only when a thin layer of ice formed over the creek.

Snow came. Hava and I redoubled our efforts for the soldiers and the poorer families, switching from socks to blankets. Every letter from Papa gave mention of the bone-chilling cold. He had moved from the steamboat to a field hospital.

"I am relieved to be among Jews again, though none are Hungarian, so I still do not feel entirely among my own. For the Jewish soldiers, I serve as both surgeon and chaplain, so that they are not confused in what may be their final hours," he wrote. "I am not sure which duty wears on me more, or where one ends and the other begins. Julius, I wish you were here to administer the chaplain duties, for your counsel on such matters is far more valuable than mine." Julius read that letter out loud to me, the despair in his voice uncontained.

We had still not received correspondence from Levi, though the Goldstein letters assured us he was fine. "He regales the troops with jokes and songs," wrote the sergeant, leaving me to wonder if, in fact, he was referring to my brother after all. Or perhaps war really did change a person. Hava continued to write to him, despite his failure to reciprocate. She told him that he would have to teach her some of his jokes, and that the children were growing by leaps and bounds, Izsak in particular.

Izsak was indeed growing quickly. He was his father's child, mercurial and stubborn. As far as he was concerned, he could not age fast enough. He fashioned himself a blue cap and took to sneaking around with a knife he had stolen from his mother's kitchen. He watched me when I practiced with Papa's sword. I made him swear not to tell anyone.

"I'll teach you how to use it as soon as you have the strength to hold it," I told him.

He frowned. "But I want to be a soldier now. My father will be back by then, and I will have missed the war."

I hoped so. In the meantime, I hoped my promise would steady him and hold his desire to fight at bay.

Instead, he ran away. Hava roused him one morning in December, but he did not come down to breakfast. When she went upstairs for the second time, she discovered his bed empty. She ran to our house wailing; her crying roused me from my own sleep. She had left the babies alone to come find us, so Mama went back to mind the children. I walked to the rabbi's house to ask for assistance from the congregation, or those who were still home.

The reinforcements I collected were a mixed lot: the rabbi and the mail carrier, and after that the women (most of us more robust than the rabbi, but less so than the mailman), the older men, and the infirm. For once, Julius was among the fittest in the group, and it was agreed that he and I would search the woods while the others searched the streets.

Oh, my brother. His sharp mind, his withered leg. We walked slowly, and though we did not need pretext, he would pause on occasion to catch his breath and examine something. A footprint in mud, a broken twig. His path meandered. He could not be far ahead of us, but a young boy would always be faster than Julius. The clues, real or not, at last brought us within earshot.

The cries were faint, but we followed them. We reached the creek, and had no doubt what had happened. Izsak had ventured out across the creek, and the ice had not been thick enough to support him. He clung to the side of the hole he had fallen through, cracks radiating from his position. His sobs had already begun to weaken.

"We're here, Izsak," I called to the boy. He looked up at us and seemed to summon new strength to struggle. "Stay calm," I added. "Be still, and we'll come get you." He was at least thirty feet out from the edge of the creek.

Julius shook his head. "You can't go out there. The ice won't hold you. Your skirts will drown you if you fall in."

"What do you suggest?" I asked. "We have no rope, no branch stout enough."

"You walk faster than I do. Go get help. I'll stay here and keep him calm. Go, quickly."

I ran until I was out of breath and my muddy skirts weighed me down. Then I walked, nearly as fast as I ran. I emerged from the woods screaming and heaving for breath, alerting several members of the searching group. We fetched rope from the nearest barn, and some blankets to wrap the child in when he was safely out of the water. I led the group back to the creek.

We were too late. Not for Izsak, but for Julius. I should have known that he would try to save the boy. The small hole that Izsak had created was gone. Most of the ice from our side of the creek was gone, broken away by Julius when he fell through. The water rushed past, clear and cold. They both lay soaked on the muddy, snowy bank.

We tried to save them. We stripped their wet clothing from them and wrapped them in blankets, and I lifted Izsak into my arms. The mail carrier and the rabbi together helped Julius to his feet. He was not a large man.

We stumbled back through the woods. Izsak stirred slightly in my arms, his face and lips blue with cold. His body began an uncontrolled shivering. At some point, perhaps when I reached the street or perhaps before, someone took the boy from my arms. I had my eyes on the backs of the two men struggling with Julius. Julius stumbled as he walked, his lameness more pronounced than ever. He did not talk, and he did not shiver.

I don't know why Izsak survived and Julius did not. Maybe because he was younger, maybe because his body was stronger. Julius lived just a few days more, speaking occasionally. Mostly he was incoherent. I stayed by his bedside and tried to warm his hands with my own, and listened as he spoke of nefesh and neshamah and ibbur, spirit and soul and that strange concept of benign possession that he had raised once before. His hands were so cold.

Only days after we buried Julius, we were informed that Levi had been killed in a battle at Stones River. Three letters arrived from Levi behind the news. There was one for Mama, one for Hava, and one for me. I thought at first it was a mistake, but my name was printed on the envelope. There was a second reason I thought it a mistake. Though the name signed to the letter was Levi's, the handwriting was unmistakably that of Julius. I knew his penmanship as well as I knew my own.

"Dearest Frieda," he wrote. "We are writing to tell you of the miracle that has happened. Ibbur. I (Jul.) had it backwards. I was so concerned with inviting a soul to comingle with my own, with making my own soul and body fit for such a task. I could not have realized that in doing so I purified myself, for even the realization of such a thing would have made me unfit for the burden of it.

"I found myself cohabitating with Levi. I cannot put another word on it, for we have no recollection of my arrival here, only that such a strange thing had occurred. We were on a battlefield. Even as we fell back, we stopped to help the injured, or at least those who could be helped. We amputated a foot while loud reports sounded around us. We walked with that soldier leaning on us – and oh! I will admit to the joy of having two strong legs that he might lean – until we reached a medical station. Then we turned around again to help others find their way. We found a soldier whose boots were gone, and we gave him our boots. We walked barefoot through the battlefield, helping men to safety.

"I felt so many things, Frieda. I was frightened, so frightened that I recited shma yisroel beneath my breath, for at any moment it felt we might leave this world (I, for the second time). But I also felt the assurance of a surgeon, and deep anger that we should find ourselves retreating. A different kind of righteousness, the kind that comes from fighting for a cause I believe is just. I have apologized to my brother, in our way, for though he is a boor, his motivations are pure. He is a good person, despite his failings as a brother and a husband and a correspondent. I don't know if he would have given away his boots without my presence, or returned so many times at such risk to his own safety. But I feel a great completeness at having done these things. We are both here now, and both safe, for the time being. I love you, and I will perhaps see you again at the end of this war."

The letter was signed by Julius and Levi both.

Hava and Mama's letters were from Levi and in Levi's hand, apologizing for his silence. I suppose we cannot know how much Julius had to do with that. Levi had never listened to him before, but neither had he put pen to paper for his wife and mother at any point in his long absence. Whatever the motivation, the sentiments he expressed seemed sincere, and they were a small comfort to my family.

We had mourned Julius, then Levi, and then Levi afresh when the letters arrived. I retreated to Julius's study to grieve for him alone. The room looked much as he had left it the day before Izsak ran away. It still smelled of leather and ink, the scents I most associated with Julius. One of his journals lay open on his table. In it he had written, "We live in the present, fleeting. We speak of past and future, and both weigh heavily upon us. My frailties began when I was a child (past), and will continue into the future. But if we find oneness of soul, will we also find oneness of time? Past, present, and future, existing in an eternal now."

I have begun to read my brother's books when nobody is looking. I believe in the oneness he spoke of, and the wholeness and the eternal now. If I find my own way to righteousness, maybe I will see him again. My brother, who is perhaps gone but not gone, who may yet reveal himself to me if his soul still has unmet tasks. My brother, who might even now guide my hand, his heart my heart, and his soul commingled with mine.

Art by Esme Baran

IT'S WAR
NNEDI OKORAFOR

April 21, 1929
Aba, Nigeria

The smell was hot, humid, wet and earthy. This night, a storm poured rain somewhere nearby. Arro-yo had spent much of the evening cooking, sweeping the floors, and dragging in hunks of fragrant wood for her next series of carvings. Now tired and pensive, she nibbled a bit of boiled yam as she watched Margaret across the small plastic table. The old woman ate quickly, a meal of boiled ripe plantain and yam with stew. She was already dressed in her best outfit, leaning over her plate as she ate so as not to soil her green gold rapa with a matching top. When she finished, she smiled at Arro-yo, got up, and left.

A half hour later, Arro-yo went flying. She was restless. The air was still heavy and static, even above the low clouds. Her dress grew sticky with sweat and humidity. She circled low over Nwora's house and considered visiting. She hovered just above the roof and saw Nwora, his father's arm linked with his.

Nwora held up a kerosene lantern as they walked slowly around the house. Nwora's father walked bent slightly forward, his feet shuffling under his navy blue rapa with white squares. In the near dark, the white squares glowed. He grumbled something that made Nwora smile and say, "No, Daddy, she's not here." He grumbled something else and Nwora laughed and said, "No, not even on the roof."

They turned around and went inside. Arro-yo hovered there for a moment, trying to ignore the ache in her heart. She missed home. Her grandmother would probably be sitting on her wooden stool in the doorway humming to herself and weaving a basket. Her grand-uncle would be sitting outside brooding and smoking his pipe as he watched the heavy clouds pass the half moon. Her mother might be making love to her father, or her father might be with one of Arro-yo's other mothers.

She crouched down but was not at the right angle to see inside Nwora's home. Nevertheless, she knew the oily flicker of the kerosene lantern would be in the front room. Nwora's father liked to sit near the door in his favorite chair and watch people walk by.

Arro-yo flew on. When she saw the small adobe house brilliant with light and loud voices, she descended. Inside was so bright that it looked as if it were on fire. Even from where she was, she saw that the house was packed. There were several women standing outside on the porch leaning forward to hear what was being said inside.

Arro-yo landed on the roof and pressed her ear to its tin roof. She didn't have to listen hard because a woman inside was shouting. It took her only a moment to realize the booming voice was Margaret's.

"...all saw what they did last time," Margaret bellowed. "It was only a few years ago." Arro-yo always thought that the best language for yelling was Igbo. Margaret's voice easily carried to the women outside and to the skies above. Efik, Arro-yo's native language, sounded best when sung.

Margaret continued, "They taxed and taxed our husbands and sons and fathers until they had nothing left!"

The women clapped and grunted agreement.

One woman shouted, "My sons, Okechukwu and Chinedu, were arrested!"

"Eh heh! You see? They take all the money, then they take the *men*!" Margaret said. "And look at these stupid warrant chiefs who join with the white men and sell out themselves and their own people! Warrant chiefs take wives without paying the full bride wealth! They take land that doesn't belong to them. They take the census and act like they are just getting to know us. Humph. They treat us like we are stupid. Like bush meat! Now they want to turn around and disrespect the people *more* by taxing us women? No, we will not *allow* that!"

Many of the women shouted, "NO!"

"We are the trees which bear fruit!" someone shouted.

"And look at our men now," Margaret yelled. She sucked her teeth. "Cowards! Look at your husbands, sons, fathers. They are not here. They are afraid of these traitorous chiefs and these white men with their guns and idiotic magic book. Are we afraid?"

"NO!"

Arro-yo leaned forward, pressing her cheek closer to the roof, her heart beginning to race.

"Our men are behaving like women, so we must behave like men! The colonial administration is still treating us like chattel, like slaves. But we are free!"

"Yes."

"Nwanyeruwa sent us this!"

Arro-yo heard something crinkle, and then the women begin murmuring loudly. She could hear Margaret laughing.

"You all know what happened with Nwanyeruwa, two days ago," Margaret growled. "That nonsense chief Okugo was going about taking his... census... and he came to her house where she was hard at work pressing palm oil."

Margaret paused and Arro-yo was sure that every listening woman was holding her breath.

"He asked her to count her sheep and goats. She replied 'Was your mother counted?' "

All the women laughed loudly. Arro-yo smirked.

"But then... oh then! That man seized her by her throat and began to squeeze. She is a strong woman, so she fought him off. And now it must start!

Ah-ah, you see, what this means? No? This palm leaf means we've talked enough to these warrant chiefs who lap at the white man's feet. It's time for action! We will sit on that damn warrant chief until he has resigned. Tomorrow they will know that we are like elephants, marching to battle, crushing obstacles on our way! *Nzogbu, Enyimba Enyi*!"

Arro-yo flew several feet into the air, her eyes wide, as the entire house exploded with cheers and shouts and the sound of stamping feet. She hovered like a frightened hummingbird, and then she turned and flew into the sky. *Whatever they are planning, it has nothing to do with me*, she thought.

Nevertheless, her heart was still pounding. The white men made her angry, too. Always playing the role of stopping people from doing what they wanted to do. First they came and worked with greedy local men to capture people and kill them with work. Then they stayed to further muddle things by causing people to forget the deities of the forest, sky, and water. Now they wanted to tax the financial wealth away. To tax the women of the land, after unfairly taxing the men was beyond insult to the foundation of the people.

Hours later, she headed home. As she drifted off to sleep, she still angrily thought about the colonial administration. When she finally slept deeply, she dreamed of a choppy ocean, grey and white beneath a churning stormy sky. Even as she dreamed it, she knew it was a bad bad sign.

***

Margaret returned a few hours before daybreak. Arro-yo was in her bed trying to forget her watery nightmare. For a while she listened to Margaret moving about the small house. She even considered getting up and asking Margaret how her night was, but she did not. Instead, she fell back asleep. When she awoke, the sun was up. Margaret was gone.

Arro-yo ate a breakfast of a mango and leftover yam. She had no birds to sell today, but she wanted to buy a chicken and some plantains. She put on her third favorite dress, a long European style blue one she'd designed and sewn herself after meeting and befriending two Catholic nuns. She'd liked the length and flow of their habits. She added her own personal flair by using blue cloth, taken in the waistline so that it nicely hugged her figure and lowered the bust-line. She slung her blue satchel over her shoulder and was off. It was a cool morning and the roads on the way to the market were practically empty. A man carried a bushel of sticks on his head as he walked and another had an armful of cloth. She saw no women. When she arrived at the market, it was nearly deserted. There were few open umbrellas; no women sat shaded in booths.

"Arro-yo!" Nwora's voice echoed through the mostly empty market as he ran to her. "They've all gone to the Native Administration Center."

"Your mother, as well?"

"Yes. I... I knew she was involved. She was gone last night. I didn't know they were planning something so big." He took a deep breath. "I had to leave my father to come find her. Are you coming?"

Arro-yo nodded.

***

They heard the women before they saw them. There had to be over a thousand of them. The open area before the large adobe building was packed with so many women that Arro-yo felt dizzy just looking at them. Many were dressed in sackcloth, their faces smeared black with charcoal. They carried sticks wreathed with palm leaves and they were singing a song that Arro-yo couldn't make out through all the noise. There were other groups of women dressed in white and red rapas and tops dancing vigorously, wooden cooking spoons in hand. Other women milled about just looking angry.

A woman's voice rose high above all the others and immediately everyone stopped what they were doing. Margaret stood on something that raised her short body a foot above everyone else. Arro-yo could feel the tension increase and the air pressure rise. She looked at Nwora. He looked back at her and mouthed, "I don't know."

"What is that smell?" Margaret shouted, waving her fists in the air. "*Death* is that smell if they don't come out and hand us that chief's cap. When they do, we will tear it apart like the piece of nothing it is!"

Margaret's fuzz of grey white hair stood on end, for today she wore no head wrap. Never had Arro-yo seen her look so invigorated.

"Maybe we should step back," Nwora said.

"Death is that smell!" Margaret shouted again and another wave of agitation rippled through the audience. Arro-yo stood mesmerized by the energy before her eyes. They were only a few yards from the peripheral of the crowd. Arro-yo stood on her toes. She could easily fly up but there was already enough hysteria. She was taller than almost all the women, so she still managed to see much of what was going on. There were British soldiers stationed in front of the administrative building. They had guns. Several women were taunting them by throwing rocks and poking them with their sticks. Arro-yo smelled smoke.

"You see that?" Nwora said, pointing his stick. Arro-yo frowned at his fragile weapon, wondering when he'd grabbed it. "My mother's in there!" he said.

Suddenly the crowd of protesting women surged forward. *CRACK! CRACK! CRACK!* Arro-yo saw Margaret fall. Then the crowd burst in all directions. Panicked women came right at Nwora and Arro-yo and he pulled her into the bush beside the road. Flames leapt from the administration building and several of the others around it. Arro-yo could see a British soldier tumbling on the ground with one of the dancing woman. She was kicking, scratching, and screaming; he was punching and shouting.

Some women lay dead or limped away injured, but just as many didn't run from the bullets. Like crazed elephants, they ran at the soldiers. Others looted the British-owned store next to the administration building. Arro-yo saw a woman running out with packages of biscuits. The chaos continued to trample the area, but Arro-yo's eyes only searched for Margaret. Nwora was gripping Arro-yo's arm. He turned to look at her just as she began to rise. For a moment, his arm held tightly, then he let go, his eyes wide.

He watched her ascend, his jaw slack, madness on the road before him. Arro-yo looked down at him, holding his eyes until she was above the trees. From above, she saw burning buildings, bodies lying in the street, women fighting with colonialists, screams, sticks, cooking spoons, cudgels, palm switches, terror and blood. She spotted Margaret crumpled next to the stool she'd stood on.

Arro-yo swooped down like an attacking owl, her blue dress billowing around her as she landed.

A woman nearby threw one of the white men over her back and kicked away his gun. She pointed at Arro-yo, sweat and blood pouring down her face, and said in a hoarse voice, "Amuosu!"

"Arro-yo is amuosu!" someone else shouted.

More women looked up. Something smacked Arro-yo's arm but she ignored it. She linked her arms under Margaret's and quickly lifted off. She didn't know how long she flew or where she was going until she set Margaret down in the garden beside Margaret's house. Then for the first time, she really looked at Margaret. Her face and neck were covered with blood. A tiny red hole with singed black edges was in the center of her forehead. Her brown eyes were open.

Arro-yo touched Margaret's face. It was still warm but the skin felt tight. She touched the old woman's neck, her chest, her belly. Her legs were bent, limp.

Arro-yo gasped, holding her own chest. She whimpered, leaning forward to hold Margaret's head to her belly, her shoulders shuddering. She closed her eyes and inhaled deeply, but that only increased the pain she felt in her heart. She opened her eyes, her jaw set. She looked down at Margaret, the woman who had opened her home to Arro-yo as a favor to Arroyo's grand-uncle; the woman who had been her grand-uncle's lover during a different time; the woman who had always lived passionately. She was gone.

"You have gone," Arro-yo said to Margaret's corpse. She got up and picked up Margaret's body. She brought her to the front of the house and set her down inside. A sharp pain in her arm made her glance at it. Her sleeve was soaked with blood. She pushed the door open so people would come to the house more quickly. Arro-yo had no doubt that Margaret would get a proper burial of a dignified Igbo soldier.

She placed one of her blue wooden birds in Margaret's hands. It was one of the two she'd made for herself. An owl in mid-flight. She kissed Margaret's cheek and went to her room to get a jar. She placed it in her satchel. Then she turned and slowly walked out of the house and flew off. The town of Aba was ruined for her. When she'd taken Margaret's body, she'd been seen and she knew she would not be forgotten. Once again she'd be labeled a witch, an amuosu. She knew what would come next. She did not want Margaret's house to be burned down because of her. This time she wouldn't even stay for the accusations.

"Nwora," she whispered. Would he understand? Doubtful. But one thing was clear: she was alone again.

She wore her bluest dress, her beaded satchel slung over her shoulder.

She stopped at the river to wash her wound. Though the bullet had only grazed her, the mark looked as if a small beast had taken a bite out of her arm. She rinsed it with water and took out the jar. She applied three dollops of salve she'd made for scrapes and cuts. It smelled strongly of mint.

Then she flew off again. She didn't see the world around her. She didn't look where she was going. She'd closed her eyes, and the tears flowing from them dried almost instantly in the rush of wind against her face.

Art by Kasey Gifford

FIND ME UNAFRAID
SHANAÉ BROWN

1905
Charlotte, North Carolina

"Shhh."

Booker's eyes are two wet, white marbles in the black black dark of my small room, illuminated only by the candle in the corner forming a halo around itself. The pointer finger pressed to his lips warns me to swallow the startled yelp he senses erupting. I was not expecting him tonight. Hoping, longing even, for his company and the way he carries my name in his mouth, long and drawn out like he is singing his favorite hymn, but Friday isn't his day to come visit.

How did he get in?

I search his face for the half-smile, half-smirk that has somehow managed its way into the sweet side of my heart, but it is absent. Only the wild-eyed, frantic look I and every Negro for fifty miles have come to take as a warning sign to run, to hide, to become invisible, is present on his tight face. The look that says it is time to try to blend yourself into the dark trees, the stained walls of your house, squeeze yourself into a dark corner of nothingness.

I am quiet, panic seizing my heart like a rough hand on a cow's udder. My eyes grow, became as large and white as his, match his alarm. I ask him without speaking, the danger that is on the other side of these walls.

"Lay back down," he whispers, silently running across the hard floor to the lone candle. He is curiously light-footed and impossibly fast for his frame, standing nearly as tall as my doorway. By the time my back reaches the dingy sheet he is back and the candle is out, the North Carolina night cloaking the house in an even blacker darkness. This time, I cannot see his eyes. I only feel his heavy lightness, always like a pillow stuffed with drapery, sink in beside me on my small bed. The thin mattress just barely fits us both.

"Hold on to me, and don't let go until I say it's OK, you hear me?" His voice is low. Grave, but calm. I know better than to question him right now.

My skinny arm reaches around him, his dark body firm and angled from chopping wood most of his nineteen years, and I squeeze my eyes shut so tight it hurts.

That's when it comes.

The rumbling, gathering sound of live thunder on the ground, like a thousand stampeding horses all running towards you. Then, the loud, crushing boom of lives being shattered around me, the screeching of glass as it bursts into pieces, the swallowing of wood by angry, forced flames.

I cannot breathe.

My grip around Booker tightens so much that I am sure I am forcing the life from his lungs, but I won't let go. He told me not to, and I won't. I suppress the screams welling inside, try to focus on the steady inhale, exhale of his sweat-soaked chest, the musky, salty pine smell dripping from his collar mixing with the tears rushing from my eyes. I try to close my ears, shut out the wailing coming through the walls.

Terror smells like burnt wood and charred grass. Like hate.

The boom is so loud, so immediate, I am sure I have taken my last breath. This is It. I will die here with Booker, holding tightly to him as the men in white robes, so full of disdain and hate for me and anyone who looks like me, finally carry out their threats.

A moment passes, the blink of an eye, and I am not dead. I press my chest, damp with Booker's sweat or maybe my own, make sure my heartbeat is there. A second later I recognize a voice I've known my whole life, pleading for mercy through loud sobs. The sound comes from next door, from Miss Grace's house.

"Oh please Lord, not Miss Grace!" Booker's big salty hand is on my mouth then, stifling my cries, holding me tighter to still the violent shaking my body has taken to.

Miss Grace. A loving, smiling old woman as sweet as the peach pies she makes and sells each week. She's lived in that house my whole life.

"Shhh!" He warns again, this time force trembling in his whisper.

The guttural screams of life being snatched from a person isn't a sound I should be familiar with. No sixteen-year-old girl should know what it sounds like to be engulfed in flames while sitting at the dinner table with your family.

But I do.

That sound took my parents away. I've seen with my two eyes what they do to Negroes, can *never* un-see that. And two years later, the white robes are here again. I say a small prayer, ask God and my parents to welcome my spirit in peace. I pray for my niece, baby Elizabeth; I cry for my sister, Essie, for my brother, Jacob. Pray that they are safe, even if I am not. Try to be grateful that I've made it to sixteen; I know too many girls my age who didn't.

"Be thankful for the sunrise, child. Plenty don't get to see today." Miss Grace's high, wavering voice is in my head, her favorite saying both calming and upsetting now. I want to go to her, to be brave enough to open the door and see to it that she's safe, but fear has a hold on me that won't let go, almost as tight as Booker's arm pressing my back.

And then, almost without motion, I am free and he is sitting straight up in the bed, eyes bearing on the door so intently, it seems if I touch him he'd feel like stone and yet fall to ashes. I can see the whole of him now, the terrifying bright outside allowing my eyes to let in the damp room around me; the small reading table Jacob built me when we all lived in the other house, the fan-backed chair given to me by the man my father worked for before he died. I expect to see fear on his face, the wild-eyed look that spread to mine when he woke me, but there is none.

He is angry.

Not in the loud, bustling way that sometimes happens when the boys play field ball, but a sort of focused, searing fury, aimed at the door, the windows, and anyone who might dare come near them.

I open my mouth, but the shock from seeing my jovial, toothy-grinned Booker so serious and stone-jawed has taken all my breath.

Another boom follows the first, this time definitely at, *on* the door to my small home. I shriek, sobs raking my body, and try to fling myself from this corner, this trap of a bed. I have to get to my family, to Essie. Booker's arm stops me, catches me in the fiercest, most painful grip I've ever felt, and I flail my body about, expect his sweaty fingers to slip, lose their grasp on my small wrist. But they don't. Like shackles on sore brown ankles, they hold me hostage firmly in his reach.

The most alarming thing, even more so than the boom that quaked the house, is Booker's reaction.

He doesn't have one. Booker doesn't even blink.

That dark, stormy stare is steadfast, still on the door. The door that is... still there. Amazingly, impossibly still intact. My eyes flash from Booker to the door, and back again, and it occurs to me that there is something happening here that my mind cannot conceive just yet. Something bigger than Booker and myself, bigger than this little wood-planked shotgun house and bigger than the blaze outside that seems to have surrounded us, to have destroyed everything in its wake but this one-room home and me, and... Booker. And whatever this bigger thing is, it seems to have taken over him, or maybe only his eyes, unblinking and focused on one thing: the unmoving, unyielding door.

I am still now, daring not to move, awestruck at this witnessing of this Bigness, and even as I tremble down to my toes, I am calm. Swaths of air likened to a fan sway back and forth in front of my face just so, flooding cool into my very bones.

***

The smell of Burnt awakens me when daylight wafts in, shedding a gray light on the charred walls, telling the night's secrets. I jump from the creaking bed, Booker nowhere in sight. On a normal night's visit, this would not be cause for alarm; Booker prefers the cover of midnight to aid the three mile trip back to the small house he shares with his father and three brothers.

Today is different. I have no recollection of falling asleep or what happened after the coolness flooded my body. I cover my nightclothes, pull on a blue dress I made from the extra fabric I collect as a seamstress for Mrs. Mary Davidson.

The rickety door, so sturdy and solid last night, groans open with a light pull of the doorknob. Outside, a war has taken place, and from the look of things, we did not win. The air is stagnant, stale and thick with dark smoke. People are gathered, distraught faces huddled in groups looking at one house or another, taking stock of the damage. Two houses completely gone — charred remnants of a full life, windows vacant like hollow eyes. Mr. Henry and Ms. Josephine's house, identical to the one Essie and I live in and every other house on this street, is only a shell, frame and foundation standing wearily. Ms. Josephine's head is pressed to her husband's chest, tears falling. Seeing these faces, I remember what urged me from bed this morning, the terror from last night suddenly hits me, and I run frantically down the street, call out for Essie.

Essie is long. Five foot nine and lanky, skinny like me and our mama. I know her gait anywhere. From a crowd several yards away, I see her head break away, turn towards the sound of my voice. My younger sister runs like her upper half is playing catch-up with her legs — I've teased her about so it many times — and I've never been so happy to see that ridiculous stride. She barrels toward me, and I her, across debris and ash and wood chippings, around a large wooden plank that has been removed from Ms. Josephine and Mr. Henry's house, and we crash into each other, become a mess of tears and limbs and fabric. I hold her like she is the last thing I'll ever hold, and relief, so much relief washes over me to feel her hot cheek pressed on my face, her heartbeat racing in her chest like it's trying to escape.

"Miss Grace," she says over and over, her voice is broken, my heart heavy with the sadness of this day.

I kiss her dirty face, streaked with tears, trekked with a day's worth of dirt. "It's OK," I whisper, "she's with Mr. Harvey now."

Miss Grace's husband, Mr. George Harvey, died a few years ago due to old age and, I have an inkling, whiskey. Everyone misses his lined face, his laugh that bellowed for blocks. There was no having a bad day around him. No matter the situation, even when he was sad, he'd offer a smile. With Miss Grace gone too, the world is less bright.

"Where is Jacob?" I ask her when she calms.

My brother, twenty-one and married now, has a home a few houses away with his wife, Sarah, and their baby, Elizabeth. He named her after our mother, said it was the most beautiful name he could think of.

"Down the road there." Essie points far down the rough dirt road and I see Jacob walking slowly towards us. Beside him, Sarah holds Elizabeth against herself protectively in her white bundle. The day, despite the gray, is hot, smoldering. The air smothers thoughts, slows everyone down to a weary pace. Slung across Jacob's thin shoulder is a gray sack, heavy against his back. He holds it tight at the mouth with his right hand, elbow up and facing me.

I forget the heat and run to him like I ran to Essie, hug him just as tight. He holds me with his free arm. "I tried to come for you, Charlotte. I swear. There were just so many of them." His eyes are sad brown probes staring into me, pleading for forgiveness. "A man told us it was coming. Told us to get our valuables and run." He rubs his forehead with the rough pads of his long fingers like he's trying to erase the memory.

"I'm fine, I'm here." I hug him tighter to let him know I mean it. "What man was it?"

"I'on know. Just a man."

"You didn't see him?" I ask, bunching my eyebrows at his answer.

"Naw. Just heard a tap on the window, real quiet tap, then a man telling us the Klan was coming, and to get out now. I grabbed the books and the baby stuff and we got out. Hid in the field real low behind the houses. Next thing, whole gang of white robes trampling through."

I know. I know deep in myself when he says this, that it was Booker. Remembering the Cool, the breeze that wasn't really a breeze, those intense eyes, the calm I felt in the face of impending death, and I know.

***

Booker came to be my friend like most stray dogs come to be your pet. You notice them one day, and you're not quite sure if they've always been around and you've not been paying attention, or if they've just shown up. He with his grin so wide it spread through his whole face, and the prettiest teeth I'd ever seen on a man.

I was walking home from tending to a dress for Mrs. Davidson and he was there, on the other side of the narrow road, tall as the sun is bright, dressed like a city boy, with long shiny shoes and a leather satchel. A thick book rested in his large hands, which by all appearances had him completely engrossed. I tried not to stare as I passed, pulled my sewing bag closer to me, and kept on my way, leaving the tall man with the handsome face to his books. He didn't even look up.

Working on several dresses for guests of a wedding Mrs. Davidson was coordinating meant me working each day that week; missed school and twelve-hour days. He was there each day, sitting with long legs stretched out in front of him, standing with a wide-brimmed hat, or leaning under a far off tree bending to lend shade. Each time, with a book in his hand. It was a Wednesday when our mutual silence was broken. He was there in his usual spot, shielding his face from the sun, a small book this time, squinting at me with curious eyes.

The ground was so hot it was like the sun was alive and walking down the road.

"Sure there's plenty places you could read 'cept the side of the road." I couldn't stop myself from speaking with sass to this huge man, looking like a plum fool in his nice trousers and jacket and polished shoes underneath this blanket of heat.

"Now why would I do that when I could stand just where I am and see a lovely face like yours pass me by each day?" He smiled with affable eyes and a wide grin, then went back to his book.

A slow smile formed but I quickly regained myself, chose not to respond to his slick comment. I didn't know this man. No one knew him, it seemed. Whenever I asked Essie or Jacob or the others in my neighborhood about him, no one knew who I was talking about. No one had ever noticed the tall stranger with the nice clothes and satchel of books.

This tradition of small exchanges as I walked past continued until one week I began taking the long way, a different way home, around the winding park where little white boys snuck and played ball, running around before and after school, collecting dirt stains and scuff marks on freshly pressed clothes and new shoes. If this man was after me, I suppose he would've taken that chance already, so fear wasn't the reason for the change. I wasn't scared of him. I was only interested in seeing if the man with the books, appropriately named Booker, was following me on my walks. He'd told me his name one day before asking for a mention of mine – I'd refused, of course.

He was nowhere to be found on that route, neither that day nor the next several, and I felt a comfort settle in the next time I chose my normal path and there he was, tree legs crossed underneath him on the yellow-green grass like a school child, reading. How he even managed to procure a whole bag of books, I didn't ask. I guess I just assumed they were given to him by whatever rich family he worked for. His clothes were too nice, shoes too shiny, and hands too clean to work for anyone other than a rich man.

"What you reading over there?"

His head snapped down at the book like he was startled to see it sitting in his lap. "Oh! This? Well it's just a little poetry. A Mister Paul L. Dunbar. Heard of him?" He stood hurriedly, then took a cautious step towards me, still across the road. "I'd love to read one to you, if you don't mind my coming over there." Delivered with that toothy smile and his squinting eyes, he held the small book up high to show the front.

"I can read just fine, thank you," I said, sass still swimming in my eyes before my face softened at his lowered head. "But I don't mind looking."

And just like that, it was like he was never not there. He began walking me to and from work, taking small steps to keep his long legs from leaving me behind. We talked of the plans each of us had, him to open up his own bookstore for Negroes, and I to make the prettiest, finest dresses and sell them throughout the state to colored people and whites alike. I liked his company, settled into our routine like a perfect fitting shoe, and dreamed, always knowing his convinced, serious response: "You only need to focus your mind, find your magic inside, Charlotte, and you can do it."

He would visit and read poetry and prose to me by candlelight, sometimes sleeping on the floor next to my bed until dawn awakened us, but most of the time slipping away into the night, never too concerned to be home by midnight to avoid the white robes. I'd get fresh peach pie from Miss Grace and we devoured it, gooey and sweet and warm on our tongues, under the big oak tree by the field where the kids played. I laughed at the stories he would make up when we got tired of reading, tales of men fifty feet tall with feet as small as mine and cotton spinners who spun themselves to the sky; ridiculous tales made even more so by this big man hopping and turning and clapping as he acted them out. Booker became my best friend under the North Carolina sun.

***

After any incident involving racial violence, the Negroes in our community are on high alert. We know some of the faces behind those hoods belong to the police officers, the people who are said to "protect us." We rely on each other to watch us, we protect each other. The men, quiet ire in their eyes, carry guns on their person or set them by the door; the women don't allow the children to play farther than twenty feet in back of the house.

A mass of flowers and written notes lays out in a neat pile on Miss Grace's yard, a collection of tiny colorful pillows fashioned like peaches atop it, made by myself and a few other girls who looked to Miss Grace as a mother figure. I do not see Booker for several days after the fires. My stomach aches with worry wondering if he's OK, if evil has struck his farm as well, wishing he'd show himself, come back and dazzle me with that smile.

I spend this worrisome time with the people I love, try to busy myself tending to little Elizabeth, teaching the younger children to read in the church up the hill, plaiting Essie's thick hair over and over. If there was ever a replica of our mother, it is Essie. Her brown skin, the color of a new penny, her nose that is neither keen nor wide, but tall and sharp in profile view, her legs that just don't seem to end, and her hair, inky black and coarse, a voluminous mountain that cannot be convinced to stop growing.

I look like Jacob, who looks like my daddy. We both inherited his deep maple skin, strong bone structure, "royal bones," as my mother used to say with pride in her eyes, and hair that is slicked into waves deeper than the Atlantic.

I am braiding Essie's long hair in the front of the house when Freddy Miller, a boy visiting here for the summer, walks up trying to make conversation. He is red. Wiry red hair, smooth red skin, all red. It's said his grandfather is a mulatto, son of a slave mother and an overseer, and the red has traveled through his father's side of the family.

"Miss Essie, Miss Charlotte, both as pretty as the sunset. How are y'all doing today?"

Essie giggles, looks up at him from her seat between my legs on the chair, and back down again quickly, her crush on Freddy made known from the first day we saw him at church with his grandfather.

"I'm well, thank you." I say, eyes focused on the long braid I'm finishing.

"I was heading to buy some of those tasty friend green tomatoes from Mrs. Robinson. Care for one?"

"Why thank you, I'd love—"

"No, we're just fine, thank you." I cut Essie's giddiness off, ignore her rolling eyes.

Freddy looks around, his wide face grasping for something else to say besides a complaint about the heat, but finally concedes and bids us a good day.

"You wasting all your good mind on that Booker character, whom I'm rightly not even sure exists, when you have Freddy right here. A northern boy at that!"

"I've no inclination to keep company with Freddy Miller, Essie. So you can stop that now." My nose turns at the very thought of sharing space and time with that boy.

"OK. But one day when you're old and raggedy and no one wants to marry you, you ain't living with me!"

She's been teasing me about Freddy Miller ever since he arrived here to stay the summer with his grandparents, his father's mother and father. His father owns two barbershops up north in New York and he's smart as a whip, but I'm not too fond of his flamboyance. It's rather off-putting, flaunting his smarts and looks around like he's the only black boy to ever pick up a book or inherit a decent face.

He came up to Essie and I after church one day, telling us all about his daddy's shops and bragging on how a white man even let him cut his hair for him once. I wanted to remind him that his daddy is more likely to have a rope hung around his neck than ever have his hair cut by a white barber, but I reserved it for my own thoughts. I have no room for Freddy Miller. My mind is too consumed with reading with Booker, with drawing outlines of dresses that I'd make if I could afford more than scraps of fabric. I haven't even ever kissed Booker, but he's far more liable to achieve that than Freddy will ever be. So I let him go about his business and I go about mine. He speaks when he sees me and I offer the same courtesy, and when he tries to get me to stay and talk, I pay him no mind.

***

Two weeks of hot days and hotter nights pass, and then there is Booker towering at my door step after dusk, like nothing ever happened. Smiling wide, his other facial features pushing up and out to make room for all that smile.

"Charrrlotte..." He sing-songs my name, like he always does.

I only stare. I want to cry and hug and hit him and squeal and yell because he is alive, and here before me, but I can only stare.

"What... happened?"

"I don't know what you mean." He looks down at me, his eyes expectant. He brushes past me and ducks into the room, sets his worn satchel down next to Essie's empty bed. She chose to spend the night at Jacob's as always, sitting with little Elizabeth.

My stare remains, my mind back on that night, and the stark difference in his eyes, so amiable and friendly now. It's like it was a dream, like I imagined the whole thing.

"That night, with the white robes. You... and the door."

At that he becomes serious. A line stretches across his forehead, forms two hills above his brows; it makes him look at least twice his age. "I've told you. You have to harness your magic, and you can do anything. It's all here," he taps a long finger on his temple, "and here." His finger travels down to his chest. "You have it, Charlotte. That's all. There's nothing else to talk about that night, really. It's done and you're safe."

Before I can process what he's trying to tell me, his eyes light back up, and he's talking again, on to the next thing. "Oh, I've been traveling. Had to go up north, saw my uncle in Detroit!" He is excited, jittery with a nervous buzz.

"What? How did you get there?"

"My uncle sent for me, I said. And Charlotte, let me tell you, you gotta go. You just *have* to go. There's so much opportunity, so much life. So much freedom! Come! Come with me, we can leave tonight." And then he's moving around the room, grabbing items at random, gathering my life in his arms to pack.

"What? No. I can't just *leave*, Booker. What about Essie, Jacob? My family is here. My life! You're crazy." Now he has my books, most of them gifted to me by him, diligently stacking them in a neat pile by the door.

"How can you say no to this?" His words are breathless, full of promise and anticipation. "There's a train leaving tonight, Charlotte. My uncle has given me enough to cover us. All you have to do is pack. They can all come! Can't they come with us?"

"We have debt here, we can't just up and leave. Don't you understand that? What about the crops!"

"Sure you can. You just leave."

"Oh I'm positive you've just up and gone crazy now." I clamor past his serious eyes, pick up the books he's stacked and bring them back to my bedside.

Deflated, he puts both large hands on my arms. Holds me in his intense gaze. "OK, not tonight, but promise me. One month, we leave."

"One month is too soon, Booker." His excitement, usually infectious and inspiring, is simply exhausting tonight.

"One month, Charlotte. A new life, a new world. Your own dress shop. You can do that up there! They don't treat Negroes up north like they do us down here. Don't you wanna have... more? Don't you want your *children* to have more?"

"That's a silly question. Of course I do."

"Well, let's go. You can bring Jacob and Essie. You both will be university age soon, right? You can go to college as smart as you are! One month."

I consider his words, imagine Essie in college studying English like she's always wanted to do. "OK. I'll go."

I fall asleep in Booker's arms this night. Still never having even kissed, I feel closer to him than I ever have. The intensity and conviction in his clear brown eyes convinces me that there is only yes. One month.

***

That is the last time I ever see Booker.

Eight days later, I return home from teaching lessons at church to a little book on the floor just inside my door. It is worn, pages faded and edges torn. A small, loose piece of paper rests within its pages, which I turn to with urgent, nervous hands. Folded inside the paper, small and neat, are bills. Money. A *lot* of money. Enough for the lot of us to board a train north and have extra to boot.

Tears well as I unfold the paper, see the tall, slanted handwriting I've come to recognize as Booker's.

Beyond this place of wrath and tears
Looms but the Horror of the shade,
And yet the menace of the years
Finds and shall find me unafraid.

It matters not how strait the gate,
How charged with punishments the scroll,
I am the master of my fate:
I am the captain of my soul.

***

Three weeks later, my brother frantically pounds on the door to his home, shirt dampened by sweat, clinging to his body like a garment overcome with static.

"They're coming back," he heaves, breathless when he enters the house. "The white robes. They're coming back." Sarah rushes to him, helps him to a seat at the small table, fixes him a glass of water with nervous, shaking fingers. She and I both rush to the window, relieved to see empty roads in all directions.

"But, why," I cry, "what do they want?" I pace the cold wood floor, feel the cool under my soles and think of Booker. Wish for him to come protect me, protect us again.

I have started sleeping here now; with Essie back in class each day I find it comforting to be around people. I rest easier with the smell of Jacob's work boots polluting the air, mixing with the soft smell of baby Elizabeth's untainted newness. I don't even mind Essie's long arms swatting against my shoulder, my face, when she shifts in her sleep during the night.

"They think I've been stealing from the mill," he says, face stone, jaws clenched tight.

At this Sarah's dark body is crumpled on the floor, crying. She knows, just like Jacob and I know, what it means when a Negro is accused of a crime. He's guilty, whether he did it or not.

***

"Charlotte, come in here for a moment, will you." Mrs. Davidson is a portly woman, her love for pork cooked every kind of way most likely the cause, and has a kind face. My mother was Mrs. Davidson's personal seamstress before she died, and I grew up watching her make dresses within an inch of alteration just by looking at a woman's body, she was so skilled with a needle and thread. Mrs. Davidson said she was the only one who could get a dress fit to right over her bosom the first time around. She took me in to replace my mother after the first fire. I still can't measure by sight like my mom, but my lines are just as nice.

I leave my sew station she's set up in her home for me, a small table in the laundry room, and walk into the kitchen where she's eating a lunch of boiled pork sausage cut into squares.

"I'm sorry, darling, but we won't be needing you here anymore." She avoids looking at me completely, just turns her head in my general direction, plays nervously with the spoon in her pea soup. This has to do with Jacob, I feel it in the air, this tension making her display nervous habits I've never seen before.

My eyes become ice, let her know that I know this is nothing but her mean old husband, convinced in his prejudice that my brother did something he did not. "That's fine, Ma'am. It's been my pleasure." I offer a slight smile and make my exit, her still sitting there, pea soup on her bib and pity in her eyes, and I almost feel bad for her.

***

"We have to leave. Tonight," I tell Essie and Jacob when I get home, both packed for the train leaving in the morning. It's not hard to convince them. Everyone is packed by 8 p.m., and we have an hour to get to the station. Our neighbor John has agreed to take us for a rather handsome fee that I am more than happy to pay.

The night is balmy, September arriving with a breeze that offers reprieve from the particularly scorching summer. Relief thins the air as we load our things, our books, the lone photo we have of our parents, one my father had taken when Jacob was just six and I was no bigger than Elizabeth. We gather as much food as we can carry for the long trip. I send thoughts to Booker, thank him again for this amazing gift.

The small wagon has just begun its journey when we hear that familiar rumbling. The entire neighborhood is empty save for us, as the word has reached ears throughout the community that Jacob is a wanted man.

I've been waiting for this.

Resolve settles in my spirit, a coolness seeping into my bones as I turn in my seat, focus on the road, the field, in the direction of the sound. It gains momentum, grows louder as they near, sounds like a hundred ancient trees collapsing in defeat behind us. I tell John to stop, to let me off the wagon. When he refuses, I fling myself off, roll along the gravel until I am standing again, facing the robed army.

There, with the wailing and pleading of my family for me to return to the wagon behind me and the thunderous roar of fifty angry white men before me, I see only the road, the field, and orange. My eyes narrow, focused as Booker's that night in my small room, and I feel the ground nearly trembling beneath my feet. My heart is a drum on fire, and still the coolness, the breeze like a slow fan floods my arteries, settles in my chest.

And then.

The earth listens. Miraculously a thick trail of beautiful, brilliant orange erupts from the swaying grass, from the pebbled dirt road, neat and straight between me and the angry mob. It snatches across, blazing left and right as far as I can see. The men halt, clumsily fall over themselves with fear and bewilderment as the flames begin to grow and change colors, become long ropes of blinding, hot, white. Tails of white form every few yards, reach out to them like tongues. I see the glowing fear in their eyes and keep my stare, dare them to come closer. They bumble, turn and flee, tumble backwards on horses, fall into flames of pure white, perish to dust before my eyes.

I know at this moment what Booker meant. I know now, that this is his goodbye.

***

Detroit is nothing like Charlotte.

A bustling, smart city, rich with people and tall, tall buildings. We arrive with uncontainable joy. The money lasts; seems each time I unfold a bill, another shows up between the thin pages of the old book Booker left. We are able to rent the upper floor of a home, and Jacob takes a job at an automobile factory. It is not easy by any means. Our skin is still black, and there are many who do not want us here, on their streets, in their neighborhoods, at their jobs. But we smile in the face of it all, because it is... better.

I've settled into a life in the north now, finding work as a seamstress in a textile factory, with wages I am saving to create dresses I will sell in my own dress shop soon. Life is better, still.

That is when I see him.

Two years after leaving, when the smell of the wind in North Carolina is no longer in every inhalation, and I do not remember the cool soil under my feet nor the exact path to Mrs. Davidson's home, I see him. Plain as the cold day we are in, a tall, gangly man with a big, toothy smile. He stands across the road, buying a newspaper from a small black boy manning a local stand, black overcoat accompanying his ever present leather satchel and shiny shoes. I march over to him, awestruck, tears gathering to cloud my eyesight.

"You devil!" I slap the padded shoulder of his thick coat and he turns, startled, facing me. His face is his face, but both younger and older somehow, a mature youth resting in his eyes.

He looks me over, smiles that big smile.

"Well that's not much of an introduction." His voice is deeper than I remember, smooth like warm coffee has softened his vocal chords.

"Introduction? It's me, Charlotte, fool." My hand travels to my hair, newly coiffed and pinned to my head at the sides, it's a different look for me. A new hairstyle can't possibly be preventing him from recognizing me, can it?

"I'm not sure I understand," he says. "But it's very, very nice to meet you, Charlotte. I'm Samuel. It's not everyday a beautiful woman walks up to you and slaps you silly."

"But..." I start.

"Here, do you have somewhere pressing to be right now? Let me buy you a coffee." He folds his paper and places it under his left arm, leads me to a small storefront shop in a building at least ten stories high.

My head is shaking. I rub my temple, stare and try to make sense of this Booker that isn't Booker.

"So, you are not Booker... but you look just *like* him," I say, a question and a statement in one.

He pauses, head tilts to the side, eyes narrow with confusion like I am playing a joke on him.

"I... am not." He shifts on his stool as two coffees are placed in front of us on the long counter. "Did you say Booker?"

"Yes. Booker. From North Carolina." I look at him expectantly. He meets my gaze and confusion is still there in his eyes.

"Hm. My grandfather's name was Booker. He was a slave in North Carolina. My mother says I look just like him, but I never met him. He died in a fire when he was nineteen, right after she was born.

"My goodness." My heart beats so fast I can hardly hear him speak, one hand covers my mouth.

"Yeah. His name is a sort of legend in those parts. They say people took to calling him the Magical Negro, used to sneak into the big houses and kill the masters without a sound. No one knew how he did it. My father says he saved a lot of Negro lives along the way. I'm proud to look like him. But this is... strange, don't you think?"

And suddenly it makes sense. I'm terrified and relieved and panicked and... happy. I cannot stop the tears that well as understanding filters in, floods my senses.

I reach out, touch this stranger's face, make sure he is real. "I'm sorry." I say, smiling through clouded eyes. "But... I think that we were *supposed* to meet, somehow."

His face pushes up and away, makes room for that wide grin. Booker smiles at me. His eyes wide, glistening like they used to under that big oak tree.

"I am inclined to agree, Miss Charlotte, I think I do agree."

Art by Eric Orchard

A WEDDING IN HUNGRY DAYS
NICOLETTE BARISCHOFF

1900
Rural village outside Shandong province, China

"Your daughter wants a husband," Mother says one day, after they have found another dead chicken. "I know it."

"How can you know it?" Father asks her, smiling small. Father always has small smiles for Mother, even while he stares at the bottom of a bowl of hard rice with no chicken or fish or egg in it. "How can anyone presume to know what she wants? The minds of *all* children are unknowable."

Mother's eyes become narrow and black. She thinks he is making fun of her. Or else this is just how her eyes go when Father smiles, now. "She brings me dreams... terrible, urgent dreams that I can never quite remember when I wake. Dreams where everything we have becomes a black ruin, and all our family living and dead wanders like lost ghosts..."

Father's smile spreads dolefully. "I do not think you need our daughter to bring your dreams of ill omen these days," he says, and pats her hand in the way that tells her he will not talk of this anymore.

But Mother will not have her hand patted today. "She brings sickness, Husband! To my stomach, to my head. The only pains greater are my hunger pains."

Father relinquishes what is left in his rice bowl. He eats less and less as the days pass. "It is this house. The wind-and-water of this house has always been bad. We should have gone from here long ago."

"Wind-and-water does not kill our chickens!"

"No," Father agrees, "the drought kills our chickens. And makes our neighbors to sell their houses off piece by piece, and makes our neighbors' children to fill their bellies with dry grass and tree bark like in the years of the Great Famine..."

"You see? She even visits misfortune upon our neighbors!"

Father laughs, which makes Mother's eyes turn to slits. Mother understands his laughs as little as she understands his smiles. "You have always been soft with her, and blind," declares Mother, "always turning your head when she made mischief, praising the vain thing straight to her face. It's as though you thought she was a son—"

"I never mistook her for our son," says Father, now without a trace of laughter. "I know where our son is as well as you."

He is so grave that Mother is silent a moment before she chooses her next words. "Then you know that a daughter cannot stay," she says. "A daughter belongs in her husband's house, with her husband's mother. Where

291

they will not starve to feed her."

Father's gaze lowers. He did not know until now that Mother watches every scrap placed at my tablet with narrow black eyes. He makes no immediate reply, and this or something else makes Mother suddenly go hard in the face. "It must be time," she says with pinched determination. "She must be old enough. I have seen it done for daughters much younger. I have *seen* it."

"All places are not Taiwan," Father reminds her, in a voice far away. "Who would take our poor unlucky daughter to wife in this place, in these bad days? Who would keep her? There is almost no one left here, living *or* dead."

They think I will not hear them, where I am. My tablet is small, and made of a cheap, warped wood. It faces a wall, behind a door, where no guests will see. And so they think I will not hear, facing the wrong way. But the tablet is not where I truly live. Not truly. In the place where I truly live, I hear almost everything that is said, whether I want to or not. Words leave living mouths so carelessly, and we come across them all sooner or later, here in the City of the Ghosts, floating on and on forever into space.

***

For one day out of the year, on the fifteenth day of the month they call Ghost Month, we are allowed out. This is the day of our Festival, the day the world opens for us. No matter who we are now in the City, even if we are now the wildest and hungriest of Hungry Ghosts, we are permitted on this day to go among the living, and see the sights, and hear the sounds, and smell the smells of who we were.

If I concentrate, if I send enough intention to my arm and hand, I can even touch things.

And so, on the day of my eighth Festival, just days after I have heard Mother and Father plotting my marriage through the little warped-wood window of my tablet, I am walking in the village where I once lived and died, touching everything I can find to touch: cobbles and straw, and birds' feathers and hot coals, and warm dung. The heads of some small boys who turn from pissing their names on a wall to see who has touched them, and find that there is no one there. I will collect it all. I will not lose one single thing.

I walk better now that I am dead. I am not so small, and toddling and bowlegged. And now that I am dead, I am free to walk where I will. I am free to smell the dust of the road, the damp of the water, the woodsmoke of a thousand different ovens, without anyone saying to me, "Little Ling, where do you go in the road all by yourself? You will be run down by a horse and cart!" or "Little Ling, the bottom of a river is nowhere you want to go! Stay there, where the bank is dry!" or even "Little Ling, don't you see this flame burns blue and hot? Stand back, stand back!" For this one day, it is like I have been allowed to grow up, and to learn what there is to learn about the world.

You cannot learn very much about the world when you have only been alive in it for four years. And no one ever did say to me, "Little Ling, you must be very careful of a fever! A fever may come hot and cold at night, and take you faster than horses and carts, or rivers, or blue flames." And so now I have to do my walking and growing up and learning while I can, while the sun shines on this day.

This one, small day. In the month which has been called ours. Oh, the living are so generous, so extravagant to believe we might be allowed to stay with them so long. But in this even the Ancestors must obey.

When the sun goes down, I will go, as we all must go who are not Hungry or forgotten, to the place of my family home, and I will sit in the chair father has kept empty for me even though I am not an Ancestor, a chair he once cut down to my small size. I will breathe the steams of all that Mother has cooked, the rice and fruits and warm buns she might have made in the days before my brother went away. I will listen to the clatter of old, familiar plates and old, familiar talk, the grumbling and begging of an old familiar dog, if the dog still lives. And I will be able to watch Mother's eyes and Father's small smiles, and know that I was alive here once.

After that, it will be back to the City, where I am alone in the gray streets, in a strange, gray, crooked house I have built myself, waiting for the next scrap to come through my window. I can bear going back, though. I can bear almost anything, as long as there is a place to return to when the world opens again.

But if I am married, if the place I must return to is just another strange house...

To end my walking every year in a house with its own dusts, its own dim light, its own unfriendly smells, its living faces who would feel no more walking through me than they would passing through a current of cold air... it would only ever be like wandering.

I *won't* be married, I decide now, as I pass through the scattered rice and withered peaches that someone has already left in the road for any passing Hungry Ghosts. I can't be married. Married to whom? Who would marry me? I'm dead. I have been dead twice as long as I have been alive. I have never even been engaged. I am a thin, funny ugly girl even now. I do not know how to be a good wife. I do not even know how to be a good ghost. No other ghosts come to visit me. No one comes to drink tea in my gray little house. I am nothing. I am nobody. It is all I can do to hold my walls up, and to keep the Hungry from my door.

No, I won't be married. Tonight as Father sleeps, I will talk to him. I will scream and tear my hair and beg him to let me stay behind the door facing the wall. And maybe today, on this day of ghosts, he will hear me. Until now, I have only ever come into my father's dreams mute, unable to make even the smallest sound that might keep him from forgetting me in the morning. And I have never been able to come into Mother's dreams at all, whatever she might say about her dreams of omen. But I am young for a ghost. I have time to learn how to make them hear me. And when I do, Mother will not dare to argue, even if she does find a some far-flung strangers willing to clear a place on their family altar for a dead farmer's daughter.

Cheered by this thought, I turn my face to the sun, breathing the warm air in, breathing it out. It has been a long time since I breathed.

It is a quiet Festival day. There are no street operas, no parades for us ghosts to watch. Most of our neighbors have now gone away into the cities as my brother did eight years ago, leaving the shells of houses and farms, long ago stripped of roof tiles and fence-posts and anything else of any value at all. But monks still light small altars for us (how hard they chant to retrieve us all from Hell! I wonder what they should say if they saw where we really lived) and there are still enough households to send up comforting clouds of incense and food smoke, and the smoke of burnt paper.

Perhaps some of the paper offerings are for me, and I will go back to my gray house to find solid, bright festoons of flowers, or a chair or two to sit in. Perhaps by and by, I will be able to fill my house with shining lamps, and rugs, and ornaments, and then the great old Ancestors in their paper mansions will deign to drink my tea, and not pass me by with such stony faces. Probably not, but I find it is a nice daydream.

As the sun climbs, I stop and sit in a tuft of dry grass by a little inlet of seawater that still trickles in from the great ocean. There are some ghosts drifting up and down over the water, aimless, yet somehow preoccupied. Perhaps they drowned here. Or perhaps they are just Hungry, quenching their ghost-thirst where they can (most fresh water has either dried up or turned foul).

I keep my eyes on the water. If they are Hungry, I do not want to look at them. I meet enough of them in the gray streets, growling low in their throats as they think of tearing me apart for my food.

The inlet is the last place where my brother held me, covering my fevered head with droplets of salt water while he made crosses in the air and said Christian prayers from a book he had found. I wish l remembered what his hands had been like. But I remember only how black Mother's eyes became after that, how hard her voice. She hissed and raged. She called him names I did not understand. She spat words I had never heard before, with hatred I never knew she had. And then my brother was gone, and shortly after, so was I.

Of course, now he is gone away from her, trapped in Peking with angry, hungry men who would do more than spit on him and his Christian book — who will tear him apart — and she cannot say he is dead to her without thinking how close he is to becoming a ghost. And there is no one to carry her worry and anger but my father. My father and I. I come here on this day to make sure my brother is not one of us. To make sure I do not meet him. I have never found him yet, in the City or anywhere else. And when I have learned to speak in Mother's dreams, I will quell all her black worry. I will say to her, "Your son is not here. He is alive, and I am alone."

I lose track of time, sitting there on the bank, not finding my brother's ghost, and the sun is gone before I know where it goes. The inlet begins to fill with the lit paper boats and lanterns that are meant to guide ghosts here and back again. It is the paper that makes me realize. All at once, I understand just how my mother intends to find me a husband.

There is no time... there is no time. I only pray — if ghosts can pray — that I am not too late.

***

The Fisherman's Boy once had an older brother and a name, and now he has neither. This is just how it happens, the Boy decided. When you have a brother, when you are one of two sons hauling in the fishing nets, your father must call you each something, so that you know when you are being called, or praised or punished.

But his brother, Tao, came to him one night, standing very tall, and told him that a brotherhood of great men had come to take Tao away with them to the city. These were powerful men, he said, part of a secret Society that would bring back righteousness and strength to this land. The Boy asked his brother where righteousness and strength had gone. "Are you *stupid*?" Tao asked him. "Do you not see that there is moral degradation and Christians and Imperialists and yang guizi everywhere, bringing this drought down upon us?"

The Boy looked around him, but saw none of these.

"These brothers are of the highest discipline," said his brother with shining eyes. "They keep the strictest schedule of prayers, and cleanse themselves with the most secret of rituals. They are invulnerable to all the foulest weapons of the foreigners and the Imperialists–"

"What about the yang guizi?" asked the Boy.

"Yes, yes, them as well! And when I am one of the Society, I will be invulnerable as they. Our father may be angry to find me gone in the morning, but he will know what I have done when I and my true brothers sweep this land, unable to be cut down."

Tao spoke half the truth. Their father was angry in the morning, but he would never see his son sweep the land. Only a body, three weeks later, and a letter with no name that said the body was Tao's. And a neat little hole where the bowels of the body had come out. The Boy used to wonder whose magic had failed, whether the Imperialists had found a weapon strong enough to kill even Tao and take the long life from his name, or whether his brother had become a shape-changer and left something else that was not him at all to die in his place.

By and by, though, it did not matter. Gone is gone, and now the Boy is the Fisherman's only son. He must haul in the nets and mend them. He must gut the fish, and clean the fish, and make the fish into soup. The Fisherman does not need a name for him when the nets break or come up empty, or when the knife slips in his hand, or when the soup boils and burns. The Fisherman only ever says "You," and so that is what he is called. "Come, you! Idiot child, what makes you so stupid?"

And the Boy answers always to himself, "I do not know what makes me stupid. I do not know what makes me anything that I am, except that perhaps I think too much about paper."

Tao used to say that his little brother had a head full of paper, that he dreamed about paper instead of wealth or feasts or women. And Tao was right, the Boy decided. There is always paper, even when there is nothing else. Hanging like lanterns and flying like kites, and whipping around in dusty streets. Red paper, and yellow paper, and blue and green paper. Paper can be made into anything, can make whole worlds of anything, if you are patient and you collect enough: meadows of flowers, flocks of birds, fleets of ships, an entire province full of houses.

The Fisherman hated for his son to collect so much paper. In the weeks after the body and the letter with no name, the Fisherman would throw all paper into the fire. He would flatten the ships and houses, and scream and hit the Boy until he bled. He would ask why it was their fate to starve, why the lower realm had taken his good, strong son and left him only one skinny, brainless boy with dead-fish eyes and fumbling hands and a head full of paper. And when the Boy would answer that he did not know, the Fisherman would cover his face and go away to weep. In those weeks, the thirsty days were very thirsty, and the hungry days were very hungry.

And then one day, the Fisherman met a man who would trade him a pipeful of opium for a bowl or a teacup, or a polished stone figurine, or whatever else the Fisherman could find in the house. When the Fisherman has his pipeful, an empty net or even a broken one cannot anger him. He does not complain about burnt soup, because he almost never takes soup when there is any. He does not scream, or ask the Boy questions he cannot answer. He almost never stirs from his chair to go out onto the water. He only sits and watches the Boy shape his paper, making dreamy smoke rings in the air. Sometimes, if he has found nothing to trade, he will weep, and hit the Boy on the ears, and call out his missing son's name – or the name of his wife, though she died years and years ago. But the whole house is a little less hungry when the opium smoke hangs.

The Boy goes out in the morning, now, with all his paper treasures, walking around and around until he finds somebody with food to trade. There are always people who want paper treasures to send to the world of the dead. Even in these hungry days, he can always find them. Perhaps because everything in these days is brown and withered (grass and people and blossoms on trees) the people will take away a little food from their bellies to feed their eyes with something bright. The Boy has no priest to bless them, but the people take them anyway, even if it is only to be kind. And whenever the Boy returns home with a dumpling or a peach or small bowl of rice, his father almost smiles.

Today, on the Festival of Ghosts, the Boy plans to bring home their ghost-day feast. Today, the air will be filled with the smoke of the things he has made.

In the morning, he fills his father's pipe and leaves him in his chair to smoke, and he walks the six miles to the next village with all his most beautiful paper. He has thought of everything: paper chairs for paper tables, and paper vases for paper flowers, and paper pots and pans on paper stoves.

The sun is high by the time he reaches the first houses, but the air smells already of feast food being prepared, and everyone is generous to guests on Ghost Day. Already, a woman opens her door for a few bright paper flowers, and offers the Boy tea and a dumpling for his trouble. He has not eaten since yesterday, and he refuses only twice before he takes what she gives him and consumes it in violent bites.

After that, he is more polite. He does not accept so eagerly, and he tucks away some of what they trade him. Soon, he has bread and dumplings and red bean cake in all his pockets. But there are fewer people living in the houses than there used to be.

Eventually, he reaches a place where most of the houses stand empty on bare brown farms, and those who are at home do not look as though they wish to lavish more than a small meal upon the dead. The Boy sees many pale, unhappy ghosts drifting here and there, as he always does on this day, but he does not show them his wares: ghosts never have anything to trade themselves, and nobody living ever seems to know who he is speaking to.

At dark, long after the feasts are supposed to have begun and the offerings supposed to have been made, the Boy still has plenty of his paper, and nothing like a feast. He is invited in to eat by a few tired faces, as is proper on Ghost Day, but when he properly refuses, they make no protests, retreating into their houses to shut out the night. And so the Boy walks on, wondering what to do. He might return home to make boats or lanterns, but nobody will want more of those until fourteen days after the festival, when they say it is time to send the ghosts home again (though the Boy knows the ghosts are long gone by then).

It is only because he is thinking about making boats, and because he is passing by the only lighted house on that side of the road, that the Boy happens to spy the red envelope.

The Boy is stupid, as his father says, but he is not foolish, not greedy. He does not pick it up to take the money inside. Even a stupid man knows better than to go snatching up money he finds lying in the middle of the road on Ghost Day. Who knows what wandering spirit might have left it there, and to what purpose? No, no, this Boy only wishes to see if the envelope is made of good paper that might be re-used.

He has not held it in his hands for longer than a moment, when he sees her, rushing bright out of the darkness, a tiny, skinny girl of a ghost. She halts when she sees him, standing absolutely still in a way he has never seen a ghost do, and stares, eyes meeting his eyes. Until now, the Boy did not know that a ghost could feel dread. But she is so clear and plain to him, with her half-opened mouth, and her bright hands clutched to her heart, her eyes so terribly wide, blinking at the red envelope. It's as though he has caused her a second death. "No!" he hears her say, clear as anything. "Please, no!"

The Boy does not know what to do for her. He holds out her envelope so that she can see he does not mean to keep it. "I am sorry. I am very stupid. Take this. I did not know it was yours."

But the ghost girl makes no move. She stands so perfectly still and begins to cry, silent silver ghost-tears making furrows on her cheeks. "Please," says the Boy, "please, you must not be offended by me. I am my father's most worthless son."

And that is when the girl's mother and father emerge from the lighted house, drawing him to their table with loud congratulations, and calling him "Son-in-law" before they know his name.

***

On the island where my mother was born, there is a way to trap a living boy into marrying your daughter's ghost. Even if they were never engaged. Even if he knows her not at all. Ordinarily, the envelope has only a card with the ghost-girl's birthday in it. But Mother has filled this one with money.

I ought to have known Mother would try to trick someone. It is too easy a hope to nourish, that some unwitting greedy person would come along and take up this money they believed to have no owner, and find themselves bound to take her dead daughter too. Much easier than believing anyone would volunteer to marry her dead daughter knowingly. She must have told herself as she stuffed the envelope with every spare note she had saved, that this was the day my spirit would finally leave her. Perhaps she has wanted this ever since the day my illness turned her son into an unfilial stranger, forcing her to drive him away, into a city that is now burning. Like the angry, hungry men who light Peking on fire, my tired mother only hopes. She hopes I am a cause, a reason. That when at last I am flung away, she will have live chickens and a live son again. And perhaps she is right. What do I know? I'm dead.

"Such blessings!" says Mother to the skinny, fish-eyed boy in a voice I know she has practiced many times. "Who knew there was such a fine young man destined to be husband to our poor daughter? Bless you. Bless you... Have you eaten yet? No, do not go away without sharing our feast." But once she has him inside, eating from our table, her words dry up, and her face becomes pinched as she pours out the tea, as though she has done all she means to do, having caught the fish and pulled it in.

It is Father who makes all the toasts – barely smiling – and asks questions while the boy stares into his bowl and fumbles his teacup. He answers every one of Father's questions in a halting mumble, as though he is afraid he will give the wrong village when asked where he lives, or the wrong name when asked who his father is. And he will not stop turning from Father to stare through me with his dull, dark fish eyes. I want to hit him hard. I want to shake him and shout, "Do not look at me, fool, I have no answers! Look at the one who speaks to you, before he decides there is water leaked in your brain!"

I am ill with the smells of the feast, though it is almost the same feast as it has been every year since I died. The light of the house feels already dim and unfamiliar, as though my lonely marriage has already begun. As much as I try to collect it all, as much as I say to myself, *It cannot begin yet! You must seize your last night and keep it with you!*, I cannot seem to stay in the same moment as Father's small smile, or Mother's hands on the teapot. There are too many dangerous silences.

Am I already lost? Am I Hungry?

When the boy finally fumbles his teacup badly enough to break it, when he mumbles out a stupid apology, causing his own hand to bleed as he gathers the pieces, I feel I have already begun to waste away.

I make the plates rattle when I shudder, and the tears come again, even though I have vowed they won't. And that stupid, stupid boy offers me the corner of his napkin, holding it out like he had held out the red envelope, as though I could simply take it from him. My mother's face only becomes more pinched, my father's smile only more of a silent laugh. And I am forced to remember that I am an empty seat to them, unseen as I am unheard.

When at last the terrible feast is over, the boy is given a carefully written proposal to take back to his father along with the envelope, and he is shuffled, with very little of the mask of politeness, back out into the night. Mother turns on her husband. "Do you dare to judge me?" she challenges him. "I won't bear any more from you! I tell you I won't bear it. She must be old enough!"

Father says nothing.

***

They have to give the Fisherman two pipefuls of opium along with all the money in the envelope before he will take the ghost girl's tablet. But in no time at all, on a day that is both hot and gray, the Fisherman's Boy is married.

It passes like a funeral, full of solemn light and unsmiling faces. The Boy is even hungrier than usual, skeleton-skinny in his brother's blue and black robes, and the bright paper effigy they have made has none of the girl's face in it. It has no person's face, living or dead, that the Boy has ever seen. It is well made, pale, with graceful dark paper eyes, and deep red paper lips, and thin red paper bride's robes. Before he had seen her — before he had seen the skinny ghost girl that is the real Ling — he might have thought this paper thing was beautiful. As it is, he does not want to look at it, all the way to his father's front door.

She herself is missing. She is hiding, all through the wedding feast, the Joyful Wine that is not joyful. The Boy sits by an empty chair to eat a thin bowl of shark's fin soup with nothing in it. And he waits, and he waits for her.

It is only after all the guests have all made excuses and gone far away from the dark little fishing hut, and the bright, doll-like effigy burns along with its paper bride gifts, that the Boy finally sees her, standing deathly still on the high shelf where he has placed her tablet. Her eyes are dry this time, but she does not look at him.

"Hello," says the Boy, and he knows it is not the right thing for a husband to say to his wife.

She nods at him, unsmiling.

"Do you like where I have put your tablet? I have put you near to my mother, and to my great-uncle who used to tell me very good stories..."

She nods again, but dips her head, and he can see her shuddering, a bright, silvery ghost-shudder. The Boy shifts in his worn red wedding shoes, not knowing at all what to do.

"If you would like it better," he tries, "I will move you to the window so that you can look out over the sea... or perhaps you will want first to see more of your house...? Do you like the house?"

Her shuddering grows worse, and she cradles herself, head still bowed.

The Boy chews his lips, afraid to see her cry her silent silver ghost-tears again. "I am sorry that I gave you no proper letter of betrothal," he says suddenly in his stupidest voice. "I am sorry that I have no proper bride gifts to give to you. I am sorry that my house is dark and small and stinks of fish guts. I am sorry you are dead... I am sorry that I can only wish you were not dead. I am sorry that my brother is not here to marry you. I am sorry that you have only a weak, stupid husband with no brother and no name. But please... say something."

***

I do not know what to say. It isn't only that the house is the darkest, barest house I have ever seen. It isn't only that it is cold and fireless, or that I can no longer distinguish the gray of the City of Ghosts from the gray seeping in at my window. I do not know what to say because the house seems changeless. It seems as though the man sitting in the rickety chair with the smoke hanging thick around his head has been sitting there for years, thinking of nothing. He does not even seem to know anybody else is alive.

But the boy is alive. "How is it you can see me?" I say, quiet as a flea. "And how is it I can stand here, outside my tablet, when the Festival day is past?"

"I do not know," he says, and thinks for a long moment. "Perhaps it is because we are married, and this your home now."

"This is my home now..." I do not mean for my voice to sound so faint, so sick.

"Do you hate it very much?" His eyes suddenly do not look dull or dead at all.

"I do not *know* it, that is all," I say quickly. "It does not seem a home to me. Do not be offended. I am a very rude little ghost."

"You are not rude. You are very quiet and very sad, and beautiful."

"You are kind," I say. I try hard not to look at the man sitting still as a statue in his opium dream. "Is there... anyone else who lives with you?"

"Me and my father, only."

"Oh."

He blinks a nervous blink. "Do you... you must have a splendid house in the Lower Realm."

"No," I say, my voice feeling hard in my throat. "I have nothing in the Lower Realm. And no one. No one even comes to visit me."

"I cannot believe that no one comes to visit you." His smile is so funny and slanted. Not like Father's small one, but somehow I feel it means the same.

"And I cannot believe you have no name. Why do you say you have no name? I do not even recall what name you gave to my father."

"I don't need my name. You only need a name if someone must tell you apart from your brother, and my brother is gone, and will not come back."

I want suddenly to touch his arm, but I do not know what he will do, if he will flinch, or twist away. "My brother is gone also," I say. "My mother believes he has burnt up in a Christian temple and gone to the City of Ghosts. He hasn't, but I search for him every day, half-hoping that he has so that I will not be alone anymore. So you see, I'm wicked as well as rude."

"You are not wicked. And you are not alone," the boy says. His eyes are so earnest they make me shudder. I want to believe he is right, that I have not entered such a terrible and desolate place.

"You must give me your name, now," I tell him, because I know it will make him smile at me again. "If you are to be my husband, I must call you something to tell you apart from all the boys who are not my husband."

"My mother called me Qing Yuan," he says, his mouth nicely slanted.

"Then," I say, bowing bravely and gracefully as I can, "I am Ling, wife of Qing Yuan."

The man — my father-in-law — begins to twitch in his chair as soon as his pipe is empty.

***

Qing Yuan hardly feels the days pass, he is so busy being a husband. He brings home rice and dumplings and sometimes fish for them to share, and he makes for her everything he can think of, with every fine bit of paper he can find: joss paper robes as bright as flowers, a great joss paper bed piled high with paper cushions. She refuses him every time. "These beautiful things only serve to make my gray little house look like a decorated grave!" she says. But a wife never really refuses her husband, and he can see her eyes dancing like the eyes of the living girl she used to be.

On the day he presents her with her own small paper inkstone and writing brush, she forgets that she is not solid enough to kiss him, and they fall into each other like lapping pools of water. That is the day Qing Yuan decides he will build her a home, in the way a true husband would. He will change his father's house. He will make it into a house she belongs in, a house that makes her feel she is come home.

He begins that very day, an exact and clever replica of the Fisherman's cottage, with shining joss paper roof tiles, and shining extra windows to rooms the cottage does not have. Even the Fisherman stops smoking to smile on what he has made, and touch his son on the top of the head.

They are together every day, and every night they walk and talk together as a husband and wife should. She cannot stray too far from her tablet on most nights of the year, and so Qing Yuan carries it, Ling flowing beside him like a quiet stream.

It's only the Fisherman's moods that make her disappear into her tablet and not come out.

"They are just exactly like storms," Qing Yuan tries to tell her. "He will only scream and weep and hit me until he remembers, and then he will collapse into his chair to dream again."

But Ling shakes her head. "The dreaming is worse," she says, as she reaches to touch the blood on his face.

301

***

Somehow, I have stopped counting the days of my death, and Ghost Day is upon me again before I know it. And because I am a wicked ghost, and a wicked daughter, and a wicked wife, I decide this morning to run away.

After all, I can go out and wander the world every year without anybody knowing or caring. What could possibly happen to me were I to keep on wandering? Who will make me enter that dark changeless house and sit in silence with that weak, bleeding boy and his father on this, my only day among the living? Who says I belong to them? Who says I belong to anyone?

Who can make me face this day? I say to myself, as I drift in the morning mists, following them out to sea. I am as good as a Hungry Ghost, with no mother, no father, no brother. I haven't got a family. No one can make me say I have.

But then, the boy, my silly, stupid husband, smiles nervously behind my eyes, and something in me is sighing. There are so many Hungry Ghosts, both living and dead, growling low with hunger, or quietly aching in rooms full of smoke.

When the sun goes down, I make myself go back to the Fisherman's house.

It is only when I am inside that I realize the house is changing. It is becoming somewhere else, full of ghost-bright beauty. Full of rugs and lamps and beautiful screens that only Qing Yuan could have made. There is a whole wing of bright rooms that was not there before. I sob horribly as I watch the smaller house, the one my husband must have blistered making, burning away in a living fire. *He has done all this for you, you ungrateful, wicked little ghost,* I say to myself, *he has made all this great, beautiful, sad empty house for you.*

It must be enough. A bride must learn to say goodbye to her old life, and enter the new without shedding a tear.

"There you are," he cries when he sees me. "I was afraid you would not come back in time. Do you like our house? Have I made enough rooms?"

"It is the most beautiful house any wife ever lived in," I say, and blink away the blur of tears, and make myself sit at the great empty table.

He smiles then, the widest, crookedest smile I have ever seen. "Oh, but don't sit down!" he says. "They will arrive, soon, I think."

I quell a churning sickness, slap away a tear that has escaped. "Who?"

But then I see the Great-Uncle. For a moment or two, he is a brightly wavering light coming down the road, and then he chooses an empty seat, flickering suddenly into a chair across the table: a smiling, well-wrinkled old ghost loudly demanding to make the first toast. His wife is not far behind him, small and delicate as a smiling bird.

There is barely time to stand and greet them ("So wonderful to meet you, Great-uncle... have you eaten yet?") before a pack of boisterous, laughing cousins and great-cousins flicker into seats of their own. I am flitting like a silver comet to greet them all ("Have you eaten yet? Have *you* eaten yet?"). And after them, there come a dozen more: not only Ancestors, but others, too.

Ghosts so young, they are still learning to speak. Ghosts so ancient, they hardly need to speak at all. The spouses, the nieces and nephews, the sons and daughters of a hundred years past are all around me, exchanging stories, telling sly jokes. I finally belong enough to see them all. My family.

And there's one who sits with the stillness of a white jade statue, as though she has existed long enough to have collected all the graces and beauties and strengths worth having in the world. Even before Qing Yuan kneels to kiss her hand, I know who she is. But she laughs, unexpectedly, to feel his solid kiss. "My son, who taught you to do that?"

"Mother," he says, "this is my wife, and your daughter, Ling." I am a little sick as I bow, not daring even to meet the bright, still eyes.

But she takes both my hands firmly. "Yes, of course she is." She looks at me, her smile very serious. "Yes, I have waited long for my son to meet a good wife. I see I don't need to worry about him so much."

"Mother's not been here for years and years on Ghost Day," says Qing Yuan. "She has only just found us again."

"I could not recognize the place, it was so full of sadness and smoke. I was lost, as your brother Tao is lost. But we all find our way, eventually." The Matriarch reaches for an empty teacup, and with a quiet thrill I reach out and take up the teapot, filling the cup like a proper, living daughter-in-law. She nods, and I know I have done well. But suddenly, I remember the Fisherman, slumped in his chair nearby.

"Do not worry about your father-in-law," says the Matriarch. "He will not be disturbed by floating teapots or drunken ghost-uncles. I give him dreams. There are things I need to say to him that he will not hear any other way."

"Will you teach me?" I ask her. "There are things I need to say to my mother."

Art by Esme Baran

MEDU

LISA BOLEKAJA

1877
Ellsworth, Kansas

Lil Bit found the two missing long-horned steers cowering between some weathered-down boulders. Their six-foot-long horns scraped against the granite, sending tiny sparks into the night. Lil Bit was so relieved to see them after riding around for nearly thirty minutes in the moonlight, she didn't stop to wonder why they were cowering and not responding to her whistles.

"I found 'em, Papa," she yelled and rode forward her four-year-old mare, Daphne.

The baby rattlesnake was curled in a tight ball, its hind quarters shaking violently. Lil Bit missed the warning rattle. Daphne reared up, bucked Lil Bit off her back, and hot tailed it back to camp.

"Dammit," she said, and then caught herself. Papa would be upset if he heard her cussin' like a man. Her tailbone ached, but nothing else was bruised. The fall knocked off the rabbitskin cowboy hat that Vicente the cook bought her before they crossed the Red River back in Texas. She reached for her head kerchief. It was knocked askew, revealing her bald scalp.

She heard the rattlesnake again. It was closer now, right next to her hand.

Lil Bit's scalp throbbed.

Tiny raised bumps from every root shaft on her head pulsed and opened as adrenaline rippled through her.

"Babygirl, don't move. Calm yourself."

Papa's voice sounded like God's voice above her head. She couldn't see him, but she heard his horse, Bear, breathing hard and neighing behind her.

Lil Bit sighed, her eyes glued to the snake. She couldn't even round up two lost steer by herself without falling off her horse and having to play damsel in distress in front of her father.

"Lil Bit! Make your head stop moving, gal. Now."

Lil Bit closed her eyes. She tried to think of something peaceful so the pin prickly root shafts would close themselves back up. Already the slender filaments of her twisted black hair trembled, ready to shoot out in full force at any second. She didn't know how to control her hair yet; until she could, Papa made her keep the locks inside. She wore a bald brown head with tiny bumps to keep him happy.

She fastened her mind onto that thought, making Papa happy because he took care of her. Why, he had bought her a big ole book back in Texas. It had all kinds of strange stories and pictures. She already knew about Brer Rabbit, and stories about the Boo Hag and La Llorona from Papa and Vicente, but this book had stories she never heard of from clear across the world.

The more she thought of the book, the more the skin on her rippling scalp relaxed. She thought of how the first story she read in that book was about a girl named Daphne who didn't want a particular fella chasing her and she turned into a tree. Lil Bit liked the name Daphne, and she named her trail horse after the girl in the story.

Lil Bit opened her eyes.

The rattlesnake was sliding on its belly away from her hand. She smiled and turned her head to look up into her Papa's hazel eyes. Pain erupted in the ruddy brown skin between Lil Bit's thumb and index finger.

She felt the toxin in the venom being absorbed into her bloodstream, and then she throbbed.

The hair slithered out from deep within her scalp. Each serpentine strand was over a foot long and it only took three of them to strike the upper half of the rattler. She pierced its skin and injected it with her own neurotoxins steeped inside the needled tips of her hair. The snake's head and midsection spasmed once, went rigid, and then hardened like petrified wood. The bottom half shivered; its rattle jangled a few more times then stopped.

Lil Bit's Papa swung down from his horse and grabbed the snake by its tail. He bashed the head against a boulder and the front part of the snake shattered to pieces. He threw it on the ground and mashed it up with his boot heel.

Gabriel looked down at her. Lil Bit was thirteen but looked younger.

"Put away your hair," he said.

While her Papa rustled up the longhorns, Lil Bit felt a new emotion sink down into her body like the hair retracting into her scalp: shame.

***

Lil Bit knew that her father was frightened of her.

She walked alongside his horse, using a stick to help guide the longhorns back to the rest of the herd.

It was her blood that scared him, and it came from her mother, Odetta. Only women in their bloodline were born *Medu*. Both her parents thought Lil Bit had bypassed the lineage when she was born with normal black corkscrew curls. She had her mama's dark skin and her father's light eyes. But when she was six months old, Gabriel had bathed her in a wooden bucket with her Mama laughing at him because he looked so stiff holding her with his big hands. He had wiped her wet hair with a damp rag and all her corkscrews smeared away in thick black clumps.

Water had fallen into her infant eyes and she cried. It was the first time both her parents saw her newly bald scalp move – it writhed under Gabriel's light-skinned fingers and then the first slender threads of new baby hair sprang out and stung him. Odetta told her that she was so proud, despite the fact that she hid her own venomous hair wrapped tight with leather strips under a calico scarf. Gabriel never held Lil Bit again until she was three and knew how to keep her head bald by retracting the hair.

Lil Bit took in the shadowy flat plains. They were on alert for trouble tonight. She thought it was the main reason why he went looking for her in the first place.

The herd and the men were being watched.

As trail boss, her father had to be aware of everything concerning the drive towards the Ellsworth stockyards. And everything that Gabriel knew, Lil Bit kept track of too: Head count of the entire herd (3,000). Head count of all the men, and her (16). How much food Vicente had left on the chuck wagon to feed the predominantly black and Mexican cattlemen (40 pounds). How many horses the horse wrangler and the wrangler's son controlled for the entire crew (90).

Her father rode ahead of everyone searching for watering holes, Apaches, Comanches, cattle rustlers, wolves, and anything else that would prevent them from getting fattened meat to payday. They were only a few hours' ride away from Ellsworth where the men could take baths and wash away grit and crusted shit, visit a barber, and eat a decent meal.

The full moon was out, and nothing could really be hidden on the wide open Kansas plain. Gabriel opted to take the twilight watch and let most of the men bed down and dream of good pay and the whorin' they would do at the cathouse in Ellsworth.

Walking beside her father, Lil Bit thought about their life together on the trails. They were on the run from bounty hunters. Two years ago her Papa was a member of the Tenth Cavalry Regiment. A Buffalo Soldier. He shot and killed a white man to save a Kiowa-Apache who had crossed paths with his unit. The Kiowa-Apache lived to tell his people about the black man who shot a white man to save a red man. A white lieutenant from another regiment tried to cut her Papa's throat as punishment. But then her Mama stepped in, hair quivering, calculating and deadly.

Lil Bit wasn't present when her parents killed the two Cavalry men. An older aunt was caring for her, and without warning, Lil Bit was taken to Texas by two uncles. Other Kiowa-Apaches helped spirit her father away from the law, and her mother was transported out of town hidden among dry goods headed west. The plan had been for them both to meet in Texas to retrieve Lil Bit.

Only her father had made it there. After months of failed searches and furtive inquiries, Gabriel had to give up looking for her mother and keep Lil Bit safe. They had been on the move ever since.

When Vicente the trail cook saw Lil Bit's hand back at the chuck wagon, he dug into his chuck box and pulled out liniment, and a full bottle of whiskey.

"Chica!"

"It don't hurt no more," she said.

She held up her hand to the kerosene lamp hanging from the wagon.

"See, concinero, just two holes. It's not bleeding."

"Take a swig, chica," Vicente said, handing her the bottle. She glanced over at her father. Gabriel nodded, and she poured it down her throat.

"Aye! I'm not tryna get you soaked." Vicente snatched back the bottle. Lil Bit laughed. Vicente cleaned her wound with the whiskey and ointment. After dressing it he handed her a bedroll and stared into her eyes.

"You get pissed?" he asked. Her gaze dropped to the ground. Vicente shook his head. He looked over at Gabriel.

"Anyone see?"

"No," Gabriel said.

"Good, we're fine then," Vicente said as he pushed Lil Bit away from the wagon. "G'night, chica."

"Night, chico," she said, grabbing a spare lamp from under the wagon. She glanced back at Gabriel. He raised his head up slightly in her direction. She stood with shoulders less slumped and waited for him.

"You want something to eat?" Vicente asked Gabriel.

"No," said Gabriel.

Lil Bit watched her father turn on a small tap on the side of the wagon. He cupped his hands to catch cool water. He drank deeply, turned off the tap and wiped excess water on his forehead.

"One more day, jefe," said Vicente.

"She was getting better," said Gabriel.

Lil Bit felt her cheeks flush with heat. He spoke as if she wasn't there. It was his way of shaming her.

"She is! She is! She's better, she'll get better."

Gabriel ignored Vicente and stepped behind the wagon. He reached inside a side panel and pulled out a fresh box of rifle bullets.

"You spot anything unusual when you were ahead of the men this morning?" Gabriel asked.

"No."

"We're being followed. Felt it the last few days."

"Rustlers?" asked Lil Bit, happy that the conversation wasn't about her anymore.

"They would've made a move on us by now, babygirl," said Gabriel.

"And we would've been ready," said Vicente. Gabriel stuffed more ammunition into his vest pockets.

Lil Bit looked over the widespread encampment. The cattle were staggered out over seven miles in groups of twenty to forty. Seven men on evening watch circled the herd on horseback. The horse wrangler had corralled their resting mounts in a roped off space one hundred feet from the wagon.

Vicente had the tongue of the chuck wagon facing toward Polaris, the North Star. At dawn he would feed the men and hitch up his four horses to the wagon. The crew, along with the herd, would follow after him. Gabriel would already be ahead of them, only a few miles, waiting for the herd to kick up dust before mid-morning the next day.

"I think you should bed down and watch your kid. Enough men are on shift. Schultz can do your time. I'll tell him you said so."

Vicente walked towards a smoldering fire pit and reached down near the hot ash of dead brush and cow dung, pulling up a tin plate with a wooden spoon in it. He walked over to Gabriel and handed him the warm dented plate.

"Her favorite. Slumgullion," said Vicente, winking at Lil Bit.

Gabriel took the plate filled with leftover biscuits mixed with sugar water and raisins. A poor imitation of bread pudding, but she liked it.

Gabriel flicked his tongue against his front teeth. Bear followed them. Gabriel's horse was never corralled with the others in the evening because he was a night ride, used only for emergencies. Along the trail her father used five other horses interchangeably. But tomorrow morning he wanted to ride Bear. Just in case.

Lil Bit couldn't shake the feeling of unease that descended over the area. As they walked through the camp, there was no good-natured laughter from her father's off-duty men after they finished eating boiled beef and pinto beans. No card playing or dirty joke telling. No Spanish or Irish or Negro songs shared over a harmonica or spoons slapped on knees. She didn't want to look like an old croaker in front of him, but there was a tightening in her bowels and chest. Camp didn't feel right.

They found their spot and unrolled their bedding. Lil Bit lit a kerosene lamp near her head, took off her hat, and clutched the book Gabriel bought in Texas that was shoved inside her bedroll. Gabriel handed her the plate after she was settled. She felt so much smaller without her hat on. The others thought she had suffered an illness that made her hair fall out. She was grateful they all liked her and respected her presence on the trail. She was a hard worker and she knew her father valued her contribution as a wrangler. She could ride her tail off just like her mama. Only Vicente knew the truth about her "illness".

Lil Bit ate, picking out the raisins that had gotten too hard to chew. Her father surveyed the landscape again. The moon was a fine lady. Whoever was out there, her Papa and his men would see them coming miles away.

Bear snorted, stamped his front hooves on the ground. Some of the bedded down cattle responded to his agitation with anxious moans.

"Papa."

Lil Bit's scalp rippled under the bluish-white moonlight and the red glow of the kerosene lamp. She touched the top of her head.

"I don't know what's happening. I'm not upset. Honest," she said. Her eyes were wide and her lips trembled.

Gabriel grabbed the pistol hidden in his bedroll. The night drovers circled around the groupings off cattle in opposite directions, rifles ready, searching for signs of wolves, or worse, rustlers. A new concern entered Lil Bit's mind. Bounty hunters. She felt herself shudder thinking of them. How long could her Papa run from the law? Two years was a lifetime of running from a lynching. If her Papa ever got caught, what would happen to her?

"It stopped throbbing, Papa," she said, rubbing gentle circles across her scalp.

"Shh," he said. Bear settled down and Gabriel grabbed the loose reins and pulled the animal closer to them for cover. Peace settled over the clusters of steer close to them. Lil Bit heard relieved chuckles from some of the resting men. Total sleep was hard to come by on the trail. Even tired bones came awake at the slightest hint of trouble.

"What do you think it was?" asked Lil Bit.

Gabriel took off his vest. "Probably coyotes or wolves most likely." He scooped his feet out of his boots and loosened the bandanna around his neck. He spread out his bedroll and plopped down on it next to her. Bear backed himself away from her father and flicked his tail. The horse would stand guard over them for the night.

Gabriel tucked his gun under his bedding and placed his Stetson over his face.

"Read me some of that book, babygirl," he said.

She obliged by curling up closer to him, book in hand. She flipped open a page, then looked up at Gabriel's hat.

"You listenin'?"

"I'm listening, babygirl."

"No you ain't. I can't see your eyes."

"I don't need my eyes to listen. Now read."

She waited a full minute and then she heard the familiar trembling snores escaping from under Gabriel's hat. She rolled her eyes and laid the book on her chest. She stared at the night sky.

"Estrella, luna, sol..." The Spanish words Vicente taught her about the sky helped her relax. Because it was a light night, it was difficult to see a lot of the constellations.

She picked up the book again and slid her fingers along the cover. She loved the feel of the heavy gold embossing and the musty smell of the pages. Even though she didn't understand all the words, she was grateful that Gabriel bought the book for her. It cost four days' wages, and she squealed when she saw him pay the German merchant in Texas the full amount.

Lil Bit stuck a finger on a random page and opened the book back up. Her breath caught short. Her bandaged hand rubbed the picture she stared at. The black ink of the drawing was so detailed that Lil Bit thought she saw the woman in the picture moving. Especially the woman's snake hair.

The woman looked just like her Mama.

Lil Bit read for the rest of the night until her eyelids drooped and the oil in the kerosene lamp burned out.

***

The screaming woke them up. Gabriel grabbed his rifle and shoved a pistol into Lil Bit's trembling hands. The moon had risen to the top of the sky, its light a dim glow across the plains. Three gunshots cracked the still night, then more screams. The cattle stirred and stamped their feet.

Two men ran up towards them from the south.

"It's Schultz," one yelled, "There's something wrong with his eyes."

"Who's shooting?" asked Gabriel.

"Casey, maybe," the other man said. "He was with him."

They found Schultz on his back, clutching at his eyes and screaming in pain. Gabriel pulled Schultz's hands apart as Vicente held a lamp above his head. Schultz's eyes were squeezed shut. Blood was splattered across the top half of his face and they all saw the skin there sizzle and break open with dark red pustules as if someone had thrown boiling water onto his face.

"Don't touch it," Gabriel said, pulling the men back.

"Papa look." Lil Bit pointed to Schultz's neck.

The bloody pus slid away; black lines like tiny blood vessels stretched under his skin, across his pale throat.

"Schultz, what happened to you?" asked Gabriel.

Schultz's voice came out in a garbled whisper. His breathing slowed down. Vicente leaned in to hear him.

"He say, *demonio*," said Vicente. "Demon."

"Gabriel! Over here!"

Lil Bit saw Juanez, one of the drovers, waving at her father.

Schultz's brother Casey was dead on the ground. His face was like Schultz's, and his work shirt was ripped off revealing a perfectly round hole in his stomach the size of two fists. His intestines lay strewn next to him.

"Christ. Stand back, Lil Bit," said Gabriel.

Lil Bit saw that Casey was missing the rest of his insides. Gabriel kneeled down to look at the wound.

"Where's his gun, Papa?"

"No man did this," said Gabriel.

They went back to Schultz. He was dead.

"No one sleeps for the rest of the night," said Gabriel.

After the men buried the bodies, Lil Bit stayed awake wondering what kind of animal ate everything inside a man except for his intestines.

***

The herd stampeded into Ellsworth with a spent and shaken crew. Gabriel guided them to the stockyard as the men forced the long horns into tight lines, packing them into the fenced pens. Lil Bit hustled the horses into a separate holding pen where some would be sold with the cattle. She rode back and forth behind the stragglers, gripping the reins and adjusting Daphne's gait when one of the horses got out of line.

When her work was finished, she helped Vicente secure the chuck wagon. Gabriel found her when she was done.

"Keep your eyes open, babygirl," said Gabriel, pulling his hat low on his face.

***

They ate in a quiet tavern where the owners didn't want to know the patrons, most of whom looked rough around the edges. They sat furthest away from the entrance and tucked into plates of sourdough biscuits, baked chicken with white gravy, and mashed butterbeans. Lil Bit topped everything off with the driest piece of vanilla cake she'd ever eaten. She had to down three glasses of water to rid her mouth of the taste. She wanted so badly to talk about the dead men, ask her father about the missing body parts and how a wolf or a coyote could make a hole in a man so neat and so round.

In late afternoon, after potential buyers had looked over the herds all morning, Lil Bit and Gabriel watched the auction, drank water in the oppressive heat, and listened to the rapid-fire slurred words from the auctioneer as he described the animals. Lil Bit kept mimicking the auctioneer's voice in Gabriel's ear, making him chuckle. She loved how the auctioneer would stomp his foot after yelling "Sold!" in a nasally twang.

Some of the herd would become beef, some breeders, and others were designated as future oxen. They watched men run their hands across flanks of cows and steers, bicker over starting bid prices, and saw their eyes glaze over with the amount of money they would make once the herds were loaded on the trains nearby and shipped back east. Lil Bit knew from her parents' stories that it was less than ten years ago that her own people were up on those auctioning blocks too, Negro bodies shackled in lots, scrotums fingered, breasts prodded, human chattel bought and sold. She knew that some of these same men had bought more than beef in their lifetimes.

After five hours, all three thousand heads of cattle were sold, the majority going to one particular meat packing company in Pennsylvania.

Gabriel completed the financial transactions, divvied up the money to the crew, and admonished them to keep some cash in their pockets for the trip home. The easy leg of the journey was done for them. Getting the money safely out of town without being robbed was a whole new mission. And now her father had to think of a new safer route to travel, this time with two dead cowpokes on his mind.

Gabriel and Lil Bit met up with Vicente at the chuck wagon. Gabriel gave him his cut and, for the first time, allowed Lil Bit to hold onto her own hard-earned cash.

Lil Bit and Gabriel took their horses to the old livery stable. It was a ten-minute walk from their rooming house. Vicente chose to spend the night in the chuck wagon inside the stable and save his money. They left him clutching a bottle of applejack cider and munching on a piece of old hard tack.

***

Lil Bit bathed and washed her hair with hard brown soap in cold water inside the rooming house wash room on the first floor. When she returned to their room she hopped onto the big lumpy bed and watched Gabriel mark sales figures in his small ledger book.

A sharp knock at the door startled them both. Lil Bit grabbed her pistol off the nightstand. Gabriel's rifle was propped up against his side of the bed.

When he opened the door, a young thin-lipped woman stood there holding towels and an extra blanket.

"I don't need anything else, thank you ma'am." Gabriel eased the door shut.

The woman stepped forward, her ginger-colored hair pulled tight unto an upswept hairdo.

"They don't always cater to niggers and Mex'cans in town."

"Oh," Gabriel said.

Lil Bit kept her hand on the pistol beneath the blanket. If the woman made a false move, Lil Bit would take her out without hesitation the way her Papa taught her.

"You don't look much like a nigger up close, and I'm clean and all—" Her eyes were on his chest.

"I just want to sleep, ma'am."

"Change your mind, my name's Arlene." Her gaze lingered on his shirt-less mid-section and then she glanced up at his face. "I swear, you have the prettiest eyes."

Gabriel locked the door. He shoved his gun back under the pillow.

"Papa, she ain't even care I was in the room." Lil Bit placed her pistol on the nightstand.

"That's just nasty."

Gabriel smirked and moved his rifle over by the door.

"That's how they nickel and dime us to death in this town. Food, drink, and entertainment."

"And women," said Lil Bit.

"That's entertainment, babygirl."

"Ewwwwww," she squealed, giggling afterwards.

Gabriel walked over to the open window in their room and pulled back the curtains a few inches. Lil Bit saw him frown.

"What is it, Papa?"

He didn't answer. She climbed out of bed and peeked from the other window that was closed.

A negro cowpoke stood in the shadowed alley beside the tavern. He was looking up at their window. In the darkness they couldn't make out his features but they could tell by the clothes that he wasn't one of their crew.

Lil Bit glanced at the deep strain lines on her father's forehead – the expression she knew meant he was weighing several near-impossible options. They'd often skipped town to avoid confrontations with thieves or bounty arrests.

Before he even said "Pack up," she was putting on her denims and shoving her feet into boots.

There was another knock on the door, this one quieter. Lil Bit looked at the door, and then stared back out the window. The man outside was still watching their window.

"Ma'am, I said no thank you." Gabriel grabbed his rifle and opened the door.

The brown-skinned man in front of them was taller and thicker than Gabriel. His hair was dusty and he reeked of horses and dank sweat.

"What do you want?" asked Gabriel as he pointed his rifle at the man's chest.

"It's all right," said a husky voice behind the dusty man.

Lil Bit felt her heart fold into itself from the sound of that rich drawl. The man stepped aside and Odetta walked in from behind him.

"Mama?" said Lil Bit, brushing past her father.

"It's me," said Odetta.

Lil Bit threw her arms around her mother's waist and buried her face into her chest. Gabriel moved behind Lil Bit and gently pulled Odetta's face to his lips and kissed her. Lil Bit was smothered between her parents, her eyes blurry with long-held tears. She felt the world stop, wasn't sure if any of them were breathing anymore.

Odetta reached behind herself and closed the door shut. She untangled herself from them and removed her cowboy hat. Odetta's coiled hair fell down to her waist like spaghetti-thin ropes made of soft black skin. The stingers stayed retracted inside the tips of her locks.

Lil Bit had forgotten her mother's girlish sloe-eyed dark beauty. Odetta's hair slid across Lil Bit's lips then trailed up wiping a tear away from her eyelashes, the tactile sensation making Lil Bit's skin shiver with the thrill of seeing her mama again.

"We thought you were dead." It was the first time Lil Bit had ever heard a tremble in her father's voice. "How did you find us?"

Odetta swept into the room with urgent steps. She wore denim pants with leather chaps and a heavy duster covered her entire body. She was tall and could be mistaken for a man if she kept her head down and body covered. Only her eyes and high cheekbones gave her away.

She reached inside her duster and pulled out new beige wanted posters with Gabriel's clean-shaven face on it. The reward money was a hefty $1000. It revealed that his last known sightings were Houston and Abilene.

"We leave now," she said.

"I have to get money back to Texas," said Gabriel.

"You can't go back there."

"That money don't show up on time, more trouble comes for us."

"If these posters in Abilene, they damn well in this town too," she said.

Gabriel frowned. "Where can we go?"

"Nicodemus," she said.

"Nicodemus?"

"It's an all-Negro town one hundred and twenty-five miles from here. We can make it in ten days if we push it. It's safe."

"All Negro?"

"We don't have time for all this talking, I can explain on the way. But there's something else." She glanced at Lil Bit.

"What?" asked Gabriel.

"There's trouble out on the prairie. People been finding bodies ripped apart."

"We lost two men yesterday," said Gabriel.

Odetta rubbed Gabriel's shoulders with her hands. Lil Bit saw her father's body soften.

"My brothers will go ahead of us and clear the way. We have to be gone before sun-up."

Lil Bit watched Gabriel's eyes close. He looked hesitant.

"Gabriel, now," Odetta said, grabbing Lil Bit by the arm and pulling her towards the door.

***

It was a tense walk to the livery stable. Lil Bit took shallow gulps of air through her mouth, afraid her own breathing would be loud enough to alert trouble their way. At the stable, Odetta lit a few coal oil lamps that were set in wall brackets while Lil Bit quietly saddled up Bear and Daphne with Gabriel's help. Odetta's horse was hidden behind the building. When they were ready, they woke up Vicente from inside the wagon. Vicente reached under the wagon, where Juanez dozed between the wheels in a dingy blanket, and shook him awake.

Lil Bit felt heat seeping into her scalp.

"Papa..."

"Let's go!" hissed Odetta.

"Don't move, nigger!"

Three white men walked out from the horse stalls, their rifles drawn. Lil Bit recognized two of them from the cattle auction.

"Where's the money?" said the taller man with a bulbous nose. His voice sounded strange to her, like his mouth was stuffed with food making it hard to enunciate.

"We don't have any," said Gabriel.

The tall man laughed. "Don't lie to me, nigger."

Odetta placed herself in front of Lil Bit.

"Bitch, keep still," said the shorter man. His pockmarked face twitched. He sounded just like the tall man. The third muscular man kept his two guns trained on Juanez and Vicente.

Odetta slipped off her hat.

"I said keep still!" the tall man yelled.

The short man shot a round into the ground. The horses whinnied and reared their legs. Lil Bit felt her knees buckling, but she made herself stay standing. She saw Odetta's hair unravel and discreetly slink down her back.

"You got money. We watched you. Just toss it on the ground," said the tall man. The short man walked closer to Odetta, aiming his gun at her head.

"Slowly," said the tall man.

Gabriel grabbed the satchel from Bear's saddle and tossed it on the ground. The short man picked it up.

"Good and heavy," he said.

"Nice doing business, folks," said the muscular man. He opened his mouth wide, and a surge of blood splashed into Juanez's eyes. Juanez shrieked, reached for his face, and the muscular man knocked him to the ground. He ripped open Juanez's shirt and buried his mouth into his stomach and ate.

The hair on Odetta's shoulders rose up. The tall man's eyes squinted as if he were seeing Odetta for the first time. He backed up a few steps. Gabriel grabbed a gun hidden in the small of his back.

Blam!

315

The thief stumbled, clutching at the wet hole in the middle of his chest. He fell to his knees, opened his mouth and a torrent of red liquid gushed from his lips in a thick stream that splattered onto Gabriel's right leg. Gabriel screamed as the acidic blood burned through his denim and seeped into his flesh.

Odetta leaped onto the tall man and released her hair into his neck and face. The tall man spit blood onto her cheek, but she wiped it away with no sign of pain. Lil Bit saw Odetta's hair spasm, and then the tall man stopped moving.

The two other thieves grabbed the money and ran out of the stable. Odetta snatched the tall man's rifle and ran after them.

Lil Bit knelt by her father. Vicente grabbed a kerosene lamp and held it over them.

She ripped apart what was left of the pant leg. The skin was oozing with bloody pustules and darkening as spidery black veins ran up his thigh towards his groin. He was slipping away.

"Papa," Lil Bit whimpered. She was crying so hard that snot and tears were falling on him and mixing into his wound. She slapped his face to keep his eyes open.

"It won't stop, Papa."

"S'OK," he said.

"No it ain't."

His eyes were gazing at her hair. Her locks were waving around her face freely. A weak smile animated his lips.

"So pretty. Just like your Mama's."

He reached out and stroked a few strands that looped around his fingers. Lil Bit looked at her father's face, then at his ravaged and festering leg.

"Sorry, Papa."

She struck his leg with the barbed tips of her hair. The needle points went through his flesh from the top of his thigh down to his toes. She pushed her venom into his body. She could hear Vicente praying in Spanish. Gabriel shuddered then gritted his teeth as her toxins surged into his leg. She reached for his hand and held it tight. Closing her eyes, she focused on sending her venom down his leg. It was her first time spreading the neurotoxins without anger. She squeezed Gabriel's hand tighter.

Unhooking herself, she touched his leg. Gabriel's flesh was rock hard. She traced her finger along the skin that was still alive above his thigh, and the dark hardened mass below. She took the lamp away from Vicente and brought it closer to Gabriel's skin. She had to make sure the infection stayed frozen in place. No more pustules formed. The black webbed lines didn't spread. They had faded away.

He was alive.

Lil Bit touched her father's sweaty forehead. He was conscious, watching her the entire time. Staring at her hair. She pulled her tendrils back down inside her head. The bumps on her scalp were hot to the touch. But they felt good. So good.

***

Vicente helped Odetta lift Gabriel into the back of the chuck wagon. Odetta took the herd money and placed it underneath Gabriel.

"When we get to Nicodemus, I'll have my brothers go back with you to return this money for my husband. Tell your rancher that he's dead," said Odetta.

"Sí," Vicente said. Lil Bit could tell that he was afraid of Odetta. He spoke Spanish when he meant to speak English, and he stuttered a bit when Odetta spoke directly to him.

"I'll pay you for going with us," said Odetta.

Vicente couldn't keep eye contact with her. Her living hair was too much for him. He saw what she had done to the monstrous thieves. They didn't look human anymore. They'd stuffed the thieves in blankets and carried them out of town in the back of the wagon.

Odetta rode Bear and Lil Bit rode Daphne alongside her. Vicente followed Odetta's lead with her own horse tied and following the back of the wagon. Lil Bit's uncles were staggered a few miles ahead of them.

Lil Bit couldn't keep her eyes off her mother's profile. One of Odetta's locks lifted towards her.

"What you thinkin', babygirl?" said Odetta.

"I never wanted to forget what you looked like."

"All you gotta do is look in a mirror, chile. I be right there."

Lil Bit glanced back at Vicente and the wagon. He held his hand up and waved to her.

"He scared of you, Mama."

"I know."

"Can he live in Nicodemus with us?"

"If he want to."

"What's it like there, Mama?"

"Everything owned by Negroes. Hundreds of colored people living on they own land for the first time. And they free. That's what it's like."

The sky lightened for a new morning and Lil Bit helped Vicente dig up the graves. Her mother tended to Gabriel. The digging didn't take long. When Vicente was about to roll the last body into the ground, Lil Bit moved closer to the tall man's face. His mouth was parted open. She picked up a small stick and stuck it inside. Wiggling it around, she dragged out a thick forked tongue. There was a bulging dark gland under the tongue. It still dripped blood. She noticed something else.

"Be careful, chica."

"They have no teeth. No wonder they talked funny. See here? There's a hole under the tongue, that's where they spit. Their blood eats away the skin."

"Bury it," Odetta said.

Vicente trembled from the sound of Odetta's voice. He gently nudged Lil Bit aside and shoved the thing into the grave.

"What were those men, Mama?"

"I don't know."

317

"Do you think they are like us?" asked Lil Bit.

"Those things eat people," said Odetta.

"No, I mean... they have blood that injures people, and their mouths are made like lizards... and our hair can do things like their blood..." The words were not coming out the way she wanted them to.

"Let's go, Lil Bit. There might be more of them around."

Vicente grabbed the shovel and walked back to the wagon.

"Papa?" asked Lil Bit.

Odetta smiled.

"Weak, but he'll be fine. You saved his life."

They both climbed on their horses. Lil Bit eased Daphne a little closer to Bear. She thought about her book and the picture she saw of the woman with writhing scales for hair. If she and her mother existed, and those white men who ate human insides existed, maybe the book wasn't made up. She side-eyed her mother for a few minutes as the horses settled into a comfortable trot.

"Where do we come from, Mama? The *Medu*?"

"When my grandmother was alive, she called it the bright lands. A place called... hmmm, how she say it... *Rebu... Rebu Tehenu*. A dry hot place. Like Texas. Desert country. She said we were something to see."

"In Africa?"

"Yes, somewhere there."

In the rising sunlight Lil Bit stared at her mother's plump lips, her glossy black ropes of living hair, and her blue-black flashing eyes. Mama was nothing like that old mythology book said. Nothing like it all.

Odetta shook her tresses, and every lock spiraled out, dancing around her face and defying gravity.

"We *Medu*, babygirl. Be who you be."

Lil Bit threw back her hat. She let her scalp throb and pushed out. Every dark strand from her head tasted the morning air, never to be hidden again.

Never.

Art by Eric Orchard

LONE WOMEN
VICTOR LAVALLE

1914
Montana

Adelaide Henry and her steamer trunk had come a long way but still had much farther to go. They'd left the family farmhouse in Redondo behind, burned down to its foundations. They escaped on a San Francisco–bound steamer; a second ship from San Francisco to Seattle, then the locomotive inland. Now there were just two more days on Mr. Olsen's rattletrap wagon. Soon Adelaide, and that steamer trunk, would finally reach the small cabin. Their homestead. Their hideout. Their exile.

She checked the padlocks on the trunk every time the wagon hit a hard bump, which meant at least once an hour. When the Mudge family joined her on Olsen's wagon she checked the padlocks every ten minutes. The Mudges. A mother and four boys. The oldest looked to be seventeen and the youngest about six. The boys all wore blindfolds. At first Adelaide thought they were playing a game, but the blindfolds never came off. It was everything Adelaide could do to keep from lifting each one and peeking at their eyes. A mother and four blind boys headed for the wilds of Montana. Adelaide's anxieties about her own homesteading were put into perspective.

The Mudges huddled down in the wagon just like Adelaide. The winds out here were stronger than sea currents. At one point a gust got hold of Adelaide and actually lifted her to her feet. Nearly flung her out the wagon. Mrs. Mudge didn't move to help and the four boys couldn't see anything with the blindfolds. Mr. Olsen, up driving the wagon intently, hardly even turned back when he told her to be careful. If she'd actually fallen out she felt sure she'd be dead and then the Mudges and Mr. Olsen would have the Seward steam trunk sitting right there in the middle of the wagon. How long before curiosity got them to open it? Before they pried the padlocks apart? Adelaide couldn't help imagining the violence that would come next. A vision of the six year old with his stomach torn open – really just a memory of what her mother had suffered in the farmhouse – made Adelaide go tight.

They overnighted in a derelict hotel. One empty entranceway, one empty parlor, ten empty bedrooms. Adelaide had expected to find a few strips of cloth, a broken chair or two, but everything had all been sold, stolen, or withered away. Like fools, no one had brought lamps or matches in their travel bags. The supplies were sealed up tight in the boxes buried in Mr. Olsen's wagon. Late night hardly seemed like the time to scavenge their resources and besides they were all exhausted. The wagon had tossed and crashed the whole way and each of them, even the children, limped as they moved inside.

321

The darkness outside became worse indoors. Not even the stars in here to guide them. To Adelaide every room felt fathomless and she felt truly alone.

Suddenly it was too much. Adelaide fled out into the wind. Her only companion here in the wild country was that steamer trunk, and wasn't that funny? She reached the wagon and crouched behind it. The wagon, even when weighed down with hundreds of pounds of baggage, rattled as easily as an infant's toy.

She would have to go back inside, impossible to spend a night in the open. Still she didn't think she could go back in, couldn't sleep, without some sense of protection. She had no gun. She had brought something else, though.

Adelaide climbed up into the wagon and produced keys from the inner pocket of her heavy skirt. She unlocked two of the padlocks on her trunk then hesitated at the third.

"Know what happened at this hotel? Before the town shut up for good?"

Mr. Olsen appeared beside the wagon. She dropped her keys, they *thunked* on the floorboards. Her fingers clawed for them in the dark.

"Man named Vardner got hanged right on the front porch," Mr. Olsen said. "He rustled cattle and got caught. Thieving is serious business around here. Understand me?"

Adelaide looked up at him. "But I wasn't trying to..."

Mr. Olsen nodded though his eyes showed he wasn't listening. "You climb on down now. Get inside and get to sleep."

"I lost my keys," she said.

He gestured for her to move and she did.

"I'll find them in the morning. If you dropped them like you say."

Adelaide Henry walked inside the hotel, crossing the threshold where a man had been hanged. She crossed the parlor and climbed the stairs. She found the door to the Mudges room, closed, and patted along the wall until she found the next open door. Inside she unfurled a flannel blanket she'd kept in her travel bag. She folded the blanket over to double the nominal comfort.

In the morning Mr. Olsen rapped at her door lightly.

Once Adelaide rose and opened the door he stood there smiling. "Found 'em."

Her ring of three keys sat in his palm. She snatched them up. "I told you," she said.

He dipped his chin. "Never should have doubted you."

After she dressed, Mr. Olsen met her at the wagon with a bowl of beans and a wooden spoon. She ate quickly even though the beans were hot enough to scald. Mr. Olsen watched her.

"Out here you'll be earning your hunger every day."

"How long have you been awake?"

"Me?" he asked with feigned nonchalance. "Hours already. Had to let the horses out to graze. Had to find your keys. Then there's the Mudges. They're gone."

Adelaide stopped chewing. "Gone where?"

"Went ahead, my guess. Wagons come through most days. If there's space drivers'll always give a ride."

"To five people?"

"Does seem like a lot. But anyone would have sympathy for a mother and four blind children. They left all their things so I'm bound to bring it to them. After I get you to your claim I'll keep on."

Adelaide nodded, ate more beans, but tasted nothing. *The Mudges are gone.* She wanted to scramble over Mr. Olsen's shoulders and check her steamer trunk. *The Mudges are gone.*

A mother and four children.

She decided to believe that they'd gone ahead or even turned back, gone home. Either option was better than the third. She was able to maintain this fantasy until they struck camp and Mr. Olsen helped her back into the wagon. She almost didn't want to check the steamer trunk, but knew she must.

The third padlock had come off. She found all that remained of it: a portion of the curved shank. It had been stretched until it snapped.

And now the Mudges were gone.

She tested the steamer trunk and felt the familiar weight inside. Wherever it had gone, whatever it had done, it had returned. Mr. Olsen tried to make conversation on the second day of the journey, but Adelaide couldn't bring herself to speak.

When they passed through a small township Adelaide bought a replacement padlock.

***

The first Sunday after Adelaide took possession of her Montana cabin, she heard the snort of horses. She'd been working in the wicker rocker, stitching the holes that had developed in her gloves from digging up soft coal for the stove. Now she moved to the stove and began a fire. She brought down the teakettle and filled it with water from a jug. Tea for a neighbor, that was just polite. The nearest homesteader, a woman named Grace Price, had come to visit three days ago with her five-year-old boy, Stan. It had felt more like an inspection than a friendly chat. If Grace and Stan were back, then Adelaide must've passed the exam.

But when she went to answer the door she found two men standing there.

Two cowboys.

Each one rangy as fence wire, their cheeks and foreheads a brownish red from years of outdoor work. Their fingertips all stained brown. Both wore denim overalls and boots. The cuffs of the overalls were threadbare, the soles of the boots worn thin. The man at the door had a clean face and the one behind him, a little older, wore a beard. When she opened the door they removed their hats.

"We don't mean to surprise you," said the clean-faced cowboy. He smiled and his teeth were small, stained. The one behind him nodded gently. "But we heard you were out here all on your own."

Grace had been talking, it seemed.

"You make me sound like big news," Adelaide said, laughing..

The man with the beard gave a short laugh. "Ma'am, you are this week's headline."

The teakettle blew on the stove.

"You were sitting down for tea," said the younger man, hinting disappointment.

"I was expecting Grace and Stan," Adelaide said.

Adelaide stepped back inside to get the kettle off the stove. She shut the door on both men because her bed was right there, unmade. She didn't want them to see it. She set the kettle on a stove plate to cool. When she opened the door again the bearded man was already walking toward the horses.

"You're leaving?" Adelaide asked.

The younger man said, "We came to see if you were free."

The bearded man returned, leading not two horses but three. All of them saddled.

"We hoped." He paused. "*I* hope you'll come out for a ride."

Matteus Kirby – who insisted on being called Matthew, a proper U.S. name – took her out for a wonderful afternoon. His uncle, Finn, rode a few lengths behind the whole time. She'd thought of them as cowboys but the men worked on threshing crews. Matthew's uncle operated the straw-burning steam engine, and Matthew worked as a separator man.

In the next weeks Adelaide was visited by other men like Matthew and Finn. Word spread about the new "lone woman." Adelaide had come out to Montana for the seclusion, but her seclusion quickly ended. Most men asked her to come on a ride, bringing a saddled horse for her. They might take her to a ranch, where they lived and worked, and she'd spend the evening eating dinner and making conversation. She realized they were all just profoundly lonely, and grateful for her time. She enjoyed the time with them, too. They were often a better option than reading one of her novels all over again. Adelaide spent fewer evenings penned up inside her cabin, watching the locks rattle on her steamer trunk, listening to the wind howling outside the shack and something else howling within.

***

She enjoyed the company of nearly all the men, but Matthew was special. One evening he invited her to a dance nearby. She agreed to go because Finn was bringing Grace Price and Stan. It felt, in a way, like a grand family outing.

Because of the cold and a layer of newly fallen snow, the dance was held in a granary. The place was actually smaller than the home on the property, a two-story palace with four bedrooms, but the granary had been cleared out so it made a better dance floor. A corral sat on the property as well, with nine horses, and a large barn. Adelaide understood this family had done well. The husband and wife had each filed for a homestead so between them they'd proved up on 640 acres. Matthew joked that he could file for a plot alongside Adelaide's and they could amass a property that was just as impressive. Adelaide laughed along but she guessed Matthew was sincere.

They all wore their rough clothes for the ride. Adelaide and Grace kept their dresses for the dance in bags on the backs of their horses.

Musicians had been brought in to play;a woman on the piano and her husband on the fiddle, a guitarist came down from the mountains for the night, and there were rumors a man was on his way with a horn. They'd put cornmeal on the granary floor and by the time Adelaide, Grace, and the boys arrived people were dancing. Adelaide and Grace changed in the main house and returned to dance with their dates, while Stan ran off to bop around with the other kids. This dance would go all night. When the children got tired they'd sleep in the main house, girls on the second floor and boys on the first.

Adelaide shared many dances with Matthew. Sometimes she and Grace traded and Adelaide enjoyed herself with Matthew's soft-spoken uncle. She always addressed him as Mr. Kirby. He, in turn, only asked questions about "Mrs. Price."

But most of Adelaide's time was spent alongside Grace. No one could dance for that many hours. Every little while the men would go off to yap with other men and the women would be free to make conversation. Grace brought Adelaide around to meet all the women who'd come. These were her closest neighbors and almost all of them were "lone women," even if only on paper. Some, like Adelaide, had been lured out by Mattie T. Cramer's "Success of a 'Lone' Woman" — Adelaide was unsurprised to hear it had been reprinted in newspapers around the country — and the women now referred to its many exaggerations with mingled humor and chagrin.

It was in this way — with Grace leading her around like a protective older sister — that Adelaide came to shake hands with a very pale, sharp angled woman and immediately lost her breath.

"Mrs. Mudge?" Adelaide asked.

The woman, who'd only been paying the faintest attention during the greeting, tensed for an instant. No one else would have noticed, but Adelaide held the woman's hand, and for that instant, the grip tightened like a bite.

"This is Rose Morrison," Grace corrected.

The woman's grip loosened then her hand fell. She watched Adelaide carefully but turned on a tight smile. "That's right. Rose Morrison."

"She's even newer to the territory than you."

Adelaide nodded. "Well then, welcome to Montana."

"Aren't you kind," said Mrs. Morrison.

No doubt about it though, this was Mrs. Mudge.

Why do this? Why pretend to be someone else? Did it matter? Adelaide had come out here to keep her secret, locked up tightly in that steamer trunk, so maybe Mrs. Mudge had her reasons, too. Adelaide told herself to share a pleasant farewell and turn away. Say no more. But she couldn't stop herself.

"You left those boys all alone?" Adelaide asked. "How will they manage?"

Grace held Adelaide by the elbow, a grip to snap wood beams. "Mrs. Morrison is a widow. She and her husband never had children."

Now Adelaide laughed. Actually laughed at what Grace said. Grace let her arm go. Adelaide realized how cruel, or insane, she must look. Mrs. Mudge watched in silence.

"I must have been thinking of someone else entirely," Adelaide said.

This seemed to calm Grace, who nodded awkwardly.

Mrs. Mudge said, "That's quite all right."

"I mean really," Adelaide said. "I must have been *blind*."

Mrs. Mudge, or Morrison, gave a tight-lipped glare then walked off.

***

Adelaide, like all the other women who stayed the night, was invited to sleep in the main house. The bedrooms filled fast so Adelaide and Grace slept in chairs in the parlor.

In the morning Matthew Kirby woke Adelaide up. He leaned over her. She reached out and touched his face and he seemed to glow under the tenderness. While dancing, he'd told her he was all of 23. She was 31. When he helped her up, led her out of the house, she felt relieved he hadn't tried to kiss her last night. She wondered if he, too, understood that they were never going to go steady. Was it the age difference? Partly. But even more, there was a way he seemed so naïve, or maybe just cut off from some of the world's ugliness. He'd seen enough hard times; she didn't doubt that. He had a life of labor to look forward to, and hardly any money, more than likely. But all night she'd been trying to imagine the moment when she would bring him to her home and lead him to the steamer trunk, take off the padlocks, and show him the thing inside. He was too straightforward, too rational a man to bend in the face of something so impossible. He would break or he'd break it, and for Adelaide Henry neither outcome would do.

Now, in the morning light, Matthew led her back to the granary, already swept clean. Men were hauling equipment back inside. Grace and Stan were on their horse and Finn, looking still half asleep, led it by the reins. Matthew brought Adelaide to her horse and helped her up. He pulled the reins of her horse and led it forward.

They'd gone a quarter mile before Adelaide realized Matthew and Finn weren't leading them to the other two horses.

"Horses gone missing," Matthew said when she asked. The words came out weary and she realized he and his uncle must've been up hours already searching.

"Well, you're not going to walk our horses all the way back, are you?"

"Weren't sure how you'd feel about riding with me."

"I don't want to see you drop dead from exhaustion, Matthew."

He stopped and looked at his uncle, who had a few words with Grace.

"Why didn't you just say so? Of course it's all right, Finn!"

The men climbed up and got the horses trotting.

"What happened?" Adelaide asked.

Matthew grunted as they rode. He remained quiet for another mile.

"Kids," he finally said.

"Kids what?" Adelaide asked.

"Four horses gone missing this morning," Matthew explained. "Both of ours and two from the family who owns this property. Folks said they saw four boys riding off real early."

"Four boys," Adelaide repeated.

Adelaide had her hand around Matthew's middle and she squeezed so tightly he coughed with surprise.

***

When Matthew reached her home he insisted on standing at the threshold of her shack and inspecting the interior. Adelaide told him what she knew about Mrs. Mudge and her boys, but Matthew had a hard time believing both that Mrs. Morrison was really Mrs. Mudge and that four blind boys could steal four horses. Though he wasn't convinced, Adelaide's story left him twitchy and protective. Adelaide didn't argue when he asked to look inside her place. She invited him in. He left his rifle out on the horse.

Adelaide offered him tea, but he didn't say yes or no. She realized, in that moment, that he wanted to stay. And she, to her own surprise, wanted him there. She doubted either of them felt true passion. Not love, but affection. And caution.

It occurred to Adelaide that she was the only person, besides Mr. Olsen, who could testify that Mrs. Mudge had four boys. And if these people stole horses, in a place where stealing livestock was a hanging offense, what might they do to silence a witness?

The ride back to Adelaide's had taken them the whole day Very soon it would be that fathomless Montana night. Matthew looked out one window. "I guess I can make it to the ranch if I leave right now," he said.

Wasn't company a fine reason to keep a man around? Even just for tonight? If she was a different woman she might even have wanted him close for the promise of protection, but she had her own means right here in the room, in that steamer trunk. Compared to that, Matthew could only offer closeness, a night of warmth. But she reminded herself how long it had been since she'd been held.

"Go get your things," she said. "I'll make us something to eat."

Matthew tried not to smile but couldn't help himself. His chest rose and fell with enthusiasm. Just then he seemed even younger than 23.

"You're sure?" he asked.

"Don't make a woman offer twice."

***

Matthew secured his horse while Adelaide went down to the root cellar for potatoes and beans and eggs that Grace had given her. Adelaide felt more ashamed of surviving on Grace's charity than she did about the very young man sitting in her cabin. When the winter passed — presuming she made it through the first winter — she would have to become self-sufficient.

"What will you do first?" Matthew asked.

It didn't sound like a question, more like a quiz. To Matthew and Finn and Grace Adelaide remained a newcomer, a tenderfoot, a pilgrim. Matthew's tone played like Grace's when she'd first visited with Stan. He'd probably asked what she planned to do only so he could overwhelm her with advice about what she should do. But Adelaide had been reading her secondhand almanac and planning quite seriously.

"I'm not required to plow up a whole forty acres when I plant for my first year, so I'm going to have just enough land broken for a garden," she said. "That way I'm not setting myself up for the whole thing to fail in the first year. Especially if there isn't much rain."

"You'll hire a man to break the land?" Matthew asked, as if insulted.

"I would pay a man to do it even if I knew him very well," she said.

Matthew blushed and looked down at his plate. He cut into a small potato.

"I've got a few vegetable seeds I've ordered, but I'll make sugar beets at least half the garden."

Matthew raised his eyebrows, a piece of potato held high on his fork. "They'll grow even if there's drought. That's a smart choice, Mrs. Henry."

Now that was the tone she wanted to hear. Esteem. Respect.

"You'll call me Adelaide if you're here this late." Then she set down her utensils and touched the top of her head and, for the first time in his presence, she let down her hair.

Matthew set down his fork, the potato uneaten. "Adelaide," he said.

They were awkward together. She stood taller than him, and heavier as well. But though Matthew was small and slim, the man was strong. He climbed over her with a playful grin and when they wrestled each other flat neither of them held back. He touched her arms and found the small scars that ran along both forearms. More than a dozen little divots in the flesh of each one. He almost asked the question – *where did you get these?* – but was smart enough to read the expression on her half closed eyes. This wasn't the time for telling histories. This wasn't the time for words.

Afterwards she put the kettle on, and he brought her tea in bed. She had neither cream nor sugar, and the tea was bitter, but his smile was kind. *I could get used to this*, she thought.

***

Adelaide opened her eyes. She wore nothing and the covers were still drawn up around her. Someone was screaming somewhere, the howls faint and muffled. For a moment, she wasn't sure where she could be – in Eagle Pass, Montana, or back home in Redondo.

Her home had gone madhouse. The great chair lay on its side and the top half of the wicker rocker was shredded, serrated, as if it had been bitten off. Her books were little more than shreds of paper scattered on the furniture like ash. The pans on the walls had all come down. Matthew's blood spread on the floor and across the walls and windows.

The steamer trunk sat open and empty.

How had Adelaide slept through all this? When had the world gone so wrong? Her head ached. Outside it was still nighttime. The Montana wind howled as it crept up the side of her cabin and looped under the roof then crashed down to chill the room.

And there, in the corner, she saw it. It was out of the steamer trunk, its back to her, the mighty body pressed against the cabin wall. Great folds of leathery skin hung from the bottom of its arms. And just below those folds were a pair of bare feet. Matthew Kirby's feet. Listlessly kicking. Not the sign of someone fighting, but of someone fading out. This thing, Adelaide Henry's secret burden, the weight she'd been carrying her whole life was consuming him.

Adelaide felt, very quickly, the utter exhaustion of her life. Almost all of her 31 years had been spent like this. Catching up, cleaning up, covering up. If she couldn't save her own mother and father, what did it matter if she let a man she hardly knew die?

But this was only a moment of weariness. She wouldn't abandon Matthew.

She reached for the body, the thing, she knew so terribly well.

Her sister.

Its skin wasn't really skin, but thousands and thousands of tiny gray scales, linked so tightly they became a natural armor. Impervious to blades and bullets, a fact her father and mother had tested that awful, final night. The scales felt like sandpaper to the touch, but rougher, so even grappling with Adelaide's sister could make a person, any person, bleed.

Except Adelaide.

Ever since she was a child Adelaide could grip her sister's scales and come away unscathed. Even their mother hadn't been so lucky. Breastfeeding had been a short-lived experiment. Adelaide was sturdy enough to yoke the creature, the only living thing in the world who could restrain it. Their father once said that nature had designed Adelaide, their surprise second child, for this righteous purpose, to be a kind of living leash.

Now she flung back the covers and went after her sister as a veteran rodeo rider might approach a bull. Except Adelaide didn't need the aid of a flank strap to make her sister buck and jump. Adelaide squeezed the throat with one arm and pulled backward with all her weight. Her father had often blessed the fact that Adelaide had been born so strong, wide from the shoulders to the hips. One more proof, to her parents, as to her purpose. She had the mass to peel her sister away from Matthew Kirby and to twist the massive head.

Her sister's legs were short and thin, a trait they both shared, so she buckled when Adelaide pressed all her body weight down. But with the head turned there were the teeth to contend with. The teeth. When Adelaide was young there had been so many times when she let her arm stray too high, too close to her sister's maw. Those dimpled scars on Adelaide's forearms were the proof of all her practice.

With her sister turned away from Matthew, Adelaide climbed higher onto her sister's back. It was like scaling a pterodactyl. Adelaide's sister crashed forward, onto her softer belly, cracking some of the floorboards beneath them. But now the head was flush against the ground and this was the trick Adelaide had figured long ago. Monstrous or not, her sister's jaw still worked like any human being's, biting was done by movement of the lower jaw, not the upper. If the lower jaw was pressed to the ground and 180 pounds of Adelaide lay against the back of the head, well, that head wasn't coming up. She'd learned this trick after watching alligator wrestlers in a traveling show.

He sister sputtered and snorted but Adelaide held her down.

Adelaide looked back to Matthew. Hard to tell, in the darkness, if he'd lost any limbs. She heard him choking and coughing so she knew he still had a head. Better than how she'd found her mother.

"Can you hear me?" she asked him between heaving breaths.

More coughing. Was he nodding or suffering a spasm?

"How did Elizabeth get out?" Adelaide asked. "Did she break the padlocks?"

Her sister hissed and belched, and through her clenched teeth she brought up a spray of blood that soaked the floor.

Matthew's blood.

Adelaide had worked so hard to get her sister into the steamer trunk back at the farmhouse. If she'd done it once in Redondo then she could do it again now. She wrestled her sister forward, pushing Elizabeth toward the trunk while keeping one hand against the back of the head so the jaws wouldn't lift from the floor.

And now her sister, seeing the trunk, gave a choked wail. It looked like an open casket. Elizabeth would be buried alive again. This was the worst part for Adelaide. The physical strain was terrible, of course, but this noise felt worse. A kind of sobbing that might last for hours once Elizabeth got locked back in.

When Adelaide was very young she had trouble sleeping because her parents kept her sister on a short chain in the barn behind their farmhouse. Her sister might wail throughout the night or she might simply whimper and go to sleep right away. There was no predicting it. Her father had learned to sleep through the worst of the bawling and her mother would sit up all night reading the Bible, not for solace but to remind herself that demons had always roamed the world. And Adelaide would sit at her bedroom window looking out at the barn. By the time she was seven she understood that when her parents were gone responsibility for Elizabeth would fall to her. It was like knowing a drop off a cliff was in the future but never being sure of where or when it would come.

Matthew Kirby fell forward at the waist like a child still learning to sit upright. Adelaide couldn't look back at him right then; she and her sister were at the trunk and this was the trickiest part. Adelaide reached for one of her sister's arms and pulled it backward until her sister shivered and gulped with pain. Now Adelaide sang, trying to keep her voice gentle even though she huffed from the exertion.

"*Your mother wants you to sleep. Your father wants you to sleep.*"

Elizabeth whimpered, the vigor seeped out of her frame. Adelaide's sister had spent most of her 40 years in chains, stuffed into root cellars, locked inside a barn. She was used to it. Conditioned. Perhaps she didn't even realize there was any such thing as freedom. It was the captivity, at her family's hands, that was normal, and breaking loose as rare as a good dream.

"*Your sister wants you to sleep, to sleep. Now it's time to sleep.*"

Elizabeth climbed inside. As Adelaide closed the lid they looked into each other's eyes. Both sisters held back tears.

Adelaide closed the lid and found all three padlocks on the ground. She held them up for inspection. They weren't broken open.

They'd been unlocked.

Her three keys no longer hung on a nail by the stove but were on the ground, right here, by the trunk.

"You opened this," Adelaide said quietly.

When she looked back Matthew was propped against the overturned great chair. He held his rifle at his waist — the rifle she thought he'd left outside. The barrel was aimed at her.

"Move aside," Matthew said, though his voice was weak. "And I'll kill it."

Adelaide slipped the padlocks back into their slots. Inside the trunk her sister sniffled. "You opened this," Adelaide repeated.

"Only thing in here that's all locked up," he said, the rifle barrel quivering with the weight. He held the rifle in his left arm but he was right handed. His right arm was tucked against his side, the sleeve of his shirt sagged loosely up by the shoulder. But then Adelaide realized that he was just as naked as she, and the sagging fabric was actually his skin practically falling off the bone.

"How did I sleep through all this?"

He stayed quiet a little while but finally said, "Laudanum. In your tea." Another pause. "I just wanted to see what was inside the trunk."

"You wanted to see what you could take."

He shook his head stiffly. "Call me a thief, but you've got a devil in your home."

Adelaide wasn't even angry with him. Not truly. Every man and woman out here, every child and even every beast, was well acquainted with desperation. He'd thought to pilfer her treasure but found only her curse hiding in there.

"You're bleeding," she said. "Let me help you so you don't die."

The rifle dipped down, as if it was nodding off and not him, but rose once more.

"Will it get out again?" he asked.

"Not if you don't steal my keys again."

Adelaide brought down a lamp near the stove and lit it. She scanned his right arm, his head and back. "I've seen her do worse," Adelaide said.

She dressed his wounds and set him on her bed to sleep the last of the night away. As she cleaned the cabin she felt strangely relieved. She didn't know what Matthew would do with what he'd seen tonight. Spread the news around his camp and be dismissed as a drunk? Wrangle up his uncle and try to kill her sister? Matthew would have to bring a lot of cowboys if he hoped to hurt Elizabeth. She doubted there were enough in all of Montana.

While he lay in the bed, eyelids half closed and eyes swimming, Adelaide spoke.

"The first time I saw my sister I was two years old. I don't remember it but my mother told me. I snuck out of the farmhouse and wandered into the barn. I heard all this noise. She was inside tearing apart a chicken. My mother finally realized I was gone and ran out to the barn, but she said she found me right there on my sister's back, yanking her ears. And Elizabeth was laughing. Or, at least, she hadn't killed me. I started sneaking out there all the time."

Adelaide felt good. She'd never spoken of her sister to any stranger. Now, for once, she told it all. Was it silly to find comfort, relief, in sharing? Her family had taught her to barricade herself from the rest of the world. For the safety of all sides it was better to be silent, live in solitude. She'd accepted this for decades. If she needed to just *speak* of it all for one night – with a young man who was practically delirious – then surely she'd earned the right. Matthew babbled in a hazy sleep and Adelaide gave this woozy priest her confession.

***

Matthew Kirby recuperated in her cabin for a week. When he left, Adelaide helped him stow his rifle and gear. She even filled his pack with food and water. They spoke only in willful pleasantries. What more was there to say? As he turned his horse Adelaide felt sure she'd never see that man again.

After he was long gone, Adelaide busied herself with the business of survival. She put on her boots and heavy coat and brought two buckets to the nearest coulee and filled them both with snow. They were still far from a true Montana winter. The fact that she could march to the coulee and back on foot served as proof.

Once back with the snow she took stock of her soft coal. The supply was nearly exhausted.. She needed wood. When the temperature dropped lower, a few handfuls of coal in the stove wouldn't keep her alive. Maybe Grace knew a place to find firewood.

Adelaide washed the bed sheets that had collected Matthew's blood. Between the washing and collecting snow, the short day was done.

In the night she felt a new cold, ten degrees chillier at least. Adelaide wondered if her sister felt the cold, if she was just as vulnerable – in that way, at least. She remembered looking down into that face, seeing them both holding back tears. Weren't their eyes the same shade and shape?

Adelaide flipped back her covers and knelt before the steamer trunk. She wore the padlock keys around her neck now, looped through a length of string. She undid the locks and lifted the lid. Her sister slept inside.

Adelaide stepped back and returned to bed. She watched the trunk and waited. Her sister stirred when a burst of cold air came down under the roof and scoured the cabin. The grey, scaled skin rippled with an electric thrill. A yelp of surprise, even fear. Maybe her sister thought it was Matthew Kirby, scavenging again, but this time she held herself in check. It was easier to stay inside the trunk than be disciplined by Adelaide again.

Adelaide watched her sister with a farmer's patience. In all her life she'd never tried to let her sister *out*.

"Elizabeth," Adelaide whispered. She had no idea what she should say.

That first night Elizabeth lifted her head out of the trunk, but nothing more. She watched Adelaide closely. Adelaide returned the gaze. Neither sister slept. Both shivered from the Montana cold. They needed that wood, no question.

At dawn Adelaide pulled left the trunk open, the padlocks in a pile on the floor. She dressed and set out for Grace Price's home. She had no horse. She'd be going on foot.

***

After walking an hour Adelaide felt she might have to crawl. The wind just wouldn't let her keep her balance. She stopped to adjust her wool scarf, cover her mouth and nose. She unwrapped it and before she could loop the wool back around her face the wind pulled it away like a strong-arm robbery. She watched as the green scarf rose into the sky. The wind just took it. She started again but she looked west now and then to see the scarf fluttering to the earth and then lifting again, off into the long distances.

Another hour and it hardly seemed like she'd left her cabin behind. So tough to judge scale and distance out here. Did she have two more miles to go or ten? She'd brought water and pilot bread, what her father would've dismissed as "dog biscuits." She crouched down to eat and drink so the wind wouldn't steal her meal too.

By the third hour she felt nearly delirious. The cold turned her exposed face and neck raw. She couldn't feel her nose or her lips. She should've invested in a horse as soon as she'd arrived. But there were always people coming by with one for her to ride. The folly of this march was evident. Walking 15 miles to get firewood? Why not just wait until Grace came by for her next visit? Was it really that she'd just wanted to get out of that cabin, leave behind the conflicted feelings now stirring for her sister? What a silly reason to risk one's life.

This line of thinking turned into a kind of long-form harangue. She had done so many things wrong, so many times, and in so many ways. Simply showing up in Montana being one of the biggest. But there was also that night when her parents called to her from their bedroom. Had she known what they were going to do when she saw them lead Elizabeth into the farmhouse, both her parents carrying pistols? If they'd succeeded wouldn't it have meant that, finally, at 31, Adelaide would've been free? Is that why, when they began to scream Adelaide's name, she didn't come running right away? Her deepest secret, her worst sin, was that she'd stayed outside the farmhouse praying that her parents would succeed. Then when it became clear they were being mutilated, destroyed, consumed, she'd decided not to save them because, in a sense, they would now be released. It had almost seemed like loving kindness to finally let her mother and father go, with all their guilt and self-blame.

She'd stood by as her parents tried to kill her sister.

She'd abandoned her parents to suffer violent deaths.

There it was. The truth of it. There it was. Three hours on her feet and she went to her knees in the snow. For all this she could never be forgiven.

For the first time since she'd arrived in Montana the winds died down until the world went quiet. The snow under Adelaide's knees squeaked as she looked backward to her cabin, too far off to see anymore. Sunlight reflected off the snow and burned the horizon.

If she fell here, in all this nowhere, who would find Elizabeth? What might they do to her when they did?

Adelaide got back to her feet.

***

She walked another four hours before she reached Grace Price's place.

There were two small cabins, side by side, both 10x10. An outhouse with two stalls right behind that. Nearby, a horse shed with a corral. No horses. What if Grace had gone off for a visit? What if, right now, she and Stan were at Adelaide's place?

By now Adelaide had developed a limp in her right leg. Her foot hurt badly and she felt nothing but a constant burning on her cheeks and forehead. Burning was better than numbness. Numbness meant death.

Adelaide had finished her water and pilot bread two hours before. She hoped to find Grace and Stan sitting down for dinner. She fantasized about the meal. Maybe they'd even have meat. She hadn't eaten any since coming to Montana.

Adelaide did find Grace at home. Curled up on the floor of one cabin. Stained with blood.

"Oh, Grace!" Adelaide shouted as she stumbled into the shack.

Grace Price had fallen into a kind of trance, breathing faintly and fast. Adelaide's voice didn't even register. It was only once Adelaide got down and touched Grace's head that the sharp breaths ceased. The eyes fluttered but finally focused. She looked at Adelaide. Her face had gone pale with loss of blood; it was whiter than the lace curtains on Adelaide's windows.

"What did she do?" Adelaide said. Had this all been some trick on Elizabeth's part? Lull Adelaide into loving kindness just so she could slip out and attack others? Grace's blood spread across the cabin floor just as Matthew's had done.

"Stanley," Grace whispered. "Find him for me."

Adelaide looked around the cabin. The oven had been tipped over. Pots and pans tossed everywhere. There were two beds, one for a child and one for an adult, both flipped over. Two of the cabin's windows were shattered, fragments of glass sprinkled inside the cabin.

"She broke in," Adelaide said.

"Get Stanley," Grace said. "They threw him in the root cellar."

Grace had her right hand pulled tightly against her belly. Her blouse had soaked up so much blood. Adelaide, in shock, crawled on the floor and across the threshold. Only as she stood up outside did she look back to Grace.

"*They?*"

But Grace ignored her. Back to the short, sharp breathing. Back to that meditative state.

Adelaide scrambled to the root cellar. When she opened the door she saw a pair of small feet there at the bottom of the short stairway, the rest of the body lost in the shadows.

"Stan," Adelaide said as she came down.

His feet, bare and nearly blue, shook at the sound of her voice. From the darkness came a cry, shrill and terrified.

"It's Adelaide. It's Adelaide."

When she reached him she found his hands tied behind his back and a pillowcase thrown over his head. He'd thrown up inside it. She wiped at his face with the hem of her dress. He lay against Adelaide.

"That boy took my shoes," he said quietly.

***

"Mudges."

Grace said the name as if it was a poison.

It was fully nighttime now. When Adelaide brought Stan back into the cabin Grace wept with relief. The sight of her son gave her strength. She couldn't very well lie there and let her son witness it. To protect him she composed herself. She let Adelaide help her up and dress her wound.

"Shot me right through my hand," Grace said.

Grace's limp right hand lay in Adelaide's lap. The loss of blood had been bad but all the broken bones would be worse in the long term. The hand was bloated and almost purple. Adelaide tore apart a pillowcase and used the strips to wrap the palm. Stan sat next to his mother, his face pressed against her left shoulder.

"Why would they shoot you in the hand of all places?" Adelaide asked.

"He meant to get me in the head, I think," Grace said. "But the shooter was a damn six-year-old."

Elizabeth hadn't done all this. Was it wrong to feel relief?

"I'm surprised a blind boy could even hit you in the hand."

Stan pulled away from his mother. "Those boys can't see?"

"They found my horses sure enough," Grace said. "That woman came knocking at my door like she was just over for a visit. Meanwhile her children were in the corral."

Adelaide stayed and cooked for them, cleaned up, tended to the property with Stan as her helper and, just as often, her teacher. Stan explained, as best he could, why there were two cabins side by side. "Mother Price" had come to the territories with Grace and Stan. Grace and Stan lived in one cabin while Mother Price had her own. One afternoon Adelaide asked where Mother Price was now. Had she gone back home to Washington?

"She's behind the corral," Stan said. And that was all.

Mrs. Glover rode over on the second day. Her regular visit turned into a rescue operation. Mrs. Glover's property lay 10 miles west, and as soon as she was apprised of the situation she rode off again. By midday she returned with reinforcements. Six more lone women. Adelaide had seen some of these women at the dance but other faces were new. They cooked and cleaned and made repairs around Grace's home.

On the third day Mrs. Glover pulled Adelaide aside. "Grace has asked me to lend you my gelding. But come next week you and I will ride into Sumatra and file for a loan so you can purchase your own. And we might as well get your equipment ordered then. If you wait until the spring you won't get it soon enough."

Mrs. Glover said all this casually, but Adelaide felt nearly crushed by the kindness. By the care into which she'd stumbled here among the lone women. She accepted the gelding gratefully and rode back to her cabin. She tied the horse up and when she went inside she crouched by the steamer trunk.

"Come out, Elizabeth. You don't have to stay in there anymore."

It took Elizabeth half the night to accept the invitation. By then Adelaide had fallen asleep in the great chair. She woke after midnight when she felt pressure on her thighs. Her sister was sprawled across the cabin floor, her enormous head cradled in Adelaide's lap.

***

Adelaide became quite used to her sister spread out across the floor. Elizabeth liked to lie on her back and scritch herself side to side, grinding her scales against the wooden floorboards. The floor already showed scuffmarks. Letting her sister out was going to lead to more repairs. The wicker rocking chair was all but dust by now. Elizabeth liked to clamp her teeth down on it then thrash her head like she was bringing the chair down for a kill.

Funny how quickly this kind of thing became normal, or at least typical. Adelaide now let Elizabeth out night and day as long as they were alone. But where would it end? That was the question. Sooner or later her sister would want to go outside.

Adelaide was worrying over this point as she ate dinner. She'd tried giving her sister scraps from her plate, but root vegetables made Elizabeth vomit and she sniffed disdainfully at beans.

Adelaide was halfway through *The Tenant of Windfell Hall* for the second time. As she sat in the great chair with the book in her lap she watched her sister creep over to the spot on the floor where Matthew Kirby had almost lost his life. Where his blood still stained the boards. Elizabeth opened her mouth, unfurled her slick, gray tongue and lapped at the spot like a cat at milk. The tongue scratched on the boards again and Elizabeth purred so warmly it sounded sensual.

Looking away from her sister was what led Adelaide to glance out the nearest window. The lace curtains were closed but Adelaide could clearly make out one of the Mudge boys standing right there on the other side. She hadn't heard anything. Just like that he appeared. Her lamp had nearly died out so she sat in shadows.

The Mudge boy went up on his toes.

No bandana over the eyes.

"Looks empty," the boy said.

His mother's voice hissed back. "Then why is there a gelding out front?"

Adelaide stayed in her seat. Elizabeth remained on the floor, lapping lazily.

Then a loud knock. "Mrs. Henry, please open your door."

Elizabeth stirred. Snorting softly and opening one eye. She looked up at her sister.

"Should I call you Mudge or Morrison?"

As soon as Adelaide spoke, sounding tense, Elizabeth lifted her head, alert.

"You know my name," Mrs. Mudge said. "Let me show you my pistol."

Elizabeth rose up on all fours. Her great, gray back stiffened. Adelaide stood and Elizabeth circled her legs protectively.

"I see her!" shouted the youngest. He stood at another window, high up, riding on the eldest brother's shoulders. They were treating this like a game.

"I think she's got a dog," the six-year-old added. "I want it."

"What happened to the blindfolds?" Adelaide shouted to Mrs. Mudge.

"Tell me what you remember about my boys? Height? Hair color? Accents? Or just a couple of blindfolds?" Mrs. Mudge laughed with satisfaction.

Now a new sound. Rain splashing the windows.

Not rain.

The Mudge boys had all opened their trousers. They were peeing on Adelaide's windows. The youngest, the six-year-old, had come down off his brother's shoulders. Adelaide couldn't see him but she heard him shout.

"I'm making on her wall!"

This is our house, Adelaide thought. *Those boys are defiling our* home.

"If you were anyone else we would've just gone off with your horse," Mrs. Mudge said. "But you and that big Mr. Olsen were privy to some details I prefer to keep private. We already had a talk with him."

Elizabeth watched the front door with a slavering intensity. Her lower jaw hung open, saliva dribbled down onto the floor. Her teeth gleamed whiter than a full moon, each one sharper than any blade. Adelaide grabbed her sister by the back of the neck and led her toward the front door.

"You boys will be sure to bury this one deep in the snow, you hear? Like the wagon driver."

The boys shouted back as one as they buttoned their slacks. "Yes, ma'am!"

Adelaide opened the front door to find Mrs. Mudge wearing a grin. But then Mrs. Mudge saw Elizabeth.

"Oh my," she said.

Elizabeth leapt out and tore off Mrs. Mudge's left arm.

All four boys scrambled around the cabin to find Elizabeth crouching over their mother, a beast guarding its kill.

In that instant Adelaide saw them as they truly were. Four boys. 17, 16, 10, and 6. Blood ran from their mother's shoulder like oil erupting from a well..

Mrs. Mudge panted. Her eyes swam wild in their sockets. Her lips moved but she addressed no one. The two youngest couldn't look away from their mother. They didn't cry or scream. But the older boys recovered more quickly. And what did they do?

They ran.

Left their two young brothers there. Sprinted to where the Mudges had tied up two horses. The two youngest only looked to the eldest brother when he was already on his horse.

"Edward!" they shouted.

Edward rode away.

The second oldest followed. They rode north and in seconds disappeared into the cavernous gloom of Montana night. The rumble of the horse's hooves was all that remained.

Elizabeth barked once. She rose onto her legs – hard not to think of them as hind legs – and spread her arms. The loose skin under there expanded like sails being let out. That unstoppable Montana wind gathered in Elizabeth's loose skin and when she snapped her arms down she shot up, into the sky.

Elizabeth Henry took flight.

Adelaide watched with as much shock as the two little Mudge boys. She hadn't know her sister could fly.

Elizabeth's barking echoed. It came from farther north. Another bark then a horse whined and snorted as it went down somewhere out there. A young man's voice called out once – *Edward!* – but was quickly silenced. Only one horse galloping now. There were two pistol shots. Then silence.

Adelaide came back to herself. She'd been so busy listening to the darkness that she'd stopped seeing what lay in front of her. Mrs. Mudge. The body not yet cold, but the soul already gone.

The remaining Mudge boys had split. They'd mounted Mrs. Barlow's gelding together. Adelaide watched them ride to her. The 10-year-old held the reins. His younger brother in front. They stopped at Adelaide's door. The boys looked at their mother then back to Adelaide. The 10-year-old's eyes showed bright with rage, but it was the gaze of the 6-year old that chilled Adelaide. He watched her with a dispassionate eye, colder than a Montana winter.

"Mudges never forget," the 6-year-old said.

His brother gave the gelding a kick and the two boys stole off on Mrs. Barlow's horse.

***

First winter was the hardest test for any homesteader. First spring counted as the hardest after that. Eventually summer and fall would challenge the homesteader, too. And if you survived the first year, then the second loomed. After the third the land was legally yours. Many homesteaders, once they owned the property outright, returned to their home state and sold the land for profit. Others managed their resources and stuck around.

Adelaide and Elizabeth emerged from that first winter to find that by May the land had thawed back to its raw grace. They'd almost forgotten what the world looked like without its shroud of snow. Adelaide took Mrs. Barlow – Violette, as Adelaide called her now – up on the offer of help to secure a bank loan, and used some of the money to buy a gelding that Adelaide named Redondo.

A plow and harrow had been the next. Adelaide picked up an ax and hoe, rake and flail. She bought a four-burner stove with an oven so she could cook larger meals. She bought a rifle. She repaid Mrs. Barlow for the gelding the Mudge boys took. With the start of spring Adelaide planned to hire a man to come out and build a small barn but Grace and the other women built one for her. It rained nearly every day so this was soggy work.

None of the women would let Adelaide do much because she was eight months pregnant. She'd been wrong, thinking she'd never see Matthew Kirby again. She wondered whether the child would have his face, his hair, his shy smile.

Elizabeth stayed hidden in the root cellar when the barn was built. She never slept inside the trunk again. Adelaide used it to hold the baby clothes she'd sewn.

Grace and Stan were last to leave after the barn was complete.

"How're you going to break the soil up with Redondo?" Grace asked. Stan, now six, held the reins of their horse and snuck bits of beet into its mouth.

"I'm going to get the plow on him," Adelaide said. "Then after we're done I'll use the harrow."

Adelaide tried to sound confident but at eight months pregnant she didn't feel like much more than dead weight.

"I think you could guide the plow, even now," Grace agreed. "But you can't control your horse and slip that heavy thing on him. Let us stay."

Stan pulled at the reins and the horse tugged back. The boy stumbled and dropped the beets in the dirt. He bent quick to snatch them, looking to his mother with worry. Grace must've warned him against this, for her own reasons, but now the boy brought himself within inches of the horse's hooves. He stood exactly where Mrs. Mudge's body had bled out..

"Be careful there, Stan!" Adelaide said quickly.

Grace turned fast and swatted her son, and he fell backward onto his ass. The horse was a good one; it stayed calm. Stan held his head and cried out, overplaying his pain.

"That's what you have to look forward to, Adelaide." Grace smiled. "Lots of theater."

Adelaide touched Grace's shoulder gently. "I appreciate your offer. Ride over on Wednesday. I'll let you know if I need help."

Grace agreed with a grunt and helped Stan onto the horse. Grace's hand never had healed properly and she had enough trouble tending to her own land because of it. Adelaide didn't want to add to Grace's burden even if she had no idea how she'd manage plowing on her own.

Adelaide let her sister out of the root cellar when Grace and Stan were blotted out by the distance. For dinner Adelaide made rabbit, mountain cottontail. Elizabeth had turned out to be a talented hunter.

In the morning Adelaide woke to the sound of her barn doors rattling open. By this point in her pregnancy she couldn't sleep deeply and her mind felt fuzzier than a mossy stone. She was too tired, too dazed, to act immediately. Instead she listened to the sound of something heavy being dragged from the barn. She wondered if the Mudge boys were back – *Mudges never forget* – stealing her equipment.

She sat up with some trouble. Elizabeth wasn't inside. Maybe off hunting, patrolling the sky. Adelaide retrieved her rifle and looked out a window. She laughed at what she saw.

Elizabeth on all fours in the dirt and growling with intent. She had pulled the plow out of the barn and slipped her head through the harness.

Adelaide hadn't even eaten breakfast yet, but these days she had a hard time keeping anything down. It was a sunny morning. A Montana homesteader should always take advantage of a morning without rain. Adelaide stepped back in for her coat and scarf and hat. She set down the rifle. She walked out to the plow. Her belly pressed against the high bar between the handles. Elizabeth tested the harness with a pull.

"I'm ready, Elizabeth!" Adelaide shouted.

The Henry sisters got to work.

Art by GMB Chomichuk

THE DANCE OF THE WHITE DEMONS

SABRINA VOURVOULIAS

1524
Guatemala

I dream in shades of green. The dusty hue of swallow herb; the new growth of little hand flower; the deep forest shade of cat's claw. Plants are my calling and, as in waking life, they sprawl across boundaries.

The old woman dreams of deaths to come.

I wake to the sound of little explosions – ta-ta-ra-ta-ta – of copal cast into flame. When I come into my full power, the old woman will teach me the secret prayers, the ones only our kind intone because none other have such need to see under and beyond the world.

Perhaps the priests do too, but theirs is a much different calling. Though the incense that carries our prayers up to the heart of heaven is the same as the one they use, the words given flight are not.

I rise from the mat, secure my skirt with a sash, and pull my tunic over it so only a few inches of skirt shows above my ankles. I sing the names of my ancestors as I weave a ribbon through my braids: Names like vines that twist through leaf and branch; names like bits of cloud caught on the fingers of trees; names like the sound of air displaced by a bird's wing.

It is nobody's ritual but my own to sing this litany, but I – granddaughter, great-granddaughter, blood heir to generations – use the names to knit my bones more solidly to my flesh with each rising.

Every day of every year I've been with the old woman has started this way.

When I come out of the house, the old woman doesn't even turn around. She's on her heels by the fire pit, dropping copal into it. The smoke rises heavy above her head, then spreads wide instead of up.

"I noticed we're almost out of snake's broom," she says to me, without looking around. "And thunderer root. And chicken herb."

"Won't we be preparing achiotl today?" I ask hopefully. We haven't yet gotten the call for it but the old woman has assured me we will.

She looks at me then. I know she's irritated at me by the way her crossed eye moves even closer to the inner corner. "Yes. But preparing for war doesn't mean the people won't run fevers, or bleed, or give birth."

She gets up and comes to stand next to me. She's not much taller than me, for all that I'm only twelve and she's lived years beyond my counting.

343

"The Sun will soon show his face," she says as she takes the cloth folded on her head and places it on mine. She adjusts it so the stiffest fold overhangs my eyes. Its shadow will keep them from watering.

I prefer to go bareheaded but the old woman's gift is not to be ignored. She doesn't need to mention again that she has foreseen people from other towns passing through our lands on their way to Utatlán. The people from our village are used to the way I look, but if these others chance to see me their eyes will slide over my white skin and white hair and freeze on my pink eyes.

Curses are passed along through prolonged eye contact. And fright, which is hard to treat and sometimes fatal.

The old woman is not my mother. She is not my grandmother, nor any relation that can be traced in straight lines. But the tree of life has crooked lines too, and her crossed eyes and my ghostly appearance tie us together in more worlds than just the one under our feet. My father brought me to her still tinted dark by my mother's blood, but the old woman knew me anyway. The gods have made us family.

***

The paths I have worn through scrub and brush are so familiar I don't pay attention to where my feet land as I trot down to collect the herbs. I look at the dawning sky instead and at the mountainside above me, still burrowed in the blanket of clouds it pulls over itself to bide the night. If the old woman's visions are true and the message carried by the northerners prophetic, I wonder if the mountains themselves might be roused to arms at what is coming.

I find the patch of snake's broom first. It is tall, with tiny yellow florets topping the bony stalks. It is a useful plant: we decoct it for massages that reduce swelling after childbirth. I pray before I start picking, and then I'm careful about how much I take. Plants are like villages, dependent on each other for well-being. Even far-flung seedlings know when their colony of origin has been decimated, and they stop thriving.

I move on to the stand of chicken herb, a styptic. The properties of the two plants partnered call up memory of my mother. If someone had mixed them – three parts chicken, one part snake – and administered a bolus, maybe her blood would have stopped flowing during my birth.

It is farther to go to get thunderer, and harder work to dig the roots from the earth whole. But it is important to do it well. The old woman long ago predicted that plague would anticipate war, and so it has. Fully a third of the people have died after burning so hot their bodies erupted in pustules – like volcanoes opening second and third vents to release what boils within. Thunderer, given in the right measure to the newly afflicted, is our best defense.

A light step and moist exhalation sounds midway through excavation of the third root. I look up. The doe's eyes are dark and liquid, but the rest of her – small body, white pelt, reddish skin stark inside big ears – is me in animal form. She snuffles again, then butts my hand.

"I'm not done," I tell her.

Her regard is steady, unblinking.

"Oh, all right," I say. I put down my digging tool and get to my feet. I take off at a run behind the doe. She stops every so often and rises on her hind legs, feints toward me, then tears off in the opposite direction. We pursue each other, away and back, in a dance we've done together for as long as I can remember.

When I am too winded to continue, I drop to my back on the ground and close my eyes. I stretch my arms out to take advantage of the tender heat the Sun floods down this early in the day. I feel the doe nibble on my hair, then step away to a patch of something more savory.

I don't know how long I stay like this, but too soon I hear her footfall again. She is an excellent timekeeper; I must go back, she's telling me with her approach, to finish digging that root.

Only, when I open my eyes, it isn't the doe who stands over me.

The boy is older than me, but not by much — fourteen at most. He's a noble; his sandals and breechclout are bright with decoration.

"Where am I?" he says. Then, "Are you a white demon?"

I'm a girl, and as common as dirt despite my unusual look, so I shouldn't venture to fully meet his eyes, much less with challenge. But I'm annoyed that he's confused me for one of the gnomes that live under our mountains and hills. I've seen the carved white demon masks and there is nothing uglier.

"No," I say. "My name is K'antel. And how is it that you don't know where you are? Did someone knock you about the head and scatter your thoughts?"

"I was walking alongside my father's house in Utatlán," he says, "and after enough steps, I was in this clearing."

He is a liar.

Utatlán, where the king's fortress-palace stands and warriors are massing in preparation for war, is a two- to three-day trek from here. He does not have the look of one who has walked that far.

He casts himself on the ground next to me. That's when I see it. The way the light sneaks through his flesh.

I scramble up. "You better come with me," I say. "And hurry."

He scowls. It turns his eyes shiny and hard, like the shells of the big, black beetles I find when I upturn certain roots.

"Nobody talks to me that way," he says after a moment.

"I know," I say, "but we don't have much time. I must get you to the old woman. Else, you'll wake from your trance in Utatlán and whatever wisdom your spirit knew to seek here will be lost to you."

He shakes his head again but gets to his feet. "Maybe yours is that wisdom." There is an odd sort of challenge in his voice as if he's daring me to admit I think more highly of myself than I should.

When I don't rise to the taunt, he says, "Lead on. I've seen you run, I'll labor to keep up."

I do, and he does, and he is a beautiful runner even when his feet don't know the way.

The old woman knows, as she always does, when someone approaches our compound. She meets us with two cups of steaming liquid. Mine is frothy with honey, ground squash seeds, and corn. His will undoubtedly have some addition dictated by her foreknowledge of his arrival.

"Tekún Umám," she says, then inclines her head a little in acknowledgement. I start. The boy isn't just a noble, he's royal. The prince.

"Umám," he says. "I haven't earned the Tekún."

"It's not earned," the old woman says, "and you'll vouch for it soon anyway."

He catches a sigh before it fully leaves his lips. "Your granddaughter has made me run my heart out to be beneficiary of your wisdom before the trance that brought me here breaks."

The old woman looks at me with her crooked eyes and for a moment I'm scared she will tell him that I am not her granddaughter, just a girl she's cared for because she did not want to see me abandoned to the wild. But she doesn't. She walks over to the fire pit, and we trail her. The smoke huffs up as if she has thrown something flammable on it; she follows the smoke with her eyes.

"Son of kings," she says, "you know my gift of doubled vision just from looking at me. Your gifts are more carefully hidden. Tell me what they are."

"I have a strong arm for sling or spear," Umám says after a moment. "And enough breath to be a good shot with the blowgun."

When she doesn't say anything, he adds, "Warriors follow my lead without hesitation."

"What else?" she turns to fix her eyes on him.

"He runs like the wind," I interrupt.

"I wasn't asking you," she says.

Under her continued scrutiny, he finally answers, "My nahual isn't like any other."

"How?" she asks. I've never heard the old woman impatient before, which makes me search her face. Her crossed eye is where it always is, huddled near the inner corner, but her other eye... it's in a mad shimmy from one corner to the other.

"My nahual lives outside and inside," he says slowly.

The old woman nods, falls into thought.

"The message from the north warns that, like that great kingdom, ours will fall to the foreigners," Umám says presently. "My father's spies say there are not many sent forth to take down the K'iche', but I fear they will try to gather our enemies to their ranks on their drive down."

"Perhaps if your forefathers had not made enemies of so many..." she starts acidly, but doesn't complete the comment

"I have been given many visions already," the old woman says after a moment. "The foreigners have sent their hawk against you. And while hawks are swift and cruel when they hunt, smaller birds still dare harry them and drive them away. Even when those birds normally crave only song and peace."

He stares at her. "You know which my nahual is."

She nods.

"I would have preferred a jaguar. Like my father."

The old woman's smile is mocking. "Because yours is more commonly associated with women? I have known some with this same animal twin and I assure you, there is courage in it. Have you ever seen what happens to these birds when they are caught from the wild and caged?"

"They die," he says.

"They choose death over subjugation," she corrects.

"I have seen far into the future," she adds. "Your name is still alive, even on the foreigners' lips. And your nahual takes wing, they say, to fly higher than the eagle of the North or the condor of the South."

"In truth?"

"In song," she says. "Which holds a different kind of truth."

After a long silence she asks, "What do the priests and advisors say to your father?"

"To fortify Utatlán when I march into battle. To make the capital like a trap that will close around the foreigners if I fall."

Then, "I'm ready to bleed, but I don't want to fall." For the first time he sounds like a boy. Like me, he's waiting to transition fully into adult status, and the wait is by turns too long and too short.

"There is no reason to dwell on falling, only on leading your warriors," the old woman says, but absently, as if she is thinking of something else at the same time. "There will be others, in any case, who will help you stand."

"Others?"

"Us," she says.

He laughs — a contemptuous sound like I haven't heard from him before — and shakes his head.

The old woman turns her back on him and returns her eyes to the smoke. "K'antel, lead Umám back to where he stumbled upon you. And while you're there, retrieve the tool you left. It might not look like much but none other can do what it does."

We walk silently down the path as the Sun turns the fierce side of his face toward us.

"Those last words weren't meant for you, were they?" Umám says when we're nearly to the clearing.

"She must expect better of you than she does of other men," I say, looking up at him, even though the angle makes the Sun get in my eyes and they start to water.

His expression grows concerned.

"I'm not crying," I say irritably. "It's just the Sun."

After a moment, he nods. "I am sorry to have laughed at you."

"You think we haven't heard worse?"

He reaches for my hand, wraps his fingers loosely around two of mine. I'm so shocked he's deigned to touch a commoner I don't pull away.

His lips move to shape words but then thin to nothing and he's gone before saying whatever he intended.

Somewhere in Utatlán, the prince is coming out of his trance.

***

Achiotl is a hard, intensely red seed, smaller than a kernel of corn. Grinding it to a fine powder is hard work. Normally we wouldn't pulverize the seeds, we'd just crack them to coarse chunks and set them in water to soak, then use the liquid to treat headaches and mouth ulcers, or to dye cloth.

But the gourds full of seeds aren't for village use. We are grinding them into powder to send to Utatlán, so Umám's warriors can paint themselves red before battle. The couriers who carry the demand for tithe bring news in trade. Reports place the foreigners at a good distance from us, though moving fast. The leaders ride on animals like we have not seen before — bigger than the great cats that live in our mountains, with hooves three times the size of the ones on deer.

We know animals. They are our neighbors. We dance them, and gratefully accept the gifts they offer the people. Gifts like no other people receive: their spirits twin with ours. The arrival of an animal with unknown strength or weakness and no tie to us is no small matter. With every crush and slide of stone on seed I think on what this might mean.

We grind on our knees, pushing a heavy stone roller over a flat rock base held not even a hand's length above the ground. The old woman's stone base is much more beautiful than my plain one. The front edge has a carved bowl to catch the pulverized matter, and beneath that, where mine has only a conical foot, hers has the carving of a coatimundi with legs splayed above and tail coiling below. I know her nahual is a coati, but the grinding stone is much older than she is, harking back to the first of our ancestors.

"When I journey to the tree of life, it will be yours," she says when she catches me eyeing it.

I shake my head. "I was just wondering what use is a coati, or a small doe, against an animal like the one the spies have described?"

"Chssst." It is her expression to shut me up, or to let me know I've said something so wrong a correction must follow. "The gods have given the people many gifts," she says. "Never think the gifts they've given others are greater or better."

"Stronger."

"The people are like this stone," she says, slamming the end of her roller hard against the base. Its thwack is loud as thunder in the thatched, open-walled pavilion where we do some of our cooking and most of our herbcraft. "Like the heart of the world, we do not break. No matter if we're the ones crushing, or the ones bearing the weight."

"Have you seen which we will be in the coming war?" I ask.

But she doesn't answer because just then we hear the rustle of dry corn husks. When we look up Umán is there, head dragging on what hangs from the rafters. This time he wears an embroidered double length of cloth over his breechclout. It is ceremonial clothing, so his trance must be taking place during a ritual enacted by the priests in Utatlán.

"You have found us again," the old woman says, stilling her stone roller.

"This time by intention," he answers.

"What would you have us do for you, young lord?"

He shifts from one leg to the other. "I have been able to gather eight thousand men to me, and as many slingshots, bows, and spears. I have need of your sight to tell me if that is enough."

"And if I say it isn't?"

"Then I will go to our closest enemies with the offer of riches if they will join with us against the foreigners."

The old woman gets up and walks over to the house. When we follow her inside, she's on her knees in front of the small, elaborately painted chest that sits next to the larger, plain one that serves as our everyday storage.

"Go with K'antel to the river," she says to Umám. "Take the largest gourds and bring back enough clay slurry to fill one of our soaking troughs. Then go to the village fields. Make offerings in gratitude for the corn — you yourself, not K'antel — and come back with enough ears to fill the drying cribs. When you have done all this, I will have your prediction for you."

"I hadn't intended to stay that long," he says.

"You hadn't intended many things, and yet they are demanded of you." She lifts the lid of the chest and pulls out a handful of beeswax candles dyed to the colors of the four directions and lays them on the ground next to her.

"Cover your head," she says to me without looking, "the Sun likes to follow him."

We're halfway to the river before he speaks. "Is it difficult?" he says. "Always being tormented by the Sun?"

"Yes," I say. "But the Moon loves me better. I glow like a beacon in her light."

He stops, pulls a pouch out from beneath the ceremonial covering of his breechclout. "I want to show you something. I had one of my father's most skillful artisans make these for you," he says.

They are two rounds of obsidian — so thin they are a translucent grey instead of opaque black — rimmed and held by fine woven fiber, which also attaches them to each other. Long fibers on the sides are meant to be tied around the head.

It's hard to know what to do or say to him. "They are strange," is what I finally manage.

He nods. "But this way no one will think you are crying when you are not." He ties them to my face, then fiddles with their positioning a bit when I complain they make my eyelashes hurt.

When he's done I whip off my head covering and look toward the Sun. There are wavy lines on the air where there shouldn't be, but the Sun's face is clouded enough by the volcanic glass that I don't immediately start tearing. And when I look down and around, nothing radiates enough light to bother me.

I drop to my knees, then touch my forehead to the ground in front of Umám's feet.

"I prefer the friend to the subject," he says after a moment. "And be careful. They break easily. The artisan was left with shard and powder in his hands when he tried to chip the shape in attempts that came before."

When I get back to my feet, he studies me. "They make your face look like a mask."

"A white demon."

He nods. "You're quite monstrous."

I pull my features to what I've seen on the masks. "Enough to scare off the foreigners?"

"And the people too," he says, but with a smile.

It is the last we say about it, but I think on the unexpected gift during the hours it takes us to fulfill the old woman's demand. "Have you no siblings?" I say finally.

He looks at me. "No. Nor real friends either. Just those who would curry favor by proximity."

Later, standing before the old woman, both of us muddy and abraded from the rough harvesting, Umám reaches for my hand as he had that first day. I think I love him for this brotherly touch. The way of witches is lonely. The way of the only ghost witch born in a generation, more so.

"I have seen that eight thousand men will not be enough to secure victory," the old woman says to Umám. "And you will not find help from the Kakchiquel by promising them riches. You will only send them to the invaders' side in hopes of ruining us."

Umám hangs his head. "You are telling me I cannot win."

"No," she says. "I am telling you the ways of men are not enough. Send couriers to every village, to every woman like us who walk between worlds. We will make men of corn to swell your ranks."

"You are not gods to make men."

"Chssst," she says, but Umám doesn't know to go quiet and hear what she'll say next.

"I will consult with the priest-advisors," he rushes to say, then disappears even faster than the first time.

"The priests will say no," the old woman says to me as she gathers her ritual things and ducks back into the house to return them to her chest.

"That is ever the way between men of power and women of power," she adds when I follow her inside. "So they become priests to kings and we stay witches hidden among the people. But we will do what we will anyway."

She closes the lid of her chest and turns to look at me. She motions at the obsidian rounds. "What are those?"

"He had them made. They let me see the Sun without hurting my eyes."

She smiles, a tiny little sliver of smile.

"I will be teaching you the ways of making life, K'antel," she says. "And the ways of taking it. This you will learn because I have seen your future."

I feel a shiver climb my spine. "Will I be a part of Umám's victory?" I ask.

"You'll help him live forever," she says. Then, before I can say anything else, she points at the open door. "There is corn to shuck."

***

Black, red, yellow and white. The kernels of corn look like multicolor teeth pulled from their gums and set out to dry.

We grind and grind and grind. When the trough is filled with meal, we mix it with the slurry and shape our warriors out of corn and clay. They line up in our compound, rank upon rank, hardening under charge of the Sun.

Umám's and my first haul of corn and clay is not enough, of course, and the old woman and I carry more raw ingredients up to the compound. The villagers mark the corn we take from the terraces and are respectful of our need even when they don't know the why of it. But they don't help us, or follow us up to the compound. Witches are part of them, but always apart.

The obsidian rounds make the Sun friendlier, but I still love the Moon best, and the white doe and I go out under her gaze to dance to the music I hear in the earth. One night, the old woman catches us at our dance – around and through the rows of waiting men – and watches us wordlessly.

"I have confused you for a child when in reality you are a white demon," she says later that night, as we're both laying on our mats.

"Can white demons love?" I say. "Because I love you."

I hear her get up and come to the edge my mat. She strokes my hair, as she did when I was four or five and crying from the work, or the Sun, or some remark I'd overheard on market day. "Not everything that seems human is human," she says.

"But I am," I say as I fall asleep.

The next day she grabs a blade and cuts my braids off. She wraps them carefully in a cloth and stores them in her chest. What's left on my head is so short it is soft and prickly at once, and I can't stop myself from running my hands over it.

"Promise me one thing," she says. "Promise you will come back to me."

"Am I going somewhere?"

She nods, but doesn't say anything, and moments later she leaves.

That night I see Umám, standing with his back to our frozen army as if he's already leading them. His skin is painted red and his hair is half pulled away to stream down his back. His headdress is every shade of green – pale jade cabochons and strands of mixed dark nephrite and turquoise beads, topped with the three-foot tail feathers of a male quetzal. They arc high over his head and down his back.

"It is time," he says. "Two days from now I will meet the invaders on the plain of Olintepeque."

"We will send our battalion to meet you," I say, motioning behind him.

He turns around, looks at the strange, still figures. "Do you dream?"

"Yes. A color, mostly. What about you?"

He turns back to me. "I've been dreaming the same dream every night for the past three months. Corn kernels pouring out of men like blood."

"That's good," I say. "We created them from corn so they would bleed instead of you."

"But the gods created us from corn as well," he says.

As Umám steps forward, into the light the Moon streams down, I see for the first time his nahual perched on his shoulder. Not even the majestic tail

351

feathers on the headdress have prepared me for the bird. Neither too small nor too large, it is uniformly green. But it is a green not of this world; a green made by the gods for the gods; a green that burns my eyes worse than the Sun ever has.

The bird raises its wings, lifts and coasts over to me for a moment. Then, instead of returning to its perch, it flies straight to the center of Umám's chest and dives through his hardened cotton armor – and behind that his muscle and bone – as if all were as tender as a barely unfurled leaf. The nahual disappears into the boy warrior. For a few instants the eyes that look into mine are hard and inhuman, as they were once before, and now I know why.

Then, they are just Umám's eyes again.

"Promise me something," he says.

Unease rises in me and seals my lips, but I manage to nod.

"Promise you'll remember me as Umám, not the Tekún or whatever I become."

"I will," I say.

He fades out slowly this time, as if he is reluctant to go.

I don't know how long I stand there until I feel the old woman's hand on my arm. She leads me up the mountainside, past a rock covered with wax drippings from the blessings we've asked there. Past the slender, silvery tree to which the Moon ties her loom when she takes to her daytime weaving. Past the cave where the Sun goes to change into a jaguar and stalk the night.

We're almost to the top of the mountain when we come upon a space formed by the roots of a tree so enormous no more than its trunk can be seen. Its branches are hidden in a garment of clouds.

This is her cavern. The first grandmother. The eternal grandmother. The grandmother who has loved me from the day she held me, and shaped the tool that I am to be to her hand.

***

It starts with one drop, and then another. Soon it is a steady drizzle. The ranks of mud and corn men take in the wet. Their pallid yellowish-grey cheeks flush. Their fingers flex around the figured handle of slingshot, the long hollow of blowgun. Their sandaled feet lift as one, stamp as one. It is the tún, tún, tún of the hollowed log instrument with the same name as sound; and the bom, bom, bom of drums calling to war.

All at once the statues open their mouths, and the rain falls on their outstretched tongues – this red rain, blood rain, rain of the living and of the dead. The cry that issues from each throat at the same time has the quality of song. A song meant for a road that opens only once and for a short while. The song of a body brought to life.

***

I run faster than I have ever run. At my side, the white doe matches my stride. Behind us are the grandmother's corn men, in formation three abreast, silently keeping pace.

I cannot say what the people think as we pass their villages on our way to Olintepeque. I imagine they think it is a white demon — boyish, naked and absolutely colorless except for the black rounds where eyes should be — leading an army of ghosts. But as each night of our run turns to dawn, the people come to the edge of the trade road to throw flower petals under our feet. The children sprint alongside us for a stretch, and the women walk behind them, stoic and thoughtful. We start with five thousand corn men and march thirty thousand onto the battlefield.

Arrows, darts, and stones pierce the sky. Black powder flares. The foreigners shoot charges as the animals below them rise on enormous hind legs and tear at the people with hooves tipped in metal.

I see one of our men catch a foreigner's shot mid-torso and then the mud and corn pours out until it is no longer a man standing but a mound of dirt and husk and kernel on the field. The foreigner stops to push another shot into his gun, controlling his animal with the pressure of his knees.

I drop to my haunches, place my palms flat on the earth. I've always known the way of what roots beneath the ground, but this is no ordinary harvest. I sing as the grandmother has taught me and the earth itself becomes a weapon. Blades of obsidian push out of the ground where the foreigner's animal is set to step. I hear a bellow as volcanic glass points bury themselves in the soft under its hooves.

I pull two long blades from the ground for myself. Even after he slides off the tremendous beast, the foreigner is much taller than me, and encased in metal armor. But every plate weighs, and I jump where he can't follow. I stab up between seams. He twists, then goes down on a knee.

The people prefer prisoners to corpses, but the foreigner brings his musket up and I know I cannot afford to keep to custom.

I make another obsidian blade rise and drive itself through skin and bone where the jointed knee of armor opens the foreigner to earth. The sudden pain makes his shot go wide. The blades in my hands slash one way, then another, across his throat. He gurgles, then flops forward and the ground takes his blood.

The next foreigner — only half-armored — looks confused when I step up to face him. His eyes slide over my skin, even paler than his own. He hesitates, I do not. The next one does much the same.

As I step over their bleeding, dying bodies, I put it together in my head. The foreigners know nothing of the white demons, so they do not fear me for my semblance. They fear me because I look like one of their young, turned against them and repudiating the savagery of this invasion.

Rightly is the grandmother known for her foresight.

I keep dancing with my blades and beside me the white doe distracts and bewilders, buying me time to slash wider, pierce deeper. We will never be taken.

***

When the silence falls, my body is as red as if I had been smeared with achiotl.

At the heart of the plain of Olintepeque, a red-haired foreigner with a dark red animal beneath him meets a lone standing warrior. They are like statues, the light caresses them with love.

Then blowgun and musket rise to sight at the same time.

Umám blows his feathered dart with enough force that it slices half through the animal's eye and lodges its long thorn in what rests behind. As the beast topples, the foreigner still caught on its back buries his shot in Umám's thigh.

Umám leaps forward anyway. He reaches for the animal – down and snorting and sneezing as if it could rid itself of the pain in its head that way – pulls a blade and slits its throat. It brays its death, and the foreigner scrambles to get out from beneath it.

I turn back to my own fight. I have a foreigner to unseat, and following him, one of his allies – who looks like one of the people and probably has ancestors in common with us. I'm humming and singing with power, as the grandmother knew I would be when she sent me into battle.

The soles of my feet are hard, but not so much that I can't discern what I step on as I make my way from one end of the battlefield to the next: kernels of corn; dirt slicked to mud by blood; gobbets of flesh, some squishy, some firm.

Then, my toes curl around something smooth, cold, unyielding. I look down. It is a large nephrite bead – dark green and glossy like the leaves of certain trees. Not too far from it is another bead, this one the paler blue-green of turquoise. And then another.

At the end of the trail is a little mound of beads and cabochons, broken feather and iridescent herl. Umám's cotton chest armor is covered with bright red blood that pumps weakly from a tremendous hole the foreigner has blown in him. He's been abandoned to an undignified bleeding out, despite the trappings of royalty and honors due.

I yank the obsidian rounds off my face and drop them to ground so everything can be seen in the harsh, real light of this day: the boy-prince fell before securing victory; the skinny girl confused bloodlust for purpose.

We have failed.

I go to my knees, take Umám's face in my hands and turn it so what we see is still harsher. Both of us are losing our only friend.

Umám's eyes meet mine. They are hard and black. Even though he can chose to do so, his animal twin has not abandoned him.

Because even the supernatural can love this life. This earth. These broken human beings.

The grandmother taught me the song to make weapons spring from the earth. The grandmother taught me the song to make life rain from the sky. But the song I sing now is all mine.

I sing for the boy-warrior and his nahual, and for the only certainty that can be wrested from the future: that they will never be forgotten.

Umám's bones shift with the melody. His shoulders draw back and his arms stretch by another full length. Barbs of brilliant feathers poke out from his dying flesh.

Green, green, green. And red.

Even without the gift of foresight I know that every quetzal after this will bear a red breast in imitation of Umám's lethal wound.

A deep, rumbling bird call issues from Umám's beak at the same time as his wings catch the wind. He lifts and makes a slow circuit over the battlefield. Weapons forgotten, the people, even the foreigners and their allies, follow the great bird's trajectory with their eyes. When he has shown himself to all of them, when he has stilled the battle with his passing, he flies toward our mountains.

I lift my arm in farewell. One of the mountains lifts its arm in greeting.

The battle resumes. My friend is gone. There is only this.

***

The grandmother waits for me at the tree of life. She looks long into my pink eyes.

I found the obsidian rounds Umám had made for me ground to powder under the heels and hooves of battle, and my eyes are swollen because the Sun shines on without regard for what happens on earth.

"Even the trap at the palace in Utatlán failed," I tell the grandmother. "It was a rout. We are finished."

"Chssst," she says.

I slump to the ground, looking up the shallow hillside to the dark cavern formed by the roots of what stretches so far below and above I will never knows its end. The grandmother comes to sit behind me. As I lean back, I feel her body – ancient and strong, soft and hard. She strokes my head, comforts me as if I were human. I'm not. Not anymore, if I ever was.

"I promise, the people will not be vanquished by the foreigners," she says.

"But they will keep dying."

She nods. "But they will keep living too."

After a long silence, she taps me on the head to let me know she's getting up, then walks to the tree and traces the root-cavern's mouth with deliberation.

"Tekún Umám had become your friend, so you danced your dance of the white demons for him. And with him. And because of him," she says. "But he is not our last hero. The dance cannot end with his life."

"One puny white demon," I say, "is not a dance."

Her laugh rumbles so it shakes the earth.

She beckons me to the cavern. "Come. Meet my other granddaughters. The dance of the white demons changes when it is danced in unison, and they are waiting for you."

I don't budge.

"Hundreds of years from now," she says, "the white demons will dance again. For women heroes this time. Tenacious ones who discover ossuaries

355

full of bones and the stories that can be read in the remains of bodies. Courageous ones who speak aloud the forbidden history. Righteous ones who will not flinch when calling for justice.

"Surely you will want to call those heroes friends too," she says. "Surely you will want to dance for and with and because of them."

I get to my feet, but don't step toward her. I am slicked by gore, and sickened by its stench on my skin. If I dance again it will not be wielding blades to draw blood.

But she must know this already, for she is the grandmother, the one who came before all others, and nothing is a surprise to her.

"When will your other granddaughters and I stop dancing?" I ask.

"When you grow tired," she says.

I stay where I am.

"When you lose hope."

Still.

"When you forget what it is to love."

"That'll be never," I say.

The white doe and I trudge up the little incline until we stand by the grandmother's side at the root end of the tree of life. She puts her arm around my waist, and with that she's just the old woman again, and I am just the odd girl who has a way with herbs and things of the earth.

We are ordinary. Our battles are human. Our bodies know this earth from first step to last, and each step demands justice.

This is our dance.

AUTHOR BIOGRAPHIES

Sofia Samatar is the author of the novel *A Stranger in Olondria* (Small Beer Press), winner of the 2014 Crawford Award. She is nonfiction and poetry editor for *Interfictions: A Journal of Interstitial Arts*. You can find out more about her at www.sofiasamatar.com.

Thoraiya Dyer is a three-time Aurealis Award–winning, three-time Ditmar Award–winning Australian writer based in the Hunter Valley, NSW. Her short fiction has appeared in *Clarkesworld*, *Apex*, *Nature*, and *Cosmos* and is forthcoming in *Analog*. A petite collection of four original stories, "Asymmetry," is available from Twelfth Planet Press. Find her online at Goodreads or thoraiyadyer.com.

Tananarive Due is the Cosby Chair in the Humanities at Spelman College (2012–13). She also teaches in the creative writing MFA program at Antioch University Los Angeles. The American Book Award winner and NAACP Image Award recipient is the author of 12 novels and a civil rights memoir. She recently received a Lifetime Achievement Award in the Fine Arts from the Congressional Black Caucus Foundation. In 2010, she was inducted into the Medill School of Journalism's Hall of Achievement at Northwestern University. Due lives in Southern California with her husband, author Steven Barnes, and their son, Jason. Her website is at tananarivedue.com. Her writing blog is at tananarivedue.wordpress.com.

S. Lynn has been wrestling with Multiple Chemical Sensitivity for most of her adult life; to keep herself busy in the absence of the capacity to spend an eight-hour day in a work environment, she has been serialising Trevor's present-day stories at hiraeth.dreamwidth.org. She lives with her Mum and an evil-genius-cat with attendant unwitting-minion-cat, and her friends are beginning to worry about how quickly she knits. This is her first professional fiction sale.

Sunny Moraine is an occasional author of various flavors of speculative fiction; the flavor in question depends upon a complex conjunction of different variables, the exact nature of which they have yet to specify or untangle. Sunny's short fiction has appeared in *Clarkesworld*, *Strange Horizons*, *Shimmer*, *Daily Science Fiction*, *Ideomancer*, and the anthology *We See a Different Frontier: A Postcolonial Speculative Fiction Anthology*, among other places. They are also responsible for the novels *Line and Orbit* (cowritten with Lisa Soem) and *Crowflight*, the sequel to which, *Ravenfall*, will be released in 2014 by Masque Books. They live just outside Washington DC in a reasonably creepy house with two cats and a husband. They are on Twitter as @dynamicsymmetry, and can be found making words at sunnymoraine.com.

Rion Amilcar Scott has contributed to *PANK*, *Fiction International*, *The Rumpus*, *Washington City Paper*, and *Confrontation*, among others. Raised in Silver Spring, Maryland, he earned an MFA at George Mason University and presently teaches English at Bowie State University.

Meg Jayanth is a freelance writer and digital producer living in London. Cani Theruvil and Munira Begum appear in Samsara, her storygame of dream-walking, courtly intrigue, and war in 18th-century Bengal, online at samsara.storynexus.com. Find her @betterthemask and megjayanth.com.

Claire Humphrey lives in Toronto, where she works in the book business, and writes short fiction and novels. Her stories have appeared in *Beneath Ceaseless Skies*, *Interzone*, *Strange Horizons*, *Crossed Genres*, *Podcastle*, and other fine magazines and anthologies. She is also the reviews editor at *Ideomancer*. She can be found online at clairehumphrey.ca.

L.S. Johnson lives in Northern California. Her fiction has appeared or is forthcoming in *Interzone*, *Corvus*, *Mirror Dance*, *Fae*, and other venues. Currently she is working on a fantasy novel set in 18th-century Europe. She can be found online at traversingz.com.

Robert William Iveniuk is a Toronto-based author, screenwriter, and columnist. His works have been published in Schlock Magazine and both of the Alchemy Press's *Pulp Heroes* anthologies. He is also a contributor to *BlogTO* and *Archenemy Magazine*.

Jamey Hatley is a native of Memphis, TN. Her writing has appeared in the *Oxford American, Torch Poetry*, and elsewhere. She has attended the Callaloo Creative Writing Workshop and the Voices of Our Nation Writing Workshop; received scholarships to the Oxford American Summit for Ambitious Writers and the Bread Loaf Writers' Conference; and won the William Faulkner-William Wisdom Award for a Novel-in-Progress. She has an MFA in Creative Writing from Louisiana State University.

Michael Janairo's work has been published in various newspapers and literary magazines. His story "Out of Japan" won the Tsujinaka Fiction prize and was published in both English and Japanese in the *Abiko Quarterly*. Recent publications include the poem "Aswang in Eye to the Telescope," the short story "The Advanced Ward" in the anthology *Veterans of the Future Wars*, and the short story "The Duck" in *Bartelby Snopes*.

He lives near Albany, NY., with his wife, son and dog. (His family name is pronounced "ha NIGH row.") He blogs at michaeljanairo.com.

Benjamin Parzybok's second novel, *Sherwood Nation*, is forthcoming this fall 2014 from Small Beer Press. He's the author of the novel *Couch*, and has had a number of short stories published. He has been the creator/co-creator of many projects, including *Gumball Poetry* (literary journal published in capsule machines), *The Black Magic Insurance Agency* (city-wide, one night alternate reality game), and Project Hamad (an effort to free a Guantanamo inmate and shed light on habeas corpus). He works as a programmer and lives in Portland with the artist Laura Moulton and their two kids. He blogs at secret.ideacog.net.

Kima Jones is a 2013 PEN USA Emerging Voices fellow in poetry, a Voices at VONA alum, and 2012 Lambda Literary Fellow in poetry. Kima has been published at *The Rumpus* and *PANK* among others. She lives in Los Angeles and is writing her first poetry collection, *The Anatomy of Forgiveness*.

Christina Lynch is the co-author (with Meg Howrey) of the *New York Times* bestselling novel *City of Dark Magic*, and the sequel, *City of Lost Dreams*, both published by Penguin under the pseudonym Magnus Flyte. She is a graduate of Harvard and has an MFA from Antioch University Los Angeles. A television writer and journalist, she teaches writing at College of the Sequoias and UCLA Extension. She lives near Sequoia National Park with too many animals.

Christina says, "While touring Ambras Castle in the mountains of Austria one summer, I came across portraits of the real-life Gonzales family, who had a rare genetic trait now called Ambras Syndrome. All of the historical figures named in the story are real."

Troy L. Wiggins is from Memphis, Tennessee. His short fiction has appeared in the recent anthology *Griots: Sisters of the Spear*. He currently resides in Daegu, South Korea, where he teaches English.

Nghi Vo currently lives on the shores of an inland sea, and her fiction has appeared in *Strange Horizons* and *Crossed Genres*. Her current interests include old gods, new gods, papercutting, candymaking, revenge tragedy, and the Ottoman Empire. She can be contacted at bridgeofbirds@gmail.com.

David Jón Fuller was born and raised in Winnipeg, Manitoba, where he now lives, and has also lived in Edmonton, Alberta. He earned an honours degree in theatre at the University of Winnipeg and studied Icelandic language and literature for two years at the University of Iceland in Reykjavík. David's short fiction has been published in *Tesseracts 17*, *In Places Between*, *The Harrow* and *The Mythic Circle*. David currently works as a copy editor for the *Winnipeg Free Press*, and as time allows he blogs at www.davidjonfuller.com.

He would like to thank Cindy Lavallee at Aboriginal Languages of Manitoba, and Roger Roulette for his translations into Island Lakes Dialect Ojibwe for "A Deeper Echo".

Ken Liu (kenliu.name) is an author and translator of speculative fiction, as well as a lawyer and programmer. His fiction has appeared in *The Magazine of Fantasy & Science Fiction, Asimov's, Analog, Clarkesworld, Lightspeed*, and *Strange Horizons*, among other places. He has won a Nebula, two Hugos, a World Fantasy Award, and a Science Fiction & Fantasy Translation Award, and been nominated for the Sturgeon and the Locus Awards. He lives with his family near Boston, Massachusetts. Ken's debut novel, tentatively titled *The Chrysanthemum and the Dandelion*, the first in a fantasy series, will be published by Simon & Schuster's new genre fiction imprint in 2015.

Kemba Banton, a writer of fiction, poetry and nonfiction, was born in Kingston, Jamaica in 1983. In 1989, she moved to the States to join her parents who had emigrated several years before her. Since then she has moved frequently between Jamaica and the States. Banton earned a BA in Anthropology at Columbia University. In 2007, she was a semi-finalist for a Fulbright grant in the creative arts field. In the same year, her short story "Zebra's Trod" won a silver medal award in an annual Jamaican national creative writing competition hosted by the Jamaica Cultural Development Commission. She is a freelance writer for *Heart and Soul Magazine* and the co-founder and editor of TheNobantuProject.com. She is also pursuing an MFA in Creative Writing at Antioch University, Los Angeles. Banton currently resides in Georgia and is the mother of three children.

Sarah Pinsker is a Baltimore-based singer, songwriter, and author. She has three albums on various indie labels and a fourth in production. Her short stories have been published in *Strange Horizons, Asimov's, Lightspeed, Fantasy & Science Fiction, and Daily Science Fiction,* among others, and she has stories forthcoming in several anthologies, including *The Future Embodied* and Crossed Genres's *Fierce Family*.

Nnedi Okorafor is a novelist of African-based science fiction, fantasy and magical realism. In a profile of Nnedi's work titled "Weapons of Mass Creation", *The New York Times* called Nnedi's imagination "stunning". Her novels include *Who Fears Death* (winner of the World Fantasy Award for Best Novel), *Akata Witch* (an Amazon.com Best Book of the Year), *Zahrah the Windseeker*(winner of the Wole Soyinka Prize for African Literature), and *The Shadow Speaker* (winner of the CBS Parallax Award). Her children's book *Long Juju Man* is the winner of the Macmillan Writer's Prize for Africa. Her short story collection *Kabu Kabu* was released in October 2013. Her forthcoming works include her science fiction novel *Lagoon* (scheduled for release in April 8, 2014) and her young adult novel *Akata Witch 2: Breaking Kola* (scheduled for release in 2015). Nnedi is a creative writing professor at Chicago State. Find her on Facebook, Twitter (@nnedi), and at nnedi.com.

Shanaé Brown is a writer and blogger in NYC. This is her first published story and she's currently hard at work on her first novel, *Naima*. She's represented by Sara Camilli. You can find her most days on her blog, becauseimwrite.net, or on Twitter @muzeness.

Nicolette Barischoff's greatest achievement, prior to being published in this awesome anthology, is graduating *magna cum laude* from the Literature / Writing and Religious Studies programs at the University of California, San Diego (0.001 away from *summa*, goddamnit!). She is as skilled in the art of love as she is in the art of storytelling. Her smile powers the entire state of California. She lives with her husband and a multitude of faeries in a shoebox under the stairs. Call her Nicci. (Yes, her husband wrote this).

Lisa Bolekaja is a recent graduate of the Clarion Science Fiction and Fantasy Writer's Workshop and was named an Octavia E. Butler Scholar by the Carl Brandon Society. She is an affiliate member of the Horror Writers Association, and an active member of both the Black Science Fiction Society and the Organization of Black Screenwriters. Her first published story, "The Saltwater African," appeared in *Bloodchildren: Stories by the Octavia E. Butler Scholars*, edited by Nisi Shawl. She's currently adapting her horror screenplay *Skin* into a short story for wayward children.

Victor LaValle is the author of one story collection and three novels. His most recent novel, *The Devil in Silver*, was a New York Times Notable Book of 2012. He has been the recipient of numerous awards including a Guggenheim Fellowship, an American Book Award, and the Key to Southeast Queens. He teaches creative writing in Columbia University's MFA program.

Sabrina Vourvoulias is the author of *Ink* (Crossed Genres, 2012), a speculative novel that draws on her memories of Guatemala's armed internal conflict, and of the Latin@ experience in the United States. It was named to Latinidad's Best Books of 2012. Her short stories have appeared in *Strange Horizons*; the anthologies *Fat Girl in a Strange Land, Menial: Skilled Labor in Science Fiction*, and *Crossed Genres Year Two*; and forthcoming in *GUD* magazine. Her poetry has appeared in *Graham House Review, Dappled Things, La Bloga's Floricanto, Poets Respond to SB 1070*, and *Cabinet des Fées*, and forthcoming in *Bull Spec*. Sabrina is also the managing editor of Al Día News in Philadelphia, and was the editor of Al Día's book *200 Years of Latino History in Philadelphia* (Temple University Press, 2012).

For bibliographies and author notes on the stories, settings, and history in *Long Hidden*, visit longhidden.com.

EDITOR BIOGRAPHIES

Rose Fox is a compulsive magazine editor with a lifelong love of genre fiction. Credits include: reviews editor for *Publishers Weekly*, co-host of *Publishers Weekly* Radio, editor-at-large for *#24MAG*, and dissociative editor of the *Annals of Improbable Research*. They also provide freelance manuscript editing services to unpublished authors. In a few occasional moments of spare time, they help to run Readercon, an annual conference on speculative literature. Rose lives in Brooklyn, in a cozy apartment full of loving family, opinionated cats, and a great many books. You can find Rose on Twitter @rosefox or at copymancer.com.

Rose dedicates *Long Hidden* "to my parents, who gave me books edited by Terry Carr and Judith Merril, and smiled indulgently when I said that when I grew up I wanted to make anthologies."

Daniel José Older is a Brooklyn-based writer, editor and composer. *Salsa Nocturna*, Daniel's debut ghost noir collection, was hailed as "striking and original" by *Publishers Weekly*. He facilitates workshops on storytelling, music, and anti-oppression organizing at public schools, community organizations, and universities and worked for ten years as a New York City paramedic. His short stories and essays have appeared in *Lightspeed*, *Salon*, *The New Haven Review*, *Tor.com*, *PANK*, *Strange Horizons*, and *Crossed Genres* among other publications. His forthcoming urban fantasy novel *The Half Resurrection Blues*, the first book of the Bone Street Rumba series, will be released by Penguin's Roc imprint and as an audio book on Audible.com. You can find his thoughts on writing, read his ridiculous ambulance adventures, and hear music by his band, Ghost Star, at ghoststar.net and on Twitter: @djolder.

Daniel dedicates *Long Hidden* to Sheree Renée Thomas, who lit the way.